I0760635

THE LADY'S LAST SONG

SHADOWS OF CAMELOT BOOK 1

BREE MOORE

INNATE INK PUBLISHING

This is a work of fiction. Names, characters, places, events and incidents are used in a fictitious manner. Any resemblance to actual persons, living or dead, or actual events is purely coincidental.

Cover Design by Moonpress | www.moonpress.co

Previously published as "Woven" by Phase Publishing, LLC

First Ebook & Print Editions

August 2017

ISBN 978-1-943048-34-2

Library of Congress Control Number 2017947436

Cataloging-in-Publication Data on file.

Second Edition by Innate Ink Publishing

January 2022

Ebook ISBN 978-1-956668-14-8

Paperback ISBN 978-1-956668-14-8

CHAPTER ONE

Guinevere trailed her fingers along the window ledge, gazing morosely at the empty fields and the green hills beyond.

"Lady Guinevere, sit down. They won't be in sight for another week, at least."

"It shouldn't be this way, Mary. Don't women have the right to defend their homes and families?"

"You're not saying you want to be out there fighting, milady?"

Guinevere turned away from the window, giving up the idea that she would catch a glimpse of whatever was happening. Her father would return and give her the full tale, complete with embellishments of his deeds and of his favored knights. *If* he returned.

"No, the sword isn't for me. I just wish I didn't have to pretend I was interested in sewing flowers on clothing and sheets while something so important is happening." She held her embroidery at arm's length, staring at the tiny blue flowers she had been so proud of the day before. "We don't *do* anything, Mary."

Mary tsked, sliding her needle effortlessly through the cloth she held. "Sure we do. We sew, make beautiful embroidery, we clean and cook and..."

"You clean and cook," Guinevere said.

"You are more than welcome to help," Mary replied.

"You know what father would say if he caught me at work like that! Besides, the maids don't like me." Guinevere eyed her own needlework with distaste. She had been trying to embroider while talking, something she was clearly not good at. She had no fewer than three knots in her thread, and the flower she was working on looked more like a bird. A fat, lumpy bird.

"They don't know you. If they did, they would love you."

Guinevere slumped in her seat and jabbed the needle into the fabric, chewing her lip. "Why do you think the men make all the decisions?"

"Not this again. Lady Guinevere, sit up and focus on your needlework, would you? We have talked about this many times. When you are married you will make most of the decisions regarding the way your house is run and how the land is cared for."

"But not about anything important!" Guinevere protested, pushing her needle up. It came through crooked, but she ignored that. It would get worse if she tried to fix it. "Making sure the mead is well-seasoned and the cheeses aged, solving domestic skirmishes between moonstruck pages and arguing cooks. It's no way to live when the men decide our fates on the battlefield and in throne rooms. Marrying us off to their friends or reluctant allies. Forcing us to bear heirs until our bodies go to ruin and we're only fit for the solitude of nunneries. All while they drink and fight and take any woman they like any time they like. Even you can't make that sound more appealing than it is."

"True, I have no experience in marriage. I've been too busy taking care of you, much less a husband!" Mary glanced at her.

A small smile grew on Guinevere's face. "Have you ever wanted to marry?"

"Once. I was your age, a stable hand I fancied used to kiss me in the fields on our days off, and in stolen moments when we were alone. He promised to marry me someday."

"What happened?" Guinevere asked, giving up on her embroidery. She would have Mary sort it out later.

The maid shrugged. "He became a page for your father, then a squire. His duties kept him too busy for me. By the time he joined your father's men he had married another woman. Even so, he was killed young in battle. I wonder if those few short years of happiness would have been worth being his widow the rest of my life."

"I'm sorry," Guinevere said honestly.

"No need." Mary replied. "The way I see it, I'm better off unattached. That way, I can go to bed with whomever I choose and be none the wiser." She winked and Guinevere laughed. A lady should balk at such talk, but Guinevere liked it. It was honest, real. None of the flowery chatter other ladies indulged in when they visited.

"You know, if you want to make real change in the world, you should marry a king." Mary's brown eyes sparkled.

Guinevere laughed. "There's not a king around that would have me."

Mary set her embroidery in her lap. "Why not? You're as lovely and intelligent as any other eligible lady they could find."

"You've ruined me for it. I'm too rough for elegant company. Just a country nobleman's daughter." Guinevere adjusted her skirts. It was good she would never be the wife of a mighty king; she hadn't the patience for politics. She glanced out the window again, wondering if she should take her horse out for a run. At least then she'd feel less like an ornament and more like a living, breathing being.

Mary clicked her tongue. "Well, I still think you ought to consider -"

"Mary, look! They're back!" Guinevere rushed to the narrow window opening, leaning out to see as far as she could.

"Already? Your father said this battle would last months." Mary joined her at the window. "But you speak rightly. There they are, after a single moon, and far more of them than I expected. I'd better tell the cook."

The woman grabbed her skirts and ran from the room, leaving Guinevere staring at the approaching army. It was definitely her father's; his flag flew high on the standard. Next to it, a standard bearing a red dragon on a field of white blazed in the sun. The red dragon of the Pendragon house. The dragon represented the High King's banner.

His Highness Arthur Pendragon had come all the way to Carmelide to help Guinevere's father? The battle must have been terrible indeed to warrant the presence of the king.

The king. He was young, as kings went. And looking for a wife, if the rumors of several moons ago still held. Guinevere flew to her closet and pulled out her red dress. It was her favorite, for it complimented her black hair and fair complexion, giving her dark eyes a mysterious allure that men couldn't help but notice, or so she imagined.

Since Mary was busy, Guinevere brushed through her own hair, wishing she had time to put it up. She dressed herself, working her way into the flowing gown with some struggle. The laces weren't as tight as she would like, but it would do. The king would be coming back from battle, after all. The sight of any woman half-pretty would be sure to please him.

She had her hand on the dress, fully intending to wear it, when she stopped, a chill running through her. Was she really going to parade herself before the king like a jewel to be admired and added to his treasury?

Guinevere dropped the dress and turned, spotting her everyday dress still on the floor where she had discarded it. No, she couldn't wear that for the king. Something nicer, to show the proper respect. She went back to the closet and noticed a simple, pale blue gown hanging on the far side. It was nice enough, though the color washed her out. It was one she didn't particularly like and only wore if she had to.

It was perfect.

As was proper, Guinevere waited in her room until Mary retrieved her. The maid clucked without satisfaction at her chosen dress.

"You could at least try, milady. His Highness has yet to choose a queen, and even you wouldn't begrudge a crown, despite our earlier conversation." She sighed. "I suppose there's nothing to be done for it. They're waiting for you downstairs."

Guinevere followed Mary, trying to keep her pacing unrushed, her expression indifferent, though her heart pounded in her chest. Men filled the hall, their stench coating the inside of Guinevere's nose, the scent of dirt and metal and unwashed men. Most of the men had been out for well over two months. Guinevere tried not to wrinkle her nose as she walked through the crowd to where her father stood.

"Ah, Guinevere! It is good to see ye, daughter. A sight for sore eyes, eh?" He nudged the man next to him and chuckled.

Guinevere curtseyed, ignoring the anger that flashed inside of her. Whether she primped or not, she was on display. She tried not to think about the men that milled all around her, their eyes lingering unchecked and unnoticed in the crowded hall.

"As are you, father." She tiptoed and kissed his cheek. "I am glad to see you return. Victorious, I assume?"

"Eh? Of course! Of course. King Rience never stood a chance, and the timely arrival of our king's knights sealed the deal. He saved me, in fact, from many a death blow. It's all thanks to him yer father is alive, my dear." He clapped the man beside him on the back.

The Pendragon removed his helmet, and Guinevere's eyes caught on his sun-colored hair. Her gaze trailed to his lake-blue eyes and stopped on his smile. Though it was hidden in part by a weeks-old beard, it dazzled her so she forgot to speak. His warm fingers took her hand in his, and his lips brushed her skin. A gentle tingle traveled up her arm. She almost regretted not wearing the red dress.

Silly thoughts. Silly, useless thoughts.

"Many thanks to you, my liege," Guinevere stammered, curtseying.

"My pleasure, milady." The king replied, nodding to her father. "He was loyal to my father and has ever triumphed in protecting this border of our kingdom from the Saxon armies. I am glad to have been here to prevent losing such a noble man."

Her father's chest puffed out like he was a red-breasted robin about to burst into song. Guinevere wouldn't have put it past him if he had, either. He was not subtle in receiving praise.

He managed to humble himself enough to bow with a hand in a fist over his heart. "Ye'll always have me and my armies, my king." He straightened, armor clanking. "That is, if these blasted Saxon hoards don't wipe us off the map! Where do they get their men, I want to know. They are endless. They must breed like rats!"

The king shook his head, stroking his pale beard. "This was not the work of Saxons, Lord Leodegrance. King Rience of Wales has wanted my beard hair to trim his cloak as long as I've sat on the throne. He made deals with the Saxons, bringing them into this army, but I recognized his insignia on many shields. We ride to hold him accountable for this battle after a brief respite here."

"Of course, our king and his knights are always welcome within our walls," Guinevere's father declared. He turned to the steward standing near the stairs. "Fire up the... er... fires! Bring out our best and finest. Our swords have feasted well enough on the flesh of our enemies. Tonight, we feed ourselves!" He bellowed loud enough to be heard by all, and the men roared their approval, banging gauntlets on shields and stomping their feet.

"Might I propose a requirement for dinner?" Guinevere shouted above the din.

"Eh?" Her father grunted.

Guinevere's mouth quirked up in a smile. "A bath before the stewards let you in the feast hall!" Then she *winked* at the king

Her father looked stunned. Beside him, the king burst into laughter, and Guinevere blushed. Despite all her attempts to pretend his opinion didn't matter, it pleased her that she could at least make him laugh, inappropriate though her comment was.

Her father caught on after a moment and chuckled before sending her off to see to the preparations with Mary. It was all she could do not to glance over her shoulder to see if the king was watching her with his striking blue eyes.

The feasting began long after the sun went down. The cooks hadn't had much time to prepare the meal, but the hunting had been fair, despite the war, and meat was plentiful. Cider and mead even more so, and it seemed the men could drink endlessly, the way they downed pint after pint, getting louder with every empty mug. Her father was possibly the loudest, and she wondered if the king wouldn't go deaf sitting beside him.

Guinevere glanced at her plate and shifted in her seat. Mary had managed to convince her to change into her red dress after all, and raised her eyebrows at Guinevere's poorly feigned indifference. The matronly woman sat beside her now, occasionally smiling to herself in a way that had Guinevere wondering if she had picked out Guinevere's wedding flowers yet.

Guinevere let her eyes wander about the hall, skipping over groups of drunken men singing bawdy tunes. It wouldn't be long before she was sent to her room, to be kept out of rough company. She might as well enjoy it while she could, and not draw attention to herself.

One figure caught her attention, standing in the shadows. The figure hunched over a cane. Guinevere squinted, trying to see who it was. None of the stewards or maids were so old, and it certainly wasn't a knight. Though perhaps one emptying his stomach of alcohol...

She blinked and the figure was gone, and though she scanned the crowd again, she found no sign of the figure. She did, however, catch the eye of the dark-haired knight sitting across from her at the table. He grinned at her, not unfriendly, and she found herself smiling back.

Maybe it was the wine, but his face was familiar to her, and she stared without concern for who might be watching, trying to place him in her memory. He spoke to a burly knight at his side and they both laughed.

The room rushed at Guinevere, colors blurring together until the scene changed to a leafy forest. The same dark-haired knight approached her in her mind, wrapping his arms around her and kissing her. The vision blackened.

She came to a moment later, slumped in her chair against Mary's shoulder. It must not have been long, for Mary seemed to be the only one who had noticed her collapse.

"My dear, are you all right?" Mary asked.

"I am fine." Guinevere mumbled, and she reached for Mary's arm. Except that it wasn't Mary's arm she grabbed. She was pulled to her feet and came face-to-face with the dark-haired knight. She couldn't look away from his lips. Had she dreamed about kissing him? She glanced away quickly, her face burning at the lingering sensations from the vision.

“I saw you tumble and came to your aid. Are you all right?” he asked. His voice was like a melody, gliding through her thoughts. Guinevere met his eyes. Recognition flashed in their depths. It was fleeting, but she had not imagined it.

“Thank you for your quick thinking, Sir...?” Guinevere tilted her head expectantly.

The knight smiled. “Lancelot. I am Sir Lancelot.”

She realized she still held his arm and released it, folding herself into a curtsey. “Thank you, Sir Lancelot. I am indebted to you. I must retire now, however. The drink has gone to my head and I feel ill.”

“Very well.” The curve of his lips straightened, and his face reverted to a more reserved expression.

Guinevere was too befuddled by the heat and noise to think of a wittier exit. She followed Mary from the room, her mind spinning. The vision that had come to her mind had felt so real, but she had never kissed a man in her life, much less one of the king’s knights.

There were those that believed in past lives, and that sometimes the very observant or those skilled in magic could tap into them and see the life they had lived. She had never put much thought into it before. But what if she had known this knight, not in this life, but in one long past?

Her heart fluttered at the thought, and she shook her head, laughing. Soul mates. Life-partners. Past lives. She was being a silly girl, imagining herself in the arms of a knight. Ridiculous romance.

Mary finished undressing Guinevere and tugged a nightgown over her head. Guinevere fended off her questions, protesting exhaustion. Mary didn't rest until Guinevere was tucked in bed, and Guinevere finally dismissed her.

She closed her eyes and was almost asleep when a shadowed figure moved across the room.

She sat up. "Mary?" she hissed, clutching the covers. "Is that you?"

The lights were out, the fireplace burning low for the night. Mary had most assuredly gone by now.

"The time has come," a voice, so hoarse that it might not have been used for a hundred years, rasped from a dark corner of her room.

"For what? Who are you?" Guinevere demanded.

A fire flared in the grate and revealed the stooped form of an old woman. The figure in the shadows at the feast sprang to Guinevere's memory. Had it been this woman? How had she gotten in Guinevere's room?

The hag tilted her head to one side. "Have you forgotten everything? Fortunate that Mordred fared better. Tell me, is Guinevere your true name?"

"Of course it is, it's the only name I've ever..." Guinevere paused, frowning.

The woman whispered words that itched Guinvere's mind, dredging up something she knew, something she had known, someone she had been, once. Blue light leaked from the hag's flexing fingers, and Guinevere opened her mouth to scream, but the magic reached her first and Guinevere's mind cleared like smoke in the wind.

Morgan. Her true name was Morgan. The thought came with no other information, but she knew it with a clarity she could not deny. The blue magic dissipated, drifting around the room in a mist-like form.

Guinevere looked back at the old woman, who revealed her missing teeth with a wide grin.

"What name did you hear?" The woman croaked.

"Morgan," Guinevere said slowly. "But how did you…"

The woman waved her hand dismissively. "I know much about you. Far more than you do, apparently. The spell isn't meant to take one's memories. Unless there was much you wished to forget."

Guinevere's head ached. "Who are you?" she demanded again.

"My name is Niviane. You knew me once, and you will know me again, in time. For now, it is vital that you remember. Your name is a beginning. Do not be troubled as the memories come back. You will remember with enough time to finish what you started."

Guinevere clutched the blankets. "Finish what I started? What are you saying?"

Niviane chuckled. "You will see. When you do, you will call me friend. For now, sleep."

Suddenly the woman was at her bedside, without Guinevere seeing her move. The crone waved a hand over Guinevere's face and her demand for answers left her lips as she lay down, eyes closing against her will.

"Sleep well, Morgan le Fay. Next time we meet, it will be as friends."

CHAPTER TWO

Willows whiten, aspens quiver,
Little breezes dusk and shiver
Thro' the wave that runs for ever
By the island in the river
Flowing down to Camelot.
Four gray walls, and four gray towers,
Overlook a space of flowers,
And the silent isle embowers
The Lady of Shalott.

Elaina lay in bed, eyes shut tight against the light pouring into her room. Her body was rested after a rare night of uninterrupted sleep, and yet she was loath to wake. For a moment, all was still, and she was left to her thoughts, to simply breathe and lay quiet.

Outside, a bird sang. Elaina's heart wrenched at the lovely sound. It sounded so close; if she turned her head and opened her eyes, she knew she would see the delightsome creature.

She turned her head towards the light, towards the window and the song, but her eyes did not open. Her fingers flexed, as if she could take the sky from the scene outside and bring it in to look upon. Just this once.

If Elaina opened her eyes, the enchantment holding her would be broken; but a single glance out the wide, circular window that looked out toward Camelot would kill her. Or so the sorceress in the mirror had claimed.

It had been years since the fateful day that Elaina had come upon this tower, desperate for shelter from a freak storm. Years since she had been accidentally caught up in a powerful enchantment. Mordred had not come for her. No one had. So what did she have to lose by looking?

She remembered the face in the mirror as it had appeared that day. A beautiful woman, like one from a story, the mirror's surface swirling with ethereal mist.

"You cannot leave," the woman in the mirror said. "Nor may you so much as look out the window of this tower. You are the Weaver, chosen by fate to record the story of Camelot."

"Let me go!" Elaina pleaded. "I am to be married to a man I love. Surely you would not keep me from him."

"I do not keep you, but the loom does. It demands a Weaver. And that Weaver is you. Look out the window or try to leave and you will perish."

"No," Elaina gasped. She ran to the door and pulled at the latch, but it had somehow locked behind her. She whirled towards the room's window and a force like a great rush of wind struck her, slamming her against the door. She crumpled to the ground, crying in pain.

"You force my hand. I do not wish to harm you. But I am the Weaver's keeper. It is my job to ensure this position does not remain unfulfilled. You must record the doings of Camelot and its people in tapestry."

"I do not know how to weave," Elaina cried, rising to her hands and knees, looking at the mirror through straggled

strands of hair. "Choose someone else. Surely there is someone better suited."

The woman in the mirror smiled. "You found the tower. It is not visible to most. You heard the music. There are few who can hear it. You have been chosen. But not all is lost. You will enjoy an extended lifespan, nearing immortality. You will pass the time in comfort, all needs met. No sickness will befall you. There will be no need for you to do anything aside from eat and sleep and weave. Such a life would be the envy of many."

Elaina sat back on her heels. She dared not attempt to look out the window again. "Why can't I look out the window? Why have one in the tower at all, if the Weaver cannot look?"

"The tower was here before the curse. It is a test. The Weaver must be dedicated to her task. No distractions, nothing that might convince her to abandon her duty. Once you look, you are severed from the loom, but its threads do not let go easily. Those threads will strangle the life from your body, and you will be dead before your feet touch the grass outside."

"Surely there must be a way out." Elaina looked back at the mirror, but the woman was gone, and the room was filled with sunlight and silence.

Faintly at first, then growing in volume, the beautiful music from the previous night wove its way around Elaina. She tried to ignore its pull, but could not; a magical force drew her to the loom, forced her to pick up the shuttle, place her feet on the treadle, and weave.

She did not have to thread the shuttle; it was already done, and the thread appeared to change colors before her eyes. It was nothing like the weaving she had done in the past, which required much work on the weaver's part. She was no more than a vessel moving the shuttle and treadle, pounding a rhythm with wood and thread.

A bird chirruped outside and she turned instinctively to look, then stopped herself so quickly it made her neck ache. What the woman had said haunted her mind: if you look, you will die. Where would she be then? No one could save her if she was dead.

It wouldn't be long before Mordred came for her. Once he realized she was gone, he would stop at nothing to find her. He would come, and when he did, together they would find a way to free her.

Elaina had stopped hoping for Mordred long ago. Her former lover no doubt assumed she had jilted him, and he had surely wed another. But Elaina still held hope in a vice grip. Hope that, after all this time, someone would find her. That the curse could be broken and she could stop weaving without the loss of her life. That she could finally leave this tower and live.

There had to be a way.

Elaina's eyes finally opened. Grey stone glittered through a haze of dust-ridden sunlight. From the far corner of her room, soft harp music drifted into the air. Anyone else listening would have heard a happy tune, but Elaina had heard it enough to recognize the subtle undertones of the enchantment weaving itself around her.

No, Elaina thought, closing her eyes again. *Another moment... please.*

Her hands and arms moved of their own accord, pushing her out of bed. Her feet traitorously dragged her across the floor, but she knew better than to fight. The music would win; it always did.

Rubbing the sleep from her eyes, Elaina sat on the hard bench, facing an unremarkable wooden loom. She forced herself to look into the glassy eye of the mirror. For the briefest moment, she saw herself, hair mussed from slumber, eyes circled and weary.

She grimaced as the image wavered, as if she looked into a pond that had been disturbed by a leaping toad, and when it cleared, she was staring at a field of young, green barley stalks, waving gently in the same breeze that rustled the trees outside the forbidden window.

Her hand found the shuttle, and she passed it through the two rows of warp thread. Her foot on the treadle brought the beater sliding down to compact the new row. Magically, the thread had changed, and was now a bright, spring green color. She never changed the thread herself, and yet, each day when the sun faded, intricate images had been woven so incredibly that they seemed to come alive.

Often, when she was allowed a moment to sleep or eat, Elaina caught the shuttle moving out of the corner of her eye, weaving without a hand to wield it. As soon as she looked full on it would stop, but each time she returned to the loom, a new length of tapestry was woven. The loom did not need her, but it held her just the same.

As she worked, she inspected what had been woven while she slept. It was a night scene depicting the same stretch of road she was being shown in the mirror now. The same field of barley, and across from it the glistening river, winding idly by the dirt road that led towards the great city Camelot.

Elaina sighed and watched the market scene outside the city gates. It was some distance away, but the mirror had magnified it, as if to taunt her with what she could not have. Peasant boys ducked and weaved, snatching apples and tarts and stuffing them down their shirts or into their hungry mouths. Stall keepers shouted as they paraded their wares, trying to convince the haughty, passing noblemen and women to open their purses and buy.

Elaina let herself get caught up in what she saw, pretending she was standing among them smelling the freshly baked goods and basking in the noises of the market.

The reflection was a poor substitute.

All she could hear in reality was the bird, still trilling in the tree outside; all she could smell was the earthy wool beneath her fingers. Her only access to the outside world was the mirror, both a blessing and a curse. It showed her everything there was to see as the world passed by on its way to Camelot. It also showed her everything she had lost when she first came to the tower.

She closed her eyes, not needing sight to guide the shuttle through the tunnel of threads as the enchantment wove the tapestry. When she opened them again, a group of young girls passed in the mirror, their straight and shining hair held back by jeweled combs. They wore long, beautiful dresses made of shimmering, colorful silks and borders of bright white lace.

Elaina paused her weaving and watched them move, their pretty mouths open in silent laughter and cheerful chatter in her mirror. Glancing down, she smoothed her own dress, which was rags compared to the finery the other girls exhibited. She had been one of them, once.

A twig snapped outside her window and a male voice cursed, interrupting Elaina's reverie. She gripped the loom to keep herself from turning around and looking through the window. She listened in the stillness, hoping to hear another sound, another word, anything that might indicate someone had come for her at last. Leaves rustled, but that could easily have been the wind. Had she imagined the voice? Had she finally gone mad?

CHAPTER THREE

Gereck glanced over his shoulder, across the river and towards the road. He could still see the men he had been with, standing on the road with their horses. He watched them search the river, and then turn away, talking among themselves.

Let them search. They wouldn't find him. Not for the rest of the day, at least.

No one would look toward the faerie's tower. He wouldn't dare approach it on a normal day, but today... today he couldn't take the knights' condescension any longer.

But he would have to face it later, because he was just a *squire*. And today he had been the fool of all squires, losing Lancelot's shield like that. If he had been paying attention instead of make-believing that he was a knight like a foolish boy, he could have controlled his horse when the snake appeared and none of this would have happened.

Trying to ignore the sense of shame rising inside of him, he turned back to the tower wall and found another foothold. Wet as he was, his foot slipped and his forehead hit the hard gray stone. He let out a curse. A muffled sound, like a small gasp, came from inside the tower.

The faerie? There was a legend...

He shook his head, angry with himself. It was probably the trees in the wind. Or, at best, some old hermit woman spending the last of her days within the broken-down tower.

From this height, he could see the length of the road and the river winding beside it, leading to the great city of Camelot, just visible above the trees. He shook his head, coming back to the real reason he had scaled the tower.

He glanced over the riverbank, looking for the gleam of silver and yellow that marked his master's shield. He squinted his eyes against the sun, but half of the waterway was obscured in deep shadows cast by the trees. He would never find it up here, and Lancelot would never forgive him. He began to climb down, cursing his own thick-headedness.

"Is someone there?"

The voice made him look up and his hand slipped, causing him to grasp the nearest handhold in a panic. He clung to the wall, one hand gripping a vine, the other clinging to a tiny lip of stone. Had he imagined the voice? It sounded so young; certainly not belonging to a crone, but a sorceress could change her voice to sound young, to lure up a handsome, unsuspecting man and... no.

Gereck stopped his thoughts. He would not fear magic. If he had any chance left of becoming a knight, he had to be thinking like one. One of King Arthur's knights would never allow such a thought to freeze him with fear.

The wide, half-circle window above him wasn't much farther than where he had climbed before. Perhaps if he looked inside, he could set his mind at ease. He might discover some great asset to the kingdom, like a valuable treasure, and the king would forgive his indiscretion.

Gereck climbed with more vigor, his mind feeding him optimistic visions of being knighted by the king the moment his valiant discovery was announced. He would earn a knight's keep and finally be able to move to the city of Camelot itself. He would be the greatest knight ever to sit at the Round Table, greater even than the insufferable Lancelot.

He was so caught up in his thoughts that he hardly noticed when he reached the window, and without thinking, pulled himself up over the sill and stepped into the room.

Everything fell silent, except for the sound of the loom, which appeared to be moving on its own. He stared at it in wonder and the moving parts halted, but as soon as he looked away he could hear its steady thrum start up again. The bench, he noticed with ever-widening eyes, was empty of any person, as was the room.

It was large in size, and circular. He stood in front of the room's window, which gave the room most of its light, although a few empty torch brackets adorned the wall. A modest bed stood to his right, the sheets crumpled and recently slept in. A small tin tub filled with dirty water sat outside a dressing screen on the far side of the room. And in the middle, the loom stood erect.

He studied the now quiet and still loom carefully for any sign of enchantment, but despite the vast and detailed tapestry in the midst of being woven, the loom itself seemed ordinary. Whoever had been weaving must have been the one who had spoken to him.

He noticed, for the first time, the mirror.

It was tall, and ovular in shape, resting on a stand that kept it steady. He couldn't figure out how he had missed the ornate golden frame and clear glass surface. It would be worth a fortune. He squinted, noticing intricate designs and symbols carved around its edge, but he couldn't make them out from the far side of the room.

He moved closer, inching away from the window, ready to leap out if anything should attack him. He didn't have a sword, after all, and would have little use for one if a sorceress lived here. The flame of his curiosity muffled his voice of reason and kept him moving toward the mirror.

Two bare feet, visible beneath the mirror's ornate frame. Gereck stopped and pulled a small dagger from his belt.

He cleared his throat. "Hello?"

The feet shuffled, but the person they belonged to did not make a sound. He glimpsed the hem of a pale pink dress, plain and un-embroidered. *So, it is a woman,* he thought, *and a poor one, at that. Certainly not someone who could afford such a mirror. Had she stolen it?* He believed it was his duty to apprehend her, if she was a thief. He grew bold. No woman could possibly harm him.

He moved to the left of the mirror, feinting as if he meant to round it. The feet edged the opposite way, as if the person there might run for it if he tried to come around. He moved suddenly, feinting to the left, then bolting right, putting himself directly in the path of the woman in the pink dress. He caught the young woman in his arms and she struggled, kicking and flailing her arms.

Gereck pinned them down, sputtering as he got a mouthful of blonde hair.

"Calm down, would you? I mean you no harm." The maiden stopped moving. Her lungs gasped for air, and for a brief moment, her heart beat as fast as a bird's. He set her down, releasing her arms and stepping back to look at her. Her eyes cast downward at the stone floor.

"If you don't mean to harm me, why do you have a knife? And what do you make of your sneaking about, then?" she said.

"I thought to use caution, entering a strange tower in the middle of the woods by myself. Are you not an enchantress?" he sheathed his knife.

She laughed. "An enchantress? If I were an enchantress, do you think I would have put myself in this tower, cursed to weave on this loom for eternity?"

"You are cursed?" He wished he could see the rest of her face. Her honey-colored hair tumbled over her fair-skinned cheeks, creating a tent perfect for hiding. *But why was she hiding*? "Perhaps I can help you."

"If only you could," she said quietly.

She then turned her face upward, her eyes closed tight. Her face, once fair, now looked pale, as if it hadn't seen the sun in years. Tiny freckles, barely noticeable, graced her cheeks and nose. On others, they could be unsightly, but on her they were wonderful. Her hands clenched and unclenched; her bare toes curled against the wooden floor.

Voices, shouting, carried through the window to his left. It sounded like Sir Tristan, perhaps. Gereck reached toward the woman, excitement building inside of him. "But I can. I mean, I can try. You'll have to tell me about the curse. Who trapped you? How did you come to be here? What forces bind you?"

She hid her face in her hands. "It is useless, sir knight. I cannot be freed by you. Do not waste your time here."

"But I can help you."

"You cannot."

"Please, let me try." The shouts grew louder. *Would they try the tower?* he wondered. No, they would not think of it. If they looked for him this intensely, it must be because Lancelot wanted him. He didn't want his master to be angrier than he already was. He had to go.

He looked back at the woman. She had turned away from him. She was thin, but not frail. Did she have enough to eat? He reached toward her, to touch her, then thought better of it, and cleared his throat.

"I must go. They call for me. Can you come with me?"

She shook her head.

"Then I will return."

She did not respond.

"May I have your name?" A long silence stretched between them. The voices that shouted, no doubt for him, faded as the callers moved away from the tower. He could not wait for her answer.

"Then I take my leave. I will be back as soon as I am able." He turned away, toward the window, throwing his leg over its ledge and reaching out to the tree branches he had used to climb up. From behind him, a quiet voice, one he almost didn't hear, spoke.

"Elaina."

He turned back to look, but she had disappeared farther into the room and was nowhere to be seen. He smiled.

"Farewell, Lady Elaina. I will see you again," he said, and then he continued down the tree, careful to keep his footing on the smooth branches.

Gereck was still deep in thought about Elaina when he found the knights. They handed off his horse, and Gereck mounted, riding with them toward Camelot.

"When will Lancelot return?" he asked. The knights exchanged looks.

"You didn't find it, I presume?" Sir Elyon said. "He is furious, you know, and I think he has a right to be."

"It was an accident," Sir Leon said, cutting in as he rode up beside Gereck. "We all make mistakes. Knight or squire makes no difference when we are all mortal."

Gereck gave him a grateful smile, and Sir Elyon, for once, did not respond with an insult. They rode in silence, the tree-lined trail they followed dappled with sunlight. It was peaceful. It stilled the pounding of Gereck's heart after his encounter in the tower.

"What were you doing in that crumbling old tower?" Sir Leon asked.

"Looking around. The window had a great view of the river. I thought I might find Lancelot's shield," Gereck said honestly.

Sir Leon exchanged looks with Sir Tristan, who had ridden up on the other side of Gereck, and they both grinned.

"I think Gereck found the faerie lady, and he's fallen in love!" Sir Tristan said.

"That's it!" Sir Leon agreed. "Besotted. No, enchanted!"

"He doesn't stand a chance," Sir Tristan said, shaking his head in feigned sorrow. "You have a wife, do you not, Gereck? Sir Leon, we ought to send a messenger. She deserves to know his terrible fate."

"Aye," Sir Leon agreed.

Gereck clenched his fists. "Oh, go jump in the river, both of you. And if I hear anything about a message of that sort from Winna, you will both answer for it."

The two men burst into laughter.

"Is that any way for a squire to speak to a knight?" A black-haired knight rode up, his handsome face stern. He brought his white steed up alongside the others. The laughter stopped. Lancelot had returned, much sooner than anticipated.

Sir Tristan glanced at Gereck. "It is all right, Lancelot. We were giving him a hard time. Our fault."

Lancelot remained stone-faced. "If he does not learn to control his emotions with you two, how will he ever have the composure worthy of a knight? He will rise to every taunt of his enemy."

"It was a moment of fun, Lancelot. No need to be so serious," Sir Leon interjected.

"There is every need to be serious with Gereck. He does not understand how serious life can be." The knight gritted his teeth. "Did you find my shield?"

"No," Gereck said, gazing steadily ahead. Lancelot's eyes darkened, but he said nothing. He would wait until no one else was around. Gereck had to be sure that there was no opportunity for that until Lancelot had cooled down.

"Well, keep looking." The knight kicked his horse's sides and surged forward, ahead of the group.

"He can be a prat sometimes, eh?" Sir Tristan said, glancing sideways at Gereck. "I mean, we all think so. He is a brilliant knight, but we see how he picks on you. I'm not sure that it's befitting a knight to act that way, but he doesn't do it with others of your station. I think he feels threatened."

"By me?"

Sir Tristan shrugged. "Why not? You hold a lot of promise. And King Arthur talks about you from time to time."

"He does?" Gereck looked up, heart pounding. "What does he say?"

"Just that he is waiting for you to prove yourself, that you would be worthy of knighthood. He knows how much you want it. He needs a really great reason to knight you. A valiant effort, a quest, you know," Sir Tristan replied.

"Thank you for telling me. At least someone appreciates my efforts." He hesitated a moment. "What did you do to be knighted, Sir Tristan?"

"I ran him over."

"What?"

The knights around them laughed. Sir Tristan grinned. "He was in a tight spot. I came along and bowled him over in my attempt to join the fight. That was back when he was Crown Prince and Uther still lived."

Then the other knights regaled him with tales of how each of them met the king and became one of his knights. Gereck wondered how it would come for him. Would his story be like any of these? Brave and daring, or perhaps amusing, tinged with the immense loyalty each man felt for his king. He longed for the day he joined their ranks, each day facing the possibility that it might never happen.

CHAPTER FOUR

A bow-shot from her bower-eaves,
He rode between the barley-sheaves,
The sun came dazzling thro' the leaves,
And flam'd upon the brazen greaves
Of bold Sir Lancelot.
A red-cross knight for ever kneel'd
To a lady in his shield,
That sparkled on the yellow field,
Beside remote Shalott.

Elaina paced the floor, legs chilled by the cooling air. Twilight settled over Camelot and the sunlight faded, its golden shadow performing its last dance across the stone floor beneath her feet. The air coming in her window curled around her ankles, making bumps rise on her skin. She ignored them, for the most part, her feet continuing their march back and forth.

Ever since that knight had interrupted her solitude, she found her heart turning once again to thoughts of escape. It had been many years since she had felt desperate enough to attempt anything. Her last suicide attempt had frightened her enough that she had sworn off escaping and reduced herself to hoping someone would rescue her, or that someday the curse would simply wear off.

And then *he* had come. Without warning, like a rainstorm on a clear-sky day. Like the first spring bud after a heavy winter.

She had spoken to a human being other than herself, remembering what it was like to have an unpredictable conversation. The thrill of it had taken hold of her and would not let her go. She fevered, waiting for him to return. With each rise of the sun, her heart would quicken.

Often she woke before the music called her to the task of weaving, and she forced herself to stay awake long into the night, even if the loom's binding spell released her. Each rustle of the trees outside made her leap to her feet, and every whisper of the breeze caused her to look around.

It was never him, of course. By the end of several weeks, she was as jittery as an abused dog, and it was perhaps a good thing that she kept no regular company, for she would have made a poor companion.

Her irritability had reached a peak this night. She had undressed for bed in a fury, flinging her clothes about the room. A piece of tough bread and a wrinkled apple made her meal, but she hardly tasted it in her hasty chewing. And now, the sun finally giving way to shadow, she paced.

"It's hardly reasonable to act this way, Elaina," she told herself, feet slapping on the cold stone. "Mooning after a man you just met. It's not like he's the first man you've seen, after all."

She choked on a hysterical laugh that tried to escape her throat, wishing that statement didn't feel so much like the truth.

"I mean, you don't even know his name," she continued, turning before she hit the wall on the far side of the room and heading back toward her bed. "And he's probably never coming back, after what you said to him. You were awfully rude. You should have invited him to stay. Only for tea, of course."

She dipped into a curtsey. "How do you do, sir? Don't mind my eyes, they have trouble focusing on handsome men. Please, have a seat. Do you prefer hard bread or moldy cheese? Warm water to wash that down? For dessert, we have the finest Desperate Woman who would like to go home with you. Do you happen to have room on your valiant steed? Don't mind if I do."

She flopped onto her back across the disheveled covers of her bed, staring up at the ceiling. It was almost too dark to make out the crisscrossing beams of the conical roof above. Gradually, the dark took on its own faded blue glow as the last light of day vanished. She didn't reach over to light her candle, but she didn't make any move to pull the covers over herself and go to sleep, either.

Instead, she focused on the feeling in her limbs. The cool air, turning colder, made her skin icy to the touch. The slight numbness tingled through her legs as they dangled over the side of the firm mattress.

In a moment, the cold stopped bothering her, and she felt lost in a whirlpool of mindfulness, where only she existed in this moment, and everything past and future had ceased to exist. For a split moment in time that passed like a brush of lover's lips on her cheek, she was happy.

"Faerie, are you awake?" a male voice whispered through the darkness, flashing through her awareness like lightning.

She bolted upright, then scrambled to find tinder and flint to light her candle. In her fumbling she dropped it, the hard flint clacking against the wooden floor. She dropped to her knees, fingers searching in the dark, until her hand bumped it, sending the flint skittering towards the wall, underneath her bed.

Well, that was that. In any case, she couldn't look upon him, so what was the point? It would be so much easier if they had no light.

"You are back," Elaina said, finally sitting back onto her knees and brushing hair from her face and mouth. Good thing he couldn't see her. She likely looked a mess.

"Can't you predict the future? Didn't you see me in your magic mirror?" he asked from somewhere behind her, near the window. She shook her head, forgetting he couldn't see her.

"I see only the present like you." Her eyes wandered the darkness, seeking out his form.

He was so quiet she thought he had gone, and then he shifted his weight, boots shuffling on the stone. He stood by the wide window, off to one side so she couldn't see his silhouette, but now that she knew where he was, she could gaze at least in his general direction.

"Why have you come?" she asked.

"Because I said I would. Did you think I wouldn't?"

She didn't know how to answer that. She had hoped he would come, had wished it, but she didn't want to frighten him with her desperation.

He continued. "In any case, I couldn't sleep this night, and I wondered if you might be awake, and here you are. I hoped to find out more about you, about this enchantment. You seemed... trapped."

"I am," she replied.

"How long have you been in here?" the knight asked. His question startled her, although it should have been obvious that he would ask.

"I don't know," she said. "Who is king now? Did King Aurelius have a son?"

"You knew King Aurelius's reign?" His voice cracked.

"Yes," she said slowly. Now she wished she could see his face.

"Arthur Pendragon reigns now. King Aurelius's reign ended forty years ago."

Elaina put a hand to her mouth, tears welling in her eyes, emotion choking her throat. Thirty years. She knew it had been a long time. It had felt like a lifetime. She didn't know that it had actually *been* a lifetime.

"Elaina?"

Her body shuddered. She let her breath out, then took another to calm herself. "I am sorry. The realization... everyone I love is likely dead now, or so old it doesn't matter. They have lived full lives, and I..." She choked again. "I have been trapped in here. My life full of nothings."

He knelt, and his hand landed on her shoulder. "I am certain it has not been nothing. It was something to those who knew you. And... and it could become more again. We need to find a way to help you out of here."

Hope swelled within her again. "Do you think you can? I have tried for years. But perhaps you know of something, or could get something that I can't, being in here."

"There is a sorcerer employed by the current king. I could speak with him. He is old and knows many magics." The excitement rose in his voice. It was infectious. Elaina stood up, and the knight stood with her. She paced about the floor, mind reeling.

He cleared his throat, startling her. "Er, Elaina? Do you have a candle?"

She hesitated. "I dropped the flint. It rolled under the bed."

"I will get it." He grunted, and something rattled across the floor.

Her eyes adjusted to the dim light, and she could see his outline as he sat up. "Got it!" he said triumphantly, breathing heavily. She took it from his hand. "Elaina? Could you light it?"

"I would rather not," she replied.

"Why not?"

She rubbed the rough, familiar surface of the flint with her thumb. "I cannot look upon any man from the outside world, and I would not risk it happening by accident."

"So, earlier, you weren't being shy? You really cannot look at me?" His voice floated through the dark. It sounded closer.

Elaina's heart pounded. "No. The very thing that would break this enchantment would also mean my death."

"Then why not risk it? You choose staying in this tower forever over attempting the one thing that would save you?"

"Despite what you might think, I have things to live for, reasons I would still want to escape here alive. I am not keen to die. Are you?"

"No," he replied. Then, after a moment, "I cannot believe you are unable to look at me. Who told you that?"

"When I first arrived here, there was a woman in the mirror. She told me about the enchantment, and is, perhaps, the one who cursed me. I cannot look out the window, only upon the images I am shown in the mirror. They are a shadow of reality, a poor substitute for reality."

"Could you light your candle so that I will have light to see by?"

"I will not. Come back during the day if you want to see," Elaina insisted.

"I have little time during the day," the knight argued.

"Maybe it can wait?"

He paused. "If it frees you, do you really want to wait?"

The thought of freedom brought a small smile to Elaina's face. Could she dare to hope? "No," she replied.

"Light the candle, then."

"I told you, I won't risk seeing you and breaking the curse."

"Do you want to be here forever?" Footsteps brought him closer.

Elaina's heart prickled with both excitement and warning. "No, but I want to go about it the right way."

His warmth passed behind her, and then he was at her side, hands moving over the surface of the table. He would realize in a moment that she still had the flint, and then what would he do? What if he wasn't a knight, bound to uphold her honor? Her hand gripped the smooth flint, sweat making it damp. She backed away. Her throat stuck, dry despite her swallowing.

"Where is that flint?" he muttered. Then, in the darkness of the room, her eyes adjusted. His form turned toward her. "You still have it. Give it to me, Elaina."

"No," she brought her closed fist to her chest. The man's form moved quickly, coming at her.

"Give it to me."

"No!" she yelled and threw herself to the side. She had the advantage of knowing where everything was; he would never find her in the dark if she was silent enough, but he was right there in her path and she ran straight into him. They went down in a tumble of legs and arms.

His fingers snagged in her hair, and she shrieked, ramming her hand into his face. He went limp and she untangled herself, scrambling off him and scooting away on her bottom until she touched the wall behind her. To her left was the only door to the room, unfortunately locked as it always was.

Sitting in the dark, heart pounding, she listened. Nothing could be heard besides the rain on the trees outside. Her eyes scanned the room, looking for any indication of where the knight hid. It didn't take long.

She caught a glimpse of his outline, standing near enough to the window that light from the cloudy gray evening outlined his shadow. And she could look at it. She could *see* him.

Well, not truly.

He stood taller than she, and his shoulder-length hair was disheveled. The outline of his axe rested at his waist, and he wore boots on his feet. No extra weight hung around his middle; at least as far as she could tell. Who was she to say? She hadn't seen another mortal being in decades, and when she finally could, he was nothing more than a shadow.

Her breathing slowed. Emotion choked up into her throat. She sniffed, despite her resolve to remain stealthy.

The knight's head turned in her direction and she stiffened. He didn't move. "I am sorry I frightened you. Elaina? I want to help you."

"You have a ridiculous way of showing it," she said, pushing off the floor to stand up. She held the flint tight and rubbed it with her thumb. "If you truly want to help me, you must understand something. I do not look because I cannot. I could no sooner look upon you than fly from this tower like a bird."

"I do not believe that. What if it is what will free you? What if the sorceress told you that so you would not look, so you would never be free?"

Elaina's breath caught in her throat. "You were not here when I arrived. You do not know that. I believe there must be another way, one that doesn't risk my death."

Elaina's heart pounded in her ears; even her breath was loud.

"Do you want me to return?"

Of course she did. She couldn't imagine going back to the way things had been. Silent. Alone. Talking to herself and a bird. She had waited so long for someone to come, and if he succeeded in freeing her, she could finally live the life she had been imagining.

"Yes," she said quietly.

"Then we will do this your way. I will return tomorrow, and you can tell me more about the curse. I will bring some things that might help."

"Thank you," she said, and she meant it. Her fear from earlier was gone. It had been a simple misunderstanding.

He did not mean her harm.

"The night has worn late. I must return, but I will be back tomorrow, perhaps, in the afternoon."

"I would like that," she said. She wished she could see his face. Was it the trustworthy sort, round, warm, and friendly? Or perhaps bearded and rough, with years of battle etched into the skin? "Sir knight, I realize that while you know my name, I have yet to learn yours."

"Oh! Of course. I am Sir Gereck."

She smiled. Having his name made him more real, somehow. Less like a phantom that might disappear into the night and never return. "Then, Sir Gereck, I bid you good night."

"Good night," he replied, and then he moved toward the window and she had to look away.

She lit the candle as soon as she was certain he was gone. She found herself wishing that the loom would force her to weave. It would keep her hands busy, at least. Instead, she brushed her hair, made her narrow bed, relieved herself using the chamber pot, and then sat, staring at the mirror. She wasn't really looking. She wasn't even thinking anymore. She felt numb, empty now that Sir Gereck was gone. Why continue with this life?

This wasn't a new question. It was, in fact, one she had asked many times. She wondered if she would be able to do it, to look out the window. It was such a simple thing, but even as she twisted her head towards the light, she found her neck muscles tensing, becoming stiff and immovable, and her eyes shut of their own accord.

She swallowed hard against the emotion in her throat. Even if she wanted to break the curse and end her life, she couldn't.

Once, she had tried to throw herself out, but fear had stopped her. What if the tower wasn't tall enough? She could end up maimed at the bottom, to die a lonely and agonizing death. If she was going to end her own life, it had to be quick and painless. So jumping was out of the question. She had tried, once, pulling the yarn off the loom's shuttle, but it would not unwind. There was nothing sharp in the room. The mirror would not break; at least not when she threw the chamber pot at it, and she had nothing else to throw.

Elaina lay back across her bed, eyes shut. She fell into a fitful sleep as thunder rumbled outside her tower.

She woke up hours later, the room dark and cold. The loom's familiar clacking sound filled the room, accompanied by the sound of the steadily falling rain outside. She felt chilled and fevered at the same time. Was she sick? Something Sir Gereck had said, a name, was stuck in the back of her mind. Her head ached, trying to remember. When he spoke of King Aurelius, he had said another name...

Arthur.

At that moment, a forgotten memory erupted in full color in her mind, vivid as the day it happened.

Her belly was round and full, carrying the product of a night nine months before. She rubbed it as she wove, relishing in the feeling of strong kicks and the knowledge that soon she wouldn't be alone. She had started feeling pressure that morning, but it was no different than what she had felt the past several weeks.

She knew little about birth, having had no mother to teach her such things, and part of her feared that it would go wrong. She would be all alone. No one was here to help her. No midwife, no wise woman. She only had herself to rely on. And yet, she found that she was calm as her time approached. Birth sometimes went wrong, but when it did, there wasn't much anyone could do even if someone was there. Fear certainly wouldn't make it any easier.

Now it grew, swelling, filling her belly with waves of pressure. Elaina had to stop weaving while the intensity passed, and in the midst of it, the loom released her. She stood and began to walk around. What did she have?

The tub of water brought to her room this morning sat untouched. She had gotten into the habit of not bathing as often, so she would have clean water for after the birth. It would be cool, but the day was warm and she had blankets. She glanced at the small table near her bed, on which sat a ribbon, unthreaded from one of her dresses. She didn't know why she had it, she just remembered hearing women speak about birth and mentioning that one needed thread of some kind, and since the loom wouldn't give her any, she had found something else. She hoped she would know what to do with it.

The waves grew steadily more powerful and closer together as the day wore on. The golden light of late afternoon lit the room, and a rush of fluid gushed to the floor. She walked, she swayed, and she breathed. Then she pushed.

The world lost focus; all she could see was the tiny area of the room she stood in. All she was aware of were the sensations moving through her. She leaned against her bed as a rush of force overwhelmed her and she cried out, her body instinctively falling into a crouch. The baby moved through her, her pelvis widening to allow it through.

Then, without thinking, she reached inside and touched her baby's head. Soft hair. Another gush of fluid, and blood trickled down her leg. A wave hit, overwhelming her with its intensity. She yelled, begging for deliverance from the pain. She would split in two. She could not get wider, the baby would get stuck; she was going to die.

The sun was setting outside, but she was unaware of anything other than the sensations throbbing through her body. She could not stop it. She screamed, gripping the backboard of the bed while the baby's head crowned. Then, in one final burning thrust of her body, it emerged.

She reached down and the rest of its body slid out, slippery with blood and a strange white coating. She held her baby to her chest. Little arms flailed and it began to cry, perhaps feeling the evening chill. She pulled a blanket off the bed and covered them both before collapsing, her back leaning against the wooden bed frame. As she did, the afterbirth flowed from her trembling body. It was finished. Her baby was born.

It wasn't until some time later, with a single candle lit beside her bed, that she looked at her sleeping baby and discovered it was a boy. He had light, fine hair, even lighter than her own. The next morning, the newborn had his first bath.

Just as she finished nursing him and laying him on the bed to sleep, the music of the loom wove its enchantment around her. Tired though she was after the previous day's laboring, she dragged herself to the bench, bringing a small pillow to sit on.

She spent the day weaving, and was surprised to find that occasionally the loom let her stop to calm or feed her crying son. As if it knew what had happened, and yet, it still controlled her. Sometimes she had to let him cry because the enchantment held her too long. Would she be able to take care of her child despite the limits of her curse?

She didn't have the chance to find out. Day four was deceptively bright and sunny and normal, as the other days had been. She still hadn't decided on a name for her baby boy, but she loved him more than she had loved anyone. Her heart felt full and complete for the first time since that fateful day she had been trapped in this tower. Then the door opened. A crouched figure stood in the entryway, a basket on her arm.

It was her. The old woman who brought her food once in a while, emptied her chamber pot and brought the bath water. She was here. Elaina clutched at her baby, a sudden protectiveness rising in her. The woman ignored her at first. She set a tray of food on Elaina's bed, enough for several days. She then gathered the soiled sheets that held the afterbirth, and placed them in her basket. Then, she looked at Elaina and the new mother knew what the woman wanted. She held her son tight to her chest.

"No. You cannot have him."

The crone didn't speak, but her eyes softened at Elaina's plight. She held out her arms.

"No! Please, he's all I have." Tears began to stream down her face. They dripped onto the sleeping boy's face and he stirred. "Don't take him from me. Please."

The woman shook her head, then came closer, arms still reaching for the boy. Elaina looked back at the infant in her arms. Any moment his eyes would open, blue like a river, expecting to see the only one he knew. And she knew then, with the instinct of a mother, that she could not take care of him. The enchantment would not allow it.

Eventually, there would come a time when the loom would not release her, when her son would sit for a day or more without food or care or attention and he would sicken and die. She could not take care of him; not while she was cursed. Besides that, children needed attention to grow. They needed care and nourishment, and other children to play with. Who knew how long she would be trapped in this tower? She could give him none of what he needed. She kissed his soft skin, stroking his cheek with her hand.

"I love you, little one," she whispered.

He yawned a baby yawn and began to squirm. Elaina handed him to the old woman before he could wake and watched as he settled, once more falling into slumber. Her heart constricted. She hoped he would wake and cry, reaching for her, wanting her, but it was better this way. Her heart emptied as the woman walked away.

"Wait!" Elaina cried out as the woman reached the open door. The crone hesitated, but did not turn around. "His name. His name is Arthur."

The woman gave no sign she had heard her. She picked up the basket of linens and left. The door closed behind her.

Elaina crumpled to the floor.

Tears dripped onto Elaina's shift. Her shoulders shook. Her hand was over her mouth, as if she could hold in the keening that could not be coming from her.

How could she have forgotten? Had someone taken her memories away? The crone, the old woman who had taken her son, knew something; she must. When she came next, Elaina would find out about her son. She would know what had happened to him. Was he still alive, somehow, impossibly? Did he have a happy life? Did he have a family? Where was he?

It finally made sense, her conviction to not look out the window. It had burned inside of her for years, unquestionable in its strength, but she had never had a reason. Now she did. She had something to live for. Even though he would never recognize her, and if he lived he would be old, older than she... he was her son. Mordred, without knowing it, had made her a mother.

Suddenly exhausted, Elaina climbed into bed, shivering in her shift until the blankets warmed her. Outside, the rain continued through the night.

In the morning, she woke suddenly to stifling silence. It was still gray dawn, and she wasn't sure why she had woken. She had gotten only a few hours of sleep. The loom spun on without her across the room, its familiar clack a nuisance to her tired mind. She rolled over to face the wall, trying to go back to sleep, when the door to her room clicked open.

She sat up, turning to look at the intruder. It was the old woman, the same one who had taken her son so long ago. She crept into the room, a basket of food on one arm, as she had every few days since Elaina's imprisonment.

Elaina's mind sharpened as her eyes adjusted. She stared at the old woman. Back bent with age, white hair falling in erratic wisps about her wrinkled face. The woman busied herself, setting down the basket, emptying the tub and chamber pot outside the window, shaking out Elaina's few dresses, setting one of them aside to repair it.

"Where is my son?" Elaina blurted, sitting up in her bed. The woman froze, but did not reply, then continued going about her tasks as if nothing had been said. "I know you took him. You know where he is. Tell me."

The woman's head turned to look at Elaina. "And if I do not, then what are you going to do?" she asked, her ancient voice cracking.

"I- I- I'm going to break the curse. I'll look. I'll look out the window," Elaina said. Her heart threatened to beat out of her chest.

The crone laughed softly. "Careful what you promise, my dear. I know you do not want to die."

"How do you know that?"

"You would have looked decades ago if you did." She hobbled away from the window and came toward Elaina's bed. Elaina kept her back straight and met the old woman's scrutinizing gaze.

"I know someone took my memory of him. Was it you?"

"I thought it would be less painful for you. How did you get your memory back?"

Elaina opened her mouth to respond, then closed it. The old woman was a sorceress. Maybe the same one who had trapped her, maybe not. Perhaps memory spells were easy to cast and she wasn't very powerful, giving Elaina little reason to fear her, but her gut twisted inside of her nonetheless, and she knew it wouldn't be wise to reveal Gereck's visits. At least not yet.

"It just came to me. Perhaps your spell wore off."

"No, not this type of spell. What made you remember?"

"I gave birth to him in this room! It could have been any number of things. It was raining last night, just as the night of his birth. Perhaps that was it," Elaina lied. "Did you name him Arthur, as I asked? Where did you take him? Is he still alive?" Her breath came in quick gasps, her heart pounding from the thrill of her lie going undetected.

The old woman considered her for a long time. "I told those I gave him to his name was Arthur, but I cannot be certain that is what they called him. As for whether he lives, that remains yet to be seen."

"Is he far away from Camelot? Could I see him?"

"No," the old woman said sharply, "that is not possible." She bent and retrieved her basket, now emptied of its food. Then swiftly, without another word and without looking back, she walked from the room. The door shut behind her with finality.

Elaina stared at the door for a long time after, until her arms and legs felt cold and her belly rumbled for the food that had been left. Finally, she climbed out of bed and picked up some bread and fruit from the floor where the woman had left it. She dressed and combed through her blonde hair with her fingers, mind filled with thoughts as she braided her hair, and then at last the music wove its spell around her, calling her to the loom.

It wasn't until she was seated, the tread moving beneath her foot and the arms of the loom clacking with each row of thread she finished, that the thought struck Elaina… she had been able to see the old woman.

She stopped. Her muscles, manipulated by the music, protested the halt in the work, but it took Elaina several seconds before she started weaving again. She had been able to *see* her. Not just glance around her or view her silhouette, but actually look her in the eyes. Perhaps the old woman was part of the curse, made immune to the strictures of the enchantment because the sorceress allowed it to be so. After all, Elaina could hardly avoid looking at the woman who brought her food.

She relaxed, satisfied by her own explanation, but some part of her was restless, still searching, still seeking to know. Had she overlooked something so simple? Was it true, what Gereck said, that her freedom was a glance away?

If only she could know for sure without giving up her life.

If there was such a way, she would find it.

CHAPTER FIVE

The rain poured down, drenching the countryside. Its constant driving against the thatched roof and walls of the castle drove Guinevere mad.

She lay in her bed, shivering under the covers. It had been raining all day since Merlin had arrived, and there was no sign of it letting up. Nothing Guinevere did got rid of the dampness that seeped into her bones.

The fire had burned low in the grate, down to the coals. She thought about calling for Mary, but the moment she opened her mouth, her bedroom door opened. Guinevere shot upright, clutching the blankets to her chest.

"Mary? Is that you?"

"Yes. Your fire has gone out, why didn't you call me?"

"I was about to." Guinevere watched the maid add wood, feeding the newly flickering flames until they were nice and high. It took a moment for Guinevere to feel the difference.

"This drafty old castle will be the death of us. Move over, dear." Mary climbed into the bed and Guinevere shifted over.

They had done this since she was a little girl, although in the beginning it had been for nightmares. Guinevere lay her head on her pillow, turning her back to the fire and letting it warm her.

She smiled at Mary, whose graying hair, normally wound in a tight braid about her head, was splayed out on the pillow. Her softly wrinkled face glowed in the fire's light. She still had an effortless grace and beauty that Guinevere had always admired.

"Why are you smiling like that, Guinevere?" Mary asked.

Guinevere pulled her arms out of the blankets and smoothed them over herself. "You are still so beautiful. Men must adore you."

Mary laughed. "If only it were so!" her eyes gleamed with mischief and laughter. "I do enjoy a tumble now and then, if that's what you're asking."

"I wasn't!" Guinevere replied, blushing deeply. "I didn't mean to, anyway. You're far too scandalous for polite company."

"Good thing I'm not in any, then."

They laughed together, then fell silent. Guinevere turned on her side, resting her head on her hand.

"But really, Mary. What is it like?"

"Wonderful, if he's gentle." Mary gazed at Guinevere, eyes and voice softening. "I am sure the king will be good to you."

"I'm not betrothed to him yet!" Guinevere exclaimed. "But I know these alliances are often made more from political advantage than love, and it would be nice to know... what to expect."

Mary clasped Guinevere's hand. "Your father would never choose a cruel man for you." She paused, looking at their hands. "I want to be sure my Gwen is happy, before I die."

"You're not that old," Guinevere scoffed, but the seriousness of Mary's stare made her feel guilty. "I know it's my duty to make a good match. Perhaps I've grown up."

"Or you've finally met a man to make your bosom burn," Mary said. "The king is a handsome one, and charming and kind. He'll make a good husband."

"What?" Guinevere shook her head. For some reason the image of Sir Lancelot had distracted her. "Oh, the king, of course."

Mary frowned. "You do fancy him, don't you? You've been mooning about the castle ever since he left. Or have I read that wrong?"

Guinevere smiled. "Rest assured, Mary, if I can procure the king I'll be a happy woman indeed. Marriage may not have been my favorite topic in the past, but I feel that the king, of all men, might be perceptive to having a woman of thought by his side."

"In his bed he won't care if you think," Mary said. She held up a hand to Guinevere's protest. "It's true, and you can't deny it. A man doesn't marry a woman for her brain, at least not at first, but the good ones come to appreciate it. Focus on winning him first, with your body. Then you can convince him of your mind."

Guinevere kept her mouth shut. No amount of arguing would change Mary's view. She hoped that, perhaps, King Arthur was different.

"Come now, you're tired. It's the middle of the night, after all. Let us sleep." Mary said, laying down and pulling the covers up. She rolled over and seemed to instantly fall asleep, but Guinevere found herself unable to succumb to sleep any more. She stayed awake until the sky lightened outside, and then she got up, careful not to wake Mary, and dressed herself and combed her hair.

She glanced at the letter on her nightstand in passing.

It would greatly please His Highness, King Arthur, to have your presence at the summer jousts in Camelot. Her father had given his immediate and enthusiastic consent for her to attend.

Two months away from home, longer than she had ever been away in her life, but she would go, and, as Mary put it, see if she could win herself a husband.

Guinevere crept from the room. The castle stirred with the first signs of life. Her father's wolfhounds barked outside as she walked through the corridor toward the great hall. When she was outside the doors, her father's voice could be heard as well. Guinevere pressed her ears against the doors and could make out some of what was being said.

"...sent you here to take my daughter away..."

"I would have you remember that you requested an escort..."

"Of knights! Not a blasted demon sorcerer..." Her father stopped short, then became flustered. "Begging your pardon, Merlin. We aren't used to... your type, and we've heard stories, see. Men turned in trees, entire armies silenced without a sword swung. It's unsettling."

She listened hard, but heard no answer from Merlin. He had arrived the day before, a mysterious figure cloaked and soaked from the rain. A shudder ran through her. She didn't take well to a man so shrouded with rumors of magic.

"I trust swords and good, honest men. What guarantee do you have that I will see my daughter again, and that she won't have been... altered?"

"My word will have to be enough. That and knowing I have a vested interest in keeping the king's intended betrothed alive and, as you put it, unaltered."

"Intended...? The man has only seen her once! And they've exchanged but five words in person."

"Apparently words are not needed," Merlin said dryly. "The king is young, and your daughter is fair. It is a sensible match, given your loyalty to the king."

"Indeed," her father replied. She could picture him stroking his mustache and taking a hefty swig of mead.

"Lord Leodegrance," Merlin said suddenly, "I would like to speak with your daughter. Would you have her brought in?"

"Certainly," he clapped, and the door swung open suddenly.

Guinevere let out a shriek as it caught her toe, and she stumbled out of the way. She straightened. Her father was shocked to see her standing there, and he glanced from her to Merlin with a bewildered look on his face. He regained his composure quickly, however.

"Guinevere, Merlin wanted to..."

"Speak with me. Yes, I heard, Father." She bit her lip as her father's face reddened. She shouldn't have mentioned her eavesdropping. She curtseyed, keeping her head down. "I'm sorry father, I couldn't help but..."

"Be seated," he growled.

"Yes, Father." His pride was easily offended, but just as easily mended.

Guinevere hurried to her seat and allowed the servant to pull it out. She sat across from Merlin, his icy blue stare making her colder than the damp hall. She shivered and stared at the plate set before her. Guinevere sipped as quietly as she could, but it echoed in the stillness of the hall. Even the hounds were petrified, shuffling quietly in the corner without their usual snarling and bickering.

Merlin cleared his throat. "The king wishes your presence at the summer festival, no doubt you can guess his intentions."

"Then why invite me now? The summer festival is months away."

"Ah, yes. Your father believes you need tutoring."

Guinevere opened her mouth in protest, but one glance at her father's stoic face made her think twice. She waited for the sorcerer to continue.

"I will be staying with you for some time at Cornwall, to evaluate whether you would truly make a good match for our king. You are lacking in the art of courtly behavior. You've had little experience or example, and since the king has expressed such interest, I recommend you take your tutoring seriously."

"Is this necessary?" She looked desperately from her father back to Merlin. Neither man showed a hint of changing their mind.

Merlin interlocked his fingers and leaned in towards her. She found herself unable to look away from his frigid gaze.

"In the two encounters we have had, you have shown yourself to be outspoken and unfazed by overstepping your bounds, as well as prone to surrendering to emotion under stress. None of these qualities make a queen, and unless they are rectified, you will never fill such a high position. It will take a significant amount of time, I recommend you begin now."

Guinevere's face burned with shame. She pressed her lips together, withholding the insults she wanted to hurl in the wizard's self-assured face.

"Guinevere," her father's voice growled deep in warning.

She took a deep breath through her nostrils and let it out slowly. "I appreciate the king's attention and favor. I will go to Cornwall."

Merlin studied her for a moment longer before responding. "Very good. Provided the rain lets up, we will leave within the week."

It took five days for the rain to let up, and three more before the roads were passable. Guinevere wondered why Merlin hadn't waved his hand and sent the storm clouds away. She kept running into him; he was around every corner, in every room. She couldn't escape him, but she was proud of herself for keeping a civil tongue. She hardly spoke a word to him except to wish him well every morning at breakfast, and to excuse herself from his presence.

The entire castle was in a flurry of action the last few days as they rounded up all the supplies Guinevere would need on her journey. Infuriatingly enough, no one would let her help with anything. So, she sat in her room, embroidering, reading, and staring out her window until her eyes glazed over. Even Mary was too busy to spend much time with her, and Guinevere missed her attention.

One afternoon, she found Mary going through her dresses. She sat on the bed, fidgeting, as the woman muttered over worn seams and frayed hems.

"If this is what it will be like to be the king's wife, I'm going to run away and marry a farmer," Guinevere blurted, when she could take the silence no longer.

Mary stopped and turned, a hand on her hip. “Everyone has a task to do in the castle. I have no doubt you'll be plenty busy.”

“What are the queen's tasks?” Guinevere asked, standing and swishing her dress, dropping into a mocking curtsey. “Looking beautiful? Displaying jewelry and gossiping?”

“This is exactly why your father is sending you to Cornwall!” Mary said, returning to the wardrobe. “You have no concept about how a kingdom is run and how to behave in court. The Duke and his wife, God help her, will have their hands full with you.”

Guinevere sighed dramatically and draped herself against the nearest pole of her bedframe. “Cornwall is so far away from here. What if Father needs me?” Mary didn't respond. “It doesn't make sense for him to send me there. We'll pass Camelot on the way!”

Mary slammed the lid of a large trunk shut and leaned on it. “You'll do what he says. I doubt he wants you anywhere near the king until you have learned the ways of court. Especially after what happened the last time he was here.”

“It was one comment, a teensy bit satirical... doesn't anyone have a sense of humor?”

The maid dragged the trunk over to the door, and set it against the wall with several others. “A woman is expected to honor her husband. It looks poorly when a girl does dishonor to her own father. And a king, most especially, must not look weak to his people. You'll have to curb your tongue in his presence far more than you do here,” Mary said sternly.

Guinevere looked at her shoes. There was a black scuff on one toe. How had that gotten there?

Mary sighed and came close to her, resting a hand on Guinevere's shoulder and kissing her forehead. "Growing up is never easy."

Guinevere sighed, gave Mary a small, reassuring smile, and set herself to her embroidery once more.

At least she was going somewhere. Somewhere new, different. Perhaps her life would take a turn for the better. Not that things were difficult or any degree of horrible here, just uninteresting. Being in Camelot, consorting with knights and a king and any number of noblemen and women, was bound to provide some excitement, and that was something she could look forward to.

The thought lifted her heart, and she spent the remainder of her afternoon caught up in daydreams that caused such pleasant feelings that even Mary's concerned frown did not diminish them.

CHAPTER SIX

"You should have been there, Gereck. She was stunning."

Gereck looked up from the sword he inspected. King Arthur stood before him, cutting a gallant figure in his gleaming armor.

"Aye, Your Majesty, and I hear the battle was glorious as well." His palms felt sweaty.

The king squinted into the sun, then shaded his eyes. "I suppose, as battles go. But Lord Leodegrance's daughter... well, she was a relief to look on after weeks of sweaty, bearded men."

"I don't know if that's a compliment, Sire. Are you certain it wasn't just...?" Gereck trailed off. He had to be careful. He wasn't sure how the king would react if he insulted a woman he appeared to be attracted to.

"Desperation?" A friendly grin split the king's face. "Aye, could have been, but she was an angel, Gereck. Truly. A vision from heaven." Gereck wasn't sure what to say to that. He glanced around, letting awkward silence fill the space. Between them. Birds chirped in the early morning. It was a relief when King Arthur cleared his throat and broke the silence. "Where is Lancelot? Has he slept in?"

Gereck shook his head. “He was dressed when I reported to him this morning, Sire. He might have gone for a ride before your sparring.”

The king sighed, looking down.

“Surrendering already? I accept.” Lancelot’s familiar voice met Gereck’s ears. He grimaced.

The king straightened, picking up his sword and pointing it at Lancelot. “I think you surrendered when you decided to show up late.”

“Sorry about that, Sire. I had important business to attend to.”

“In the forest at the crack of dawn?” Arthur raised an eyebrow.

Gereck pretended to wipe a spot from the sword with his rag. It gleamed by now, and well sharpened, but he wanted to watch the sparring. If it didn’t look like he was doing anything, Lancelot might send him away.

“Just an informant I needed to meet.” The knight’s eyes landed on Gereck. “I would rather discuss it in the security of your council room, away from prying ears.”

Gereck’s cheeks burned.

“Of course,” Arthur replied. He shook his hair out of his eyes. “You missed our discussion.”

“Oh? And what would you have to talk about with my squire?”

Gereck gritted his teeth at the condescension in Lancelot’s voice, but he kept his head down.

“Who else? Lady Guinevere.”

“Oh, her again?”

Gereck looked up in time to see Lancelot roll his eyes and shake his head as he adjusted his gauntlets.

“Wasn’t she the fairest maiden you’ve laid eyes on?” Arthur asked. He placed his helmet on his head, then held up his blade. “Swords today?”

“I would rather practice mace.”

“Very well. Your mace and sword against my sword.” The king grinned, and Gereck sat up. This would be interesting.

The two men circled each other. Arthur reached out with his sword first, a wide chop certainly meant to draw Lancelot out.

His blow was met by Lancelot’s shield and Arthur stumbled back with the force.

“So, Guinevere,” Arthur said.

“She’s fair enough,” Lancelot said, swinging his mace and slamming the king’s shield, “but not your type.”

“Is she yours?” Arthur asked, recovering from the hit in time to knock Lancelot’s sword from his hand.

Lancelot shrugged. “No more than others have been.”

“Are you even a man, Lancelot? Do you have eyes? You got to touch her, and you won’t claim her beauty moved you?”

They sparred, pushing too hard for conversation, until Lancelot called a stop to remove his helm. Arthur removed his as well. Their chests heaved, and their hands adjusted their grips on shields and weapons.

“There is more than beauty to be favored in a woman. And we know nothing of that,” Lancelot said, spitting into the grass.

“What more is there to know, truly? She was genteel, charming, well-mannered...”

“Until that comment of her lord in front of you.”

Arthur laughed. “And witty, then! Honestly, Lancelot. One would think you were made of ice. Someday I’ll find a woman to melt your soul as Guinevere has melted mine. Did you know she is coming for the Beltane festivals?"

"I did not think she would bother to travel." Lancelot wiped sweat from his brow and hefted his mace, as if considering using it on Arthur.

"I invited her specially. Her father thinks I might choose Guinevere as queen."

Lancelot looked up, eyes flashing. "And might you?" he asked sharply. Gereck recognized this mood. Something Lancelot wanted was slipping from his grasp.

"I would like to speak with her more, to make sure she is suitable, but yes, I might." Arthur flashed a wide grin and struck towards Lancelot with his sword.

The knight dodged smartly and his mace swung down, narrowly missing Arthur's head. The fight continued until Lancelot had at last brought Arthur to the ground, ending the fight as he did most days.

The sweaty, panting men clasped arms and grinned at one another. "I hope your conquest with her is more victorious than your sparring with me," Lancelot said.

Arthur laughed and walked off the field, chatting with his best knight about sword and mace techniques while Gereck struggled to carry the discarded weapons and shields off the field. He had been at Elaina's far too long the previous night, and with the several hours it took to get back to the castle, well, it was going to be a long day.

He spent the rest of the morning in the armory, polishing various bits of metal. The other squires, boys half his age, chatted and teased, and fought amongst themselves. He kept to himself. The others liked him well enough, but none of them considered him a friend. Besides, they were all nobleman's sons, born and bred for knighthood.

Many of them had a year or two more of service as a squire before age would automatically qualify them to participate in the knights' tourney, and perhaps win a place at the Round Table. Any who didn't make it could remain a squire and try again the following year, or choose to become part of the king's infantry as a foot soldier, with little honor to gain besides regular pay.

Winna had tried to convince Gereck for years to accept a soldier position, but Gereck could never bring himself to do it. He had watched his friends leave, either returning to their farms or joining the barracks soldiers. Some tried to keep in touch, but duty, family, and war called them away often, leaving Gereck alone in his fight for knighthood.

Most thought him insane. Winna certainly did at this point.

"Oy, Gereck!" a voice shouted at him. Gereck stood up, sending a lap full of armor odds and ends clattering to the floor. The boys around him laughed. Flustered, Gereck bent to pick it up. A cuff to his head sent him sprawling sideways on the dirty armory floor. Sir Lancelot stood over him. He turned first to the boys watching with wide-eyes.

"Get out of here, all of you."

"But, Sir Lancelot, we're supposed to…"

"Out!" he barked.

The boys dropped their polishing brushes and cloths and scattered, leaving the room empty. Gereck's head was still ringing, and his throat was dry. He looked up at Lancelot.

"Where is my shield, squire?" The menace in the knight's voice was unmistakable. Gereck started to sit up, but Lancelot hit him again, this time across his face.

“I couldn’t find it.” Gereck said, feeling his lip. It was bleeding.

“What do you mean, you couldn’t find it? It’s bright bloody yellow!” Lancelot bellowed, slamming his fist on a nearby table.

“Sir, I looked everywhere. It must be at the bottom of the river, and if so, it has washed downstream. There is no way to find it.”

“Then no one will find your body when I take you diving for it.”

The threat made Gereck nervous, but again, Lancelot had made no secret of his disdain in the past and often threatened him. He likely didn’t mean it. He would order ten lashes and forget about it.

Lancelot suddenly struck a helm sitting on the table, sending it clattering against the wall. Then he turned on Gereck, grabbing his shirt and lifting him into the air. “Do you have any idea what you have cost me? That shield is irreplaceable.”

“It’s just a shield, Sir Lancelot. The king’s blacksmith is as good as any in the kingdom; you can have another made.” His air supply was running low. He pried at Lancelot’s hands, trying to loosen the knight’s grip on his shirt.

“Not this one.”

A fist, sheathed in a metal gauntlet, struck Gereck across his face. His head snapped to one side and his jaw cracked. Blood filled his mouth. He spit out a broken tooth and wiped his arm across his mouth. Blood streaked his sleeve.

He looked up, blinking back tears at the pain blinding the left side of his face. “How did Arthur ever choose you as one of his knights?” he asked. “I know I’ll never see it.”

"Which is why you will never be a knight," Lancelot replied. He ran his fingers through his hair, other hand flexing on his sword, then thrust his way past Gereck.

Leaving the polishing things and armor on the floor for the others to clean up, Gereck made his way through the castle, ignoring the pitying looks he received from other servants he passed.

He didn't get far before Sir Tristan ran into him, *tsking* at the sight of his face. No comment was made about Lancelot's actions, but the knight was kind enough to stop a passing maidservant and enlist her help. She, in turn, took Gereck to the cook, who doubled as an apothecary of sorts. He made Gereck swish salt water in his mouth to clean the wound his tooth had left. It was one of his back molars; a tooth he wished he could have kept, but one he could live without.

After a quick wash with a warm herbal tea, Gereck convinced the cook to let him go. His face still tingled from the herbs as he left the kitchens. The scrape on his face was shallow and would heal quickly, and the cook was convinced he would suffer no further injury. Gereck wasn't so sure, as he rushed down the corridor, his head feeling as if it was under water. He slowed to a brisk walk.

He determined he would visit Merlin today. The king's sorcerer was the only one Gereck knew who might possibly be able to help Elaina. Would he be in his tower rooms? Or in conference with the king?

Bergus, the king's steward, and two guards stood outside the doors to the great hall.

Gereck stopped. "Is Merlin in conference with King Arthur today, Lionel?"

One of the knights broke his serious expression to smile at Gereck. “Indeed he is, Gereck. By the looks of it, you’re going to ask him for a new face,” the other knight, one Gereck didn’t know well, chuckled.

“Very amusing. Listen.” Gereck leaned in toward the knight and lowered his voice. The steward was watching him suspiciously. “I need to get in there. I need to talk with Merlin, and it’s important. I’ll wait until he finishes with the king, of course. I don’t know when I’ll have another opportunity. He’s liable to disappear for days at a time, you know, and this can’t wait.”

The knight hesitated. Bergus stared at them.

Gereck leaned in further. “I’ll make it worth your while,” he whispered, “the Three Arrows, tonight, my tab.”

Sir Lionel raised his eyebrows, then glanced over at the steward. “Oy, Bergus, Gereck here has been sent to replace your man inside. Special instruction from Sir Lancelot, who wishes his squire to serve the king.”

The steward gazed long and hard at Gereck, probably wondering what happened to his face, which felt hot and swollen.

“I heard nothing about this. Are you certain?”

“Yes, sir,” Gereck said, giving Bergus his most innocent expression. “It is my honor to serve his majesty.”

“I wish I had been told these things. They have started eating. It isn’t appropriate…”

“I will go tell Lancelot I’m not needed then. He won’t take it lightly that his gift was ill received. The king will hear about it.” Gereck said nonchalantly, turning to go. He winked at Sir Lionel.

“Wait!” the steward called. He sighed, rubbing what little hair he had left. “Go in. Send Dan down to linens.”

He walked away, muttering to himself. Gereck grinned at the steward's back, then nodded to Sir Lionel and the other knight before opening the doors and entering the great hall.

Inside, two men sat, their discussion clearly growing more heated, while their food grew cold. Gereck took his place beside the king's chair, relieving a young boy who stood there, and found Merlin sitting across from him. Neither man acknowledged his appearance.

"This is meant to be more than a marriage of convenience or political alliance, Merlin. I do believe I could love this girl. Is not my happiness also of import?" The king took a swig from his cup. It was almost empty, so Gereck fetched the wine off the table and poured some in. He was also expected to attend to Merlin, he supposed, but the sorcerer hadn't touched his cup.

"I was afraid you might bring that up," Merlin admitted. "You are king, Arthur. Your happiness relies on the well-being of your kingdom."

"As you frequently remind me," Arthur replied. "I understand that, but the kingdom also needs an heir, and intelligent, beautiful women of age and decent breeding are difficult to come by in these times. Few lords or dukes in the area have daughters of appreciable personality and comeliness. Many are too young, and I'll not marry one much older. Guinevere is as good a choice as any, the way I see it, and her father is loyal to me. Securing that loyalty through marriage could save our borders."

Merlin's blue eyes sparked with anger, though his voice remained steady. "You do not know her well enough to form such an alliance."

"And you do?" Arthur demanded. "You've met her once, as have I."

"I traveled with the woman for a fortnight, escorting her to Cornwall. I had the opportunity to get a reading of her while we journeyed. She is unstable and unpredictable, greatly lacking in respect, and her emotions are out of control."

"You said she was to receive training," Arthur replied. "Surely she has improved since you last saw her."

"Mere weeks will not change a lifetime of neglect in the area of courtly respectability," Merlin said. He seemed to grow taller as he spoke, and the back of Gereck's neck prickled uncomfortably. "Arthur, I have no way to impress upon you the importance your marriage holds for this kingdom. I cannot force you to choose otherwise, but I fear her beauty is what holds you spellbound and you will consider no other."

Gereck shifted his feet to keep the blood flowing through them. His head pounded, but as he refilled the king's cup a second time, he was able to keep his hands steady. The king picked up the cup as soon as it was full, taking several large gulps before responding.

"She is more than a simple beauty, Merlin. She is charming, and intelligent. There is wisdom in her, I know it."

Merlin raised his bushy white eyebrows. "More than courtly gossip provides?"

Arthur looked away. "You aren't being fair."

"Life is not about fairness, Arthur. You must listen to me. Marriage to Guinevere is the biggest mistake you could make."

"Very few options have been presented to me. It is not hard to see she is the best choice of those who have come before. Admit that, at least."

"Many of them knew their place and were comfortable in themselves. Guinevere is not. She would not suit you."

"If she can bear an heir, then that will be enough."

"If that is the only requirement, then any other woman would do," Merlin countered. His gaze, fixed upon Arthur, was steely and cold.

"And now we come full circle. Have you been listening to me? I do not want a marriage of convenience if love presents itself, and it has. You could be happy for me."

"Love has been the downfall of many a good man. I will not be happy for such a fate to befall you."

"You speak of fate. What of God's will? The bishop believes the alliance to be a wise and good choice. He wrote to the bishop over Lord Leodegrance's chapel. Guinevere is a faithful, devout woman. Surely God will be pleased enough with her. Or do you suppose to know the will of God better than our bishop?"

Gereck's ears perked up. The bishop did not like Merlin, that much was well known in the castle. He preached against the use of magic weekly. Gereck was curious to hear Merlin's own opinion of the bishop first-hand, to see if it was the same.

"I do not presume to override God's will, Arthur, and whether or not he has any bearing in your choice of wife is an argument for another time. Simply heed me when I say this; the bishop is but an imperfect man with an imperfect interpretation of life and its doctrines. He has no more knowledge than you or I in this matter, and perhaps much less, as he has not met Guinevere himself. My counsel, whether you choose to follow it or not, is this: do not marry Guinevere in haste. Another woman, any other, in fact, would give you a happier future."

"Unless you have seen the future and can tell me for certain Guinevere bears me ill will, I cannot believe you mean that." Arthur pushed away from the table, his chair scraping against the stone floor, and stood. Gereck thought he would storm from the room, but then the king's shoulders relaxed and he sighed, shaking his head. "You are too wise to ignore, and I respect your counsel. I will take some time to get to know her better."

The old man remained seated as he watched Arthur leave. Since it seemed the wizard would not be eating, Gereck began stacking dishes and preparing a load to take back to the kitchens. Silence filled the hall, and after some time, Merlin's eyes closed and Gereck wondered if the old wizard had fallen asleep. Perhaps he would not get to talk with him at all. He almost dropped the stack of plates he was holding when Merlin finally spoke.

"What do you think?"

Gereck waited for his hands to steady, and then he set the plates down at the table's edge. "About who the king should marry?" he asked, hardly believing Merlin would address him.

"Yes. Should Arthur marry Guinevere?"

"I have not met her. I cannot say."

Merlin laughed. "You are wiser than most, to admit ignorance."

Gereck set down the plates. "I do not presume to know the will of God."

"Neither do I, but I believe he gives us more say in the course of life than we think."

"What do you mean, sir?"

"Nothing more and nothing less than this: God has more important things to do than to dictate our lives down to the simplest acts of daily living."

"Then you would have me believe God does not care," Gereck said.

Merlin shook his head. "No, on the contrary. He cares so deeply that he will not choose for us."

Gereck was faithful in his church attendance, but he had never presumed to ask such questions of the bishop. As wary as he was of the sorcerer, he figured him harmless, and, in fact, found himself drawn into conversation with him as easily as an old friend.

"Then does God answer our prayers? Does he heed them, even when we pray about things that are of less than cosmic importance?" he asked.

"Ah, now you assume too little of him. He is so involved in our lives that, if we are living right, we will see Him everywhere, and thus our insecurity of being left to our own devices vanishes, leaving such power in confidence in its wake as to make us servants unto ourselves, and thus better able to serve the most high God.

"You see, young man, God created us with brains, the ability to decide. Too often, men do not use their brains. They rely on God or fate to change them, to change their situation, to solve each problem they face. What they do not realize is that God gave them the ability to do all this themselves, with a nudge from heaven now and then."

"But the bishop says we can do nothing without God. If that were true, wouldn't he dictate every decision of our lives?" Gereck asked.

"And that is why you should never listen to a bishop," Merlin said, with a twinkle in his eye. Gereck did not know whether the man was serious or fooling with him. "The priestesses on Avalon understand this. To them, the

Goddess is everywhere, available to call upon as long as you know how to ask for help. It does not do to say, 'Do this for me, and I will be loyal forever'. That is false loyalty, lacking faith. But to say, 'I am going to do this, be with me and give me strength', that is another thing, and a better one. It can be a tricky balance, at first, to know when to rely on the arm of God and when to surge forward on your own strength, but a balance that can be learned."

"You mention the priestesses, but they do not believe in God. What does their faith have to do with my own?"

"You are mistaken. The wisest of them believe that their Goddess can coexist with the Christian God. In their minds men and women rule side by side in the heavens, and on earth, women have as much power as men."

"Is that realistic?" Gereck asked.

"Think on it. You will find the answer for yourself."

Gereck stood silent, pondering. He had never before thought about it. He had been raised in a world where men ruled on thrones, on the battlefield, in the home. He remembered Winna, the strength she had in managing all the affairs of their home while he was gone. She didn't need a man to do all that. So what did she need a man for at all?

"Does this Goddess, then, rule over God? Do men serve as mere vassals for getting a woman with child when a child is wanted, or for waging wars when war is necessary?"

"We have gotten off topic," Merlin observed, finally taking a sip of his drink. He didn't continue, and Gereck began again to clear the table. "Women do not rule men in the Old Religion. They stand beside, a worthy consort and equal in making all decisions." Merlin spoke quietly, gazing into his cup. "Men and women have different energy, directed to different things. When that energy combines and a man and woman come together, powerful things can happen. They are far more powerful together than apart, but the power each brings to the table is unique and individual."

"So you would find an equal for the king, and Guinevere is not that equal?"

Merlin tipped his cup toward Gereck. "Very observant. I believe the Lady Guinevere is lost inside herself. It would be better for a queen to not be so distracted." Merlin sighed heavily and heaved himself to his feet, holding onto his staff. Gereck noticed his hands trembled, and the beads carved into the knob at the top of his staff rattled loudly. "Alas, all the theological discussion in the world, however enlightening, will not help stubborn kings choose worthy brides."

"Then you believe he has chosen poorly?"

"I believe that a pretty face causes a man to do many foolish things."

"The lady Guinevere is intelligent as well as beautiful, from what I hear. I think she would do well for him."

"One can hope that I am wrong, then." The old man smiled, then stood to leave the room.

"Oh! Merlin, may I ask you something?"

"You just did, lad." The old man's voice was serious, but his eyes sparkled. Gereck cleared his throat.

"I met someone. A young woman, trapped in the tower of Shalott."

Merlin raised his eyes. "Then legend would appear to mingle with reality."

"Yes," Gereck said, breathless for some reason. His heart pounded. "Anyway, she says she is enchanted. There's this loom and a mirror, and she's forced to weave forever... I thought..." He licked his lips. "Well, I thought if there was anyone who might have an idea of how to free her, it would be you." He stopped, waiting a long moment, trying not to stare at Merlin.

"I may," Merlin replied. "Then again, I may not. Try this first." He pulled a vial from his sleeve. It was made of blue glass, and the liquid inside was dark. Gereck reached for it, and Merlin pulled it away. "Be sure you do not spill a drop. It will burn through flesh, bone, rock, metal... anything it touches."

Gereck nodded. "Yes, sir." Merlin put the vial into his hand. "What would you suggest I do with it, sir?"

"Well, don't pour it on Elaina. There are things in that room binding her to the enchantment, disrupting one of them might do the trick."

"Yes, sir. Thank you."

Merlin clapped Gereck on the back and walked from the room, his hands tucked inside his robes while he muttered to himself.

Gereck placed the vial in a secure pocket and began clearing the table. Excitement burned inside him as he thought about what it could do. He could free Elaina. Perhaps that would be a quest worthy of knighthood. His daydreams ran away with him. It wasn't until he had finished clearing the table that he realized something strange about his conversation with the old sorcerer.

He knew Elaina's name.

Gereck hadn't mentioned it to anyone since he met her. A strange, unsettled feeling filled his chest. He stared at the door Merlin had gone through. Some believed Merlin could see into the future. Many believed that was how Camelot had come to be, how Arthur had become king, that Merlin had orchestrated it from the dawn of time. If that were true, why would someone with that much power be interested in Elaina? And how did he know her name?

The thoughts followed him all the way through Camelot's gates and down the road, to the foot of the tower, filling his head with questions about the girl who lived in the room above him. Then he began to climb.

CHAPTER SEVEN

She lives with little joy or fear
Over the water running near,
The sheep bell tinkles in her ear,
Before her hangs a mirror clear,
Reflecting towered Camelot.
And sometimes thro' the mirror blue
The knights come riding two and two:
She hath no loyal knight and true,
The Lady of Shalott.

Over the past several days, Elaina had jumped out of her skin every time the trees rustled in a stray breeze, or when she heard anything that sounded like a man's voice carried on the wind from below. Too often, it was nothing. A bird, or a man calling out to an acquaintance on the road outside.

It was like reliving the first days of her captivity all over again, every sound meaning rescue, every day her last in the tower working at the loom.

It was torture.

By the end of the seventh day, Elaina had reigned in her emotions in once more. The hope that had begun to blossom within her wilted. She hardened herself to the idea that he might break his word; that he would not return.

Then, late in the afternoon, the unmistakable sound of someone coming in through the window crackled behind her, and the man entered the room, breathing heavily from his climb.

"You're back." The words were out of her mouth before he had swung both legs over the window ledge.

"Of course I am. I said I would be." Gereck moved closer and sat on the floor near her. She kept her eyes forward, letting the thread colors fill her vision. Her fingers were nimble as they moved the shuttle back and forth, foot pressing a large pedal on the floor, making the strings compress every time she stepped on it. It was easy to get caught up in the rhythm.

"Are you ready for my ideas?" he asked.

"Ideas?"

"You didn't think I came empty handed?"

"You haven't had much in the past."

He handing her a velvet-covered bag. "Try something out."

She took it, feeling its soft surface, then reached into the bag, pulling out a small, blue glass bottle.

"What is this?" she asked.

"A potion given to me by Merlin. He said it is acidic, and can burn anything. Or anyone, so be careful."

She scrunched up her face. "What would I use it for?"

"I thought you should try burning the thread on the loom, or the wood of the loom itself. You could try the mirror, although there isn't much in that bottle. If you damage one of them enough, perhaps you'll be freed."

Elaina looked around, then stood and walked toward her dressing screen. She came out from behind it holding a scrap of linen fabric, which she wrapped around her hand before popping the cork off the bottle.

She sniffed it and gagged, then carried it over to the loom and carefully dripped some onto the threads. There was a sizzling sound, and she eagerly watched the threads, but they remained intact. Instead of burning, the threads gleamed with a strange light that quickly faded, as if they had absorbed the potion.

"Try the wood," Gereck said.

She did. It fizzed on the surface, then seeped into the wood, leaving no trace she had poured anything on it. The bottle was still half-full.

"I suppose I ought to make an attempt on the mirror," she said, the excitement in her heart dwindling.

The frame of the ornate glass surface tilted on its stand and Elaina pushed until it was angled so the potion wouldn't fall to the ground. Gereck came to stand behind Elaina, watching.

She breathed in to steady herself and then poured, the potion trickling from its bottle. It hit the surface of the mirror and pooled like water. Nothing.

"Wonder if it works," Gereck said, sounding discouraged. He leaned in to get a closer look and his arm brushed Elaina's. She startled away from him and the mirror slipped from her grasp, returning to its upright position. Both she and Gereck leapt back as the potion rushed down the mirror's glassy surface and dripped onto the wooden floor where their feet had been.

A sizzling, burning sound, then a tiny waft of smoke and the smell of burning wood hit Elaina's nostrils. She watched in amazement as a fist-sized hole burned straight through the floor. Stairs wound down the tower below. In amazement, she looked at Gereck, who stared at the hole.

"Sorry about that," Gereck said.

"Can you get any more of that potion?" Elaina said, hope building again.

"Why?"

She began pacing the room. "Stairs, Gereck! There are stairs beneath us. If we burn a big enough hole... it would take one more bottle, I think. Then I could get out and..."

"You would still be cursed," he said. "The moment you stepped outside, wouldn't you die?"

The smile slipped from her face. She sat heavily on the bed, and turned her face toward the wall. "For a moment I forgot about the curse. If I was just imprisoned, everything would be a lot easier, wouldn't it?"

"It was a good try." He dropped the bag in her lap. "There's more to try."

Elaina toyed with the bag. "I don't want to right now. Besides, this will give me something to do while you're gone."

"Right," he said.

A bird chirped outside. Elaina stared around the room. For decades she had dreamed of being rescued, of someone coming to her tower, someone she could talk with, and now she didn't know what to say. She fiddled with the drawstring on the bag he had given her, pulling it open, then cinching it shut, aware of Gereck's eyes on her. She smoothed the surface of the bag and began twirling a strand of hair around her fingers. He moved closer to where she sat and cleared his throat, letting her know he was near. Her head raised, but she didn't look at him.

"Now what?" he asked.

"You must promise to take me seriously. No laughing?"

"No laughing," he agreed.

Elaina closed her eyes and turned her face toward him. "I'm afraid."

"Afraid? Of what?"

She imagined that she could see him, longed to open her eyes and fill them with his face, his figure.

"Afraid of leaving here. I know nothing about the world today. A lot can change in half a century. For all I know your king is a tyrant and you're an ogre and..."

He laughed.

"You promised!" she exclaimed.

"I'm sorry! All right, I'm sorry. You were talking about ogres, and the thought of Arthur as a tyrant is laughable. He's the greatest king England has ever seen. Truly. Better than his father, even."

"The king's name is Arthur?"

"Yes."

She swallowed the emotion that rose inside of her. Her son shared his name with a king. "The name reminds me of someone I knew before, that's all."

"Family?"

She nodded, afraid if she spoke the tears would come. After a moment, she cleared her throat. "Anyway, I was being foolish just now, but I meant it. I have no family, no living relations left at all to take care of me, nowhere to go if I get out. I don't know how the culture has changed, the customs... Sometimes I think it would be easier to stay in here forever and not have to worry about anything out there." She crossed her arms over her chest, staring at the wall across from her.

Suddenly, he stood in front of her. She gasped and covered her eyes, heart pounding. He had been by her bed, all the way across the room. How had he gotten so close without her hearing? As her heartbeat slowed, she realized she had caught a glimpse of the blue tunic covering his chest. Would that be enough to break the curse? Was she about to die? She didn't feel any different.

His hands took both of hers, pulling them away from her face. She kept her eyes squeezed shut and her face turned away. She couldn't look, not now. Not after making it so long.

"Then I will prepare you for the day you step foot outside." His gentle voice broke through the darkness of her world, and he pulled her to her feet. "This is a dance we recently learned. It's the most popular right now."

She began to murmur a protest, but Gereck ignored her, one hand on her waist, the other holding her right hand high into the air. He moved quickly, humming an upbeat tune and guiding her with her hands. She didn't know what to do with her feet, and kept tripping and stumbling as he led her out into the room.

Occasionally, light from the window would stream through her eyelids, flashing by as her partner spun her around. She laughed out loud, a true, carefree laugh, and for a moment, there was no tower, no curse, and nothing to fear.

After a time, they halted, breathless and laughing. Elaina protested exhaustion and sat on the floor to catch her breath. Gereck's warmth whispered past her cheek as he sat beside her.

His hand closed over hers in her lap and she sucked her breath in at his unexpected touch. "Elaina,"

"Yes?" she replied.

"Look at me."

Her heart almost stopped.

"I can't," she said. It was painful to swallow, like something was lodged deep in her throat.

"I think you can," he said. She shut her eyes as she heard him move. His other hand took her free one. "What if this broke the curse? What if this is what would set you free, just to open your eyes and see?"

Elaina swallowed, the pain bringing tears to her eyes. "Truly, I can't."

"I want you to open your eyes."

Her eyelids flickered. Another glimpse of blue tunic. Could she? An image came to her, an infant's face, wide-eyed with wonder, staring up at her the night he was born. Arthur. "No," she said.

"Elaina, what's stopping you?"

She wanted to. It had been so long since she had seen another mortal being in the flesh. And the way he asked, the urgency his voice held... could he care for her? She turned the thought over and over in her mind, each time almost convincing herself she could, and would, before thinking of Arthur again and rejecting it.

At last, she couldn't take it any longer. "You don't know what you're asking," she thrust his hands away and stood, walking a few paces, leaving her back to him.

"What do you possibly have to lose? You said yourself you hate it here, you have no family, no reason to live..."

"I have a son!" she shouted. Tears streamed down her face. "I have a son. I can't die until I meet him or know he no longer lives."

"You have a son?" Gereck asked. The shock was plain in his voice. Elaina couldn't speak. Her throat felt raw from shouting. “How?”

“There was a man I loved, Mordred, and he loved me, before...” she stopped, recovering her voice. “A child was the last thing on my mind, but after a few months in the tower, I couldn’t deny that I was pregnant. I gave birth to a boy.”

“Why didn’t he come for you?”

“What?”

Gereck sounded impatient. “He was a knight, wasn’t he? This man you loved? Where was his honor?”

“I-I don’t know. I waited so long for him.” Her sobs filled her throat and she couldn’t speak for a time. Gereck said nothing until after her crying slowed.

“Where is your son now?”

She shook her head. “I don’t know. I am not sure he even lives.”

Suddenly Gereck was there, kneeling at her feet, tugging one of her arms free until he could hold her hand. “Elaina, I promise you, I will do all I can to see you free and unite you with your son.”

She sighed and looked to the mirror. “I wish I believed it were still possible.”

“It is,” Gereck insisted. “Can you tell it what to show you?”

“What?” she asked. He released her hand.

“The mirror. Can you direct it?”

“No. At least, I’ve never tried...”

“Maybe you can!” Excitement filled his voice. “You have to try. I’ll ride down the road from Camelot at high noon every day I am able. My horse is brown, with white hocks. I’ll wear armor, or at least chainmail, and I’ll wave at your tower. That ought to distinguish me from most people you see. You can focus on the road outside while you're weaving and try to direct the power of the mirror. If you see me, you can look for your son, too."

"I will try," Elaina said, biting her lip. "Promise you will return?"

"It might be a few weeks, but I will," he promised. "I have to go back now. They'll be wondering where I am." He moved towards the window.

"Sir Gereck," Elaina said, causing him to turn back, "what were you doing, that day you climbed my tower?"

"Looking for my shield," he admitted. "I lost it in the river and hoped to catch a glimpse from above."

"Why not get a new one?"

He hesitated, then, "I know it sounds silly, but I'm fond of it. When we get you out of here you can help me look. It's silver, with a yellow lion painted on the front."

She nodded. "Right. When I am free."

"Until then."

He grabbed her hand, startling her. His lips brushed her skin then her hand was released. His boot steps were loud on the wooden floor. Outside, tree branches rustled. Then silence.

She wore a small smile on her face, and her hand tingled where he had kissed her. Even as the music of the loom began to call to her quietly, drawing her to work the loom, hope blossomed within her heart. She looked at the mirror. Could Gereck be right? Could she make it show her what she asked?

She thought about Gereck and strained her mind, focusing on the sound of his voice and what she knew of his form. The scene didn't change. It showed her the same workers toiling in the field, as it had all afternoon. Their faces, bearded and red with exertion, were blurred by the watery shadows that played across the surface of the mirror. Elaina's head ached and her fingers stumbled with the shuttle, causing it to jerk against the strings of the tapestry.

With a sigh, she turned her attention back to the loom and untangling the shuttle from the warp strings she had caught it in. What was the use? She couldn't control the mirror any more than she could control the loom's power over her. She turned her head back toward the mirror. As frustrating as the unchanging scene was, it was something to look at.

Five men, weeding their barley fields. Occasionally, one turned to another and spoke. Another man picked up a hoe, digging at the golden rows with determination. Elaina let her mind wander, wondering what Gereck would say if he were here.

She imagined her conversation with him, the next time she saw him.

"Why, sir knight, I'm glad you have returned," she imagined herself saying.

"Of course. Why wouldn't I?" he would say.

She could almost see the confident, charming smiling that would spread across his face. Never mind that she had never seen his smile, much less that she knew it would be charming. That was a perk of not seeing him; she could imagine him any way she liked.

"Did you see me in your mirror?"

She would shake her head. "No, *I'm afraid not.*"

How disappointed he would be! And frustrated, to be sure. After all, as a knight he was surely used to being right and winning his battles.

What if, instead, she could say she had succeeded? What if mastering the images in the mirror was a key to saving her from the curse? Then she could look at him, look into his eyes, smiling a charming smile of her own, and say that she had succeeded, that his idea had worked, and now they could climb down the wall outside the tower window and ride off on his steed and get married and have seven children and...

Her heart clenched inside her chest and tears sprang to her eyes, the ache in her heart so strong she thought it would burst. Children. How could she forget?

The first thing she would do if she escaped would be to find her son, not ride off with some man she barely knew.

She took several calming breaths, waiting for the pounding of her heart to subside. If she could convince the mirror to show her anything in the world, it would be Arthur.

She tried, she truly did. Her eyes focused and unfocused on the mirror's surface, her mind straining to bring forth the image she wanted to see. *Show me my son. Show me Arthur.*

The mirror stayed on the same scene, the same road it always shown, lined with the barley field with its tiny sprouts, and she tried to keep tears from falling as the shuttle passed between her hands, back and forth, back and forth, just as it always had.

CHAPTER EIGHT

A sound woke Guinevere with a start. She lazily blinked sleep out of her eyes, stifling a yawn as she lifted her head and turned towards Lady Bergara.

"Lady Guinevere, you have not been paying me the least attention."

"Well observed," Guinevere mumbled, not yet fully awake. She rubbed the last of the sleep away, but she didn't miss Lady Bergara's furious glare, and then the lecture began.

"I've heard you have promise. You might marry the king. Well, with your lack of attention towards your lessons, and the disrespect you've shown me, more likely than not the knights will reject you, and you will be traipsing back to your father before the Beltane festivals are half over."

Guinevere smoothed her dress and looked back at the woman, who continued to verbally berate her. She had been appointed Guinevere's governess from the moment she arrived in Cornwall, as Merlin could not stay to teach her and a woman was more appropriate anyway. Neither had taken to each other fondly.

Lady Bergara was an insufferable woman, made worse by her jealousy of Guinevere, who had done nothing beyond be the subject of rumors about whom the king would marry. Guinevere was sure she was sabotaging her learning with false information. So why pay attention?

Lady Bergara's face purpled with anger, and Guinevere pitied the woman. She put on her best apologetic face and folded her hands in her dress.

"I am sorry, Lady Bergara. You are absolutely correct."

That stopped the older woman mid-rant. "I am?"

"Yes, you absolutely are. In the face of this sad fact, there is only one thing to be done."

"There is?"

Guinevere stood, scooting her chair back loudly, before dipping into a perfectly adequate curtsey. "Good day." She turned and walked out of the room. Down the hall and around the corner, she found an alcove and knelt on the floor inside. She put her face in her hands.

Truth be told, Lady Bergara was considered the authority on courtly behavior. If she thought Guinevere a hopeless case, how would she ever avoid making a fool of herself in front of the king? No matter how much she tried, Guinevere couldn't control herself around the woman. It was like she was another person out here, away from familiar things.

Guinevere looked at the sunlight filtering through the narrow window at the end of the hall. It had been quite rainy the past few weeks, trapping her inside. She could use some sun. Guinevere pushed to her feet and went to her room, donning a light woolen cloak with a hood to go over her riding skirts and tunic. She needed to clear her head of stagnant castle air and stuffy court behavior.

She kept her head down, but most of the people she passed were servants who hardly glanced at her twice. She made her way to the stables, waiting for the hand to bring out a horse. A nice, tall mare was brought out, her breath puffing from her nostrils as she snuffed Guinevere's hand. Guinevere muttered comfortingly to her, patting her neck and rubbing the white star mark on the horse's broad forehead.

The stable hand knelt on the muddy ground, holding his hands for her to mount, but Guinevere shook her head, smiling at him.

"I can mount alone."

To his credit, he stood and stepped back, staying near as though he were afraid she would fall.

One hand on the pommel, the other near the horse's hindquarters, a foot in the stirrup. She vaulted up easily, then sat steady while the stable hand adjusted the stirrups to better suit her height. She felt on top of the world, seated so high.

As soon as the young man finished, she nodded her thanks and walked the mare out of the yard. Guinevere hardly noticed the brisk air. She took the mare to a trot, then faster, until she stretched out over the horse's neck, the wind whipping her hair behind her as the black tresses came free of the pins holding them up. She laughed wildly, all worries of what others might think disappearing in the face of momentary freedom.

She raced like that for some time, until her face began to numb from the cold and her fingers could no longer grip the reins. The sun, so bright when she had started out, neared the horizon, making the air colder than ever. She walked the mare, whose sides heaved, and set a comfortable pace for the ride back to Cornwall. The keep was still visible on the flat landscape; she hadn't gone far, but it would likely be dark before she returned.

Guinevere looked all around, appreciating the blue cast of light that began washing over the land as the sun dipped further down. She enjoyed the silence until the telltale clatter of tack on a trotting horse could be heard coming up behind her.

She turned in the saddle. The Duke Cador rode on his black stallion. She absolutely loved the duke's horse, which stood a hand taller than her own mare, the inky blackness of his coat contrasting with the shock of his white mane and tail. She had never seen such a powerfully beautiful beast in her father's stables. She raised a hand, hailing the duke, who pushed his horse into a brief gallop to catch up with her.

"Good evening, Duke Cador. Out hunting?" She noticed a brace of grouse dangling from the duke's saddle.

"Ah, young Guinevere. The cold puts such a lovely flush in your cheeks," he replied.

Guinevere smiled. The duke was fifteen years her senior, but recently married. Which was too bad, for he was handsome despite his age. As it was, he had made it clear he thought her charming, but all within the bounds of courtly respect and candor.

"I came out here for some fresh air."

The duke moved his stallion closer to her mare, reaching across Guinevere to pat the horse's neck. "You've given my girl a good run, I see." He straightened and looked at Guinevere, his green eyes gazing at her intensely. "How are your lessons?"

Guinevere hesitated. Lady Bergara was the duke's wife. She couldn't afford to insult her. "I'm not sure they are going to help me much," she said.

"From what I hear, you can use all the help you can get," he joked, eyes twinkling. Guinevere pretended offense, looking straight ahead while trying not to smile. She urged her mare forward. The duke kept pace easily. "She's no match for Kane," he said, "so if you're trying to run away, it won't work."

The chill settled in through Guinevere's clothes as the sun vanished over the distant hills, taking with it most of the evening's pale light. A fine, misty drizzle dampened her hair and clothes.

"Are we going in the right direction?" she asked, suddenly feeling disoriented.

They entered a grove of trees. She had gone around it on her ride out, but figured it would be shorter to go through on the way back. It was thick enough she couldn't see the keep, and with night coming on, her senses were dulled. She could hear the horses snorting, stamping their hooves as they walked. Kane pressed against her leg and Guinevere tried to steer her mare away, but the trail narrowed. Suddenly she was uncomfortably aware of how close Cador was, his leg touching hers, his arm brushing hers, his hands...

Shouldn't be *there*. She reached behind her, to push them away, but the duke took the opportunity to pull her nearer, stopping the horses as he brought his face to hers and pressed his lips over her own. Guinevere pulled away gasping, her movement causing the mare to step uneasily beneath her. "Sir, this isn't appropriate. You have a wife, and..."

His lips came against hers again, hot and heavy. His hands wandered, seeking in the darkness, finding her breast... Guinevere pulled her foot from the stirrup and got enough leverage to kick at him, but he grabbed her foot, and pushed his hand up her skirt, feeling the length of her leg. Guinevere yelled, thrashing her leg, but he held tighter.

She panicked now, flailing her arms in the dark to keep him off. He let go of her leg and dismounted. His hands gripped her waist, and she knew if he unseated her the fight for her virtue would be over. The image in her mind of what he intended to do sent her mind reeling into a panic. She kicked the mare's sides, one leg still free of the stirrup, and the horse bolted.

Guinevere suddenly had the strange experience of being in her body, but not in control. *Someone else* occupied the forefront of her mind, controlling her arms and legs, holding her back inside her own body. She pushed against the strange presence, trying to take control so she could stop their wild flight across the land. Her limbs didn't respond. Instead, her feet kicked at the mare's side over and over, and a shriek erupted from her lips.

The scream of her mare came an instant before her body left the saddle and tumbled through the air. A moment later, she plunged into the frigid water of a fast-moving river. The air left her lungs immediately, and she opened her mouth reflexively to gasp, but all she got was water.

The child-like presence in her mind was petrified, unable to move, unable to give control of the body they shared back to Guinevere. Water poured into her lungs and her body convulsed underwater. The current swept her along, pushing her head underwater. Her arm struck a rock. She tried to yell but choked on the water inside her, clearing it out in time to be dunked under again. She was going to die. Her mind fogged, and she let go, drifting away. Her body stopped struggling, and a sharp pain cracked against the back of her head.

"*My name is Morgause.*"

Guinevere floated in the darkness, unable to move, unable to open her eyes.

"*My name is Morgause.*" The voice spoke again, soft, gentle, like a child's. "*I am afraid.*"

Afraid of what? Guinevere could not speak. Her thoughts seemed to echo out loud, wherever she was.

"*Afraid of hurting. That's why I ran.*"

Duke Cador, the horses…

Where am I? What happened? Am I dead? Guinevere asked, panicking.

"*You are not dead. You are protected.*" Another voice, also female, but adult. Hrarsh and familiar, somehow. "*I am Morgan le Fay.*" It spoke in response to Guinevere's silent confusion. "*I am here to protect you. We all are.*"

We? Guinevere thought. She still saw nothing. *How many are you?*

"*We are as many as you require to stay safe. Three have a name,*" *the adult woman, Morgan, spoke again.*

What are your names? Why are you here? How can I…

Guinevere woke into a sudden shock of gasping for air, eyes looking frantically from one face to another that surrounded her bed. A cool hand on her forehead slowed her pounding heart. Mary. Guinevere gripped that hand with all her might, anchoring herself in the present.

"Where have I been?" she croaked. The river had given her a sickness because of the cold. Her throat was sore and hot.

Confusion crossed Mary's face. She glanced across Guinevere's bed at someone, then back to Guinevere, smiling with some concern. "You have been here, my dear, under the capable care of the duke's physician."

Guinevere reached back and touched the back of her head gingerly. It was covered in a thick cloth bandage.

"You were fortunate the duke happened by when he did, Lady Guinevere," the physician said, "you might want to thank him."

She nodded numbly. She knew she should smile, thank the duke as he stood with his wife near her bed, but she could only stare, her entire body trembling under the blankets as Duke Cador spoke.

"I don't normally ride that direction. It was fortune indeed that led me to the river in time to see the mare throw Lady Guinevere into the water," he explained. His nose was bandaged. He had apparently struck a rock whilst saving her and had broken his nose. Lady Bergara held his arm, stroking it lovingly. Did she know? Probably not.

A thought came then, and the impression of it nearly threw her into a panic. She didn't remember anything after she hit her head. How could she be sure that the duke, when he rescued her, hadn't taken advantage of her while she was unconscious? Was she still a virgin?

Tears came to her eyes and she shut them tight, trying to swallow past the sudden tightness in her throat. Whispers around her indicated the others thought she was sleeping, and one by one they left, until only the physician was left. He added another blanket to those already heaped on her, and peeled a bandage away from her head. Her eyes blinked open.

"How bad is it?"

The physician looked at her. He had a serious, round face, the type that could be either stern or jolly as the situation dictated. In that moment, it was grave indeed, and Guinevere swallowed hard, waiting to hear the worst.

The physician sighed. "Well, my dear, it could have been much worse. If the duke hadn't gotten you here as quickly as he did, we would be having a burial."

Guinevere's entire body relaxed. He didn't have time, then. If he had taken advantage, she would be dead. At least he had that much decency, to save her life rather than satisfy his lust. He had never intended anything to happen to her, and had probably thought she would accept his advances. Hadn't she teased and bantered with him enough? Practicing the courtly love, she had told herself, but he must have read farther into her words and actions than she ever intended. Clearly, the fault lay with her.

"Milady." The physician's concerned voice brought her out of her thoughts.

"Mm?"

"Your head wound is deep, and you have lost much blood. I suggest you drink this and get some sleep."

He helped her sit up, pushing a cup against her lips. She choked on the contents, sputtering as the bitter herbal tonic forced its way down her throat. She grimaced as she lay back, but once the taste left her mouth a pleasant warmth washed over her, and she was at once quite sleepy. The physician left the room as her eyes drifted shut, and a healing sleep overcame her.

The following days and weeks of her confinement to bed passed without event. She was finally declared fit to leave bed the week before the festival, and it was a fortunate thing, as she was convinced she had begun to go mad with no one but the insufferably chatty Lady

Bergara for company. The duke made a point to avoid her, something Guinevere was glad for.

The end of her bed rest marked the beginning of a flurry of activity to ready her entourage for the several days' journey to Camelot. She spent her last days at Cornwall walking arm and arm with Mary over the grounds of the keep, the abundant spring sunshine making the ground muddy beneath their boots, but they had little care for that. Guinevere's head still ached terribly when she stood for too long, and her muscles were weak after the time she had spent abed, but she felt stronger every day.

She felt better once she got the courage to tell Mary the true story of her accident. Mary shared her sympathies, but confirmed her suspicions; most men were like that, often failing in their chivalric duties, especially in the face of a beautiful woman. She disagreed with Guinevere's assumption that it was her fault, however, insisting that rape, no matter how it came about, was never a woman's fault. Guinevere wasn't sure she believed her, but she agreed anyway, to keep Mary happy.

Two days later, they were on the road. The carriage held her like a cage, and Guinevere wished she could be atop a horse like Mary, but the physician had flat-out refused to allow her to ride in her condition, and he had given Mary a notice for a fellow physician in Camelot to look after Guinevere and make sure she didn't try to ride too soon. A fall from a horse, he said, could kill her. She would be able to ride in six weeks, no sooner.

This, of course, made her miserable. She spent the majority of the first day trying to convince Mary she was going to die no matter what, so why couldn't she ride?

But Mary wouldn't hear it. On the second day of their journey, Guinevere finally found herself enjoying the ride, despite the slight headache she had, the sickness in her stomach from the carriage's rocking, and the smell of her travel-worn clothes.

The countryside was beautiful, jeweled with dew in the early morning light, and despite how cool it had been recently, it was hot now. As the afternoon wore on, the air in the carriage became stifling. Guinevere sweated so much that she wished she could rip off her clothes and run free in her shift.

A chestnut horse trotted up to the open carriage window, and Mary's excited voice broke through Guinevere's daydream of skinny-dipping in a freezing mountain lake, and she pulled herself to the window and looked out.

"The tower, milady, isn't it beautiful? Like something out of a fae story."

It was tall, and covered in moss and ivy, the leaves a brilliant green against the dull gray stone. A wide, half-circle window arched near the top of the tower. Guinevere thought she could see someone moving inside, but from that distance and with the glare of the sun… *No, it couldn't be. No one would be living in there.*

"'Tis the faerie of Shalott," one of Cador's men claimed, trotting beside Guinevere's carriage. "The locals are extremely superstitious of her. There are many stories about how she came to live there."

"Do you believe any of them?" Guinevere asked. The soldier shook his head.

"No. There are enough people that I can see for me to worry about. It doesn't do to be worryin' over enchanted women and the like."

"A man of practicality," she said. The soldier's chest puffed out, and he straightened his shoulders proudly. Guinevere smiled. "How much farther to the castle?"

"At our pace? A few hours' journey, milady. Not far now," the man replied.

He was right. The sun was lowering when they passed through the city gate, and when the steward opened her carriage door, Guinevere just about trampled him scrambling out. Apparently, they weren't the only ones to have arrived recently; the square outside the castle gates was filled with bustling servants, horses being unloaded, carriages and carts lined the outer wall. Guinevere's eyes widened at the chaos.

"You come from the outskirts, I assume," a husky female voice said, and Guinevere turned towards it.

A young woman stood, her silvery blonde hair falling down her back in a thick braid. She wore a dark blue dress over a white underdress with sleeves that were so long, they swept the cobblestones at her feet. Around the woman's waif-like waist was an ornate metal belt, designs stamped in each piece.

Suddenly, Mary had dismounted and was standing beside Guinevere. She nudged her, and Guinevere stumbled into a curtsey. "Lady Guinevere of Carmelide."

"Lady Nimue Cavender, Northumberland."

"Northumberland?" Guinevere stared at the woman. "But that's incredibly far north. What brings you to Camelot?"

Lady Nimue rolled her eyes. "The festivals, of course. I have men in the games. And I am of marriageable age, as you are." She sidled up on the other side of Guinevere and leaned her head in towards her ear. "There are plenty of men for both of us, I wager. Although only one will win the prize." She looked pointedly in one direction, but before Guinevere could see whom she meant a voice broke out over the bustle of the square, drawing her attention.

"At last you have arrived!" It was the king. He beamed, his arms outstretched, and he looked straight at *her.*

"Your majesty," she stammered.

Mary elbowed her side and she finally remembered to curtsey, wobbling as she came up. He met their curtsey with a bow, keeping his eyes on Guinevere, the smile never leaving his face. She knew she should have practiced the curtsey more. She ducked her head, feigning modesty to hide the embarrassment in her cheeks.

When she finally glanced up, Guinevere had to try hard not to stare. King Arthur was even finer to look at now that he was dressed up, in a bold green tunic and tan trousers, Excalibur at his waist.

"I expected you to come sooner, milady. I am glad you have not missed the beginning of the festival. It starts tomorrow."

He turned to Lady Nimue, taking her hand and kissing it. "My lady Nimue, we have met. You grow more beautiful every year."

"Yes, Your Majesty," the Northumberland woman replied, a smile spreading on her face that made her face brilliant with its beauty. Guinevere noticed how many men stared at the woman. She might as well be Lady Bergara, she thought, standing next to the Northumberland woman.

"My lady met with a slight accident, Your Majesty," Mary said. Guinevere shot her a warning look, but she held her tongue, trusting that Mary knew what she was doing. "It delayed our departure somewhat."

The king's eyes creased with concern. "An accident? Of what sort?"

"My head," Guinevere said, exchanging looks with Mary. "A horse I was riding bolted and I struck it in the fall." She smiled. "I'm doing much better, however. You can hardly tell anymore."

"But she gets weak at times, Your Majesty. She will need much looking after." Mary looked so grave, Guinevere could hardly keep from laughing.

"I will see to it personally, milady. I am sure the castle physician would be glad to tend to your care while you are here," the king said. A call from the other side of the courtyard drew his attention, and he excused himself, expressing his regret and informing them that both ladies had a seat at his table come supper. As soon as he had gone, Guinevere turned to Mary.

"Was that really necessary? I sound like a complete invalid now."

Mary smiled knowingly, but before she could speak, Lady Nimue broke in.

"She has done you a great favor, Lady Guinevere," she eyed Mary appreciatively. "You are fortunate your servant knows something of courtly matters."

Mary nodded her thanks for the compliment, but Guinevere felt confused. "What has she done for me, exactly?"

"I must see to the unloading of your things, milady," Mary said.

She curtseyed to Guinevere, who excused her awkwardly. Mary had rarely curtseyed to her, it was hard to remember what to say. Once Mary had gone, Lady

Nimue took Guinevere's arm and led her toward the great castle doors.

"The king will be extra vigilant towards you now, and you will be easily remembered. He will be drawn to you in your weak and vulnerable state. He won't be able to resist checking on you often, and that will give you opportunities for intimate conversation the other women won't have."

They reached the top of the stairs, and a pair of knights pulled open the great wooden doors. The two women stepped through and walked down the hall. Something smelled incredible, and Guinevere's stomach rumbled. A hot meal would be divine after two days of travel.

Guinevere opened her mouth to reply, then closed it. She suddenly remembered Lady Bergara's first lesson: court politics. From what she said, Lady Nimue was her competition in every respect. A friend quickly made was, according to the governess, a friend to be avoided. Another woman's intention would be to scope her out, and discover her intentions regarding the king.

The prospect of tiptoeing around every subject suffocated Guinevere. And trying to evade the hatred and gossip that came with competition for a man's attention, well, she would have none of it. Better to put friendship off now than wait for a knife in the dark.

"Doesn't that put you at a disadvantage?"

Lady Nimue stared at her, then tilted her head back and laughed. "My dear Guinevere, we misunderstand each other. I am not here to win the heart of the king."

"Aren't you?"

She shook her head. "No, I am not. There are other men with far more to offer." Her eyes gleamed in the torchlight. Guinevere stared at her.

"Who do you mean?"

They came to a stop before another set of large wooden doors, and a steward asked their names. Once given, the doors opened and they stepped into a feast hall, tables laden with ornate dishes and every seat filled. Above the din of conversation, the steward called their names and they entered. Guinevere froze; every lesson she had learned flew out of her mind. She clutched Lady Nimue's arm, fully aware of all the eyes on her.

"I will take care of you," she whispered. "Do not be afraid."

Lady Nimue steered her around the tables, not stopping until they reached the table at the head of the hall. It, too, was mostly full, except for a tall-backed chair at the end of the table, and two chairs to its right. A servant took their names and appointed them those empty seats.

Sweat dripped down her neck. A quick glance around the room told her that the king was not yet in attendance, and there was no place more likely for him to be sitting than beside her. She gripped folds of her dress in her hands, trying to get rid of the panicked feeling that rose in her throat.

It was one thing to greet the king in a hall of crowded soldiers, in her own home where she was comfortable. It was another thing entirely to be seated next to the most beautiful woman in the realm, who knew the king personally, and attempt to hold his attention and regard through dinner conversation.

A hand, light and cool, found hers, and Guinevere looked up to find Lady Nimue looking at her.

"I knew when I saw you, you were set apart," the woman said quietly. "It would appear court rumor is true; the king intends to marry you."

"How do you know?" Guinevere asked.

"You are seated next to him. Only one woman holds that honor. Traditionally, this seat is kept empty if the king is not married."

"Then why am I sitting in it?" Guinevere asked. "He has said nothing of marriage to me. We hardly spoke the one time we met!"

"Your beauty speaks for you," Nimue said, smiling. "You must have left quite an impression."

Guinevere made as if to respond, but the doors opened and a trumpet sounded. The king was here. He strode confidently toward their table, nodding and smiling at those he recognized, but he mostly kept his eyes on Guinevere.

She swallowed hard and forced herself to be calm, smoothing out her dress. She kept her eyes down, daring to glance back at him occasionally. It took an eternity, but he at last stood at the head of the table, raised his goblet, and announced a toast.

"To Camelot!"

"To Camelot!" The feasters roared back in unison, and the servants came out with steaming plates of food. Everyone waited for the king to take the first bite, which he did with gusto, and the celebration began.

Guinevere's palms sweated terribly. She wiped them on her dress, then picked up her fork. She hardly noticed the food that went into her mouth. She couldn't taste it; her mind was entirely focused on the man who sat at her left.

"Lady Guinevere, how are you feeling?"

She put her goblet down and smiled at him. “I am well, Your Majesty.”

“Your attendant, she said you were injured.”

“Yes, but I am much recovered. Tell me, Sire, about your knights. I hear they are the most noble in the land.”

His entire face lit up. “Indeed they are! I hope you get to know my knights. You will not meet better men.” King Arthur was looking at her expectantly.

She glanced down the table’s length. Among the few privileged lords and ladies who sat at the king’s table, several dozen knights sat, marked by chainmail armor and red cloaks emblazoned with the king’s golden dragon.

One dark-haired knight, seated several seats away on the opposite side of the table, lit up in a grin as he laughed at one of his fellow knight’s jokes. When he saw Guinevere, he stared, his smile growing. It was his eyes that drew her in, gazing into her as if he could see what she felt.

Her heart raced in her chest, and her breath quickened. The room spun. She looked away.

“That is Sir Lancelot,” Nimue told her, “the noblest, bravest knight Camelot has known.”

“Is that so?” Guinevere asked, trying to sound indifferent. “And what has this Lancelot done to earn that admirable description?”

“He has saved my life a number of times, to begin with. Would you like to hear of one?” King Arthur asked.

Guinevere nodded, and he launched into a tale of the knight’s bravery. She was only half listening. She wanted to look back at Sir Lancelot, to see if he still looked at her and return his smile, but it wouldn’t do to be rude to the king. She tried to pay attention. Her eyes wandered over his face.

It was plain compared with the fairness of Sir Lancelot's. His blonde hair was pallid and dull compared with the knight's curling, midnight locks. The pounding of her heart slowed. Her mind wandered back to Lancelot. She picked at her food, but kept her eyes on the king.

He laughed at something he had just said, the people nearest to him joined in, and suddenly her heart perked up. His laugh had a full, joyful sound, and when he smiled, it reached out to her from his eyes.

She couldn't help but smile with him, and even though she hadn't heard what he had said, she found herself laughing.

"Lady Guinevere, would you care to join me for a picnic tomorrow? We can take our noontime meal in the forest beneath the trees," the king asked suddenly, his eyes gleaming as he gazed at her.

Guinevere's cheeks flushed. "I would love to," she said, and she meant it.

"Great! Now, tell me more about Carmelide. Do you find it much different from Camelot?"

Guinevere found immense pleasure in telling him about the hills she would ride through with her father, and all the things she loved about her home. His full attention was on her, and her alone. Others occasionally joined the conversation, asking her questions, which she answered, but no matter who she spoke to, the king's eyes never left her face.

She would have felt uncomfortable if it had been anyone else, but his presence put her at ease, and his attention made her heart warm. She finished telling him of her favorite horse, when her eyes were drawn upward.

Sir Lancelot walked towards their table. He was smiling at her, and she forgot what she had been saying to the king, who had fortunately engaged in conversation with Lady Nimue.

"Lady Guinevere."

She reached for her goblet and took a hasty drink, but her hand trembled too much to hold it steady, and a small amount of wine sloshed onto her dress. She dabbed at it with a napkin, ignoring the amused look Nimue gave her.

"Sir Lancelot, how good to see you again."

"Yes, though it would seem I have a habit of causing inconvenience for you. I do apologize for that."

Inconvenience, indeed. The last time they met, she had fainted, so some improvement had been made. Her heart throbbed again, and she feared looking into his eyes. What if she fainted again? Already her head felt heavy, and thoughts crowded into her mind in such numbers she couldn't discern all of them.

"It is not your fault," she managed to reply, though her own voice sounded far away. She frowned and put a hand to her head.

"Is milady feeling well?" Lancelot asked with concern.

Guinevere's vision swam. "I fear the drink has gone to my head. Lady Nimue, would you..." She closed her eyes, feeling an enormous throb in her head. "Would you..." Her tongue would not form the words she needed.

She looked at Lady Nimue, who wore such a concerned expression that Guinevere opened her mouth to say she just felt a bit dizzy.

Then her world darkened and went black.

CHAPTER NINE

Gereck shifted his stance, then pulled his collar away from his neck. The squire livery for special occasions was notoriously uncomfortable, and he hadn't worn his for ages.

He had managed to avoid the ridiculous tights and comical frilled collar for the past several events, but the jousts were a celebration that united the kingdom, and was not something one could circumvent for the sake of one's own comfort.

It didn't help that it was boiling hot out, one of the first real indications that summer had indeed arrived.

As a squire, he served the guests, filling cups and running messages up and down the length of the table. It was to his credit that he had been assigned the king's table. Perhaps someone had put a good word in for him. He caught the eye of Sir Tristan at the end of the table, and returned his smile with a nod.

He let his mind drift to Elaina. It had been weeks since he'd last seen her, and yet, his heart was still buoyant from the moment they had shared. And they had laughed, too. They had shared a moment of carefree happiness, such as he had not allowed himself since, well, since the day he had married Winna.

Guilt flooded his chest.

A letter from his wife sat on his bed, arrived that morning. Unopened. He had avoided opening it, knowing that what it said would likely be more of Winna's pleading for him to come home, to perform his duty as a husband and give up his aspirations to be a knight.

When he was with Elaina, his dreams of knighthood were already true. With Elaina, he could be the man he wanted to be, unburdened by the whining of an unsatisfied wife and her constant reminders that in her eyes, as long as he pursued this dream of his, he would always fall short of being a good husband.

He filled the king's cup, mind churning with thoughts, barely picking up on what was being said. Lancelot had left his seat and was speaking with the Lady Guinevere. The famous Lady Guinevere. The castle was already buzzing with words about her, rumors that the king intended to marry her. By the look on Lancelot's face, the knight had ideas of his own about whom she might marry.

As he looked at her, she put her hand to her head, but smiled assuredly at the expressions of concern from her companions. Then, she fainted. Gereck nearly dropped his pitcher in shock, but managed to keep hold and fill the proffered cup of someone at the table, he didn't bother noticing who.

Faint shouts from outside the hall drew Gereck's attention away from the Lady Guinevere, who was being attended. What could be going on? Several knights stood, hands going to swords.

With a deafening clap, the wooden doors at the end of the hall were flung open so forcefully that they struck the walls. The unmistakable sound of a galloping horse thundered through the hall. Gereck stood stunned, with wine spilled from the pitcher he held dripping down the front of his livery as he watched the rider approach. Shrill shrieks and gasps echoed around him, drowned out by the sound of giant hoofs on stone.

The rider was a giant of a man, riding on a steed that stood taller than any horse Gereck had ever seen. The ground vibrated with each step the horse took. Its great black sides heaved from exertion, as if it had galloped a good distance.

Gereck's eyes traveled from the horse to the man. He was built like the horse he rode, and his massive bulk was encased in gleaming, dark green armor. A long, scraggly beard, thick and full, fell across his chest. His eyes were tiny, dark beads, hidden in the depths of his helm.

A dozen knights leapt into action, charging towards the giant of a man. The giant raised his enormous, gauntleted hand and the knights were swept off their feet by an invisible force. They skidded across the floor in a clatter of swords, appearing stunned, but unharmed. The enchanter's hand raised again towards a second group of knights that had risen to replace their comrades. They hesitated, glancing at King Arthur, who stood at the head of the table.

"What business have you to call at the castle at such an hour of celebration?" King Arthur spoke, his voice ringing out across the stunned hall.

The rider swung down from the impossibly tall steed and landed on the floor, sending motes of dust swirling in a strong beam of sunlight.

Silence. King Arthur cleared his throat.

“I bid you, have a seat at our table for the feast.” He indicated to his left, where two servants hastened and squeezed in an empty chair. Gereck fought a strange urge to laugh. The chair would never hold the giant of a man who graced the hall with his enormity.

“I did not come for feasting and merriment,” the giant growled. His horse tossed its head and snorted impatiently.

The king’s face tightened, and his hand went to the sword that hung on the back of his chair. Excalibur. “If it is a battle you seek, then I will gladly deliver.” He drew Excalibur with a swift motion, and the ringing of blades echoed around the hall as his knights followed suit.

“No battle,” the giant announced. “A challenge.”

“If it is a challenge you want, then how will you answer to the deaths of my men outside these doors?”

“They are not dead. My blows rendered them unconscious, no more.”

Who here, among Camelot’s famous knights, would deign to fetch me one blow, in exchange for standing a return blow from my axe?”

On that word, he drew his axe as swiftly as the king had. The double-headed blade gleamed with a bright emerald sheen. The occupants of the room gasped, for who had seen steel that color in their lifetime? Its edge was sharp, as expected, its handle ornately decorated in ivy leaves of gold and green. The giant raised the axe over his head, and the room, filled with exclamations, fell silent.

Gereck looked around. Would no one take it, then? Were the knights under a spell, an enchantment, such that their brave hearts were frozen with fear?

A sneer grew on the giant's bearded face. "I must be mistaken, then. Is this not the hall of the famed knights of Camelot, of whom such mighty boasts are made, and legends spun, and ballads sung?"

Suddenly, the king thrust back his chair and stood, brandishing his sword. "I will take up your challenge, sir knight!"

Several women gasped and swooned in their seats.

The king spared a moment's glance for them, then began to stride towards the challenging knight. "You will see that we fear neither you, nor the edge of your axe."

The giant sprang forth suddenly from where he stood and the knights all stood in response, each pushing back their chairs and rushing forward to meet him. He stopped short of swinging the gleaming blade at the king, and instead knelt, offering the axe to him. "You give the first blow," he said, bowing his head.

Lancelot grabbed the king's shoulder.

"Sire, you mustn't. Head games are no fair battle for a king to fight. Let a knight take him up." Lancelot spoke in hushed tones, standing behind the king.

"I don't hear you offering to take my place."

"Think of your kingdom. Who knows what enchantments or sorcery this man might have planned to ensnare you? He knew you would not resist defending the honor of your kingdom and your men, and if he lives and succeeds in his return blow, you die with no heir. Think, Arthur."

Gereck saw the hesitation in the king's eyes, but he also saw determination in the set of his shoulders, the tension of his jaw. He was going to do it. Unless...

"I will do it." Gereck stepped forward.

Lancelot stared at him as if he had grown a second head.

Sir Tristan, who stood closest to Gereck, shot him a concerned look and mouthed, “What are you doing?”

Gereck ignored them. He walked straight to the king and stood between him and the knight. “I will take up the challenge.”

The king tightened his lips, looking long and hard at Gereck, as if searching. Then, he nodded.

“Very well,” and he stepped back, “but you will use my blade, rather than his.” He turned the hilt of Excalibur toward him and Gereck reached out and took it, numb at the offer. A surge of energy went through his hand as it contacted the hilt. He shivered, then bowed.

“Thank you.”

“Success is the only thanks I need,” the king stated. He turned to the giant, who remained on bended knee, watching with interest. “You have your challenger. Proceed with the game.”

Gereck turned to face the man. He stepped forward, trembling. His arms would not stay still, no matter how forcefully he attempted to command them, but he brought the blade up, nonetheless.

Suddenly, the giant spoke. “This is the whelp who will challenge me? Yon bold knights will cower in the corners and allow a pup wielding a sword to best me for their king?” His dark eyes gleamed as his head slowly turned about the room. Up close, his beard appeared mossy and dank, his face a mottled greenish-gray.

“Face me, giant. Or are you afraid?” Gereck tried to make his voice sound deep and rough. He wished he were bigger, with broad shoulders like Lancelot, or with great height like Sir Tristan, but he would have to make do with just being himself.

The enormous head turned, slowly, back to face Gereck. The bushy eyebrows raised. "Afraid?" the giant bellowed. Then a rumble could be heard, so low it was imperceptible until it burst from the giant's open mouth in a thundering laugh. "I, Goderick, the Green Knight of the Emerald Chapel, afraid of *you*, scrawny squire?"

"Perhaps," Gereck replied, his voice coming out in an embarrassing high pitch. He swallowed. "In any case, I've accepted your challenge. If your honor is anything to speak of, you must continue."

"As must you, young squire." The change in tone and visage was sudden, from mirthful to deadly serious, as the giant, Sir Goderick, straightened. "Are you certain you wish to go forth with this challenge?"

"I am."

"Then let all hear and witness this young man's commitment of honor; he will take the challenge. Announce yourself, boy, and the game will begin."

Gereck swallowed, trying to rid himself of the dryness in his throat. "I am Gereck Bauer, squire to the knight Sir Lancelot and loyal servant to his majesty, King Arthur." His voice rang out, filling a room that was incredibly silent for the number of people present. Nary a whisper brushed the ear of another, only the shuffling of feet, and the occasional cough. Gereck let out the breath he had been holding and took another. He adjusted his grip on his sword, then turned and faced the king, bowing low.

"I fight in your name, my liege."

"Take care that you put all of your heart and strength into this stroke, so he may never repay you in kind. I honor your quest, Sir Gereck."

The title was spoken without flare or emphasis, but it rang in Gereck's ears. *Sir Gereck*. The king thought him worthy of such praise? It bolstered him in a way nothing else ever could have. He turned again and faced the giant. Sir Goderick may have been enormous, but he could die the same as any man. One stroke he would get, and one stroke is all it would take.

"Yours is the first blow," the giant reminded him.

Gereck affirmed the statement with a nod.

"Then we are ready, but first I must have your word: do you thus swear to receive my return blow, under any condition I set hereafter?"

"Yes," Gereck said, surprised that no flood of fear followed his consent. He wouldn't miss. The knight before him would never live to make such a demand on him.

The massive head bowed low before him. A meaty hand pulled the rope-like mat of hair aside from his neck, exposing it to Excalibur's razor edge. Gereck adjusted his grip on the sword's smooth handle. It hummed with energy, and he felt another surge of confidence as he lifted it high in the air.

It hung above his head, and then, with every ounce of force he could muster, Gereck swung the blade downward. He watched as it bit into the brawny, green-tinged neck and continued on, shearing through skin and bone until the heavy head fell to the floor with a thud. No blood sprayed or dripped, which Gereck thought strange, but still he relaxed. It was done.

The ladies of the rooms shrieked and several more swooned. Someone in the crowd retched.

The giant's body remained still and upright, as if frozen. Then Gereck watched in horror as the hands reached outward and picked up the head. The headless body sprang up as if nothing was amiss and mounted the gigantic stallion, which stamped and snorted fiercely, raising its master high as it reared. The giant held his head in one hand, facing Gereck with wide eyes, and with the other pointed at him, axe in hand.

"In twelve months and a day you will seek me at the Emerald Chapel, so I can give back what I received from you. Should you fail, I will return and your king will take up my challenge." The eyes of the giant were still fixed on Gereck. "I have thy word. Do not fail to seek me out."

The stallion's hooves thundered as they struck the ground, breaking the rock beneath its feet before galloping from the hall.

Pandemonium broke loose in the hall the moment the giant was gone. King Arthur was shouting, trying to calm the people.

Gereck slowly walked toward the king, extending out to him the hilt of Excalibur. "I thank you for the use of your sword, my liege," he said.

The king clapped a hand on Gereck's shoulder. "You wielded it well. I have underestimated you, Gereck. A change is in order."

Gereck looked up. A change? But what...

The king stepped onto the raised dais and stood before his throne. "Let all hear it!"

It took a moment, but at last the hall fell quiet. Everyone looked at the king.

"I have a decree regarding the actions of this man here. His boldness in defending the honor of Camelot and her king has shown a level of fortitude worthy of knighthood." A cheer went up. His face burned with pride. He trembled with excitement. Was this it? Was this the moment he had dreamed of and worked for his entire life?

"If he is willing to train as a knight and have duties as a knight without sharing the benefits of officially bestowed knighthood, then on the day he leaves to finish his quest, he will receive full honor as a knight of Camelot. Gereck, do you accept these terms?"

Gereck swallowed. His throat dried up like last week's bread. An agreement to take on the responsibilities of knighthood meant more time consumed with duty in the castle and on scouting missions outside of it. There would not be much time for helping Elaina. But could she give him knighthood, trapped as she was? It had been weeks since they first met, and it could be months or years yet until she was freed, if her freedom was even obtainable.

Gereck gazed upward, eyes unwavering, then raised a clenched fist to his chest. "Yes, Your Highness."

"Then let it be known, Squire Gereck Bauer has embarked on the quest of the Green Knight. In one year's time, he will journey to the named place and receive the return blow," King Arthur decreed. He looked down from the throne, eyes softening as he looked on Gereck. "May God favor your righteous cause and guide you on this journey, that this land may benefit from your service as a knight. You have shown bravery and loyalty worthy of any that sit at the Round Table."

A cheer erupted through the hall and knights, those Gereck had seen become squires and then knights ahead of him thronged him, patting his back and applauding his courage. All clouds parted, and every dream he had ever dreamt of knighthood flooded his mind, lifting him so high on the wings of glory and honor that no trouble could touch him. Even Sir Lancelot's sour face went almost unnoticed.

Yet the Green Knight's decree hung over him, and half of the drinks he downed were attributed to the certainty of death that he faced, rather than celebration.

When he returned to his room that night, heavily drunk on spirits, Winna's letter lay unseen and unopened, blown under the bed by an errant draft, and not a moment's thought was spared for the lady of Shalott.

CHAPTER TEN

Morgan opened her eyes and stared at the ceiling. A small group of people hovered over her, some of the faces ones she didn't recognize. One face, she did.

"Mordred?" she mumbled, trying to sit up. Hands forced her back down.

"What did she say?" one of the strange voices asked. "Did she ask for someone?"

"She is still confused. Give her some space while she comes around." His voice, so familiar. She turned her head, looking for his face. There, directly above her, framed with black curls. She smiled at him. He returned her smile and helped her sit up.

A woman at her right gazed piercingly at her. "Lady Guinevere? How are you feeling?"

"What happened?" she asked.

"You fainted," the woman explained. "Sir Lancelot caught you before your head struck the floor, fortunately."

Sir Lancelot? She looked to the black-haired man. She knew him by another name, but if that is how he was known here... She smiled at him. "Then I owe you a debt of gratitude, Sir Lancelot."

Did he recognize her? She searched his eyes for signs. There was a certain hesitation about him, as if he wasn't sure he saw her, or perhaps he was asking himself the same question, of whether she recognized him. If only there weren't so many people around, that she could give him a sign!

"It was my duty, milady. I performed it gladly."

Morgan inclined her head. "Allow me to thank you by inviting you to join me tomorrow for the noontime meal?"

The lady sitting beside her tried to get her attention. She ignored her attempts, having eyes only for Sir Lancelot.

His face lit up into its familiar smile. "I would enjoy that. I do believe I can get away from the jousts long enough to enjoy repast with you."

She extended her hand and he took it, bowing until his lips brushed it, then excused himself.

"That was a fool move, Guinevere. I hope for your sake you can blame it on the fall. What are you going to tell the king?"

"The king?" Her heart froze inside of her. She searched her memories but found nothing. "What about the king?"

"He invited you to dine with him tomorrow at noon. Are you telling me you do not remember agreeing?"

She shook her head. "What can I do now?"

The lady sighed. "You really are foreign to the ways of the court, aren't you?" The lady stared at her, then shook her head. "I promised I would help, and I shall. Send a message to Sir Lancelot explaining the error. He will not deny the king his right to your hand, if he wants it. Promise to dine with the knight another time, and that will leave your prospects open should the king not deign to marry you."

"Marry me?" she murmured. Her mind was still muddled, unsettled, and inside, another presence stirred. She did not yet have everything under her control, and parts of her memory were clearly being withheld. She had work to do. She looked at the lady. "I must have had more to drink than I realized. Thank you for your help. Would you find someone to escort me to my rooms?"

"Yes, I think rest would do you some good. Remember to send Sir Lancelot that message. I could ask a servant for you if you wish?"

"No, I will remember. Thank you, Lady...?"

A deeply concerned look crossed the woman's face. "Lady Nimue. Are you certain you're all right? Should I call a physician?"

"No. If I am not better after a full night's sleep, I will be surprised. Thank you for your help, Lady Nimue."

Hands helped her to her feet, and a petite woman in plain clothes curtseyed, then led her from the room. She was fully aware of the eyes on her as she left, most of them male. A brief feeling of disgust rose inside of her, tinged with the sensation of fear. She pushed the emotion away.

The presence in her mind stirred again. Panic, not her own, flooded her senses. She calmly swept it away, until it was a pulsing undercurrent below her true emotions. Then the presence found its words.

What is happening? Where am I? Who are you?

She did not respond. She could not, with the maid at her side. A tide of emotion swept through her, threatening to remove her control, but she held on, pushing against the opposing force until it cowed, like a frightened shrew before a fox.

She walked through the hallway, showing no outward sign of the chaos in her mind. The maid glanced back at her and smiled, a smile Guinevere returned with one of her own. She was more powerful. The presence would tire, eventually, and then vanish, along with the others.

Like a bird trapped in a cage, the presence renewed its efforts in a panic, trying desperately to break free, to regain control of the mind and body.

The maid opened the door to a richly decorated chamber. Inside, a fire crackled merrily.

Thanking and dismissing the maid, she closed the door behind her, then finally spoke to the presence, her voice loud in the empty room.

“I am Morgan le Fay. I have claimed this mind and body as my own, and soon, dear Guinevere, you will no longer exist.”

CHAPTER ELEVEN

Gereck stumbled to a water basin on the floor, stuck his face in, and came up sputtering. He took a long drink of the cool water. His head cleared slightly, but still pulsed with pain. His vision swam. His stomach heaved. He barely managed to keep from vomiting.

He hated getting drunk. Or rather, he hated the morning after.

He sat on the floor with his knees pulled to his chest and rested his forehead on them, waiting for the world to stop spinning. He focused on taking deep, slow breaths.

What had happened last night? A lot of drinking, obviously.

Someone had thrown a chair. Had that been him? Faces swam in his memory, laughing, crying, angry faces. Bodies passed out on the floor. Men kissing women. Women kissing men. He hadn't kissed anyone, had he?

And before that, there was the Green Knight.

Nausea rose inside of him again, this time too much for him to hold down. He turned his head to the side and vomited into his water basin, moaning and holding his stomach. He stared, sorrowful, at the contaminated water. He had nothing to rinse out his mouth now.

The Green Knight. He could still see that massive head, separated from the giant's shoulders, eyes fixed on Gereck.

A year and a day.

His heart threatened to pound out of his chest. His breath was shallow and hard to draw.

What had he done? Why had he stepped forward? He wasn't a knight. He should have let a knight do it, but he wanted to become one. And he had gotten what he desired; King Arthur had all but given him the title.

Gereck rubbed his face with his hands and blew air out between his lips, then looked around the room. It was sparse. He typically shared it with another squire, but there was an odd number of them right now, and no one was in his room with him at the moment. He would be moving to the knight's quarters now. A larger room. A chest for his things.

A horse.

A shield.

A sword.

His heart welled up inside of him. He swallowed. All of these things would be his, because he was a knight.

But in a year, he would be dead.

The weight of his reality hit him then, in full force. It was like a boulder on his chest, suffocating any joy at the prospect of knighthood.

What was he going to do? His emotions slipped towards depression. He scrambled mentally, trying to hold himself up. Physically, he stood, ignoring how the room tilted and he tried to walk. He made it to the bed and used it to hold himself up.

He had to get out. Had to distract himself before... before...

Elaina. He could go help her. Helping someone always cleared his mind, and if there was anyone with a plight great enough to distract him from this, it was her.

He made his way to the door, lost his balance and struck his head on the side of the doorframe. Rubbing the spot, he turned to go down the corridor. Late morning sun filtered in through the narrow windows.

He would go see Elaina, but first, a visit to the cook. He doubled as the apothecary and healer of the castle, and was bound to have a cure for this devil-induced headache, and by then Gereck's stomach would be ready for some breakfast.

Gereck froze halfway through the tower window. Elaina was on the floor. The wooden piece she used to move the thread back and forth on the loom was now under the loom, as if it had been dropped. Elaina's hands covered her face. She knelt in front of the mirror and sobbed. Gereck slid silently into the room, not sure if he should disturb her. It was a brief moment before he could see her arms trembled, and her hands shook as if with palsy.

Another moment and she leaned over, fingers scrabbling across the floor for the wooden piece. In her haste, she knocked it away, to the other side of the loom. She gasped and got to her feet, tripping on the loom bench. Gereck was there in a moment. He caught her under her arms before she hit the floor.

She was gasping and shaking, pushing out of his arms with such force he let her go and stepped aside. She snatched the wooden piece up and hurried back toward the bench, which he had set up. She paused, for the briefest of moments.

"Thank you." Breathless and sniffling, her eyes wet with tears, she sat and re-wound the thread in the wood piece, then slid it through the strings of the loom, and as she did, her entire body relaxed.

"What happened?" Gereck asked, settling cross-legged on the floor.

She breathed in audibly. "When I dropped my shuttle? Or before that?"

"Shuttle?"

She waved the wooden piece. "This is a shuttle. Have I not told you? The curse forces me to weave." She gestured to the mirror, then ran the shuttle back through the threads. "When I stop weaving, I get a pain, here." She paused and pointed to her heart with the shuttle, then started again. "Once, I thought I might break the curse if I stopped weaving long enough, but..."

"What happened?"

"I blacked out from the pain, woke up hours later on the floor."

"Still trapped."

Her face flushed. "I haven't tried it since."

"But sometimes you don't have to weave. Why?"

Her shoulders shrugged, the blue material of her dress wrinkling. "The loom, or the mirror, releases me sometimes. I don't think I have any control over it. It doesn't always stop when I need it to. Once it kept me weaving for three days straight, no pauses."

"How did you survive?"

"I would run to the bucket and take a gulp of water every couple hours," she said, jerking her head towards the large metal pail beside the door. "While I was up, I would grab food. I tried bringing the bedpan on one trip, but mostly I just..." She stopped.

"What?" He grinned. "Pissed where you sat?" From where he sat, he could see her cheeks flush.

"In any case, it was unpleasant. I don't have any control over it."

"How hard have you tried?"

"Excuse me?"

He stood up, walking around to stretch his legs. "Maybe it's like the mirror. Maybe you could ask to be released."

"I haven't seen anything in the mirror yet," she said slowly.

Or so she told him. She could have decided to keep it from him for some reason. He looked at her. Every time he moved around the front of the loom, to see her face, she looked down. She rarely turned her head to look toward him. She either had perfect control, or the curse held her more tightly than he imagined.

He walked past her water pail, which was just about empty. Abruptly, he turned and kicked it, sending it clanking into the wall and across the wooden floor.

Elaina's head jerked halfway around, then stopped before she saw him. "Why did you do that? I need that water!"

"It was only a few drops. I could refill it if you wanted." He set the bucket upright in its place and continued his walk around the room. He halted near her bed. "Are you doing that, or the curse?"

"Doing what?" she asked.

He picked up her bedpan. Empty, and dry. He dropped it. It thudded nicely on the floor, and Elaina's head swung again. Easier for her to stop, as her bed was behind her.

"What are you doing?"

"Seeing how extensive this enchantment is. You never look at me. You stop right before your eyes would land on me, or the window. Is that you, or the curse?"

"I'm not sure anymore," she said.

Suddenly, she set the shuttle down, stretched out her arms and stood. She must have been released. "The first few weeks, I kept myself blindfolded, terrified I would accidently look out the window and die. I thought rescue was imminent at that point. I eventually came to realize no one was coming, and I took it off. Now it's like weaving. It hurts."

"Why the window? Why can't you look?"

She moved toward an alcove across the room from him and sat on the carved stone bench inside. "If I look on the outside world, I break the enchantment and die."

"That's all you have to do?" he said in disbelief. "Look outside?"

"Have you heard nothing I've said?" Elaina asked. She was close to tears. Her hands gripped her dress, then smoothed it out. She took several deep breaths.

Gereck waited. He shifted his weight from one leg to the other, then sighed and opened his mouth to speak, but Elaina spoke first.

"Tell me a story."

"What?"

"Tell me a story," she said again, staring straight forward at the opposite wall in the alcove she was seated in.

"I-I'm sorry. I don't know how; I mean, I've never told a story before. I'm not one for tales."

"Oh," Elaina looked thoughtful. Then her face brightened. "Then tell me about you; about your family, your life."

Gereck hesitated. In the stories, the hero was never married. Gereck was, and that… complicated matters. He could tell her the truth; that was the simple thing.

He looked up. His eyes took in her face, her blonde hair curling by her ears. It would be easy. He would open his mouth, tell her about how he met Winna, about Cai and Ada, about his dream to be a knight.

Of course, he had implied he was already a knight, but she might forgive him that small lie in the midst of the rest… and then only speak to him with polite reservation whenever they were together. She might insist he bring someone with him so they weren't alone together, a chaperone, or, and this thought gave him a strange pain in his heart, she would ask him to give her up, to find another person, one less attached, to rescue her.

"I do have a story," he said. A look of surprise passed over her face.

"You said you weren't much for tales."

"There is one tale I know. It may not be very interesting, but I can tell it." His throat dried. He licked his lips, then settled himself onto the floor.

"There once was a maiden," he began, his throat dry as a riverbed in drought.

"This better not be about me," Elaina piped up.

Gereck shook his head, forgetting she wouldn't see. "No, it's not. Are you going to let me tell it?"

She sighed and slumped, putting her hand in her chin. "All right."

He began again. It was a simple love story he had heard once, about a girl who made a deal with a faerie so that her parents might allow her betrothal to the man she loved, but the faerie tricked her and turned her into a tree, and her beloved had to find her out of a forest of trees. He wandered in the forest for days, unable to find food and with little water.

The man was bruised and scraped, and could not find his way out of the forest. He leaned on a tree, convinced he was to die, but when his tears fell on the tree roots and the tree was transformed into his beloved.

It was one told so often among the circles Gereck frequented that he could recite it easily from heart. He was halfway through when he found himself getting into the story, his mind drinking in the tale, reveling in every detail as he told it. It was as if he was starved for a story. And everything, the Green Knight, Winna, Elaina, all fell away from his mind and he felt as if he was there himself, in the forest, searching for his lost love, struggling to find food and avoid the wild beasts.

His heart pounded, his blood sang as he spoke the final words of the story. "And Gelfor took Hildr to wife and they built a cottage in a different land, far away, and they did live, ever after, happily."

Elaina was silent. The last words of the story hung in the air between them, almost tangible. Gereck's heart gradually slowed. Elaina finally let her breath out.

"That was beautiful. I felt sorry for the woman's beloved, but sorrier for the woman trapped in a tree for so long."

"Yes," Gereck said, with an odd feeling of sadness creeping into his chest. Elaina would associate with the woman in that tale. She herself had been trapped similarly for so long...

A bell rang in the distance. It came from the castle, ringing out bright and clear. Gereck's heart stopped.

The bell to start the tournament. He was supposed to be there, now! He was participating in four events today, starting with a melee.

He scrambled to his feet. “I am sorry, Elaina, but I must go. I am due at the arenas. There is a tournament. It’s Beltane time, and...”

“It is Beltane time?” Elaina interrupted.

“Yes. In two weeks’ time it will be Beltane Eve,” Gereck said, turning from the window to look at her. Her face was unreadable, but her eyes, downcast as they were, spoke of a hurt that existed in the depths of her being.

He didn’t have time to help her, though his heart wrenched at the pitiful sight of her, shoulders slumped, hands limp in her lap. A tear dripped down her cheek.

“Elaina, I am sorry. I would remain here if I could, but I must go.”

“I know,” she sniffed. “Good luck.”

Gereck cursed in his head. Surely there was something he could leave her with, to brighten her up, to bring her hope of his return.

Then, an idea. He ran across the room, grabbed her hand in his, and kissed it firmly. “I will see you soon, milady.”

She seemed too shocked to answer, and still had not recovered by the time he had gone out through the window and used a tree branch to lower himself down to the ground.

CHAPTER TWELVE

In the stormy east-wind straining,
The pale yellow woods were waning,
The broad stream in his banks complaining,
Heavily the low sky raining
Over tower'd Camelot;
Outside the isle a shallow boat
Beneath a willow lay afloat,
Below the carven stern she wrote,
The Lady of Shalott.

Elaina's hand still burned where Gereck's lips had touched it. She stared at it, stunned. She hardly noticed that he had gone. Her legs began to tingle. Elaina moved at last, kicking her legs to wake them, then stood up.

She walked over to her bed and sat down. Her hand reached out and took a piece of bread from the plate on her table. She took a bite and chewed. Her mind reeled with the implications.

A loud, impatient chirrup broke through her thoughts, and a moment later a jay landed on the foot of her bed.

"Hello, dear one. How are you today?" Elaina wiped her tears away, then held her hand out to the delicate creature. It hopped on, its tiny claws pricking her skin.

She brought it up to her chest, stroking its head. It chirruped again, and ruffled its feathers.

Elaina laughed. “All right, all right. I know what you are here for. Not just a social call. I should have guessed.”

She picked up the small crust of bread she'd been eating a moment before. The bird chirped appreciatively as she held it up, and while it pecked at the bread she admired the brilliant blue color of its feathers. She had never seen a jay with blue feathers until the day this one had flown into her tower and begged for a crust off of her for the first time.

Elaina had no way to mark days, but she thought that it had been a year or so since its first appearance, and the blue jay continued to visit her. She kept a piece of bread on hand, just in case it should visit. It brightened her day to see its bright blue feathers, and it had a perky, almost cocky attitude.

She listened to it chatter, its chirps and whistles making her laugh. It was almost like carrying on a conversation…

“I haven’t told you, have I, Brennus?” she said, using the name she had given the bird.

The blue jay looked up at her, cocking its head to one side. It hopped around, cawing at her until she scooped him up onto her hand.

“You would really like to know, wouldn’t you? All right, I’ll tell. Someone came to the tower at last.”

Brennus’s cheerful chattering stopped. Its eyes gazed directly into hers, and for a moment Elaina was taken off guard by the intelligence in its gleaming dark eyes. After a moment, the bird turned to preening, its beak nipping at its feathers.

Elaina continued. “His name is Gereck. He's respectful and charming. I have no idea if he's handsome or not. Of course, that doesn't matter all that much to me. He's kind. And he has taken my curse on as a quest. Isn't that noble?"

The blue jay bobbed its head and made a deep-throated warbling sound, as if in agreement.

Elaina laughed again. “Sounds like you know him. Care to tell me more? Does he have a lady back at the castle? A large nose?”

A series of trills, followed by more warbling, followed. Brennus gave her wrist a peck, picked up the remaining crust of bread, then flew from her hand and circled the room once before flying out.

Elaina knew the bird was gone when the flapping of its wings faded into the rustling of leaves in the breeze. She sighed. Alone again.

She looked at the mirror. Its ornate frame gleamed in the afternoon sunlight. The blurry scene within showed an empty road, a cloudless blue sky. Everyone would be at the Beltane tournaments today. Even the poorest among them would take a day here and there to join the festivities. Everyone except her.

Elaina stood up, leaving her bread on the bed, momentarily forgotten. That didn’t have to be so. What if she was freed before Beltane? What if, this year, she could walk out of this tower and see, even meet, her son? She could try again; she could succeed. Seeing Gereck again had bolstered her hope. She had to keep trying and finally break the curse.

She squared her shoulders and faced the mirror.

“Show me Arthur. Show me my son.”

At first, nothing. Then a ripple spread across the mirror, like a stone dropping into a lake. The ripple disturbed the image of the empty road, making it waver until it was indiscernible, and then it cleared. It was still dark, still blurry, and it had changed. She could see him mounted on a horse in an arena filled with people. Blonde hair. Armor gleaming on his chest. He raised an arm to the crowd, and by the movement, Elaina could tell they cheered.

She watched as he took a helm from beneath his arm and placed it over his head. A man handed him a lance. Longer than a man was tall, the lance seemed to weigh nothing as he hoisted it, set it, and began galloping towards his opponent. From her view, Elaina couldn't see the man he faced, but as the horse went forward, the scene shifted so she could. The meeting of lances, she imagined, resulted in a tremendous crashing sound.

The other rider fell back along his horse and dropped his lance, but stayed seated. She watched with fascination as the man lifted his lance and regrouped. His opponent faced him again, shoulder plate dented. He was handed a new lance, and the horses charged again. Wood shattered in the air. Elaina's eyes were transfixed on Arthur, who was hit, but he kept his seat, unlike the other man. His horse dragged him a few feet, his foot caught in the stirrup.

Arthur handed off his lance and took a lap around the arena, helmet back under his arm. Elaina could see enough detail to notice his hair plastered to his face with sweat. His features were fair, but broad, his face round, shoulders strong. Could it really be him?

She touched the mirror's surface and the image wavered. She pulled her fingers back, curling them into the palm of her hand, but the image disappeared. She didn't call it back right away. Her head swam. Was it from the effort of calling up the image? She wasn't certain. She shook her head. It was crazy to think she had any control over this. Nothing had ever shown up in the mirror before. She glanced back at the blank mirror, its surface dark and reflecting the inside of her tower room. What if that had been her son? What if he was alive?

It had been so long since she let herself think, dream, wonder what life would be like when she stepped outside once more. Gereck's appearance had brought in the tide that was washing away the foundation she had built to remain sane in this place. The calm dissociation she had been able to muster for the past four decades was crumbling. She wanted. She wished. She hoped again.

And it hurt, in her heart, in a place that she thought she had closed off forever, and the impossibility of what she wanted struck her in such a way that tears began to fall down her face.

Music began, soft at first, then growing louder. Its lilting melody wove around her, and she stepped backward, one step at a time, until the loom bench bumped the back of her legs. She paused, waiting until the enchantment constricted her heart before she turned and sat down. She picked up the shuttle. She hesitated. The music strained against her motionless form, pulling. The pain came, then. She took a deep breath.

Could she do it?

Could she break the curse?

Her hand shook. She gripped the shuttle so hard her hand hurt. The pain in her heart made her gasp, and with her outtake of breath her muscles relaxed and betrayed her, putting the shuttle through the threads. Her foot moved on the treadle.

"No!" she gasped again, tears brimming in her eyes.

Hands and foot moved of their own accord. She watched as the treadle pressed the weft threads tight. The shuttle moved again. A sob escaped her. The mirror showed an empty road, and the enchantment wove an empty scene, row by row of thread pressing down. Elaina let out a light, gasping sob that grew steadily until she found herself keening with despair.

She could not look again. She would not look, only to be unable to touch.

She breathed until the catch in her throat released, and then began to sing.

"Sweet is true love though given in vain, in vain;
Sweet is true love though given in vain, in vain.
And sweet is death who puts an end to pain:
I know not which is sweeter, no, not I.
Love, art thou sweet? Then bitter death must be:
Love, thou art bitter; sweet is death to me.
O Love, if death be sweeter, let me die."

She closed her eyes and let the loom take her. In the border of the tapestry, a tiny image appeared. A man with golden hair, a circlet on his head, armored arm raised, a bold and victorious expression on his face. Elaina didn't see it; her eyes were closed tight, hiding from the world.

CHAPTER THIRTEEN

Guinevere thrashed about on the bed, crying out.

"No! Please, no! Don't let me die. Don't let me die! Let me out!"

"Guinevere!"

Mary's voice broke through her wild yelling. Her cool hand on Guinevere's brow had an immediate effect.

Guinevere calmed, though her breath still came hard and fast, and her heart pounded away in her chest. She looked at Mary, her vision blurred with tears, and clutched Mary's arms.

"Don't let me go," Guinevere said, turning her face into Mary's skirts. "Don't let me disappear."

"Shh..." Mary said, lifting Guinevere from the bed and sliding to sit on it. She took Guinevere in her arms and held her, rocking. "Hush, my dear. It was only a nightmare."

"Oh Mary, it was awful. I- I..."

"You do not have to talk about it, if you do not want to."

Guinevere pulled away and looked into Mary's concerned and loving gaze. "Really?"

Mary nodded. "We can forget about it. You hit your head on the floor when you fainted, and you weren't yourself last night. I was worried, but you seem to be back to rights, and I think it's best we don't relive it. We will simply move on the best we can."

Guinevere's head swam with memories, not all of them hers, but she pushed that unsettling feeling to the back of her mind. She smiled.

"What do I get to wear today?"

Mary stood and retrieved a breakfast tray from a table near the fireplace. "Your nightgown. You will not attend the tournament today."

"What? No! I must. What happened to getting to know the king?"

Mary's face became stern. She set the tray on Guinevere's bedside table with a definitive clack.

"Now, Guinevere, you have had too many hard falls all at once. The king will understand, and one day will not ruin your chances with him."

"But I was to dine with him at midday."

"My dear, it is practically midday already. No doubt he has heard of your condition and does not wish to distress it further. I will have a well-worded message sent, if you wish?"

Guinevere crossed her arms. She pouted. Mary eyed her sideways as she put some sliced ham on a plate and handed it to Guinevere.

"Now, don't give me that face. It worked when you were five. It's not so much befitting a grown woman."

Guinevere sighed. She took a bite of the ham and made a face. "It is cold."

"That is what you get for sleeping in." Mary handed her a buttered slice of fresh bread.

Guinevere took a full bite and added it to her plate.

"So, what..." she attempted around a mouthful of food. "Sorry." She chewed some more, then swallowed. "What will we do today?"

"Well," Mary said, turning to the chair she had been sitting in and picking up her embroidery, "this is what I am doing. I brought your latest project, if you want to join me."

Guinevere made a face. "No, thank you."

Mary laughed. "I thought not. I also have a book of tales, the ones we started back in Carmelide. I could read to you, if you like."

Guinevere sighed again and slouched into her pillow. "Very well, but I may well die of boredom."

Mary got settled and began reading aloud. Guinevere's mind wandered to the window. She imagined she could hear the cheer of the crowds watching the jousts. A breeze wandered in and she closed her eyes, smelling summer.

A knock came at the door. Guinevere bolted upright. Mary sighed and put the book down, retrieved a robe from where it hung over the dressing screen, and helped Guinevere into it. Then, straightening her own dress, Mary went to the door and opened it.

A dark-haired man, looking fully geared for battle, stepped into the room. He smiled when he saw Guinevere, showing his teeth.

Her heart lunged at the sight of him.

"Sir Lancelot," she said, mouth suddenly dry. She had nothing to wet it with. She licked her lips. "What brings you here in the midst of the tournament? Surely you are jousting today?"

"I have finished my rounds this morning and will go again later on."

Lancelot glanced at Mary, who gazed at him with stern eyes and pursed lips before she stood aside and allowed him to enter. He crossed to Guinevere's bedside and pulled up the chair Mary had been sitting in.

Guinevere noticed the furrow deepen in Mary's brow before she brought her attention back to the man beside her. Her fingers fidgeted with the embroidered buttons that held her robe closed.

"Then you have met your opponents with success?"

"Aye, I have. Arthur is doing remarkably, too. We may well meet in the final." He leaned his left arm on one knee, closing more of the space between them.

Mary, found another seat and took out her needlework, jabbing at it with her eyes mostly on them.

Lancelot sighed, then lowered his head and lifted a flower from his hand. "I brought you this. It's a silly little thing, I suppose, but I thought you might like the color."

It was a cornflower, bright blue against her bed sheets. Guinevere took the offered flower and twirled it.

"It's lovely," she said.

She looked into his eyes and her heart began to pound. Her head swam. Why couldn't she breathe properly whenever her eyes met his? She lowered her gaze and took her time regaining her breath.

"I am sorry about the other night. I appear to have a strange propensity for becoming unconscious in your presence." She finally spoke up, looking everywhere but his eyes. The rest of him was plenty pleasant to look at.

"It is I who should apologize. And you haven't fainted yet today, which I will take as a promising sign." He smiled again.

Bother. Her heart was pounding again. What was it about his eyes? Especially when he smiled. A presence stirred in her mind, like a cat stretching, and Guinevere's breath quickened. Not again.

"So what… brings you here?" she half-gasped, hoping he wouldn't notice. She straightened, trying to appear as if her chest wasn't constricting and her mind wasn't pulsing with fear. She managed a smile at Lancelot. He laughed nervously.

"Well, I was invited here by you. Although it was after you had passed out, so I should have realized you wouldn't remember."

Bother indeed. Her face flushed. "I am sorry I didn't remember, but I am glad you are here. I'll have something brought." She looked over at Mary, who stood. "Mary, would you please see about having lunch brought for us? Sir Lancelot wishes to dine with me."

"Yes, milady," the governess said.

She went to the door and put her head out and spoke to a maid in the hall.

Guinevere clasped her hands in her lap, watching Mary, fully aware that Lancelot was watching her.

Mary closed the door and turned back to Guinevere. "It will be here momentarily."

"Thank you, Mary," Guinevere said.

Mary was halfway back to her seat when another knock came at the door. Mary raised her brow at Guinevere, who gave a shrug and shook her head. Perhaps the maid was back to ask a question about their meal?

Mary opened the door and immediately dropped into a curtsey. "Your majesty," she murmured.

Guinevere stared. There, framed in her doorway, was King Arthur. Hands clasped behind his back, a surprisingly sheepish look on his face.

"I am sorry I am late, Guinevere. Might I..." his voice trailed off when he noticed Lancelot, who gave a reluctant smile. Arthur shook his head. "Might I come in?"

"Yes," Guinevere said, looking around.

She smoothed the covers helplessly, glancing from Lancelot, to Mary, to Arthur.

Mary shook her head, a smile on her face.

Guinevere gazed at the governess, trying to catch her attention, to get some help, but Mary pointedly looked away as she fetched the other chair for the king.

Arthur came into the room and waited while Mary set the chair in place on the other side of Guinevere's bed.

Before sitting down, his other arm came out from hind his back. Flowers.

Guinevere smiled and took them, but anger surged inside of her, a violent rage that made her want to throw the flowers to the ground. She looked at Arthur, shocked by the suddenness of the emotion. Her hands trembled, causing a few petals to fall onto the bed sheets.

Mary blocked Guinevere's view of Arthur, taking the flowers and arranging them in a vase on the bedside table.

Lancelot cleared his throat, glancing up from the floor. "Let me guess. She agreed to lunch with you as well?"

Arthur cocked his head to one side. "Indeed. Is that what you two were doing?" He looked at Guinevere, who was still recovering from the strange surge of anger.

She looked at each of the good-looking men and found herself flustered and utterly speechless.

"I... that is, I mean..."

Arthur held up a hand and she stopped immediately, her face hot with embarrassment.

"Do not trouble yourself, milady." He stood. "Lancelot was here first. I will call another time."

"No, it is I who should leave. After all, I believe she asked you first," Lancelot said, also standing.

"Oh now, Your Majesty, please..." She stopped, biting her lip, then glanced at Lancelot. "That is not to say that I prefer his company, or that I would rather..."

She stopped again. Her head pounded. Tears came to her eyes. Both men stared at her. "I am sorry. I made such a mess of everything."

"Perhaps it is best if we both go," Arthur said softly, after a moment.

Mary watched intently from her corner. She would offer no advice or saving, Guinevere knew. She wanted to give Guinevere a chance to save herself, as she would have to often when, if, she ever married.

Guinevere kept herself from begging them to stay. That would be unseemly. Instead, she straightened, looked at each man equally long, and then cleared her throat.

"Please accept my humble apologies. I was not well last night, and I made a mistake. I will make it up to each of you, when I am well." She lowered her head in a bow.

"Yes, milady." Sir Lancelot's fist pounded his armor, and he bowed for her. "Of course. I do hope you are well enough to see the jousting this afternoon."

She smiled at him. "I hope so too." Her voice trembled, but she thought she hid it well. She looked to the king.

His expression gentled. He was so handsome, dressed much the same as Lancelot, but the way he carried himself, with such confidence, assurance... It was unmatched by any man whose presence she had enjoyed.

He, too, put a fist to his chest and bowed. “All is forgiven, Lady Guinevere. We will leave you to your rest.”

Then he looked at Lancelot, and some sort of understanding or agreement passed between them.

Guinevere could feel it, like a tangible thing, but she wasn’t sure what the agreement was. She watched them both go, a deep regret in her heart so strong, she might have thought her heart was breaking.

CHAPTER FOURTEEN

Gereck hurried down the hall and out the doors. A trumpet sounded in the distance, the final call for all contenders to enter the ring. He was late.

He reached his designated ready tent, and claimed his chainmail, gauntlets, and sword. They were all on loan; he hadn't gotten any of his own yet, and likely wouldn't until he was knighted. With everyone else at the arenas already, only a few straggling squires remained in the tent.

Gereck slid the heavy shirt over his head, cursing the rusting links in it. He hadn't gotten there in time to choose one of the newer shirts, and he might pay for it. But not with his life; he was too good for that. He hadn't entered many of the events anyway.

He had a melee at the start, where he would fight in a large group against fifteen men, who were also fighting each other. Most men were wounded in such an encounter. He had missed the jousting, but later he would have a brief sword contact match.

As he rushed from the tent, strapping on his sword, he found himself not caring about any of it. His mind filled with Elaina, and the way she had looked in the shadows of the little alcove as he promised her the world.

Peasants and nobles alike walked or rode along the road to the arenas. Gereck ran. If he didn't get there in time to line up before the king, none of it would matter. And no matter what his quest was, it wouldn't look good for him to be tardy to a second event after missing the jousting.

Over the river in what had once been a field sprawled the arenas. Five broad, designated areas with seating surrounding each. Three were smaller, two larger. The jousts were held in the larger ones. Gereck had to report to the gate at the largest: the grand arena. He could hear the crowd now, and the people were getting thicker. The crowd bottlenecked at the bridge, and many men and boys were going around, wading through the river. Gereck couldn't follow and risk getting his chainmail wet, so he inched his way across the bridge, pushing his way through every gap that presented itself.

Once across the bridge he set off at a jog, dodging people until he came to the gate. He bent over, gasping his name to the steward in charge, who directed Gereck to a line of men just walking into the arena. He darted off to catch the end of the last line, coming in just behind the others. The gate shut after him, closing to any further contestants. He had made it.

The crowd herded him along, then finally shoved him out into the arena with about thirty other men, all carrying various weapons. Gereck eyed them, assessing strength and deftness, knowing they were all doing the same. Jitters filled his body, and he shook his arms trying to rid them of the unpleasant sensation. He was nervous. Hopefully, the king's speech would bring him around.

The crowd suddenly hushed, and Gereck glanced up to see King Arthur standing at the dais above the arena, hands held high in the air.

"I did not address you this morning, as I should have, but I address you now," he said, his voice carrying far through the silenced crowd. "Camelot is a kingdom filled with great and noble people. The spring festival is a time of celebration of life and, for many, the power of the Goddess." The people let out a wild cheer, and colorful ribbons came out of pockets and bags, waving in the air like an impossibly rainbow forest.

Gereck noticed Bishop Ernald standing just behind the king and to his left, a dissatisfied frown on his wizened face. The sorcerer Merlin stood on the king's right, his thoughts seemingly elsewhere as he looked to the sky, the ground, and anywhere else but the king. Arthur must have sensed the bishop's displeasure. He paused and cleared his throat. The people quieted, ribbons fluttering out of the air. "In all our revelry, let us not forget that God also suffered and rose again at this time, and his atonement should be recognized with humility."

Uncomfortable silence greeted his words. He motioned a servant forward, who held a cup out to the king for him to drink.

"Now, I must address a certain matter of importance," the king continued. A fly buzzed near Gereck's face, but he stood still as he could, trying to maintain every ounce of dignity he had. "The Saxons have grown bolder in the past year. We have heard tales of their conquering the kingdom of Wales, and more of them come across the water toward Britain with every passing month. They are amassing on the shores, taking everything they can find. Within a matter of months, we may have a great war on our hands, the greatest our kingdom has yet seen. We must stay strong." He shouted, his voice carrying through the silent arena, reaching every ear. "Strong as the hill Camelot is built upon, strong as the stubborn, prideful people who refused to yield to the Romans until they left our lands, strong as the strongest knights of the Round Table!"

He waited for the deafening roar to silence before looking at last on the men in the arena. "Here we have some of Camelot's finest fighters, with sword, with mace, with dagger. May the greatest among you rise victorious!"

Weapons pounded on shields. Gereck raised his sword to join the ruckus, and with a start, realized he had left his shield back in the tent. He cursed. Without a shield, he stood little chance in the melee. He would be seriously hurt.

There was no backing out now. With a grimace, he stood still until the horn blew to start the melee, and then the bloodshed began.

"You know, you really got off well, without your shield and everything." The chatty, young physician finished wrapping Gereck's shoulder and Gereck slid off the table.

Every part of Gereck ached. The physician slapped a muslin-wrapped poultice into his hand and grinned. "Pour warm water on that and dab at the wound every night. Give it fresh wrapping. You'll be right as rain in a couple weeks."

"Thank you," Gereck said.

At least it wasn't his sword arm. He could still train with the knights, when regular training resumed after Beltane. He left the infirmary and made his way down the hall, out of the castle, and into the upper levels of town. People were feasting and making merry; music floated out of doors. Laughter, mixed with drunken arguing, could be heard as it echoed among the white stone walls of the city.

Gereck wandered until he found a battered tavern at the edge of the lower town: The Three Arrows. The sun was setting, its final orangish glow dimming as the lights within the tavern flickered on, making it a welcoming and cheerful sight. It was quieter than the rest, with fewer celebratory drinkers and more quiet, solitary ones. Just what Gereck wanted. He patted his money belt to be sure it hadn't been lifted, then opened the door and walked inside.

Warm food odors wafted into his nose. Several soldiers he recognized nodded to him before returning to their drinks. When you came here to drink, you drank alone. Gereck scanned the room. His eyes landed on a familiar face. Sir Tristan.

The knight turned casually to glance at who had just entered, and his eyes widened to recognize Gereck. Tristan raised his tankard to him, then took a long swallow. Gereck came over and took an empty seat beside the knight, then motioned to the tavern keeper for a pint. He obliged immediately, setting the tankard down, the frothy mead sloshing over the side. Sir Tristan's tankard clanked on the table, and he smacked his lips. He gestured to Gereck.

"No question of what you drink to," he said, words slurred already. How long had he been drinking? There were at least three tankards on the table. "The Green Knight." He smirked. "I don't envy you."

Gereck didn't say anything, just fingered the side of the tankard before taking it up by the handle and gulping down a mouthful.

"Where have you been?" Tristan asked.

"Around."

"What brings you here?"

"Home," Gereck said simply.

"Ah, Winna. Your bonny lass. How is she getting on?"

Gereck's eyes were locked on the container that held his mead. He felt numb.

"You miss her, lad?"

Insightful. Tristan must not have been as inebriated as Gereck thought. He paused, then looked at the knight.

"No, I don't. And that's what troubles me."

Tristan squinted. "Eh? Is there another lass around these parts that's turnin' your head, Sir Gereck?" The other man grinned. That would be the drink. Gereck shook his head. He wasn't in the mood for games. He dropped a coin on the table and stood to go. An arm stopped him.

"I know that face when I see it. I am sorry to be such a drunken sot, Gereck. Sit down, finish your drink."

Gereck retook his seat.

"There is something bothering you, though. If you would like, I can lend an ear. I wouldn't listen to any advice from me though. Mead gives terrible advice." The last he said around a mouthful of tankard, as he brought the bottom up again. He slapped it down, and this time, didn't order another right away. "Go on, then."

Gereck sighed. "I took on a quest. Besides the Green Knight, I mean. A woman... she needed my help. She's caught in an enchantment, and I..." He stopped himself short.

For some reason, he didn't want to tell Sir Tristan everything. What if the knight took it on himself to find Elaina and rescue her? What if he told the other knights and the whole lot of them went and met her, and she fell in love with one of them? One that wasn't… well, married.

"And you want to save her," Sir Tristan finished. "Very noble of you. Why haven't you told a knight? One of us could take care of it."

"It sort of happened by chance that we met, and now…" He couldn't say it out loud.

He didn't have to.

"You're attached to her."

Gereck bowed his head, then took another swig.

Tristan leaned in. "Didn't you tell her you were married?"

"I never got around to it. We mostly talked about her."

"Did she never ask?"

"No, she didn't."

"And you didn't feel it was important. You must have known she would fall for you," Sir Tristan said. "It's practically a rule."

Gereck threw his hands into the air. "Do you know how hard I worked to get Winna to fall in love with me? It wasn't easy! I must have been the homeliest man in our village, and had little talent for farming. I almost traveled to the next village to find a wife. I pursued seven girls before Winna accepted my hand. I never thought anyone could fall in love so easy."

Tristan waved to the tavern keeper. Another mug was brought, and the three others cleared away. "Then you are a fool. The first man this woman has seen in four decades, who also promises to save her from the plight she is in, and it didn't occur to you that there would be a love story? Have you read no tales?"

"I have read tales, Tristan. I just never expected to be part of one."

Tristan shook his head. "I keep telling Arthur it ought to be part of knighthood training, damsel rescuing for fools. Believe me, Gereck, this will not turn out well." He paused. Both men drank. Then, smacking his lips once, Tristan turned to face Gereck. His eyes were filled with concern. It would have touched Gereck if he hadn't felt so miserable.

"You must tell her about Winna," Tristan said at last.

"She will hate me."

"Not if she still wants your help. It may hurt, but not as much as it will further down the road."

Gereck hesitated. "Perhaps you should come with me. You have dealt with enchantments and the like before."

Tristan put up his hands. "Oh no, do not get me involved. I have seen enough enchanting to last me for one lifetime. After Isolde..." A bitter expression crossed the knight's face. He stared down into his tankard.

"I know, I know. I am sorry."

"Gereck, I know better than anyone what it is like to love someone who is married. The enchantment that bound me to Isolde was strong; it tore me apart. For three years, I pined after this woman, and she was untouchable. I worked for her husband, who happened to be my uncle, King Mark."

"She loved you too, didn't she?"

"Yes, but her love was as enchanted as mine. A love potion, given to her by her stepmother who loathed her for years and felt terribly about it. To make amends, she gave Isolde a love potion that would cause her would-be husband to love her forever, blessing her with a happy marriage. Suffice it to say that I accidentally drank the potion after we shipwrecked on the shores of Britain, and she drank with me so I wouldn't die of a lovesick madness. I nearly died anyway."

"Is that why you are drinking tonight?" Gereck blurted.

The knight's head shot up. "Four years ago today was the day I first laid eyes on her." Tristan smiled, but it didn't reach his eyes.

"I am sorry," Gereck said. The words were inadequate. He never knew what to say when people were upset.

Tristan took another drink. "My experience will have been worth it if it causes you to tell that girl who you really are. A husband, and a father. Only you can decide if you still want to help her when you see her response."

Silence passed between them. Gereck finished his mead, then stood up. He put a hand on Tristan's shoulder. "Thank you, Sir Tristan." The man stared into the bottom of his tankard.

Gereck turned to go, then looked back at Tristan. His back hunched, his head hung over his mug.

"If you were in my place, would you tell her?" Gereck asked.

Tristan lifted his head and turned his red-rimmed gaze toward Gereck. His eyes were out of focus, as if he saw something, or someone, other than Gereck. "No, I wouldn't. I would never go back to see her. I would get on the fastest horse I could find and get the hell out of her life. Nothing is worth that kind of pain."

Gereck left the tavern, hands in his pockets. He looked up the winding cobblestone street towards the castle. He was injured, and unable to participate in any other events, even if his heart was in it. He looked the other way, towards the lower town and beyond it, where he could barely make out the shapes of trees in the direction of the village he called home.

Sir Tristan was right. He had a wife, and children. He wasn't about to give them up for some woman he hardly knew. He already had someone who cared for him, and he owed them a visit. He wouldn't be missed if he was only gone for a few days. After all, it was festival time. He would gather some supplies and check with the stable master about a horse. Surely Fendrel's leg had healed by now.

He made his way up the quiet street to the castle, trying to convince himself to feel something, anything, but not even the mead had been able to conjure emotion up inside of him. Hopefully the sight of those that waited for him at home would.

Two days later, the sun set as Gereck hiked up over the last hill and stood, looking over the valley where he had made his home. Two little figures ran across the rocky field in front of his house, hair flying wildly behind them. Their mother stood from her crouch in the dirt, small piles of rocks on the ground around her.

Gereck put down his sack and ran to meet his children, picking one up in each arm and spinning them around until they all fell down laughing as they rolled to the bottom of the hill.

That night, with the kids in bed and most of the candles blown out and the main light coming from the coals of a dying fire in the grate, Gereck noticed his wife acting oddly. She bustled about the house, wiping down every surface with a rag, putting every little thing back in its place. She must have sensed something was wrong.

He had been too quiet at dinner, and vague when she asked questions about how things had been. He didn't know where to start, and he certainly didn't want to scare the children, so he hadn't told her about discovering Elaina in the tower of Shalott, or the Green Knight's challenge and the deadline he now faced.

But it was more than that. There was something she wasn't telling him either. It pinched the corners of her eyes, pursed her lips and tensed her shoulders. Gereck looked up as she adjusted the positions of their few pewter dishes on the shelf.

He walked up behind her and put his hands around her waist and she tensed as if she had been struck. "Winna, tell me."

"What makes you think I have anything to say?" she said, her tone angry.

"Why are you cleaning?"

"The house is a disaster. I can't go to bed without putting it in order. You know that." She reached up with her rag to wipe the edge of the shelf, something she had done twice already since he had been watching. He intercepted her hand and spun her around to face him, but she pushed him away, walking to the table and leaning on the back of a chair.

"Winna, what is wrong?"

She bowed her head, and when she raised it, her eyes were glistening. "I want you to leave," she whispered. Her lip trembled and her fists were turning white as they gripped the wood.

Gereck took a step back. "What did you say?"

She turned her head, wisps of brown hair falling into her face. "I said, I want you to leave."

"But why? Our children..."

"Will be better off without you." She pushed off from the chair and faced him, hands still clenched. "You think all this dreaming about being a knight is going to put food on the table? We barely have enough, and what we do have I put there with these hands!" She held up her hands, red and raw from tending their crops.

Silence filled the space between them. Gereck didn't know what to say. Maybe she was right. All of his feelings for Winna had waned, and the new feelings for Elaina were there, inside his heart. He couldn't deny his attraction to her, but Winna... she had been through so much with him. And their children... Why had he come home, after all? To make amends, to clarify the feelings in his heart. To prove, to himself more than anyone else, that he still wanted his family, and a stranger with doe eyes and blonde hair wasn't going to shake him so easily.

Gereck moved close to Winna, taking her hands in his and kissing them softly. "I appreciate it, Winna, I do. What you do for us is more than any woman should have to, but you know I can't ignore this dream. I can't live my life as a farmer, trapped here without hope, without the honor of serving our king in Camelot. Please." He swallowed, then reached up and tucked some loose hair behind her ear. She turned her head away. "Please don't give up on me. Not now."

Winna slid her hands from his. She sighed deeply, all the anger apparently gone out of her, and when she looked back at him, he wished he could erase the weariness that looked so out of place on her beautiful face. "I just want to feed our children, Gereck. I don't desire anything more. My father was a farmer, your father was a farmer, and all of their fathers. They led good lives. Honest, hard working lives. What place do we have in the world of noblemen and kings? What can poor folk like us ever hope to obtain?"

"Greatness, Winna," Gereck said, reaching for her hands again. She folded them across her chest. He dropped his hands. "This is my chance to do something great."

"I wouldn't have a problem with it if you got paid."

"Well, perhaps that is about to change."

"Squires are usually young boys without families to care for. You're..." she looked up at him, her eyes widening. "What do you mean, Gereck?"

"There is something I need tell you," he said slowly. "On the first day of the festival, I was challenged to a head game." Winna gasped. Gereck continued. "The knight was dressed in brilliant green armor. I've never seen the like, Winna, it was as if the metal were forged of emeralds. I accepted his challenge on behalf of the king." The confidence in his words didn't match the churning in his gut. He swallowed it.

"What happened?"

"Well, I have my head, don't I? And it paid off. King Arthur is going to make me a knight," he said, spreading his arms.

Winna threw her arms around him, shocking him. Her touch felt foreign to him, but he returned her embrace anyway. He tried convincing himself it was just the lie. Although, he hadn't lied, not really. He just wasn't telling her the whole truth.

She looked at him, beaming. "I am so proud of you!"

"Really?"

"Of course. Finally, your hard work has paid off," she paused. "Do you still want us to come live in Camelot with you?"

"Ah," Gereck said, hesitating. "No, not yet. I know how much you love it here. How about you stay for a while longer? I'll save up enough to buy a house in town, then we can live there together."

Winna nodded. "That would be wise. We must have a place to live. Oh, Gereck," she smiled at him again, then brought his face close and rubbed noses with him. Then she gasped. "Gereck, when is the ceremony? Did they already have it?"

"No, it's been delayed because of the festival." He cursed internally. The lie fell flat even to him. He could just tell her, but then she would be more disappointed in him, and there was no telling how she would react then.

She furrowed her brow. "That is strange. They have knighted men during the festivals before."

"They have new ways of doing these things now. If the rumors of war with the Saxons become more than talk they might delay it"

She eyed him carefully. "Why would they do that? Wouldn't King Arthur need you most in a time of war?"

"I can still fight for him if I am not knighted."

Uh-oh. He knew that face. She wasn't convinced. His mind reeled as he thought of what he could say, but nothing came to his mind. She opened her mouth to give a reply, when the stairs creaked behind them. They both turned.

"Papa?"

Cai stood at the bottom of the stairs, his blonde hair mussed from sleep. Gereck squatted, holding out his arms to the boy, who came to him slowly, glancing between his mother and father. Gereck set him on his knee.

"Your voices got loud," he said.

"We are just talking, Cai. Go back to sleep," Winna said, giving Gereck a stern look.

Gereck looked at his son, and brushed the boy's hair from his eyes. Only six summers old... how would he take it when his papa left again? Would Cai miss him? What about Ada? She was three, his little darling. When he was gone, sometimes for months at a time, she would wait for him every night until her mother called her in, and even then, she would insist a candle be lit in case papa came home late. He knew this because Winna had told him. Ada would be devastated, but he couldn't stay. All of this went through his mind in a moment, and he could feel his heart getting heavier with the weight of Cai's concerned, innocent gaze.

"Your mama is right, son. I won't be leaving tonight. Hurry up to bed, and I will see you in the morning."

Cai nodded.

"I love you, son."

Cai almost knocked the air from Gereck's lungs as he squeezed him with as much strength as his little arms could muster. Then he ran to his mama, gave her a kiss, and scampered up the stairs. All was quiet once more. Gereck sighed and ran his fingers through his hair, then stood and looked back at Winna. Tears were coursing down her cheeks. He followed her gaze back to the stairwell Cai had disappeared into, then walked forward and took her in his arms.

"Why are you crying?" he asked, afraid to hear her answer. She sniffed.

"Just seeing you with him. He loves you." She laughed then, and hiccupped. "You know, the other day, he told me he wants to be a knight just like you are going to be. I never thought it possible, but you have proven me wrong. I am sorry to be such a stubborn wife. Forgive me?"

He kissed her brow. "Of course."

She embraced him and he held her as tightly as he could, determined to ignore the guilt that rose inside of him. He pushed Elaina's face from his mind. Then he kissed his wife. He kissed her shoulder, her neck, her face, her lips, until she protested that it was late and they should go to bed. He picked her up, relishing in her surprised laughter, and carried her to their room. He could give her this one happy moment at least.

CHAPTER FIFTEEN

Guinevere woke three days later with a pulsing headache. The past several days, the physician had insisted on medicating her with bitter herbs that put her into a deep, somehow restless sleep.

Voices haunted her, breaking through her dreams, and strange memory-like scenes played out before her eyes. It had been entirely exhausting.

But this morning there were no strange voices to greet her, and the only person in the room was Mary, holding a breakfast tray, which she delivered with a smile and a chirpy "Good morning!"

Guinevere was relieved to see that a plain and simple chamomile tea with honey rested on the tray where her medicine normally did.

"Good morning," she mumbled, wincing at the pain in her head. She resisted touching it, though, as that would draw Mary's concern.

Instead, she poked at the food items on her tray, then picked up her cup and sipped at the tea inside. A glimpse of white parchment caught her eye. She set down her cup. Among the dishes was a piece of parchment addressed to her.

"What's this?" she asked.

A knock came at the door. Mary went to it and spoke to the person standing outside. Guinevere strained her ears, but didn't quite recognize the voice. She turned the parchment over in her hands and found a red wax seal holding it together; a seal that held the royal Pendragon crest. Her heart fluttered in her chest.

"Send them in, Mary. I can take a visitor." To her relief, the words came out clear and strong.

Mary widened the door and Lady Nimue glided in, her flowy blue gown following with graceful sweeps of fabric. She rushed to Guinevere's bedside and took her free hand, holding it tightly.

"Guinevere, darling, I hope my company isn't too much for you this morning? I heard you were still in bed and had to come see you." She released Guinevere's hand and sat in a chair at the bedside.

"Yes, Lady Nimue, I am glad for it. Mary is overly concerned with my health and would have me stay inside all day."

Nimue *tsked*. Guinevere didn't dare look at Mary, knowing the glare she was certainly sending her way.

"It is a shame you must stay inside. You are missing all the fun!"

"Well, not entirely..." Guinevere trailed off tantalizingly. It was nice to finally have someone her own age and station to talk with, someone who might understand her.

"Oh?" Nimue looked taken aback.

"Sir Lancelot and King Arthur both visited me several days ago. At lunchtime. I apparently forgot that I invited them both to dine with me at noon, and they came expecting my exclusive company."

Lady Nimue put a hand to her mouth. "I knew I should have sent that message for you! You weren't in any state to remember, but I allowed myself to believe you would. I am sorry! Were they upset?"

"Only to be denied my company, I think. Both left in an amiable enough manner. I think my apparent condition excused my poor manners. They are good friends to each other, are they not?" Guinevere inquired. She fidgted with the parchment.

"Oh, the greatest of friends. They have been in one another's company for many years, and they have seen much together. Neither has had much interest in women. Until lately, of course." Lady Nimue said with a coy smile at Guinevere.

Guinevere shifted uncomfortably. It didn't sit well with her, the attention of the two men, for one reason: she didn't want to be the force that ruined their friendship. It didn't sit well with her that they both pursued her, but only one could have her, and if one of them did, it would cause damage that could potentially never be undone. She frowned into her tray.

"What is it, Guinevere?" Lady Nimue inquired.

"Never mind," Guinevere said, smiling. "A trifling problem. I won't trouble you with it."

"Well then, perhaps you will trouble me with the contents of that letter you are holding." Lady Nimue replied.

Guinevere looked at it. "Ah, yes." She contemplated the wax seal again.

"Who is it from?"

"There is no name on the outside."

Nimue's eyes sparkled. "Then open it, and let's see."

Guinevere broke the wax seal and read the brief lettering.

"Well?" Nimue asked, she craned her neck as if to read it, and Guinevere turned it towards her. After a moment, Nimue clapped her hands together.

"Then it has turned out for the best after all!" she said.

Mary looked up from her embroidery. "Are you going to leave me in the dark, then? What does it say?"

Guinevere smiled and read the letter aloud. "Milady Guinevere, it was a delight to see you yesterday. Regardless of the misunderstanding we had, I would still like to dine with you. Would you care to join me at a later meal, where the two of us can talk and enjoy one another's company further?" She put the letter down, her hands trembling so much she could hardly keep hold of it. "It's signed 'Arthur'."

Mary smiled. "There now, all is as it should be."

Nimue put a hand on Guinevere's back. "You deserve it, Guinevere."

Guinevere beamed. She was genuinely glad. So glad, in fact, that the darkness that had hovered over her mind since Duke Cador's advances at Cairhaise faded to the back of her mind, and she hardly noticed it. The food looked incredible, and she was famished. She picked up her spoon and dipped it into the stewed plums.

Just as she took a bite, there came another knock at the door. Mary sighed and put down her embroidery, then walked towards the door. When it opened, a young maid outside dipped into a shallow curtsey. Her arms were filled with an enormous vase of flowers, tiny things that blushed pink and white.

"Good morning, milady. His majesty King Arthur sends his greeting and inquires after milady's health," she said in a sweet, quiet voice.

Guinevere smiled and gestured towards the table at her bedside, and swallowed the bite she had taken. The maid complied, setting the vase there, then stepped back with her hands clasped in front of her.

"You may tell him I am better than yesterday."

"He has asked me to invite you to join him at the jousts, milady. Will you be attending?"

Guinevere looked to Mary, who shook her head firmly. Guinevere's shoulders fell. "No, suppose not. Please express my regret...?" She stopped. She did not know the maid's name.

"Alyce, milady," the maid said, guessing her hesitation. She brushed through the flowers, removed a wilted one, then turned to walk back to the door. "I will inform his majesty."

As soon as she shut the door, Mary returned to her chair, muttering. Guinevere caught the gist of it. Something about kings and their unreasonable requests.

Frustration, and a tinge of anger, rose inside of her. She dropped her spoon on the tray with a clatter. Mary looked up, alarm on her face.

The words could not be contained. They burst out of Guinevere's mouth. "He is hardly being unreasonable. If I went to the jousts, I would be sitting in the shade, doing no more than I am doing here. I would take water. And if you did not wish to come, I am certain someone, perhaps Lady Nimue, could attend me."

In the past, a remark like that would have earned her a tongue-lashing, but Mary only stared at her for a long, hard moment, before replying. "If you want to kill yourself to watch jousting, be my guest. I will not be there to see it. Fool girl," she muttered, dropping into her chair and returning to her embroidery.

Guinevere hesitated. She sensed Mary's distress, hidden in the front her anger provided. Mary loved her; these episodes Guinevere had been having had put a great deal of stress on her, but Guinevere would be careful. All she wanted to do was go outside. And see Arthur. The thought of him brought a smile to her face, and for a brief moment, her imagining of him was unspoiled by thoughts of Lancelot. Confusion twisted in her chest at the thought of the two men.

"Guinevere? I would be glad to attend you," Lady Nimue said. Guinevere turned to her, smiled, and pushed off her bedcovers.

"What does one wear to watch sweaty men poke each other with sticks?"

"Whatever most sets her apart."

Lady Nimue walked to a chest full of dresses at the foot of Guinevere's bed. She rifled through it, then pulled out an emerald dress with gold trimming. She shook it out and laid it on the bed, then found a pair of shoes and a gleaming hairpiece.

"Am I going to a ball?" Guinevere asked, laughing. Nimue gave her a serious look.

An hour later, she was ready, her hair done and dress on. Guinevere felt stronger than she had in days, and she hoped nothing would happen today to make Mary's concern necessary. She glanced over at Mary, whose head nodded over her embroidery. Poor woman, she was exhausted. She deserved a break. Guinevere turned away and walked to the door, arm-in-arm with Nimue.

As soon as the door to Guinevere's room closed behind them, Nimue burst into laughter. "Did you see that old woman snoring into her sewing? I thought she would to impale herself on her own needle!"

Guinevere halted, pulling her arm from Nimue's. "I didn't expect such callousness from you. That 'old woman' has been with me all my life. She's like a mother to me."

"Oh, I didn't mean..." Lady Nimue stopped. "I am sorry. You are right, I should have been kinder."

Guinevere nodded. "You are forgiven. Thank you."

"You would forgive me that easily?" Nimue's brow creased. "Why?"

"The bishop teaches us to love one another, to be as Christ our Savior and forgive. I practice what I hear preached on the Sabbath."

Nimue considered her for a long moment. "You are good and kind, Guinevere. You deserve to be queen."

Guinevere blushed. They walked down the courtyard steps and into the bright morning sun, passing a few guards, but most of the people were watching the jousts.

"I never aspired to it, you know. I avoided men for a long time before I came here. Mary encouraged me, saying the king was interested, and I decided then if I was going to get married, I might as well try to find love, and if prestige came with it, then..." She shrugged her shoulders. "That might make it worthwhile."

Nimue considered her a long moment without saying anything. They left the inner keep of Camelot and entered the market district, passing many empty stalls. Only a few were open, some farmers with their wares, and of course, the smithy had its fires roaring. They were the only ones getting great business during the jousts.

They made their way across the bridge and followed the directions of the guards at the arena entrance to find the stairs to the nobles' stand. Halfway up the steps, a wide section of wall was open, giving them a view of the arena.

Two men faced each other across the dirt arena, lances in hand, the crowd cheering as their horses galloped towards each other. The blue-shielded knight's lance struck the other knight beneath his arm, unseating the unfortunate fellow. The loser's horse trotted around the arena while the dust settled, and several men ran in to help the man up while the blue-shielded knight took a victory lap.

Suddenly Nimue gripped her arm so hard it hurt, but just as Guinevere was about to protest, the woman pointed up toward the covered stand they were headed for. "There he is!"

"Who?" Guinevere asked, squinting. Then she remembered. "The man you're courting? He's sitting with the king?"

"Yes. Just to the right. Do you see him?"

For one heart-stopping moment, Guinevere thought it might be Lancelot. Then she relaxed. Sir Lancelot would be getting ready to joust, not sitting with the king. She followed Nimue's finger and saw an old man sitting beside the king, his hair long and gray and... the next moment her jaw dropped and she turned to Nimue. "Merlin? You're courting Merlin?"

Nimue crossed her arms and smiled coyly, looking ahead at the back of the gray-haired sorcerer. "Yes, I am."

"But he's a sorcerer! He practices magic!"

Nimue's fluid laughter filled the staircase. She turned from the opening in the wall and picked up her skirts, climbing up the stairs ahead of Guinevere. "I come from the lands of Northumberland, where the religion of the

Goddess still runs thick and wild in our veins. I myself have trained in the coven of the Goddess on Avalon. Merlin and I will make a powerful match. There are things he can teach me…" She turned and saw that Guinevere hadn't moved. "What is wrong?"

Guinevere climbed a few steps, then looked at Nimue. "The bishop of our chapel back home always preached against magic. He claimed it was evil, that the women of Avalon and all other magic users sinned greatly against our Lord, blasphemed His holy name…"

"And what do you say, Guinevere? Am I evil?"

"No." Her brow creased. Then she smiled. "But I don't know you very well yet, do I?"

Nimue smiled. "All women have something of the Goddess in them, even if they don't recognize it."

She turned to continue climbing the last flight of stairs. Guinevere followed, but first glanced out on the jousting arena, where two men charged one another to the roar of the crowd, and then she looked at the stand where she could see Arthur turning to speak with Merlin. She smiled, then picked up her skirts and eagerly followed Nimue.

The king occupied his seat raised on the dais, Merlin on his other side. Lady Nimue looked around and spotted Guinevere. She smiled in a warm, friendly way, then looked pointedly across the seats to the empty one beside the king. Guinevere returned her smile and nodded, then swallowed over her dry throat. Her legs wobbled. She could only see the back of the king's head as he leaned it in one hand on the arm of his chair. Taking a deep breath, she stepped carefully behind the dais, coming around the other side and sitting in the empty chair. She wet her mouth, and spoke.

"Who is jousting today, Your Majesty?"

King Arthur lifted his head and looked over at her, a smile widening on his handsome face. "Lady Guinevere, I was beginning to wonder if you had doomed me to a lonely tournament. The maid said you would not be coming today."

Guinevere returned his smile. "Not so, Your Majesty. I couldn't stay away, truly." She gave him her most charming smile and he responded by leaning in and directing her attention to the arena.

"Sir Gwydion and Sir Lionel are in the arena now. Sir Lionel is the better horseman, but Sir Gwydion is steadier with the lance. If it came to a swordfight, well, that would make things interesting." He gestured as he spoke.

Guinevere leaned forward, intrigued, as the two men took off towards each other, their impossibly long lances painted brilliant colors to match their glinting shields.

She was far less interested in jousting than her handsome companion, and watched him rather than the men in the arena. She smiled, she laughed, and she played the part of the adoring feminine companion, and found herself rather good at it. She could ignore the piercing stare of the gray-haired sorcerer across from Arthur, and it almost didn't unsettle her to see Nimue's elegant arm draped over Merlin's.

Today, she would ignore darkness, ignore confusion, and especially ignore the pressure just behind her eyes that occasionally pained her. Today, she would relax and enjoy the undivided attention of a charming king on this sunny afternoon.

The sun dipped down towards the horizon when King Arthur stood, knelt at Guinevere's feet, and kissed her hand. Stunned, Guinevere sputtered until her words finally came out. "Th- thank you, Your Majesty."

He smiled up at her, his blue eyes like pools that she couldn't help but fall into. "I must ready myself. I am up for the jousts before sundown, milady. Do you have a token for me?"

Her hand went to the handkerchief tucked into the front of her bust. She drew it out and hesitated. It was the one she had embroidered the fat, splotchy blue bird on, but she didn't have another, and the king waited. She held it out to him, and he took it in his hand, then bowed his head. "I thank you, Lady Guinevere. This will surely bring me fortune."

"Whom do you face?" she asked.

He grinned. "Sir Lancelot. I hope you will stay to watch?"

Guinevere swallowed hard. "Of course I will."

"Good. I will look for your face from the arena."

"Luck to you," she said. Her throat felt dry as she watched him leave. Merlin excused himself as well, and Lady Nimue gestured her over to sit by her. Guinevere gladly moved, not wanting to sit there alone.

"King Arthur does you great honor. He must think you beautiful indeed."

"Must he?" she murmured. It was a silly thing to say. Of course he did. They had shared an afternoon together at most. He didn't yet know of her character, her intelligence.

"And the knight Lancelot favors you as well. No wonder. The entire court is talking about it. They have an agreement, Lancelot and the king." Her eyebrows raised at Guinevere.

"Do they?" She stared at the man in the arena who had just won the round. He would face Lancelot, who would no doubt face the king.

"Yes, it is. You're what's at stake, Guinevere. They have agreed, as friends, that whoever wins the tournament gets to pursue you first. The loser will forfeit his right to court you."

Guinevere straightened up. "Really? That's wonderful!"

"Is it?" Nimue's face creased in confusion. "Aren't you upset you won't get to choose?"

Guinevere laughed. "Not at all! I like them both, and truth be told, I dreaded coming between them and ruining their friendship. This way, no one will be hurt, it is all agreed in advance. And if I don't like the one who courts me first, I can seek courtship from the second." She clasped her hands in her lap and sat back in her chair. Her heart pounded. She was looking forward to the jousts, after all.

She sat up when Sir Lancelot rode his white charger onto the field. He turned his head towards her, and though his helm visor obscured his eyes, she knew his gaze was directed at her. She watched as he brought the stallion around and took up his lance from the squire on the field. Guinevere recognized his opponent, Sir Tristan, by the purple cross on his shield, and the two men charged their steeds towards each other, lowering their massive, heavy lances, holding them, holding them...

The wood splintered as it made contact. Both knights were flung backward, and while the grand guard over Sir Tristan's shoulder came loose, both kept their seat. They waited as the plate was reattached, then came around and charged at one another again. This time, Sir Tristan was unseated. The crowd roared. Guinevere found herself cheering, sharing a smile with Lady Nimue, whose green eyes glittered. Sir Lancelot removed his helm and rode around the arena, waving to the crowd. He stopped at the king's stand, where Guinevere sat, and he kissed his hand, gesturing towards her with it. Guinevere's face went red, and she couldn't be sure, but it seemed that the crowd got louder, cheering for them.

Then Sir Lancelot left the arena, most likely to adjust his armor and have his horse wiped down. Sir Tristan made it safely off the field, uninjured, except for his pride.

Then, they waited. The squires removed debris from the field, mostly wooden shards from the lances. They ran through the dirt with large rushes, smoothing the arena, readying it for the final match. The men entered on their horses, squires attending. Guinevere watched with eagerness, her mind reeling.

Sir Lancelot had the disadvantage, as he had just jousted with Sir Tristan, while King Arthur was well rested, but Sir Lancelot was also limber, ready to run, and the king was coming to the field cold. Guinevere scooted to the edge of her seat and put her arms on the painted wooden beam atop the low wall in front of her.

The champions-to-be trotted their horses around the arena with their helmets removed, King Arthur atop a feisty bay, Lancelot still on his white charger. The crowd was ear-splitting, but Guinevere noticed they were louder for their king, only just noticeably.

They both stopped in the middle of the arena and clasped their hands on each other's forearms. Both turned and looked up at Guinevere, who leaned out of the covered box just slightly, smiling at them. Her heart fluttered as she gazed at them. Her future husband stood before her, most likely, and the winner of this match had the best chance of winning her hand.

The king touched the handkerchief where it was tied on his arm. Guinevere's heart beat faster. She took a quick breath in.

Sir Lancelot looked away from the king, and guilt shocked through Guinevere. Lancelot didn't have a favor from her, and she knew what that must look like. He must already think she was hoping the king would win; in a way, she was. After all, she didn't tend to faint around him.

The two men about faced, directing their horses to the opposite side of the arena.

That strange presence that had plagued her mind was most active when Lancelot was around. Part of her was afraid that if she stayed near the handsome, black-haired knight more often, she would suffer more episodes, and lose control completely.

Her head ached in response to the thought. She put her hand against it, trying to keep her eyes on the arena, to watch as the men put on their helmets and took up their lances. Lancelot's was a golden yellow, the king's painted bright red. They blurred as her vision darkened.

Lady Nimue tugged at her arm. "Guinevere, watch! There they go!"

Guinevere took her hand from her head. She stared at the lances, her vision clearing until she could see with sharpness again. Lance met armor and splintered. King Arthur's strike. Lancelot's had only glanced his opponent's shoulder.

The horses circled back around, and the king received a new lance. They ran again.

This time both riders put up their lances, neither one delivering the strike. Sir Lancelot's foot had come out of his stirrup, and the king had noticed.

The people cheered as the two men rounded again. The lances lowered, the steeds charged. Both had set their lances well, and when they collided, both men were unseated.

They immediately scrambled to their feet, and the squires in the field grabbed the horses and pulled them out of the way. It was down to the sword.

Guinevere shifted. Her bottom hurt from sitting at the edge of the hard wooden chair. She stood up, leaning her hands on the beam in front of her. Her heart beat so strongly it felt like it was climbing into her throat. She swallowed.

Both men removed their helms. They drew their swords. The crowd erupted. Ribbons waved. The sun was a golden orb in the sky, ready to drop down behind the horizon any moment. They had to finish this quickly.

"Whom do you want to win?" Lady Nimue asked, suddenly standing beside her.

Guinevere shielded her eyes from the brightness of the setting sun. She chewed her lip. "I think... I think Arthur. How is he with a sword?"

"Brilliant, of course, but most of the time not as brilliant as Sir Lancelot."

Guinevere watched the arena, suddenly nervous. The heart fluttering from earlier had stopped, and her head was no longer pounding, but she felt anxious.

The men faced one another, taking offensive stances, holding their weapons ready. Swords glinted with burned-orange light from the sun. They flashed as the men circled each other.

King Arthur took the first strike. He lunged forward, arm and sword extended as one, and Sir Lancelot parried.

There was no hesitation on the king's part. He carried his momentum forward, ducked under Sir Lancelot's sword, then swiped at his back.

Sir Lancelot had whirled around just in time to leap back and avoid the bite of the blade. He stumbled but gained his footing, bringing his arm forward in a wild swing, then withdrawing as the king went to block it. Lancelot jabbed his sword forward, under the king's blade.

Arthur leapt backward, falling to his side to avoid the blade, and Guinevere gasped.

"They won't actually kill each other, will they?" she said, not knowing why she whispered. The arena was deathly silent as the fight continued. Swords clashed and clanged. Both men lost their shields. The strikes came more quickly.

Lady Nimue did not respond; her eyes were riveted on the arena as she muttered something.

Guinevere nudged her.

"What?" Nimue startled, then relaxed. "No, they won't. One must lose his sword."

Almost as she said it, it happened. Sir Lancelot's sword was knocked from his hand and it thudded into the dirt some feet away. Lancelot's hands went up, and he knelt on the ground before the king, who brought his own sword point to the knight's chest to represent the kill. Then he pulled back his sword and offered his hand, which Lancelot willingly clasped and stood. They held their arms up together to the enthusiastic onlookers.

"That's Excalibur," Nimue said in her ear, pointing. Guinevere followed her gesture to the gleaming sword King Arthur held. "The sword that made the king."

"How can a sword make a king?" Guinevere asked.

She had heard the rumors, of course, of the boy Arthur, the ward of a minor nobleman, taking up the sword from a churchyard and being named as regent in Camelot.

Merlin had come forward and vouched for his nobility, claiming he was the legitimate son of Uther and Igraine. Everyone had believed the sorcerer, or was too afraid to argue.

Nimue didn't answer. She stared at the king and his knight, eyes narrowing. Then she sighed.

"He gave it up," she said, sounding disappointed.

"What? How can you tell?" Guinevere asked, studying Lancelot's face.

His smile didn't quite reach his eyes.

"I have watched them spar many times, Lady Guinevere. Sir Lancelot has never lost in such an easy manner. He must have taken your token for the king very seriously and assumed your affection was more for him," Nimue said.

And then, Guinevere imagined she could see it. There was something stiff in his manner as he congratulated the king, then turned and walked from the arena.

Blonde hair plastered to his flushed face, the king turned to Guinevere. He touched the handkerchief on his arm, then touched his chest over his heart, and her own heart fluttered in response.

The king would court her. Sudden excitement filled her. She smiled, then, and waved to him, ignoring the warning throb in her head.

Guinevere snuck off to the stables that evening. She hadn't ridden in weeks, and she was desperate to feel the wind in her hair, and the warmth of a horse's muscled body beneath her legs.

Mary would murder her if she found out, and the elegant gown Guinevere wore was hardly fit for riding, so Guinevere convinced herself she was only going to see the king's horses to see which were good for riding. She would just look.

It was lovely and cool in the summer night, and very late. She avoided the gaze of each person she passed, hoping none of them knew her by face, or at least, that none of them would tell Mary. Her rushed steps stumbled on the long hem of her dress as she rounded the final corner to the stables.

Only a few stable boys were about, feeding the horses.

Guinevere crept in.

By the dim lantern light she could see fairly well. At least a dozen horses stalled here. Bigger stables outside of the city walls kept the rest of the king's cavalry horses, but here he kept his favorites, and many of his knights' horses as well.

Guinevere walked down between the stalls, stopping here and there to stroke a nose, pat a neck. No one bothered her. She stopped at the stall of the tall bay she had seen King Arthur riding in the joust earlier.

The horse came right up to her, hanging his head over the stall.

"You're friendly," she said quietly, stroking his broad neck. He was incredibly tall and well set, with a thick muscular chest. Everything about him was thick. This type of horse wasn't considered majestic or fast, but they were good and reliable workhorses, bred further north and prized greatly for their strength. She could see why the king would like to use him for jousting. He was sturdy, steady, and even-tempered. The strength this horse added to the charge was no doubt advantageous.

"What is your name?" she murmured, increasing her stroking.

The horses lipped her hair, puffing its warm breath on her cheek as it passed.

She giggled when the horse brushed her earlobe. She was so caught up, she didn't noticed the person behind her until he spoke.

"You are quite good with him."

She whirled around and stared at Sir Lancelot.

The horse's head bumped her from behind.

"Sir Lancelot, I saw you joust today." Of course she had. He had seen her as well, and he had lost. Fool thing to say. She caught herself chewing her lip and stopped. Mary kept telling her that she would create sores doing that, and it wasn't fit for a noblewoman to have such an obvious nervous habit.

"Yes," he replied. He shifted his stance. "I didn't expect to find you here."

"Oh? Where would you expect to find me?"

"Inside. Resting. Or dining."

"I love horses," she blurted. The horse nudged her again, and she brought her hands up, rubbing his nose. "Since I struck my head in Cairhaise I have been forbidden to ride. I miss it greatly."

"Ah, that would explain it," Sir Lancelot said. He glanced around the stables and ran a hand through his curly black hair. The stable hands had gone, leaving them alone.

Guinevere rubbed her shoe against her other leg, scratching an itch.

"Mary will be wondering..."

"Would you like to..."

They both spoke at the same time, and Sir Lancelot gave a short laugh. He looked down at his hands. "Probably shouldn't anyway, after what happened today."

He looked at her, and Guinevere was struck by the deep longing she found in his eyes. It woke something inside of her, a burning sensation deep down. And that blasted headache was back too, pulsing at her temples.

Lancelot cleared his throat. "I was coming to check on Tybalt. His leg was cut in the jousts. I wanted to be sure it wasn't serious. I thought to take a ride after."

Guinevere glanced around. Sure enough, the large white horse the knight had ridden earlier was in a stall a few paces down. Her heart pounded. Where were the stable hands? There had been at least one just a moment ago.

Her head swam. Lancelot's mouth moved, but she couldn't hear him and she couldn't respond. Then everything faded, and she drifted.

Her eyes opened again.

"Hello," she said, blinking up at him.

A smile spread across his face, reaching his handsome green eyes. "I wondered if you would recognize me; if you would realize it too. You have, haven't you?"

"How could I forget?" she murmured, tracing his jaw with her hand. Her lips ached to join his.

He leaned down, hesitating before he pressed his lips against hers.

Blood rushed through her body, heating her face, her hands, her abdomen.

He pulled her closer and she moaned. His lips smiled on hers and then pulled away, trailing along her jawbone, leaving her breathless.

"I've waited a long time for this," he whispered in her ear.

She felt her lips split into a smile. She let her fingers wander, untucking his tunic from his belt so she could run them along the warm skin of his back.

His lips found hers again, kissing her hard. She let him press her backwards, and they fell into an open stall, a sweet cloud of hay billowing around them. His weight on top of her was pure, delightful bliss. It had been too long. Her other self had never encountered a man like this; she was pious as a church mouse and had avoided men. Well, Morgan would change that.

His teeth grazed her neck. "Careful," she murmured, "don't leave any marks."

The man growled playfully but complied, caressing her throat with his lips.

In that instant, Morgan heard a scream. It came from her own throat.

The man's weight immediately disappeared as he backed away. Her entire body convulsed, pulling her into a fetal position.

Violent sobs tore from her throat. She wasn't in control anymore. One of the others had taken over her body.

Who's there? she asked, reaching toward the entity she could feel at the forefront of her mind. It lashed out at her mentally, and physically she howled in pain and misery.

What do you call yourself? she demanded. She was the one in charge here. She knew every entity inside herself. Even Guinevere didn't know them all, but Morgan did, and she would know this one.

The entity calmed, and Morgan's body relaxed.

A sigh escaped their lips. Inside her mind, she heard the voice of a young girl, no more than nine. "*My name is Morgause.*"

Ah, little Morgause. Morgan needed to reassure this one. She was glad it wasn't the other one, the violent one.

Morgause was harmless, she was just afraid.

You must listen to me. You are safe. This man means you no harm...

Immediately, the consciousness turned their attention to the man, who was crouched beside her, his brow creased in confusion. He leaned toward her, coming too close. Morgause lashed out, catching his cheekbone with her fist, then scrambled away from him.

"Stay back, stay away!" Their voice sounded so high-pitched to Morgan, so foreign to her ears. She fought for control, but Morgause pushed back at her, no longer reasonable.

Morgan backed off, observing from inside her own mind and giving the child entity full reign.

"Morgan, what is it? Are you all right?"

Her name wasn't Morgan. *Who is he? Do I know him?* His hand on her shoulder made her scream louder. She lashed out at him and he grabbed her wrist. She collapsed into limp, dead weight.

"What is wrong with you?" the man whispered, glancing around frantically.

Footsteps and voices; someone was coming.

"Don't make me!" she cried out, tucking herself into a ball. "Please!"

"What are you talking about?" The footsteps got closer. "Morgan, look at me!"

She turned her head, but her eyes wouldn't focus on the man that held her. Tears blurred her vision. "Matthias, please, don't!"

A couple of men ran in, one wearing armor and carrying a spear. The first man called for them to help, and Morgause thrashed again.

"No, no, no," she moaned. "Leave me alone!" she shrieked, trying to get away, but the man still held her wrist. Her other arm covered her body, covering herself, protecting herself. She sobbed.

Emotions crashed through her body like a wave. Terror, pain, anger, hatred... What had happened to them? More hands were on her, voices, asking what was wrong. She couldn't answer. Her head tossed from side to side, and unintelligible sounds of anguish wailed from her mouth. Her eyes rolled back into her head and she jerked backward, cracking her head on the stone floor. Everything went dark.

"Ah, Guinevere. How wonderful to happen upon you here."

Guinevere looked up with a start. Her head had been nodding over the desk where she sat, but the sudden intrusion of a male voice woke her from her almost-dream state. And Morgan, who had been dormant and bored for several days, perked up.

Merlin stood at the door. Why hadn't Mary alerted her to the sorcerer's approach?

A small snore came from the corner. Guinevere saw Mary's head bowed over her embroidery. The poor woman was exhausted; worrying after Guinevere was taking its toll.

"These are my quarters, Merlin. Hardly a coincidence you would find me here." She dipped her quill, then leaned over the page, trying to recall what she had been about to write. She chewed her lip, aware of the old man still hovering just within her doorway.

"I came to inquire after your health, milady."

"I am well," Guinevere replied shortly.

"I am glad to hear that." It must have been clear Guinevere was not going to invite him in. The sorcerer stepped in anyway, moving slowly, arms tucked into his wide sleeves.

Guinevere didn't look up. "You'll have to excuse me, I'm writing a letter to my father." She twirled her quill in her fingers, then set it to the page and wrote.

"What happened in the stables?" Merlin asked, his voice quiet.

"Nothing. I had head pains. I fainted."

"The guards who came to your aid found you screaming."

Her quill froze in its writing. "Rumor does not contain truth."

"Which is why I came to you directly."

Guinevere's head was pounding. She put a hand to it. Tears pricked the corners of her eyes. Her throat tightened. She swallowed. What could she say? *I hear voices, Merlin. Voices that claim I am someone I am not. Voices that make me have feelings for Lancelot. I don't understand what is happening to me. I am afraid.*

Merlin pursed his lips. "People claim you are mad... insane. That the devil walks in your mind."

"Do they?" Guinevere murmured.

"Yes." Merlin nodded. "You must understand, Guinevere, that I only ask these things because our Arthur cares for you. I look after his safety, and that of the kingdom."

She wanted to ask for help, but Merlin frightened her, with his piercing gaze that seemed to read her thoughts. She opened her mouth, but couldn't quite bring the words out.

He already suspected she was mad, and what she said would only confirm it. Would he help her, or would he reveal her maddened state to the court and have her carted off to a nunnery?

"I am tired," she managed to say. She pushed herself away from the table and stood. "Please understand if I don't walk you out." Her head filled with pressure, like it was about to burst. She should lie down, but she could hardly bring herself to take a step, much less make it to the bed. She sat again, massaging her temples.

Merlin knew magic. If anyone could help her, he could, and it might not mean giving up Arthur. Perhaps Merlin knew a way; a simple and quick way.

Through the pressure in her mind, she could feel Morgan inside of her, anxious for control, like a horse chomping its bit and tugging the reins. This alien presence clearly didn't want her to say anything. Of course not, if it meant her end.

That decided it for Guinevere. She had to speak now. Guinevere opened her mouth and tried to get the words out, but they caught in her throat. Morgan was pushing harder, and Guinevere was losing focus. She couldn't let her in. She had to stay present, to stay in control.

Morgan slid into the forefront of their mind, and there was nothing Guinevere could do, and then nothing she could see, and nothing she could feel...

"...will get us nowhere," Merlin said.

Morgan couldn't remember the first part of his sentence; it had been lost in the transition. She had barely been able to stop Guinevere from opening her mouth, the stupid, foolish girl. Guinevere didn't realize how dangerous Merlin could be.

Merlin stood, sighing, and walked toward the window. He stopped in front of it, washed in the grayed light from outside, hands clasped behind him.

She set her quill down and studied the parchment, eyeing her penmanship, then, to avoid suspicion, she picked the quill up again and continued her writing.

"You aren't Guinevere, are you?"

Her hand jerked, causing ink to streak across the page. "What makes you think that?" she asked, keeping her voice even.

"Guinevere writes with her right hand," Merlin said. The quill halted, firmly held in Morgan's left hand, hovering over the page until a spot of ink dripped onto the parchment. It was definitely ruined.

You can't lie to him, Morgan. Guinevere's voice was faint in the back of her mind.

How had she surfaced? Morgan pushed her away, forcing her into silence. She didn't need the distraction right now.

She put the quill away.

"Who are you?" the wizard asked.

"Guinevere, of course."

"I doubt that highly."

She stood, shoving her chair back loudly. "You are a sorcerer, aren't you? Why can't you divine the truth for yourself?"

"Some call me that. I prefer to be known simply as a wise man, and counselor to the king. I also prefer friends to enemies," he said.

"And I simply prefer to be left alone," she said sharply. "If you are done interrogating me, I wish to retire."

"No, I don't believe I am. One more question, *Guinevere*."

She crossed her arms over her chest.

"I must ask you to forgive the personal nature of this question, but understand I need to be aware of certain things. I am quite invested in the future of the kingdom."

She studied her nails while he spoke, acting as disinterested as she could.

"Should you marry the king, will you be able to provide the kingdom with an heir?" his words rang through the chamber, and despite her intention to remain aloof, to stay in control, Morgan couldn't hold back the tide that was Morgaine. Of course this matter, of all things Merlin could have said, would bring her out.

Morgaine rushed to the forefront of her mind, sending Morgan reeling back into the darkness, a mere observer in her own body, hearing and seeing everything, but unable to contribute anything of her own.

Guinevere didn't always have this ability, she was too weak, but Morgan could. She could do anything, even talk to the others. For now, she listened.

Morgaine was an injured animal, and Merlin's words had struck the wounded place in her heart. She exploded.

"I will never be able to provide any man with anything! It has all been taken from me." She rose to her feet, knocking her chair backward with a crash, her nails digging into the palms of her hands.

He cocked his head to one side, studying her. She stood from her seat and paced.

"What happened?" he asked.

Morgaine held her head high, trying to remain indifferent, but the memory of the losses overwhelmed her. Three of them, so close together, and the last one, her overdose, the pain and agony as her body expelled a stillborn child onto the earthen floor, and she had almost died of blood loss...

She snapped her head up, meeting the man's gaze. It was like he knew everything, as if he had read her heart right through her body.

"You have been mistreated," he said gently.

"You could call it that," she practically snarled. "I was mutilated, at my own hand, but not by my own choice. Necessity..." She clapped her mouth shut. "I do not have to speak of this to you."

He gave her a hard stare, then nodded his head. "Very well. If you need me, I reside in the north tower..."

"I don't need anyone's help."

He passed her desk in silence.

Morgaine relaxed, beginning to drift back inside, and Morgan stepped forward, making the transition with only a blink of their eyes. Calmness washed over her and her entire body relaxed. A benefit of being divided.

She thought he might have gone, but Merlin's voice carried over to her from the doorway, startling her. "Everyone needs help, and I believe you need it perhaps more than most. If you have any heart in your body, you will leave Camelot and not threaten our kingdom's safety with your instability."

Morgan's heart clenched inside as the door closed behind the sorcerer. He knew. He knew she wasn't who she said she was. Would he reveal her? Would he tell the king? It could ruin all her plans if he did.

Morgan stood still for a long time, searching through memories of the past few days. Some time was missing, but she was used to that.

Guinevere was strong enough to keep Morgan out for some things, but Morgan's control was growing.

What she hadn't been aware of, and what unsettled her the most, was the sudden strength of Morgaine. Morgan thought she had known every alter, every aspect of her divided mental realm, but Morgaine had surprised her. Morgaine had never come out before, had only been a voice in their mind, telling her to do terrible things to herself, to kill herself.

Guinevere hadn't even realized the thoughts weren't truly her own, but Morgan had. She had learned that Morgaine was seventeen, and something terrible had happened to get her pregnant at least three separate times. Was that the truth of her past, or a figment of the abused alter's imagining? Morgan wasn't sure. Guinevere's body had always been at the peak of health.

She shook her head. It had to be something else, another side effect of this spell that Niviane had placed on her. She really needed to speak with that woman.

Mary would sleep for a while longer yet. Morgan moved into action at last, picking up her cloak and putting it on, along with her shoes.

It was time for Morgan to contact Niviane.

CHAPTER SIXTEEN

"Where are you going?"

Gereck grimaced. Lancelot was the last person he wanted to see, but he said nothing, focusing instead on saddling Fendrel. After buckling the saddle straps around the horse's girth, he looked up at Lancelot. "Just out for a ride, nothing special."

"Ah. Then you won't mind if I come? I need to get some fresh air, myself." He didn't wait for Gereck's reply, but instead turned to a passing stable boy. "Fetch me my horse."

The stable boy bowed and ran to do Lancelot's bidding. No one questioned Lancelot.

The man chuckled and turned back to Gereck. "This will be a good time, then! Two fellow *knights*, out for a casual jaunt across Camelot."

Gereck turned away from the knight and prepared to mount Fendrel. "It is going to be a rather dull ride. I have nowhere in particular to go. Perhaps I'll ride to the monastery."

"Good. I've been meaning to speak with Brother Sephis. He and I were having a marvelous theological debate last time I was there."

Gereck blinked. Why did it surprise him that Lancelot had religious debates with monks? He wasn't the religious type. Then again, according to the rest of Camelot, he was flawless.

By now, the stable hand was leading out a horse. It wasn't Lancelot's.

The knight frowned. "Young man, where is my horse?"

"Sir, the blacksmith is attending him. New shoes today. This one is fresh and ready for riding."

Sir Lancelot looked the beast up and down, frown deepening. Then he glanced at Fendrel.

Gereck knew exactly what he was thinking, and gripped Fendrel's reigns protectively. The horse wasn't his, per se, but Gereck had favored the horse ever since it had come to King Arthur's stables. He cared for Fendrel as if the horse was his own, and rode him often. Besides, Lancelot was rough with any horse he rode, even his own. Gereck didn't want to subject Fendrel to that today.

"Sir, I..."

Lancelot laughed. "Why, Gereck, you can read my mind! I will accept your generous offer." There was a dangerous gleam in his eyes, one that Gereck didn't dare question. He slid from Fendrel's back, whispering condolences in the animal's ear and handing the reins to Lancelot.

"He is a trustworthy horse, capable of leading himself with little direction," Gereck said, though he knew Lancelot would ignore him.

Already, Fendrel stamped his feet as Lancelot swung his leg over the saddle. He did not like his new rider.

Gereck looked sympathetically at his animal friend, wishing he could console him, but there was no turning back now. He sighed and climbed up onto the gray. Truly, it was a fine horse. Not as fine as Fendrel, but not bow-backed either.

The encounter put Gereck in a quiet, low mood as the two men kicked their horses into motion and started down the road toward Elaina's tower.

Lancelot whistled, content in the silence. For a time.

"Gereck, do you know what your problem is?"

Gereck sighed. "No, sir."

"Breeding." The knight turned his head and grinned, as if he had just paid Gereck a great compliment. "Or lack of it. Knights must come from a certain stock of men. Common folks are made for potato-digging and animal-raising, and they are mighty good at it. A man like me, well, let's just say Camelot would starve if I ran a farm!" He chuckled at his own joke.

Gereck stared stonily ahead, refusing to rise to the bait.

"I don't understand why you try so hard at knighthood."

Gereck turned suddenly, looking into the knight's eyes. "Fortunately, our king disagrees with you. And after all, sir, you became a knight, didn't you?"

Lancelot's eyes narrowed. "Yes."

"Weren't you found at the edge of the lake of Avalon as a babe? With no noble family to explain your lineage?"

"Yes..."

"Then I don't see why I have so little a chance. After all, you caught the king's eye and now you're his finest, most trusted knight. I hope to live up to your great name someday, and win his attention and a place at his table with you." He kept any trace of mockery carefully out of his voice, and held his face like stone.

Lancelot's mouth was open in protest. It closed and opened again several times, making him look for all the world like a fish. Gereck stifled a laugh. The last thing Lancelot wanted was for Gereck to sit at the same table as he, much less the Round Table.

"Well, I, you see... I must come from a noble family. Otherwise, the king never would have chosen me. He has a sense for these things. Besides, there is no mystery over where *you* come from," Lancelot said, smirking.

Gereck didn't bother replying. Instead, he kept his eyes forward. They rode in silence for far too short a time, and then Lancelot waxed on about Sirs Perceval and Galahad, and the soon-to-be-knight, Bors.

Gereck ignored him for the most part, keeping his eyes open for the tower. On foot, it took the better part of a day. On horseback, it was only a few hours. The sun was at its highest point in the sky and beginning its afternoon descent when the tower loomed ahead, the river parting on either side of it.

"The faerie tower," Gereck said, pointing it out.

"Ah, yes. I suppose you believe all the locals' suspicions about the place?"

Gereck shrugged. "Some of them, perhaps. Don't you?"

"Not a one. I've seen places containing real mysteries. I would recognize an enchantment if I saw one."

Gereck snorted, then stared up at Elaina's window. He wasn't sure why he was here. After his visit to Winna, every time he thought of Elaina he was plagued with guilt. Guilt that he had let himself have feelings for her. Guilt that he hadn't been there for Winna when she needed him. And more guilt that he hadn't managed to save Elaina from her horrible situation.

He wondered if she had tried anything from the bag yet. If it had freed her, surely she would have sought him out within Camelot? No doubt she was still in the tower, but perhaps she would see him today. Perhaps the mirror would show him to her, and they would finally discover the key to freeing her and she could live her life at last.

He sat as straight and tall as he could on the back of his horse. Next to Lancelot, he was sure he wouldn't inspire anyone, and Elaina wouldn't be much impressed, but he wanted to make the best impression he could. So, he brushed the dirt from his breeches and waved. Lancelot drew Fendrel up beside him and stared.

"What are you doing, squire?"

"Waving to the faeries." It was a stupid answer, but Gereck didn't care what Lancelot thought of him. His opinion couldn't get much worse than it already was.

The knight rolled his eyes. "Really, Gereck? With your thick head, it's no wonder the king hesitates to knight you."

He stood beside Gereck, waving his arm up at the tower like an idiot. "Look at me, faeries! I'm a valiant knight, bless me with your magic! If you're going to be foolish, I'll finish my ride alone."

Gereck paused his waving and followed Lancelot's gaze. Coming down the road was the lady Guinevere, astride a horse. Gereck was surprised to see her out. According to court rumor, she was abed and very ill. He still didn't understand why Lancelot and the king were both after her. They had been at odds with one another as of late, and, not for the first time, Gereck wondered if this Guinevere would be the end of their lifelong friendship.

“Sir Lancelot, what a pleasant surprise!” she called out.

Lancelot smiled with charm, kicking Fendrel into a canter to meet the lady halfway.

Gereck stayed where he was, watching.

“Milady, it is so hot. A flower like you must be wilting.”

Guinevere laughed, throwing her head back, her dark hair glinting in the sun. “Hardly, good knight. I thrive in the sun. With winter coming, the sunny days are few and far, so I’m soaking up as much as I can before then.”

“Ah, I see,” Lancelot said. “Then you are well? I worried, after...”

“I am well,” Guinevere said in a rush, glancing at Gereck, who inclined his head respectfully, keeping his distance.

“No doubt, but certainly you would be better off in the shade of the palace. Shall I escort you back?”

“I appreciate the offer, Sir Lancelot, but no, thank you. I want to stay outside longer.” Guinevere spread her arms as if she truly was soaking in the sun’s rays.

Gereck thought she looked ridiculous, but he thought that of many ladies in the palace. None of them were like his Winna, who could be covered in dirt wearing a dress the same color, her hair falling out of its bun and a child on her hip, and yet she was still more beautiful to him than anything... until he had met Elaina.

Newfound guilt rose inside of him. It was like a battle waged in his heart. He still loved Winna, and yet he doubted she understood him or cared about him. After all, if she cared, would she ask him to forget his dreams and stay home with her?

“Sir knight, you seem unwell.” Lady Guinevere’s voice brought him out of his dark thoughts.

Gereck shook his head and stared at her, realizing he didn't know what had just been said. Had she called him a knight? Her dark, sultry eyes held his gaze as she spoke. "Perhaps you have been in the sun too long?"

"No, milady. You have it wrong, I'm not..."

She laughed gaily. "There now, there's no dishonor in admitting defeat to the sun. A sword would not defend you well there. Besides, that mail shirt must be roasting."

Gereck stuttered, searching for words.

Lancelot, surprisingly, came to his rescue. "You presume much of him, milady. He is not used to the presence of utterly beautiful and charming women. He was just talking of riding to the monastery, after all, weren't you?"

Gereck nodded. "Indeed, milady. I must be off. Pardon me."

He bowed his head again, took the reins in hand, and steered the mare around. He would go see Elaina, after all. Might as well, after riding all the way out here. Behind him, Sir Lancelot suggested they take to the trees on the other side of the river, and Lady Guinevere insisted they ride further down the road before crossing. Lancelot agreed, and glancing behind again, Gereck saw the two riding in the opposite direction together, leaning in close.

It looked like they were... no, Guinevere pulled back laughing, and watching them for several moments Gereck could see he had been mistaken. Lancelot wouldn't dare court this woman since he lost the agreement with Arthur, and no woman in her right mind would choose any knight, even Lancelot, over the opportunity to be queen.

Gereck led the mare across the river and through the forest. He wound his way along a well-traveled path until it split off onto a deer trail, which he took. The river and tower came back into sight. He tied the horse's reins off on a nearby tree, giving her plenty of lead for grazing, if she desired.

Then he walked towards the tower. The river was high today, and the grassy bridge of land that connected his bank to the tower island was covered in a shallow layer of water. He would have to get his boots wet, and he hadn't had time recently to patch them.

Cursing his luck, Gereck removed his boots and stockings, then rolled up his pants. Boots in hand, he crossed through the cold river water barefoot. He looked at the ivy climbing up the moss-covered wall. Next to it was the tall willow tree, its delicate branches and leaves brushing the rushing water below.

Gereck jumped for the first branch and missed once, scraping his hands. Then he clambered up, hooking his leg over the thick branch. Near the top, climbing became difficult, but he found his usual path up to the only sturdy branch that reached Elaina's tower window. He hooked his arms over the edge, pulled himself up, and stepped into the room.

Elaina wandered around the room, head bowed over something that she worried between her hands. Parchment.

Gereck cleared his throat.

She stopped walking, but didn't look up. A small smile came to her face. "You came back."

"I said I would."

"I know, but I don't always believe you."

"If I say I will return, I will," he said, coming closer. "Have you tried the things I gave you?"

Elaina looked at the parchment. "It's been so long since I've written anything, I almost didn't remember how, but it was nice to put some thoughts on parchment." She held the note out for him. "This is for you. I was practicing, mostly, just to convince myself I still knew how, so it might not make sense."

He took it from her, the parchment rustling as it passed between their fingers. He started to unfold it. "May I?"

"What?"

"May I read it now?"

She shrugged. "I suppose. It's just some silly words."

He finished unfolding it. Inside, written in wobbly handwriting with ink blotches obscuring parts of some words, were a few sentences.

Dear Gereck,

I've missed you. The days pass, the sun shines outside. I still cannot see it. I do not blame you for this, I know you are trying, and I know you have a life to live beyond rescuing me from this place, but I miss you, and the world, all the same, every time you go. More since I met you, for it seems real now, not like a fae tale or a life that has passed. It is within reach, and I have you to thank for that. Please do not give up on me.

Gereck closed his eyes, folding the parchment back up. He tucked it into his pocket. "Your optimism amazes me," he said at last. "Being locked up here for four decades, and still hopeful I can help you get out."

"You must have a fair amount yourself, since you keep returning," she replied.

“I am apparently not very good at it, however,” Gereck said, “since my attempts continue to fail. Did you try everything in that bag I gave you?” He looked around the room for some sign of it. There, on the bed. Its contents were scattered around the bedcovers, some on the table.

“Yes, including the naked, sacrificial dance in the full light of the moon.”

“Elaina!”

She shrugged. “I used all the kindling and the flint you gave me. The loom would not light, and neither would the mirror. Nor the thread.”

“And the dagger I gave you, it wouldn’t cut the thread?”

“Oh no, it did, but the thread immediately melded back together." She fidgeted, twisting her fingers together. "It seems to be quite powerful magic. Did you talk with the sorcerer the king employs? What did he say?”

“He is the one who gave me the vial of acid, the potion we tried together.”

“Oh,” she said, shoulders slumping. “If he can’t help us, then what can we do?”

“I will ask him again,” Gereck said. “He didn’t know everything about your situation. If I tell him more, perhaps it will help.”

“Perhaps you could convince him to come here!” Elaina exclaimed.

“Perhaps...” Gereck said, trailing off. “He is busy and difficult to talk with at the best of times.”

“But you will try, won’t you?” Elaina asked.

The weight of her asking settled heavily on his shoulders. “I will try,” he said. “While I’m at it, is there anything you need? Anything at all?"

Elaina considered. "Do you have access to any family records? I want to know something... about someone."

Gereck laughed. "I could ride to the monastery. It's far, though, and I would need a name."

"I don't want to trouble you too much," Elaina said, "but it would mean a lot to me."

"What is the name?" Gereck asked.

"Morgan Astolat."

"A relation of yours?"

Her fist flew to her mouth and she bit it, as if trying to hold back sobs.

"My sister," she said, once she'd regained some control. "Half, I guess, if you take into account we had different mothers."

"You haven't told me you have a sister."

"Had, most likely. She was ten years my elder, and will likely have passed. That's what I would like to know. My father is certainly dead, and my half-brothers... Well, they were knights, and they aren't likely to be around either." She smiled then, her eyes glistening with tears.

"I will make a trip as soon as I can manage it. I am needed in Camelot now, but I promise you that I will do my best."

"Thank you," she replied, "you are very kind." She glanced at her hands, then wandered through the room to her little alcove on the other side, sitting with her legs folded beneath her on the little stone outcropping inside.

Gereck followed her. "If you could leave here today, walk right out that door with nothing to stop you, what would you do first?" he asked.

"I don't know," Elaina replied. "What could I expect to see? The world is a whole new place now, I'm sure. My favorite places, my homestead, my family... They could all be gone."

"Then just use your imagination. What would you want to see?"

She seemed to be considering, a thoughtful look on her face. Then she looked up, suddenly, towards the loom and the mirror, and sighed and stood. She walked to the loom and sat down, taking up the shuttle and beginning to weave.

She closed her eyes, hands passing the shuttle automatically through the threads of the loom. "It's more painful than you can know, to see faces in your mind but know you'll never lay eyes on them again, and even if you did, they would have changed, aged, but you hadn't. I don't let myself entertain those thoughts anymore."

His heart wrenched in his chest at her words. There was so much sorrow in her voice. He wanted to take her in his arms, to hold her and tell her that it would be all right. Guilt stopped him.

"Then don't think of them. Think of something else. Escape into a new world." Outside, Gereck could hear the river, and wind rustled through the branches of the trees.

Several times Elaina opened her mouth to speak, then closed it again.

"I would want to see a great battle," she said at last. "I want to be there, to see the rise of heroes. To see the making, and ending, of a nation." She paused, and Gereck gaped at her. She continued, her voice taking on a wistful tone. "I'd like to be part of it, like a warrior maiden of the Celts, woad-painted and shooting arrows at the enemy, my battle companions on either side, racing to our deaths together, barefoot across the moors."

Gereck cleared his throat. "I didn't... I wasn't expecting that, certainly."

Elaina laughed. "My sister and I used to dream of what it would be like to run wild and free as they do, or did. It was hard to be stifled, forced to sit in tight, beautiful dresses and learn our lessons when we would rather be running about in the woods. She had it worse than I did, being the eldest daughter. She had suitors to sit for, and childishness was not tolerated in the least. I was given more freedom."

The loom clacked as her hands and feet moved. The shuttle shot through the threads and she caught it on the other side.

"I would run as far as I could away from home, into the woods where no one would see, and remove my shoes and socks, my apron and frock, then run naked and pretend to be a blue-painted warrior. It was exhilarating. I never quite grew out of that, I think." She stopped weaving and stretched her arms over her head. "Anyway, that's something I would love to do. In another life, perhaps."

"Naked?" Gereck blurted, before he could stop himself. "I mean, who would go into battle naked?"

"I heard that the women of the Celts do. With naught but a bit of cloth or leather binding their breasts to their chests, and perhaps across their waists for protection. They are swift and fearless warriors, among the most feared in the land."

"I have heard the stories," Gereck said. "I thought if those stories happen to be real, the women must be mad, and no wonder they have all died out."

"Mad or not, the wild abandon with which they live their lives is appeals to me... Sometimes structure gets to be dull, don't you think?"

"I like structure. I like armor, too," Gereck added, trying to keep the image of Elaina as a Celtic warrior maiden out of his mind.

He stood and walked around the room stretching his legs. He glimpsed the tapestry Elaina had been weaving, and the colors caught his eye. Craning his neck, he caught sight of the image of a man with wheat-colored hair, dressed in armor, sword raised in the air. Behind him, a colorful crowd of faceless people cheered.

It was Arthur. He was certain of it.

"Do you weave what you see in the mirror?"

"Well, the loom does the weaving, but yes, the image is what I can see in the mirror," Elaina replied. She was re-braiding her hair, still sitting on the loom bench.

"That man, there, that's King Arthur."

"Is it?" Elaina asked, peering curiously at the image. "What is he doing?"

"Beltane festival tournament. A sword-match or melee no doubt. He is incredibly skilled."

"Ah," Elaina said. There were creases in her forehead as her brow furrowed, but she didn't say anything more.

"No luck seeing me in the mirror, I suppose?" Gereck asked.

Elaina shook her head, causing her blonde hair to move into her face. She brushed it away. "No, I'm afraid not. So far all I get for trying is a headache."

"Perhaps I am wrong there, then. I've been wrong about so much else."

"Don't despair! If there is a way, we will find it."

Gereck was beginning to doubt that, but they hadn't been searching long. He would speak to Merlin again, and search the library, and perhaps there they would find something worth attempting.

It was getting dark when he left Elaina's tower. He left in high spirits, having spent the time talking about this or that, dreams they both had, things Elaina loved and remembered about her childhood outside the tower.

Her note rustled in Gereck's pocket as he climbed down the tree, barely able to see the branches he needed to use as handholds in the fading light.

Her note. He had forgotten about it during their conversation. He wished he hadn't brought it with him. He could feel the thick square of folded parchment through his pants, and each time he noticed it, guilt pulsed inside of him.

I've missed you, it said, but every word, painstakingly drawn, told him something else.

I love you.

Most disturbing of all, his heart pounded in reply, longing to say the same to the maiden in the tower, because, try though he might to ignore it, he did care for her, and he could no sooner stop seeing her or feeling for her than he could stop wanting to be a knight.

CHAPTER SEVENTEEN

Guinevere shaded her eyes with her hand, very conscious of the man on a horse beside her. She had snuck out while Mary napped, and though she knew that she would be in terrible trouble if Mary found out, she had taken a horse from the stables and rode it from the city.

To be on a horse again, hair flowing freely in the wind. It was exhilarating, and it had been far too long. Her heart was soaring for the first time since her fall in Cairhaise, but it was hot, and her water skin was empty.

A headache had crept on, a sure sign that she couldn't be out much longer, which is partially why she had let Sir Lancelot ride with her. After all, it wouldn't be amiss for them to be friends, especially if she did marry the king.

Her head suddenly swam with the heat, and her vision blurred. She put her hand to her head and stopped her horse, suddenly overcome with fear that it was happening again, that she would fall off her horse...

Sir Lancelot's voice broke through the fuzziness of her mind. "What brings you out here, milady? I would have thought to find you resting."

The headache cleared, and any trace of fear left her. Morgan was free again.

She looked across the river at the shaded bank on the far side. “I needed to feel the wind in my hair again, sir knight. One can only do so much embroidery before one risks becoming dull as an old maid.”

“I am glad you are feeling well, and that you accepted my company. I wondered, after...” He was leaning in toward her now, eyes intent on hers, as if searching.

“I will race you to the bridge,” she said, leaning across her horse's mane and urging the mare on.

She caught a flash of the confused look that crossed his face and laughed as he cursed, urging his horse to catch up with hers. It didn't take long. The horse he rode was much longer in leg and trained for hard riding, something her gentle mare couldn't make up for.

He beat her to the bridge, and then they crossed it together, chatting harmlessly about this and that. The conversation was dull, but safe, for now. A strange fluttering had started up in Morgan's chest and wouldn't stop. The nauseating heat plagued her until the shade of the trees reached out and covered her from the unrelenting eye of the sun.

They were alone.

The conversation stopped. They rode in contented silence.

She caught him gazing at her, but when she glanced back at him, he would look away. At the same time, their horses stopped outside a small clearing.

He glanced around. “Would you like to rest in the shade a moment, milady?”

“A rest would be welcome,” she replied.

He dismounted, then quickly came to her side and reached up to assist her down.

She accepted his hand, sliding from the saddle, acutely aware of the way her skirt rode up in back as she came down, but he couldn't see, of course.

He escorted her to a large moss-covered log, sitting her down before he unclipped the panels protecting his legs.

"What are you doing?" Morgan asked.

"It is hot in this armor, and difficult to sit with comfort. May I continue?" He paused at his gauntlets.

She nodded her assent. Breastplate, sword, gauntlets; everything was put into a pile nearby, the sword nearer and readier than the rest.

The final piece, his chainmail shirt, rattled as it slid over his head and made a heavy sound when it thudded into the dirt.

He turned towards her then, his eyes burning into hers.

She didn't look away this time, but kept her gaze locked on his.

"I don't understand how you can ignore it," he whispered hoarsely. "The desire… it burns so intensely, even during the day, and at night…"

Of course she knew. Or rather, remembered. Fire leapt inside of her, ignited by the cool blue of his eyes and the way his skin glowed in the dappled sunlight coming through the trees. She drew close to him on the wooden seat they shared, close enough to feel his breath on her skin.

His hand came up, hesitating briefly before he touched her face.

In a moment, she found herself embracing him, lips grasping hungrily for his, hands twining through his hair, fully consumed with passion.

His arms gripped around her waist, pulling her tight against his body.

“Guinevere,” the name on his lips sounded wrong. She drew away slightly, frowning at him.

“What did you call me?”

His eyebrows lowered as he thought. He stared at her.

She stared back, waiting. His eyes widened, and a smile touched the corner of his lips.

He tucked a lock of dark hair behind her ear. “Morgan,” he whispered.

She answered with a kiss. The fire roared inside of her like a starved beast finally being fed.

The man with her slid from the log, pulling her on top of him.

His name came, unbidden, to her tongue. She spoke, tasting it. “Mordred.”

She was filled with rapture, with joy, the sun warming her back as he reached for the ribbon holding her dress together in front. He pulled. The ribbon came undone without effort. It released its hold on her gown, and she relaxed into the body of the man beneath her.

The toll of a bell rang out across the river. His lips pulled away from hers, murmuring. “That is the king's summons. I must go.”

Morgan kissed him again. “Must you? The king can wait.”

“I'm afraid not,” he sighed, staring into her eyes.

And, as quickly as it had come, the passion died within her, replaced with horror as Guinevere regained control.

Inside again, Morgan cursed the enchantment that bound her to this divided mind, but try as she might, she could not escape. Guinevere had overwhelmed her once more.

She scrambled off Lancelot's chest, gripping her dress front. The ribbon was partially unlaced, causing her neckline to gape open. Her hair was mussed, coming out of its delicate coil on the back of her head. She stared at Lancelot, and he stared back unashamedly.

"What have we done?" she whispered. The knight stood, brushing off his breeches and moving towards her.

"Nothing, yet, but when I'm finished with the king's counsel..."

Guinevere stepped backwards, away from his outstretched arm. "Don't touch me!" Her voice was too shrill in the silent woods.

He looked at her, dumbfounded. "But you, only a moment ago, we were..."

She straightened her gown and fumbled with the ribbon, trying to lace it back up as neatly as before. "I don't know what you're talking about, or how you got me here alone with you, if you got me drunk me or, or..."

"I only responded to your advances, as I interpreted them," the knight said angrily, his fists clenching in metal gauntlets. "If you have been intentionally misleading, then what we have done cannot be my fault. Is this what you intended all along? To sabotage Camelot's best knight and his trust with the king for your own devious..."

"No! How could you think that?" She put a hand to her head. It was pounding. Tears choked her throat. She tried to remember how they had gotten here, what had happened. She couldn't. She looked at Lancelot. "Do you remember?"

"Remember what?" He slapped on his breastplate, clipping it into place. He squared his shoulders before her, handsome face rigid with anger.

"How we got here."

"Of course. Don't you? It was your idea. You invited me to ride with you." He looked at her strangely. "You truly cannot remember?"

She shook her head.

"What is your name?" Lancelot challenged.

"Guinevere. But why..."

Lancelot shook his head. "She warned me this might happen in the beginning. I shouldn't have supposed... Well, what's done is done."

"What are you talking about?"

He glanced at her. "Nothing important. Never mind."

"I don't understand. Why was I kissing you?" she asked, speaking each word deliberately.

"The heat of the day, I suppose, and we both forgot the agreement we made with Arthur. If you have feelings for me, then perhaps you ought to reconsider...?"

Guinevere shook her head. She could not trust this man. It was no coincidence that Morgan came out so often around him. She could not be alone with him again.

He sighed, bowing his head. "I should not have allowed it to happen, milady. It is I who am to blame. Forgive me?"

"You are forgiven, Sir Lancelot." Her voice shook, and she wondered how she could have let herself be so reckless. "I apologize if you misread anything I said or did. I will be more careful in the future."

"Certainly. Now, if you'll allow me, I will lead you back to our horses."

They both turned to leave the clearing, then stopped in their tracks. Someone watched them.

"So, despite our agreement made, and won, in honor and accordance with the knights' code, you go behind my back and meet together, alone. A simple word to me would have sufficed. I would not have held you to the agreement if I knew you already preferred one another."

Arthur.

Guinevere swallowed hard, heart pounding. She spoke first, her words tumbling over each other in her haste.

"I know what it looks like, Your Majesty, but..."

"It was my fault, Arthur," Lancelot interrupted Guinevere, looking at the king. Arthur turned to him, anger clear on his face. The horse beneath him shifted.

"I trusted you, Lancelot. You have only ever shown me your honor."

"You speak truth. I have ever been faithful to you, but in this, I found I could not be. I have dishonored our agreement, and I am ashamed." Lancelot bowed his head.

"Do you also speak for Guinevere?"

"She refused my advances, Your Majesty." Lancelot swallowed hard. Guinevere stared at him. She couldn't tell if his confession was real or if he lied, though what his motive for lying might be she couldn't determine. "Her honor, and her affection for you, remains intact."

Arthur looked between them. His eyes stopped on Guinevere. "Is this true?"

She bowed her head. "Yes, my king." She glanced at Lancelot, hesitating before speaking again. "Though in truth I am not entirely guiltless. I- I was not feeling myself, and I ought to have never gone off alone with Sir Lancelot. Please forgive me."

She curtseyed then, hoping her face portrayed her humility.

"Rise, both of you. You are my friends, and I would like to keep our friendship rather than dismiss it with such a small slight, but I must ask: does our agreement stand? Lancelot, you surrendered the right of courtship to me when I beat you in the jousting tournament. Guinevere, I know we did not discuss this with you and perhaps that was unfair, to assume you would submit to our whims. So, I ask both of you now, do you uphold and respect the agreement that was made, or should we seek another arrangement?"

His blue eyes pierced them both, and a shudder went up her spine. The same eyes could be so benevolent, and at times shine with joy that the king did not deign to suppress. And yet, there were times, such as now, when his gaze could pierce armor, and his face was rigid as stone. Arthur deserved his title, the Lionheart of Camelot.

He had asked a question, and he expected an answer. Guinevere looked to Lancelot.

He looked to her, then back up to Arthur. His eyes squinted with a pained expression. "My king, I cannot do as you ask. I do not trust myself."

"Then what is to be done?" The king's voice was quiet, but his entire body was rigid, his neck taut, and his tone carried an edge with it. He wasn't the type to yell in rage, then.

Lancelot swallowed hard. "Send me away," he said at last. "I can take some men and scout the outer border. It will be weeks of riding, and I will have time to clear my mind."

Arthur didn't like it, Guinevere noticed. He had pursed his lips ever so slightly, a furrowed frown showing up in his eyebrows. At last, his face smoothed itself.

“Very well. You leave in two days. Join us for the Beltane feast tomorrow, and you may depart the following morning.”

“No!” Guinevere blurted. Both men stared at her.

“I mean, Your Majesty.” She curtseyed hastily and kept her head bowed. “It is I that should be sent away. I have brought contention to your deep friendship with Sir Lancelot. Tales of the hardships and victories you have seen together are many, and I would not be what comes between you. I will leave the court of Camelot and return home. It is only right.”

“Do not think of it, Lady Guinevere.” The king said, and Guinevere looked up at the definitive tone of authority in his voice. “It is Lancelot who has wronged me, by breaking our agreement. I know your father would rather you were here, at least through the remainder of the festival. Sir Lancelot has offered to do penance, and I will allow it. Please do not think that you are at fault in this.”

She bowed her head again.

The men clasped hands, and Sir Lancelot bowed, first to Arthur, then to Guinevere. “Your leave, Your Majesty, Lady Guinevere.” He retrieved his horse, which stood just outside the clearing. He stood and stared at Guinevere for a long moment before mounting and turning the horse around, heading through the trees back toward Camelot.

Arthur sighed and ran a hand through his long blonde hair. He dismounted then, surprising Guinevere. He walked over to a fallen log, then sat down. He patted the place next to him and Guinevere walked over, accepting his offer of a seat.

He glanced at her sideways. "I sure know how to pick them, don't I?"

"What? Your knights?" Guinevere asked, thinking he spoke of Lancelot.

"No, women," he said absently. Had he forgotten to whom he was speaking? Arthur smiled. "I cannot tell you how many times in the past year a woman I've courted has chosen another man to marry. Can you imagine that? Women run over each other to get to me, and then someone they can truly love comes along and even my title isn't enough to dissuade them.

"I suppose the responsibility is a great one to bear, being a king's wife. I am rarely available, especially now that the Saxons have begun their advance from Wales. War and the responsibilities of the kingdom weigh heavy on a man, heavier because I am alone. A queen would lighten the load somewhat, at least make the affairs of the castle run more smoothly."

Guinevere could read the look on his face, plain as day. She put her hand on his arm.

He looked down at it, but said nothing, and he didn't ask her to move it.

Guinevere looked into her lap at her hands. "It is my father's burden, too. Since my mother died, when I was a little girl, he has had to run a household on his own. He is uncomfortable there. He would rather be at war, at home with a sword in his hand, that one. And in his words, 'There is no woman that would want a hardened old coot like me, 'cept a heathen, and I won't be found married to a heathen. I really think all these years he's been telling me that he loved my mother too much to marry someone else, and yet last year, he met Lady Joan and they announced their engagement at the first of the year."

She grinned at Arthur, then. "So if a fat old warhorse like my father can find someone to be his hearth and home for a second time, I assume you have no reason for such concerns!"

Arthur stared at her a moment, then the laughter burst out of him. He slapped his knees and laughed until he was wiping tears from his eyes.

Guinevere smiled, feeling warm inside, that she could ease his mind so much and give him a moment of mirth. He smiled back at her.

"Guinevere, I have not met a lady like you, and they come in all sizes and types, I tell you. Lady Akelda had a chronic case of hiccups, and no one could get anything serious done. Try sitting through a sermon by Bishop Ernald with little chirpy hiccups echo throughout the church every few words! Our courtship was not long. So many others had flaws, and most of them found flaws in me. No doubt you have noticed a few. I hope they do not deter you from considering me. Your charm, your wit, your willingness to be flawed is what draws me to you. You do not stand for anyone determining who you are. Most women are trained up to be so stiff, to have what makes them human stamped out so thoroughly, so they might fit whatever mold they are married into. But you, you have refused to be stamped out."

"It comes from too much running in the mud as a little girl," Guinevere said, "and too little curtseying and paying attention to lessons. I am a country girl, Your Majesty. Compared to every noblewoman you have no doubt met, my list of flaws is long and blatantly obvious."

She met his gaze with a steady one of her own.

"I meant it as a compliment, Guinevere. You are the most genuine woman I've met."

Pain rushed back into her head, and the voices she had recently heard all shouted together in a great cacophony. She gasped and doubled over, falling arms first onto the grassy floor. Arthur caught her elbow, lowering her more gently.

"Guinevere, are you all right? What is it? What is happening?"

Guinevere gasped for air, shaking her head. Her windpipe constricted, her chest hurt, and her head throbbed. She could not speak, could not move, could not think. It was as if her head was frozen, but heat rushed through her body, and she thought she might vomit.

Arthur whistled, and there was the sound of horse hooves on dirt. His horse came from the edge of the clearing.

Guinevere recognized the white sock-like mark below its right hock.

Arthur gathered her up beneath her arms, draping one over his neck. "Don't worry, Guinevere. I will get help for you. You will be all right." He lifted her legs, then carried her toward the horse.

Her mouth was stuck open and would not respond, her arms and legs would not obey her. Her mind was still filled with that awful chasm of sound, but how could there be sound only she could hear? The glade itself was still and quiet, and Arthur did not react as if he heard anything, so it must be only in her mind.

Grunting with effort, Arthur lifted her up, putting her as gently as he could over the horse's withers and pushing her until her upper body leaned against the back of the horse's neck. He made sure she wouldn't be moving, steadied his horse, then mounted behind her.

Guinevere was only half aware of the ride back to Camelot. He went slowly, clearly afraid to jostle her too much. She caught a brief glimpse of the gentle mare she had been riding following behind, and then the hallucinations began.

Flashes from another life. Faces she both knew and didn't know. Another mother, another father. Women and men, faces distorted by time and the corruption of memory. Guinevere's eyes rolled back in her head and darkness and silence crashed in on her. She heard nothing. She saw nothing. She was nothing.

She woke in a quiet room. There was a fire crackling to her right, far across the room from the sound of it. Something bubbled, like water boiling. She stretched her hearing as much as she could, and thought, perhaps, she could hear someone breathing, but she couldn't be sure. Was it Mary?

She cracked open her eyes. It was dim, only lit by the fire and sunlight streaming through one small window high on the wall above her. The walls were brown, earthy almost, not like the gray of the rest of the castle. She must be below ground, but where?

She turned her head, keeping her arms and body beneath the heavy blanket that was draped comfortably over her. There, sitting on a chair and gazing at her with wide, owl-like spectacled eyes, was the castle physician. What was his name?

Someone, probably Mary, had introduced her to him. He had looked her over briefly when she first got here, examining her head, but Guinevere had insisted she felt fine and refused to go to him for a more thorough visit.

"The patient awakes," the old man mumbled to himself, making a note in a small, thick book at his side. The quill scratched loudly in the silent room. "Can you sit up?"

Guinevere nodded, then brought herself slowly into a sitting position, the blanket sliding down. A cough in the corner made her jump, and when she saw Arthur sitting across the room, she gave a mousy little shriek and brought the blanket back up over her shift. Her face burned.

The physician only nodded. "Reflexes good," he muttered, making another note.

He turned to her. "May I examine you?"

Arthur stood up. "I take my leave now, good physician, and leave her in your capable hands." He bowed slightly, then hastened from the room.

He seemed as flustered as she. She was, in fact, surprised he had waited with her until she woke up. Had it been long? The sun outside could be late morning, or early noon. Had she been out for an entire day?

The physician cleared his throat loudly, and Guinevere almost leapt out of her skin. She would have to work on that. Why was she so skittish, anyway? She lowered the blanket and pushed it off her legs, sitting stiffly on the bed while the physician prodded her face with a quivering, wrinkled finger.

He turned away from her, muttering to himself and licking his lips as he made notes, then thumbed through a yellow-paged book of text on the table beside him. Everything about him made Guinevere nervous. She had never liked physicians or healers of any kind.

The physician had a fire roaring in the grate behind her. It was a wonder he wasn't sweating, with it being nearly midsummer.

"They say you have been experiencing fainting spells, milady?"

Guinevere nodded. Perhaps he could help, after all, and she didn't have to tell him about the voices.

"Have you felt like yourself lately, Guinevere?" A voice from behind made Guinevere jump a second time. She looked around.

Merlin stood in the corner just behind her.

Who else was hiding in this room? Had they brought the entire court to stare at her?

The look in his piercing blue eyes gave her chills, and she shivered, then looked away. He cleared his throat again.

Was he trying to talk with her, or…?

The physician turned around, clearly disgruntled. "Merlin, how am I supposed to deduce anything with you making such a ruckus? If you have a cough, I can prescribe a syrup, but otherwise…"

"I merely wanted to make a deduction of my own, good physician," Merlin said calmly, tucking his arms up inside his sleeves. His face was placid as a pond on a windless day. He hid any disgruntlement rather well, whereas the physician's round face was beginning to redden. "The king has asked us to work together, as you well know. I cannot very well do that if you ignore my attempts."

"Very well," the physician sputtered. "What is it?"

"Have you checked her blood for impurities?"

"I was getting around to it!" The man snapped. "This is what you get for interrupting good, hard work. If you aren't going to suggest anything that is not more than obvious, leave!"

The physician turned back to his table, knocking vials over in his haste to grab something. It was a small lancet. He approached Guinevere with it, and her eyes widened at its gleaming edge.

She swallowed. "What is that for?" she asked.

"Your arm." The physician growled.

Merlin clearly put him in a bad mood. He grabbed her arm and brought the lancet down on it swiftly.

Guinevere bit back a cry of pain, chewing her lip to hold it in as she allowed the physician to squeeze her arm, collecting the bright red blood that flowed from the cut. He filled a long, tubular vial with it, corked it, then swirled it around.

"I will be testing this tonight. I will let you know if I find anything." He spoke rather loudly, and Guinevere assumed he spoke with Merlin.

A chuckle came from the corner as the physician bandaged her arm. "And when you find nothing, Pheras, be sure to let me know. Then I will take over the care of young lady Guinevere."

Chills again. Blast that Merlin. And her headache was back.

Pheras cursed Merlin under his breath as he finished binding Guinevere's arm. He patted her head, as if she were no more than knee-high and less than seven.

"That will be all, milady. I will bring your tonic when it is ready."

"Thank you, Pheras," she stood from the bench, then stopped. "Sir, would you have a remedy for headaches? If it's not much trouble?"

"Headaches, eh?" he said, eyeing her. "You didn't mention those. Do you have them often?"

She nodded. "Every day. They come and go."

"Do they often happen before your... episodes?" Merlin asked from the corner, earning a glare from Pheras.

Both men looked at Guinevere, waiting for her answer.

"Oftentimes they do, but I get them at other times, when I'm being bothered by something or someone," she said, looking pointedly at Merlin.

Pheras slapped a small brown-tinted vial into her hand. "Tincture of lavender; apply to your temples. If it doesn't do the job, come back for another remedy. I have several. Headaches can be caused by any number of things, and it may have nothing to do with your other concern. Is there anything else I ought to know?"

Guinevere hesitated, aware of Merlin's eyes on her from behind, then shook her head. She smiled and thanked Pheras, ignored Merlin, and stepped behind the dressing screen to put on her dress.

The previous day's events weighed heavily on her mind; she wanted more than anything to have someone to talk to. She wondered, then, where Mary could be, and headed towards her rooms to find her.

Guinevere fought a headache all through the festival dinner, then excused herself to her room. Some festival week this was turning out to be. She was going to bed *early*.

Most people would be up far into the night, drinking and joking, and tomorrow night was Beltane Eve. She would rest tonight, and perhaps be able to stay up for more of the festivities. Besides, the king had invited her to dine with him privately, an opportunity she was not about to pass on, especially with what had happened the day before.

Mary helped her unlace the back of her dress, then settled in with her embroidery. She had been assisting with some of the Beltane preparations earlier in the day, which is why she hadn't been at Guinevere's side in the physician's room.

Arthur had insisted on sitting in her place, she said, which made Guinevere's heart glow with warmth. It was incredible how quickly affection could grow for a person in only a few days. Perhaps marriage to Arthur would be all right.

She slid the dress from her shoulders and let it drop to the floor. A quiet thump sounded as the dress fell to the stone. Puzzled, Guinevere reached down and picked it up. She reached into the right side pocket, and pulled out the little brown-tinted bottle. She had forgotten Pheras had given it to her.

"What is that?" Mary asked, looking up from her needlework.

"Lavender tonic, for headaches. I asked Pheras for some."

"Does it work?"

Guinevere turned the smooth bottle over in her fingers, watching the liquid inside move. "I haven't tried it yet." She turned it upright, then popped the cork out. A pleasant, strong, flowery scent wafted into the room. Her headache lessened just by smelling it.

Guinevere put some on her fingers, then rubbed it into her temples. Her entire body released tension, and she sighed.

Mary sniffed the air and sighed as well. "My, that smells nice. Like perfume."

"I have smelled it before," Guinevere said.

Mary gave her a small, sad smile. "Yes, your mother used to wear it. She kept a little bottle of the extract on her table and would wear it daily. I think she used something else in it as well, called it her secret love potion for your father. Perhaps it is good luck to have something like your mother had," Mary added.

Guinevere put the cork back in the bottle. She chewed her lip, thinking of her mother. She had been six when her mother died of a strange sickness that had caused her to waste slowly away. She remembered the smell of lavender in the room as she sat with her father, listening to him read to her mother, his booming voice too loud for the small chamber.

She remembered little else of her mother but a warm smile, the echo of a laugh. The softness of her voice often wandered into Guinevere's mind when she daydreamed, reminding her to be good, to sit up straight, to please her father; telling her she was a good girl, and someday would be a good wife. What would she think of Guinevere now? In the years of her twenties, yet unmarried...

She would be pleased, Guinevere thought, to know she had waited for love. Well, affection at least, and that of a king, no less. She smiled then, thinking of Arthur.

Mary said that most people were compatible, and that it was more likely a marriage would be well if there was strong affection between the two. Too much lust and passion, like in the tales, and it was liable to fall apart when babies came and bodies changed. Just enough love to sweeten life, Mary often said, would be enough for any person.

Guinevere sighed and climbed into bed, pulling the blankets up to her chin.

Mary kept the lamp going, embroidering in the corner, a quiet, constant presence Guinevere had known since she was a young child, even before her mother had died. She hummed a lullaby, one of Guinevere's favorites, and Guinevere drifted into sleep, smelling lavender in her dreams.

CHAPTER EIGHTEEN

Guinevere woke the next morning and lingered in bed far longer than she should have, smiling. She had a lovely warmth inside that seeped into her bones. Arthur had been in her dreams, and they had been so wonderful. It had been the first long, good sleep she'd had in a while. Morgan and the other voices were silent.

Guinevere sat up, stretching, then noticed something on her bedside table. It was a tall, blue bottle with a note tied to the top.

She looked around the room, confused. Mary was nowhere in sight, probably looking after Guinevere's festival clothing, or breakfast.

Had Pheras visited early in the morning? Or perhaps Guinevere just hadn't noticed the bottle last night.

She grasped the glass bottle and took it in her lap, pulling off the note as she did so. The scrawling, spidery handwriting was difficult to read, but she was eventually able to make it out. Especially the signature at the bottom, indicating who the bottle had come from.

Lady Guinevere,

After comparing notes with Pheras, and observing your symptoms for myself, I have concluded that your issue is magically induced. The odd way in which you have conducted yourself, discrepancies in your personality, headaches, and fainting; all should resolve as you take these "pills" I have made for you.

They are mostly herbal, with a strong spell placed on them to counteract your symptoms. Swallowing one per day should eliminate your symptoms, but I warn you, the effect is temporary. I am working on a better solution, but in the meantime, take these and let me know if you run out, or if the headaches or voices should start up again.

Merlin

Guinevere's hands shook as she put the note down. She pulled the large cork out of the bottle and reached inside. Her fingers met a layer of hard little balls.

She took one out and let it roll in the palm of her hand. It was a dark, mottled brown color, bumpy with what looked like tiny slivers of golden wheat and grass. She pressed on it, but it held firm. It looked the same as any herbal remedy might, and smelled no different either.

Had Merlin really placed a spell on it?

She shuddered, dropping the ball back into the jar and shutting the lid tight. Nothing would convince her to take that, not even the promise of clearing her symptoms. She didn't trust the magic. It was clear, after all, that Merlin wasn't overly fond of her. Perhaps he was trying to poison her?

That, of course, was ridiculous. Guinevere scolded herself as she got out of bed, feet padding across the stone floor to a large basin that was steaming with warm water.

"Really, Guinevere, Merlin wouldn't poison you," she said to herself. "No matter how poor a candidate he thinks you are for queen, he respects Arthur's decision. I think. I mean, how would I know? He is a mysterious and powerful sorcerer. Who knows what his motives might be? He seemed sincere enough in the physician's chambers."

She climbed in, exclaiming in pleasure at the warmth of the water on her skin. It was perfect; warm enough to burn, but the burn quickly faded as she acclimated to the temperature of the bath. She luxuriated, putting Merlin and the pills from her mind. The lavender had worked well enough, after all, for her headaches. Perhaps it would take care of the rest of it as well.

Mary had laid out a deep, midnight blue gown with a glittering silver trim on the sleeves and hem, and silver ribbon lacing up the front.

Guinevere, out of her bath and dry, ran her fingers along the soft material. The sleeves were long and flowy, and trailed down toward the floor when she wore it, but didn't quite touch. It was one of her favorites, and the most comfortable. A seamstress had made it specifically for Guinevere, who abhorred the tight, uncomfortable gowns many other women often wore. This one would be perfect for tonight.

She changed into a clean shift, and then Mary helped her into the dress.

Some flat, comfortable shoes, more appropriately like slippers, and a few choice pieces of jewelry. Nothing gaudy or distracting, but delicate and accentuating. She wore her hair down, but asked Alyce to braid it half up to pull it away from her face. A little silver clip clasped in back to hold her hair.

Guinevere waved away the little pot of powdered ochre that Alyce brought, but on second thought, called her back. A gentle brush dusted the pale pink color onto her cheeks, bringing life to them, and distracting from the circles under her eyes.

She rarely indulged in the ridiculous makeups some noblewomen wore, afraid it would make her look like a prostitute, as the bishop in her church back home often expressed, but a little rouge now and then couldn't hurt, just to bring the health back to her cheeks after so much time abed and feeling unwell.

She thanked Alyce, rubbing some lavender at last into her temple. She put the cork in the bottle, pushing hard. The bottle slipped from under her hand on the slick surface of the table, and crashed to the floor, shattering.

"Oh my!" Alyce exclaimed. "What a mess." She grabbed a rag and mopped up the small puddle of spilled tincture. Mary came over to observe, *tsking* softly.

"It is too bad, my dear. Shall I ask Pheras to deliver some more?"

"Yes, please," Guinevere said, looking sadly at the bottle.

What if her headache worsened later on in the evening, and she had nothing for it? She was certain the headaches were a sign of Morgan's presence, and did not think she could hold her at bay. Already she felt restless and agitated. Beltane was not an evening for the faint of heart to be out. She looked around the room. Her eyes fell on the blue bottle, the one Merlin had sent her.

Only as a last resort, she told herself, crossing the room. She pulled off the lid and took one brown orb, small enough it could fit inside a thimble, and tucked it away in one of her pockets. She loved pockets in her dresses. It was silly to her that others went without them. Just because she was noble-born didn't mean she had no use for pockets. They came in quite handy, and all her dresses had at least one small pocket sewn in.

Mary watched her.

Guinevere cleared her throat. “Merlin gave me something to try for the headaches and fainting spells,” she said, trying to keep her voice level, “in case what the physician gave me didn’t work.”

“It isn’t… You know…” Mary trailed off. Magic frightened her more than anything. Her eyes were wide.

“Of course not,” Guinevere replied evenly. The lie flowed smoothly enough from her lips that Mary just nodded, though her lips pursed and her eyes were tight around the corners.

A knock came at the door before Mary could reply. She went to the door and found a young squire outside. He bowed and stepped into the room.

“His Majesty, King Arthur Pendragon, will see you for dinner now, by your leave.”

Guinevere inclined her head. “I am ready now, thank you. Will you be taking me to him?”

The squire nodded. “Yes, milady.” He turned stiffly and walked from the room, stopping just outside the door and waiting. Guinevere exchanged looks with the two other women and smiled.

Mary came and embraced her lightly, not wanting to mess the rouge on her face. “Enjoy yourself tonight, dear Gwen.”

“I will.” Guinevere drew herself away from the old governess. “I won’t do anything you wouldn’t do, Mary,” and then she gave a cheeky grin.

Mary laughed, “You better not do anything of that sort tonight, you hear? There will be plenty of time for that after the wedding.”

Guinevere rolled her eyes. "Good night, Mary."

"Shoo, shoo," Mary said, making sweeping motions with her hands.

Guinevere went out the door, following the squire. They walked in awkward silence. Awkward only because the boy kept glancing back to see whether she was following. He must be a recent addition to the court. Guinevere wondered which nobleman's son he was, but before she could ask, he turned sharply and rapped on a door, nondescript and unguarded.

The door opened; a steward was present. They talked for a moment; the steward regarded Guinevere with a practiced stare, and then he turned to announce her.

"Lady Guinevere."

She swept into a deep curtsey as she entered the room, keeping her head down until Arthur welcomed her. She would be on her best behavior tonight.

"Milady," he said, his voice resonating in the small room. She raised her head and smiled.

"Your Majesty."

"Please, call me Arthur," he said, surprising her by standing and crossing the floor to her. He took her hand in his and bent to kiss it. His blue eyes were bright, and they gazed at her without reservation. They liked what they saw, too. "You are lovely tonight, Guinevere."

"Thank you," she replied, blushing under her rouge.

A small touch of makeup worked like magic, more for her confidence then for her features, but both were benefitted.

Arthur led her to her chair and waited for her to sit before sitting himself. He motioned, and a small stream of servants brought plates to the table, already loaded with food.

The steward poured the wine, a deep purple color. Then, quickly as they had come, the servants all left the room, door closing behind them. They were alone.

"Thank you for dining with me, Guinevere. I am glad for the opportunity to get to know you better."

"And I, you," she said. Her head felt suddenly tight, like it was being squeezed in a vice. Perhaps she was just hungry, but she had to wait for the king to take the first bite.

Arthur looked at the spread of food on his plate. "This looks incredible." He smiled at her, then picked up his fork. He gestured to her. "When you dine with me, Lady Guinevere, there is no need to wait."

She picked up her fork, twirling it in her fingers. "Thank you," she said, then she scooped some of the tender meat onto it.

Arthur did the same, and they watched each other as they both brought the first bite to their lips. The meat melted on her tongue.

Arthur smiled at her, mouth full, and looked so ridiculous that Guinevere snorted. He laughed, and then she did too.

Guinevere caught her breath. "I apologize."

"For being mortal? Don't. It's charming," Arthur said, taking a drink from his goblet.

"This is lovely," Guinevere said, fingering her cup. It was smaller than Arthur's, better fit for her hand. She picked it up. "I haven't had wine very often. I haven't preferred the taste."

"This is the best, but I will not be offended if you don't like it," Arthur said, resting his chin on clasped hands.

He watched her as she took a sip. The chilled liquid slipped over her tongue, sweet, but not too sweet, the flavor of the grapes coming to the forefront. The coldness of the drink surprised her, and she looked wide-eyed at Arthur.

"It's cold!"

"Yes. Makes it better, doesn't it?"

She nodded, then took another sip. "How is it done?"

"Ice, brought from areas still cold. Damned difficult to ship, ice. It melts in any heat, and only half of the shipment makes it, if we're fortunate." He stopped and looked at her, as if remembering whom he was speaking with. "I apologize, milady, for my tongue. It must have forgotten I was speaking with a beautiful lady, rather than the local merchants."

Guinevere smiled. "It is all well, Arthur. I would prefer that you be authentic than feign too much politeness. As you said, being mortal is charming."

The pain in her head was getting stronger, and a familiar pressure was building. Something stirred, like someone stretching after a long sleep. Morgan. She took another bite of meat, heart beginning to race. What could she do? It was happening again. She drank some more wine.

Do not think you have beaten me because I have remained silent. I am biding my time, and my strength is growing. I must protect you from yourself.

Guinevere almost choked on her wine, Morgan's voice so loud in her mind she glanced around the room. No one was there, of course, excepting her and Arthur. She blotted her mouth with a napkin.

Arthur smiled at her, fork in hand, chewing his food.

A knock at the door. Guinevere sighed with relief, which she disguised by coughing.

“Enter,” Arthur said. A page walked in, and Arthur sighed.

“Excuse me,” he said to Guinevere, then turned to the page.

Her hand went to her pocket, feeling the hard lump there. She slipped her fingers in and drew it out, then, without thinking, put it directly into her mouth. Immediately, she spit it back out into her hand. It was bitterer than dandelion leaves. She gagged, then reached for the goblet of wine at the head of her plate. She took an un-ladylike swig, then gulped the rest down. It hadn’t been very full.

Arthur turned back to her. Hastily, Guinevere dropped her hand below the level of the table, stomach churning. He only smiled, however, then turned back to the page, saying something about hiding the cider from a certain nobleman, and making sure Lancelot had the knights keeping some sobriety, so they could maintain the order. Guinevere considered the pill again.

Would it truly be worthwhile to put the heathenish sorcery into her body, to keep Morgan and the voices at bay? In response, Morgan’s presence pressed on her mind, making Guinevere’s vision swim. She gripped the table, trying to force her eyes to focus. For a terrifying moment, Morgan almost took control, and Guinevere flailed in her mind, grasping the shred of strength she had left and moving her hand to pop the medicine back into her mouth.

She swallowed hard, grimacing at the strong flavor, then a shiver shook her entire body. A strange sensation spread through her stomach, moving through her body until her fingers tingled. Her head buzzed. It wasn’t a pleasant sensation, and she felt as if she were going to be sick. She put her hands on her stomach and over her mouth, ready to throw up.

"Guinevere, are you all right?" Arthur asked with concern. The page was walking away with purpose, leaving them alone once more. She tried to smile.

"I am well enough. The food is settling, is all."

"Shall we take some air?"

Her stomach rolled. She put a hand before her mouth and shook her head. "No, I only need a moment, thank you."

Her mind cleared, and her stomach stopped rolling. She waited a moment, listening for any sign of Morgan's influence. Nothing. She smiled at Arthur. "There, all better." She went to sip more wine and was surprised to find it empty.

Arthur seemed agitated. Guinevere noticed his lips moving, as if he muttered something under his breath. Then, suddenly, he stood and came around the table, kneeling before her. Guinevere stared at him.

"Arthur?" she asked. Her head felt so light, so free, as if it might float away. Had she had that much wine?

"I admit I asked you here privately for a rather selfish purpose, Guinevere." He took a deep breath, then rushed on before she could reply. "I know it is too soon. I know we have not had much time to get to know one another. Yet I have seen enough of you to know that we would be good for each other; that you would be good for my kingdom."

"But..." she swallowed hard. "But what of my... malady?"

"Pheras and Merlin will sort it out, I am certain. Please, Guinevere." He took her hand between his.

The warmth of his touch traveled through her and blossomed in her chest. Her breath came more quickly. Was it the effect of the medicine? She could not tell. She hadn't felt so alive in all her life. Her mind was clear, her body felt so strong. She stared at their hands for a long moment before looking into Arthur's face, so open and sincere, blue eyes soft, kind, and eager. His gaze took her breath away.

"Is it fair to ask you to marry me, Guinevere? Marry me, before Lancelot returns from scouting and you change your mind? Marry me, so that I might have someone at my side through all that happens next?"

Guinevere forced herself to stop biting her bottom lip. She looked into Arthur's eyes, and her gaze wandered down his body to their clasped hands again. She glanced back up. Her heart was still pounding, perhaps from the medicine, perhaps not. What should she say? Could she be happy with him? She tried to ignore the deepest parts of herself, the dark and afraid parts. Beyond that, there was a spark. A spark of hope.

She took a deep, shuddering breath. "Yes," she said. Arthur whooped and stood up, pulling her with him. He brought her tight to him, crushing her with his embrace. He lifted her into the air and spun her around, and when he set her down his blue eyes sparkled with joy.

She was to marry Arthur, the King of Camelot.

She was to be queen.

They stared at one another.

Outside the drums of Beltane were beating to the rhythm of the earth, and blood coursed through Guinevere's veins. She let Arthur pull her near and press his lips against hers, and the drums grew louder until they consumed her. She could feel everything, his hands through her dress, feeling so hot they almost burned where he held them on her back. His chest against her chest, his...

She pulled away, her face reddening. Arthur was breathless, and there was a wild edge to his gaze. Guinevere chewed on her lip and looked down, trying to hide her blush while Arthur coughed and straightened his trousers. It was certainly a good thing they were indoors. It muffled the sound of drums outside, the castle walls interrupting the spell of Beltane.

Without that, they very well might have... well, it was said that passion burned brightest on the night of the Beltane fires. Now she knew why Mary had kept her under the strictest supervision on Beltanes past.

"It is getting late," Arthur noted.

She nodded, and proffered her arm. Arthur placed it on top of his own, and Guinevere's skin leapt to life, warmth spreading again through her body. She expected it, however, and didn't let it consume her this time.

"Would you please escort me back to my chambers?" she asked.

Arthur glanced at her, a smile growing at the corner of his mouth, that wild look back, gleaming his eyes. Guinevere's body responded with a rush of warmth and a swelling feeling in certain... areas.

It was a good thing her room was further into the castle. The drums became quieter as they walked, and with it, her blood slowed, returning to normal. Her heart no longer beat too fast, her breathing calmed, and only a pleasant warmth remained.

The effects of the pill had leveled out too, the buzzing in her mind was gone, and only quiet clarity remained. She felt a rush of gratitude for Merlin, something she had never expected to feel. She would have to thank him, next time they met. They rounded a corner, entering the hall her chamber was within, and ran straight into the sorcerer's chest.

Beltane fire, he was *tall*. He loomed over them, almost taller than usual. There was a thunderous look in his eyes. At the edge of her gaze, which was mostly focused on Merlin, Guinevere could see Arthur visibly swallow.

Merlin looked from one to the other. His eyes stopped on Guinevere, and the piercing gaze went right through her, reading everything off the surface of her soul.

"I am sorry to disturb you, Your Majesty, milady. I intended to inquire with Guinevere before she turned in, to be sure she had received my message and the bottle with it."

Guinevere licked her lips, trying to moisten them. "I-I did."

"And did you take what was prescribed?"

"Y-Yes." Fie upon that Merlin. She couldn't stop shaking.

Merlin turned his attention to the king, who had recovered from his earlier intimidation. The lion look was back in his eyes, a fierce glare that challenged anyone in his path to battle, likely to the death.

No sword was drawn, but it was clear that he meant to stand up to anything Merlin might have to say. It was like watching two birds of prey fight over a scrap of meat, though nothing was exchanged but a gaze. Guinevere looked between the two men, watching for any change in either visage.

At last, Merlin's shoulders relaxed, and his terrible appearance diminished somewhat. The hall brightened, and Guinevere's chest expanded more readily with her breath, not even realizing she had been having any difficulty breathing.

"It is done, then?" Merlin asked. Guinevere did not know what he meant.

Arthur nodded curtly, the lion glare still lingering in his eyes.

"And you are certain?"

"Yes," he said, his voice strong and sure.

Merlin's face softened further, and for a moment Guinevere thought she glimpsed his true face, more ancient and wizened than any she had seen, a thousand lines intersecting and branching off, defining each portion of his face as the trunk of an ancient tree. He seemed so fatigued, and his expression so defeated, she almost reached out to him, as if to comfort him. It was gone in a moment, and then there was an ambiguous twinkle in his blue eyes, and something like a smile creased the wrinkles on his face.

"Then I congratulate you, Your Majesty, milady." He bowed, slightly, to them both, then moved down the corridor past them so gracefully, Guinevere thought he floated.

She was still trembling. Arthur rubbed her arm. "He is not as frightening as people think. An old dog with a loud bark, but no teeth left to bite."

"I think you underestimate him," she replied, turning her head in time to see the sorcerer disappear around the corner behind them.

Arthur laughed. "I have known him my entire life, Guinevere. We are old friends. He only wishes well for me."

But what of me? Guinevere thought, following Arthur as he crossed the hall to her door. *He does not wish me so well, I think.* But he hadn't tried to poison her with his magic, herbal pills. In that, at least, he was sincere. Perhaps he had assumed their relationship had an inevitable end, and was doing what he could to make it better so he had less to be concerned about.

Arthur turned to her and kissed her chastely on her forehead at first, and then tilted her face up to meet his. It was a long, warm kiss that left Guinevere tingling all over as she entered her rooms. Mary looked up from her sewing, then set it aside as Guinevere closed the door.

"So, how long does the seamstress have to make your dress?" Mary asked.

Guinevere grinned, her heart swelling until it ached inside of her. She ran to Mary and hugged her, feeling as if she were about to burst, and then sat beside Mary on her bed, where the two women sat and talked until the lantern flickered out, and the drums outside were a pale echo in the night.

CHAPTER NINETEEN

There she weaves by night and day
A magic web with colours gay.
She has heard a whisper say,
A curse is on her, if she stay
Her weaving, either night or day
To look down to Camelot.
She knows not what the 'curse' may be,
And so she weaveth steadily,
And little other care hath she,
The Lady of Shalott.

Elaina's blood pulsed with the drums of Beltane. The loom had kept her weaving since earlier in the afternoon, and as soon as the sun set the drums began to beat the rhythm of the earth, of life, of the Goddess.

Elaina didn't know much about the Goddess. She knew that many of the people, especially common folk, believed in a wise woman with power like God, possibly greater than God, who blessed her chosen daughters with wisdom and magic to do her bidding on the earth. Her ways were the ways of herb and blood and element, and Beltane was a celebration to the fertility of the earth, the meeting of the Goddess and her escort, the great Stag.

Tiny bumps formed up along Elaina's arms at the faint whoops and hollers, the chanting and drumming that went on in the darkness outside her tower. Her fingers caressed the smooth wood of the shuttle. She hadn't been able to light her candle yet, so she wove in semi-dark, moonlit shadows confusing her eyes until they adjusted. Then her hands moved easily, sending the shuttle through the threads of the loom.

She hated Beltane. Most people thought of it as a time of festival, of rejoicing, but it had frightened Elaina as a child; sent to bed before dark, after the winding of the ribbon pole and the delightful desserts she had been allowed to indulge in. Trying to fall asleep though it was still light out, staying awake long after dark had fallen, she would slip from her bed and steal to the window and look out and watch the tiny flickering orange dots that marked the bonfires common folk had lit. The drums sang in her blood then, too, as if they were made with strange magic that called to the blood of every individual.

When she grew older, the adults whispered of the things that happened on Beltane Eve, the unholy dancing and coupling of those married and unmarried. The drums didn't care about a triviality like marriage, and neither did the Goddess. She would do whatever it took to accomplish her purposes, and she wielded men and women alike as pawns in her game.

Elaina had been protected from the mischief and evils of Beltane, always escorted, always sent to bed early. Morgan was exempt for some reason, and she would return in the wee hours of the morning, crawling into bed with Elaina and whispering stories that made Elaina's eyes grow wide. Tales of naked men and women leaping about together around the flames that grew ever higher, until the climax of Beltane was reached and in the frenzy and lust of the moment, couples bedded down together where they were, in front of everyone.

Elaina half-suspected Morgan had made most of it up, but had no proof, only what she had heard. No one was without a partner on the eve of Beltane, and marriages and babes abounded in the months following.

And then that fateful Beltane arrived, when Elaina had gone with Mordred to the hills and lain with him, the bright summer sun witnessing their union. Then she had lost him, in the rain and the darkness, and there was no knowing where he had gone or what had happened to prevent him from finding her.

Reliving that terror, that confusion and loss, every Beltane since... It was torture. A reminder that she was stuck here, while the world continued to spin outside. Love, marriage, babies. None of it would come for her, not again.

That made her thoughts turn to Sir Gereck, and her thoughts caught fire as she wondered where he might be tonight. Blood rushed inside of her. The drums sounded louder. Where would he be? Did she have to wonder? Where would any knight be? Drunk, probably, in the arms of a beautiful woman. Knights had a code of chivalry, but in the end, they were men.

Unless he had feelings for her, as their last encounter indicated, but she couldn't be sure they were strong enough to keep him inside on Beltane night, when the maidens and drink were plenty and the bishops turned a blind eye. They still let the people have their barbaric celebrations, so long as they paid penance for the sins committed.

Elaina sighed. It wouldn't do to think of that now, but the thoughts burned within her like a brand, and she could not be rid of them. The dancing of her blood in her veins couldn't be helped either. It kept her on edge, a rhythm pulsing through her, a drawn-out longing for something she could not have. She closed her eyes in the dark. Beltane was torture for a prisoner.

A knock at her door startled her into jumping. She glanced over to see light seeping through the crack under the door. The latch was fiddled with, and then the door swung open. The old woman, Niviane, entered, holding a lantern and a basket. She set the basket on the table by Elaina's bed, then turned to go. She stopped in the doorway and turned her face back, gazing at Guinevere with those ancient eyes glittering in the lantern light.

"Beltane calls many hearts tonight. Yours more than most, I think." The old woman looked toward the window, where Elaina could not.

Elaina swallowed.

From her robes, the woman drew out a bottle. It had a long, graceful neck and a cork in the top. Elaina's mouth dried up. She had seen bottles like that, long ago, in her father's cellar.

Wine. Or cider, possibly.

"I have a gift for you, young lass." Never mind that, enchantment aside, Elaina was old enough to be a crone herself.

The old woman set the bottle on the table, next to the basket of food. "A medicine, of sorts. It will muffle the call of the drums, and you might get some sleep tonight."

Elaina's managed to choke out a hoarse "thank you", before Niviane closed the door firmly behind her. The loom released Elaina.

She rushed to the table and lit her candle, and then rummaged inside the basket for some cheese. There was a hunk of salted meat as well, and several pieces of fresh fruit, resting beside a large, lovely loaf of bread. A feast for Beltane. She set it out for herself, then eyed the bottle of wine. Its glass surface glistened at her.

She had no goblet, and so it was, after she pried the cork from the top, she tipped the entire bottle up to take a drink. It was barely cool, having been out of whatever cellar it had come from for too long. She took another swallow. It was sweet, almost sickly sweet, but had a slight fizz to it that tingled on her tongue. She dug into the food as well, but after only a few bites, even the once-flavorful meat tasted like wood in her mouth. She turned away from it, looking toward the loom. She raised the bottle to her mouth.

The drums still beat through her blood, calling her. She could not answer the call, and there was no one here who could fulfill it for her. She fingered the slender bottleneck in her hand. Normally, she would not condone drinking. She, herself, had never been as filled with spirits as she was now. She had always wondered what it would feel like.

A light buzz had begun to fill her head. In the darkness, she felt as if her head was floating away from her body. Her thoughts grew fuzzy around the edges, and, just as Niviane had said, the incessant beating of drums faded. A gift, indeed. She would drink away the drums, and find herself in the morning.

She raised the bottle again, and drank until her head flew into the sky and she could see the stars, she was the stars, and far below the world turned without her, dizzy in the dance of Beltane.

She gently touched the rope. Below her, someone waited. He called to her. Elaina looked back into the room. The rope was tied to something. The man called again, asking her to come down, to be with him.

She would. She would leave this place and go with him. She threw her leg out over the windowsill and gripped the rope tightly. Elation and excitement gripped her as she slid her other leg from the room, her weight held only on the rope. She had done it. She was free. Soon she would reach the bottom. She would feel everything, see everything...

A chirrup woke Elaina from her daydream.

The blue bird had come back, no doubt flying in her window to get out of the rain. Brennus landed on top of the loom, shaking its wet feathers and flicking droplets of water into the air. Elaina laughed as they scattered across her face, and was surprised that the bird didn't startle.

"You're back," she said, continuing to move the shuttle through the threads, pressing them tight with her foot on the tread. She eyed the little blue-feathered creature, who was busy preening. "I don't suppose you're going to speak with me again? Did I imagine it last time you visited?"

Nothing. Brennus looked up at her, chirped, and flew over to the top of her dressing screen.

"Well, now I know I'm just mad in the head, and desperate for someone to talk with, since Sir Gereck is content to stay away for weeks at a time. Much has happened since I saw you last, my little friend. Did you know that it's been at least two weeks since I saw him last? Perhaps I frightened him with my note."

Brennus chirped again, continuing with a thread of cheerful notes that ended with an inquisitive sound.

Elaina laughed. "You sound as if you're asking a question. Who is Sir Gereck? If I was dreaming, a suitor. Since I'm trapped here with little prospect for release, much less marriage, he's an interested party in my freedom. Though I fear he's wasting his time."

More chirrups, and a whistle this time.

"Isn't he, though? I mean, look around. How am I to escape when I can't even glance out the window?"

The bird flew over her head again. From the sound of it, the bird had landed on the window behind her. It chirped insistently.

"I can't believe you're asking me to look over there. That would be too much to imagine, even for my deranged mind. I already told you, I can't. See?" She moved her head, deliberately, as if to glance out the window. A muscle spasmed painfully in her neck, immediately freezing her head in place.

Elaina cried out in pain, rubbing the sore spot. She slowly turned her head back to the loom, her neck relaxing as she did. "Satisfied?"

A chirp was her reply.

"I don't believe this," she muttered. "A bird. I am letting myself believe a bird is talking to me."

The flapping of wings filled the room as the bird soared around, exploring every nook and cranny. Its beak rang against her chamber pot and bedpost, it ripped a corner from the remaining piece of parchment she had. Elaina tried to ignore it. She was done pretending today, but when she looked up and saw it picking at the sleeve of her dress, which she had thrown over the dressing screen the night before, she lost it.

"Get out, would you? Shoo!" She couldn't stand or wave her arms, the loom held her bound too tightly. She whistled sharply and the bird looked up. "That's one of my only dresses, you little vermin. It doesn't need your holes in it. Go build your nest somewhere else."

The bird cocked its head, then flew towards the mirror. Elaina followed it, glaring now, and watched as it tried to land on the mirror. As soon as its feet touched the carved wooden frame, the bird shrieked and flew off. Elaina frowned. The bird flapped around the room, then came at the mirror again, but it veered upward before it reached the surface, screeching.

"What's gotten into you, you crazy fowl?"

To her surprise, the bird came and landed on her shoulder. It was trembling. She pushed the shuttle through the threads with one hand, and with the other, reached up to stroke its delicate head. The bird's head turned to the mirror, and it appeared to be watching the images that moved there.

Elaina watched with it, getting increasingly confused. The scene in the mirror was a busy corridor within Camelot's outer wall. Nothing of interest, certainly nothing out of the ordinary, and if that bird thought to convince her to look for Arthur again, well, she wouldn't. She had already decided she wouldn't, not ever again. If she saw her son again, if he lived, it would be when she finally left this tower.

If she ever left this tower.

The blue bird chirped incessantly.

"You're mad," Elaina muttered, shaking her head and focusing back on the tapestry.

I am not mad.

She looked at the bird. It chirped, then flew back to the mirror, flew around it once, then landed on the bed behind her.

"What did you say?" Elaina said, wishing she could turn around. The rustling of wings told her the bird was flying again. It landed on her dressing screen in a flash of blue.

You birthed a king. That voice... Could it truly be Brennus, *her* Brennus?

"Who is there?"

No answer, but the bird preened. Was it a sign? Or was he simply a bird, and Elaina herself was going mad?

"Are you a spirit?" Elaina asked, suddenly afraid. The room became darker, though the sun had yet to go down.

No. *I am a man.*

"Then you have magic. Are you invisible?"

Do not fear, Elaina. I have not come to harm you. Bird or not, the voice was real enough.

"What do you want of me?"

Nothing more, and nothing less, than for you to choose hope.

Elaina scoffed. Her hands moved automatically with the shuttle, and her feet moved the treadle. "Hope was lost to me long ago. You should have come sooner, if hope was what you wanted. I had enough of it when I first came here. What good did it do me?"

More than you know. Every thought you have influences the world around you. You have the power to obtain everything you desire, but in your ignorance and despair, you push it away.

"I have tried everything. If thoughts were enough to free me, it would have happened long ago."

They brought him to you.

"Gereck?"

The voice was silent. "That was an accident. He never meant to come here, and he certainly didn't know about me when he did."

There are no accidents.

"Did I bring you here with my thoughts too?" The loom suddenly released her. Elaina sighed, set down the shuttle, and stretched out her back.

In a way, yes.

"Then are you here to free me?"

Your freedom will not come from outside.

Elaina threw her hands into the air in frustration. "What good are you, then?"

To gain power one must exercise it.

Elaina was silent. She stood from the loom bench and wandered through the room, arms crossed over her chest. What more could she say to this cryptic being who chose to torment her with thoughts of freedom? What right did he have to put it in her grasp, only to refuse her any help?

You are angry.

"Well noticed," Elaina said, the anger putting a razor edge on her voice. "Can you read minds, too?"

It would be a considerable waste of energy to do so, when the stiffness of your body and set of your jaw tell me all I need to know.

"You have the advantage, as you can see my body."

And you have seen mine.

"Are you the bird, then? The one I call Brennus?" she waited, but no confirmation came. "Do you have a human form?"

Would you look on me if I showed myself? Would you risk the wrath of the curse for a stranger?

"It's not a choice. The curse prevents me from looking."

Does it prevent joy and creation as well?

"What does that have to do with anything?" Elaina asked. A breeze from the window moved across her skin. It was chilly still, even after winter had thawed. She shivered and rubbed at the goosebumps on her arms.

It has a little to do with everything, and something to do with nothing, the voice said.

"That's helpful," Elaina muttered. Her shawl was on her bed. She walked over and picked it up, wrapping it around her shoulders. She walked towards Brennus on her dressing screen, but the bird took off and flew over her head, toward the window behind her. The tower fell silent. The bird had gone.

But had the voice?

"Would you tell me something about yourself?"

I am older than you think and have more influence than you can know.

"Something more helpful, maybe? Where do you live? What do you do?"

I live in the city of Camelot, mostly, but sometimes I don't. As you might guess, my magic is my trade, although I am often more use as a counselor than a wizard.

"A counselor to whom?"

The king.

It surprised her, but only slightly. Gereck had mentioned the king kept a sorcerer as his council.

"Who told you about me? Was it Gereck? Have you come to free me?"

I know many things, Elaina. I have watched you for a long time. I did not need anyone to tell me about you. And I cannot free you. Your freedom, as I said, will not come from outside. It will come from inside.

Elaina said nothing. A cool breeze blew past her face, bringing with it the scent of water and green plants. Summer was here. Her favorite time of year, once upon a time. She closed her eyes, then thought of another question, one perhaps the sorcerer could answer.

"If you are a sorcerer, which you must be, for you have magic enough to change shapes and come here to speak with me, then perhaps you have power to see the future?" No response. "Please tell me... will I ever leave here?"

She waited a long time, listening to the silence that hung in the air, hearing the faint sound of birds outside, but an answer didn't come. Perhaps the sorcerer, whoever he was, had truly gone, now.

I can give you one answer. Look in the mirror. Ask what you desire to see. You will be able to see what is real to you, what is in your heart.

"What does that mean?" she cried. Silence again. She waited longer this time. "Brennus?" Nothing. "Sorcerer, are you here?" A bird chirped outside. Not a blue jay.

She rubbed her eyes and sighed. Her head felt heavy with the weight of what she had been told. None of it was helpful; she was still stuck. Elaina turned toward the center of the room and walked to the mirror. A crowd of people pressed forward through the streets of Camelot, cheering in the scene it showed. Ribbons fell around them. A festival or a wedding, perhaps? Elaina straightened her back, not even realizing she had been slumping.

You birthed a king, the sorcerer had said. What had he meant by that?

She looked into the mirror. *You will be able to see what is real to you, what is in your heart.* She closed her eyes and pictured the first time she had seen her baby, Arthur. Time slowed. She opened her eyes.

A man with a gleaming golden crown on his head rode a horse through a throng of people. A red cape trailed down his back and across the rump of the white horse he rode. For a moment, the watery shadows of the mirror cleared and she could see his smile, a smile that lit up his entire face, brightening his eyes as he waved to people that clearly adored him. *King Arthur. Gereck told me the king's name was Arthur.*

Elaina stretched out her hand and touched the surface of the mirror, half-expecting her hand to go through its glassy surface. Instead, the image vanished, and the mirror went dark.

She collapsed to her knees, trembling. Had she seen him? Had she really seen him? He had been young still, too young to be her son, she thought. Or perhaps she hadn't been in the tower so long as she supposed. Her heart lifted, free of some of the weight she had been holding onto. She had seen her son. He was alive.

And he was king.

King of Camelot.

CHAPTER TWENTY

Guinevere set down the brush and stroked her long, dark hair, feeling its softness. It was smooth and silky, just dried from her bath. The oils the maid had added wafted to her nose, their gentle scent relaxing her.

Today she was getting married.

Only a fortnight since Arthur had requested her hand. Her own father had barely made it that morning from Carmelhide. They had both wanted it to be soon; no drawn out engagements for them, despite what propriety dictated.

Mary's figure came into the mirror, her face starting to show graceful lines of age. Her brown hair was graying at the roots, but her eyes were the same ones Guinevere had looked into her entire life.

"How are you, my dear?" Mary asked, picking up the brush and pulling it through her hair.

Guinevere closed her eyes, enjoying the feel of the brush spines on her head. It had always comforted her. Today, it barely relaxed the surface of her anxiety, but the odd clarity brought on by Merlin's pills was with her as well, and she was certain she would not lose control. She hadn't had a headache, had a fainting spell, or heard Morgan's voice since taking that first pill.

"Guinevere?" Mary asked again.

"Is this how it is for everyone, Mary? Getting married to a perfect stranger, hoping that felicity will come? Does everyone do it this way?"

"Not everyone," Mary said softly. "Some have love first, but they often lose it and end in misery. I have no personal experience, but those I've seen start out strangers in marriage grow to love more deeply than any soul mate." Her strong, warm hands rubbed Guinevere's shoulders through the silken material of her dress.

Guinevere smiled and took Mary's hand, bringing it to her lips. "I guess I just had a different expectation. I didn't expect it to happen so fast. And I didn't expect to be so afraid."

"You don't have to do this. We can stop it, if you want," Mary said. Guinevere stared up at her, half of her heart wanting to... She shook her head and swallowed the lump in her throat.

"No, Mary. I'm ready."

They shared a long silence, holding one another. Guinevere was afraid to let go. Mary sensed her reluctance, and the older woman sighed, straightening and stroking Guinevere's hair.

"I must leave after the wedding, Guinevere, and return to Carmelhide."

Guinevere pulled away. "What?"

"I wasn't meant to stay with you forever, Guinevere. Your father's new wife needs someone to help her manage the household, especially the servants. I am returning to my old job, making sure everyone else is doing theirs." She placed her hand on Guinevere's cheek, her soft brown eyes filling with tears, but there was a smile on her face. "You are a grown woman now, no longer in need of a governess. I am confident Alyce will serve you well."

"I mourn your leaving not only for my sake. Who is going to take care of my babies?"

Two tears fell, one after the other, from Mary's eyes.

"I will come visit them, if I'm able to get away. Write to me, my darling Gwen?"

Guinevere cupped Mary's hand in her own and turned, kissing it softly. "I will." Guinevere watched her beloved governess leave.

"I have the flowers, milady."

Guinevere turned her head and smiled at Alyce, who curtseyed, a basket filled with tiny white flowers in her arms. Their fragrance filled the air. Orange blossoms were a rare and expensive flower, but for the queen-to-be, no expense was being spared. She had never seen the small white flowers before. She reached into the basket and pulled out one, admiring its five straight petals, velvet to her touch. They smelled heavenly.

"Thank you, Alyce. I am ready."

The maid placed the basket on the table and took Guinevere's hair in her hands, braiding it half back, and securing it with a golden ribbon. Then she weaved the flowers, making a wreath of them to circle around the crown of Guinevere's head.

The flower stems tickled Guinevere's scalp as the crown took shape. She stared at her image in the mirror. Her face was sallow, her eyes sunken in from lack of sleep. Did no one else see it?

The maid continued plaiting the flowers in her hair, eyes focused on her work. Sudden irritation flooded Guinevere's being. Really, they were irritating. If she had her way she wouldn't have the silly little things at all.

Just the crown, a glorious symbol of her victory over a poverty-ridden life. Now, about to marry the king, she would finally be in a position where she could make a difference.

She shook her head, wondering where those thoughts had come from. Poverty-ridden life? That wasn't her. She had lived in relative finery since birth. The maid asked her to stop moving her head and she complied, but the irritation grew. Her hands shook. When was the last time she had taken one of Merlin's pills?

"Alyce, get me that bottle." She pointed at the bottle just out of her reach.

"In a moment, if you will, milady."

"Now, Alyce."

"I must pin this exactly right. It will only take..."

"Get me the bottle, Alyce!" Guinevere said, voice rising hysterically.

She was fighting the tide of Morgan's rage, head aching, breath heaving. She closed her eyes, pressing her fingers against her temples, straining to hold on to herself... The bottle slid into view, and Alyce screwed the top off.

Guinevere grabbed the bottle and dumped it too hastily, hands shaking, causing the little round balls to spill over her hand and onto the floor. She ignored Alyce's exclamation and shoved one into her mouth, forcing it past the violent gag that her body made at the extremely bitter taste.

She shoved her chair back and ran across the room, passing Alyce on the floor gathering the pills, and gulped the tea that she had rejected earlier. It was cold, but the cool peppermint flavor washed away every trace of the bitter herbs in her mouth. She waited. One moment.

Two moments. Her heart calmed. Her breathing slowed. The headache faded, and so did any trace of Morgan's influence.

Guinevere turned. "Oh, Alyce, I am sorry for the mess!"

"It is all right, milady. I will straighten it out. Shall I throw these out, or…?"

"No!" Guinevere shouted. She lowered her voice. "No. Please, return them to the bottle. I would not want to waste them."

The maid nodded, and went back to picking them up and putting them into the bottle.

Making sure the young woman wasn't looking, Guinevere knelt and picked up one of the pills, quickly slipping it into the tiny pocket hidden in one side of her wedding dress. Handy, that. Having it made her feel safer. Nothing would happen at the wedding. Nothing on her end, anyway. Merlin's pills would make certain of that.

Alyce finished cleaning up and carefully placed the jar, cork replaced, on the table with the mirror. She picked up a pin and asked Guinevere to bend down, then secured one final strand of hair and stepped back.

Guinevere stared into the mirror. The dark-haired beauty before her seemed a stranger. Perhaps that Niviane was right about something; she wasn't the same person she had once been. She shook her head then, and fingered the pill in her pocket. No, that wouldn't be her any longer.

She faced the door, hands sweaty and gripping her dress. The trail was longer than she was tall, and she couldn't possibly gather it all up to walk properly. She was sure to trip.

"You are beautiful, Lady Guinevere," Alyce said.

"I am sweating like a pig," Guinevere replied, fanning herself.

"No one can tell," the maid said reassuringly. She gave Guinevere one last look over, staring for an extra-long moment at her hair, as if looking for any parts that had come loose. She gave a small nod of appreciation and smiled warmly at Guinevere, then curtseyed. "They are waiting for you, milady."

Guinevere breathed again, trying to expand her ribcage past the tight confines of the dress, to no avail. She nodded at Alyce.

"I am ready."

They moved through the castle silently. It was odd; even the servants and guards were missing in this part of the castle. They were all at the wedding, or helping prepare the feast. Guinevere couldn't think; she focused on breathing in the constricting dress. In, out. In, out.

The two women stopped before the ornate wooden doors leading to the throne room where the ceremony would take place. Knights on either side reached out to open them. Nerves crept up inside of Guinevere, despite the warm magic tingling from Merlin's pill. She stopped biting her lip and straightened up.

Alyce handed her a bouquet of gorgeous flowers. Guinevere's heart swelled at the sight.

What had gotten into her? She could do this! She would be fine. Arthur was a good man, good as any and better than most. She would be happy with him, happy until the end of her days.

Guinevere reached her hand out to Alyce, gripping the other woman's arm tightly and taking a deep, calming breath. The maid opened the door to the throne room, and everyone inside turned to gaze on the king's beautiful bride. Her. They waited and watched, expecting her to come down the aisle, to meet the king and the bishop where they stood on the dais.

Except she couldn't move her feet.

Alyce slipped inside the door and joined the servants at the back of the room, leaving Guinevere standing alone in the doorway. She kept smiling. Her hands slick with sweat, her heart pounding. She put her hand in the pocket of her dress and felt for the bumpy surface of the little magic pill that would take it away.

And then she saw Arthur. Really saw him. He gazed at her as if nothing and no one else existed in the whole world, and gazing back, Guinevere slipped into the endless sea of his bright blue eyes. Her foot slid forward on the velvet carpet. Music came from somewhere to her right. There were other people in the room, important people, her father and Lady Joan among them, but she didn't see them. Time stood still. She moved through the crowd, gliding, and felt as if she was in a dream.

She reached the front of the room in moments and time renewed its pace, and she was smiling at Arthur as Bishop Ernald tied their hands together with a silk ribbon, binding them together in holy matrimony.

Arthur leaned in to kiss her, their lips melding as he brought her in close, their bodies pressing into one another, and the room erupted into cheers.

Guinevere finally broke away from the kiss, breathless. She let Arthur take her hand and he raised it to the people, amid the throng of people who cried out with the chime of wedding bells,

"Long live King Arthur!

"Long live Queen Guinevere!"

CHAPTER TWENTY-ONE

Gereck made his way up the tower stairs, growing increasingly out of breath as he climbed. It was a long trip up to the sorcerer's private rooms in the northeast tower of Camelot's citadel.

After his fifth stop for breath, just twenty steps below the final landing, Gereck prayed the trip would be worth it. He didn't know where he would go otherwise. After all, Merlin was the oldest person in Camelot. Older than he looked, probably, and he looked ancient. His lungs and legs burned with the effort of the final few steps.

He paused outside the door, breathing deeply until he could do so without gasping. *How does that man make it up here every day? And at his age?*

The door creaked open as he knocked; he hadn't noticed it was open just a crack.

Merlin stood inside, flipping through a ledger of some kind, squinting up at jars filled with strangely colored liquids. The room was lit with several lanterns, but there was only one tiny window towards the peak of the tower roof, which made it dim and difficult to see even in the middle of the day.

Tiny and crammed with various shelves lining the walls, the room's space was filled with furniture: two desks, an enormous wardrobe, several wooden chests and one single chair. Not an inch of surface was bare. There was no bed. Where did the wizard sleep? Another room in the castle?

Gereck had never thought of it before. He had assumed these were Merlin's quarters.

"Why have you come?" Merlin peered into a bottle of amber liquid, not bothering to acknowledge Gereck with even a glance.

"It's Gereck, sir. I have come to ask you whether you know someone?"

"I know many someones, some of them dead and others would be better off dead. Heroes and farmers and noblemen who are less than noble. A few horses and cats, even. More birds. In any case, far too many to know if I know the one you seek. Is that all the information you can give me? Someone?"

"No, sir. I have a name. Did you ever hear of a woman named Elaina of Astolat?"

Merlin grunted, replaced the bottle on a different shelf than the one he had retrieved it from, and made a note on his ledger.

"Your Lady of the Tower, I presume?" Merlin finally glanced at him, his bushy white eyebrows raised, and Gereck stared back at him, stunned that he knew. But he was Merlin. It should have been surprising if he *didn't* know.

"Well, yes," he finally managed.

"She may well have been from a smaller noble family. There were several women around the castle named Elaina then. Or Elaine. Very common. You could try the library."

"The library?" Gereck made a face. Dusty. Dark. He had only ventured there a handful of times, and the beak-nosed clerks scowled at him the entire time, scribbling away as they copied fading and disintegrating manuscripts in various languages. It was not a place he had any desire to seek out.

"Why would I want to go to the library?"

"There are many recordings there. Clerk Tingey keeps them in good order and could direct you to the right volume. Your Lady Elaina may be listed there, and any kin."

"Why would I want to look her up? I can just talk to her about her family."

"You could, but books cannot lie." Merlin shuffled around the room, muttering as he turned jars and boxes over. Perhaps he was searching for something, but it was almost random, the way he picked one up, carried it for a time, and put it down somewhere else. No wonder the room was in such disarray.

"Why would Elaina lie to me?"

"She might, she might not. Books cannot lie, and they cannot withhold information, either. They are open to whatever eyes may see the words inscribed on the page, so long as those eyes can read." The sorcerer looked at Gereck over his spectacles. "You can read, can you not?"

"Pages learn to read, Merlin."

Merlin lifted a finger. "Ah, and you are a squire."

"Almost a knight," Gereck insisted.

"As that may be, you can read. While you look up... What was that name? Astolat? You will be in the A's anyway. Find the surname Asger."

"Asger?"

Merlin bobbed his head. "Yes. That will do it."

"Do what?" Gereck resisted the urge to draw his sword and threaten the old man to start making sense. It wouldn't make a good start to his career in knighthood.

"The best way to solve a problem is to know more about the problem, and a library is the best place to find knowledge. Go to the library."

"All right, then." Gereck turned to leave. Behind him, Merlin muttered something. "What did you say?"

Merlin looked up, a look on his face as though he was surprised to see Gereck still there. "Were you aware that Lancelot does not have a surname?" the sorcerer asked.

"What? Of course he does."

"No, he does not. He is called Lancelot Du Lac, but the surname Du Lac does not exist. There is no family by that name, no noble lord. Sir Lancelot was discovered, as an infant, on the shore of a lake."

"The lake Avalon. Everyone knows that. What does it matter?"

Merlin shrugged, and a smile broke out on his wrinkled face. "Not much, I suppose, to most people, but it should matter to you. I can promise you it matters to your Lady of Shalott."

"Why would she care about Lancelot's birth?" Why, indeed. Merlin may be old and wise and skilled at making people uncomfortable, but he wasn't all-knowing.

"Not his birth. His life."

"If you could make sense for one single day in a thousand years, I wonder, what would you say?" A voice from the doorway startled Gereck into turning around.

It was Arthur, the king, leaning against the doorframe, his arms crossed over his chest. "Do not worry if you do not understand him the first hundred conversations,

Gereck. I'm still puzzling him out, and he was present at my birth."

"I was not present. Birth is women's work." The wizard straightened his robes and snorted indignantly.

Arthur sighed. "I wasn't being literal, Merlin."

"Neither was I."

Gereck looked back and forth between the two men, mind barely grasping what they were saying. It sounded as if, possibly, they were joking with one another. A telling twinkle shone in Merlin's eyes, and a corner of Arthur's mouth turned up.

"I will go now, if you give me the leave," Gereck said.

"Of course!" Merlin said with sudden joviality. "Although I wish you wouldn't go; it's been refreshing to converse with you."

"Should I be taking that as an insult?" Arthur asked.

"Thank you, very much." Gereck bowed. "Merlin. Your Majesty." He passed the king, ducking his head.

Arthur slapped him on the back, nearly sending him down the stairs.

"It's Arthur, Gereck. Do try to remember."

After taking his rotation standing guard on the battlement in the frigid air, Gereck removed his borrowed armor in the armory and left it out for the squires to clean. The strangest feeling descended on him. Normally he would be polishing that armor, not wearing it. As an honorary knight, however, he had the privilege of wearing it.

He tried to shake the feeling off as he saddled Fendrel and urged the horse toward the monastery east of Camelot. Cold rain drizzled from an overcast sky. He closed his eyes and relaxed his body, mouth full of the cheese and bread he had snagged from the kitchens for lunch.

He emptied his mind while he rode, giving himself a rare moment of rest from thoughts about Winna, Elaina, and the Green Knight. Instead, he gave himself fully to the moment, the peace of the falling snow, eyes seeking out swollen buds and other signs that spring was here. It didn't last long enough.

He rounded a bend and saw the monastery, squatting among the trees like a farmer in his fields, short and sprawling, with strange, growth-like buildings dotted around the outside that had been added as the monastery expanded. Gereck had only been inside twice, and both times hated it. It was no place for a man of the sword.

The monks spoke reverently of histories and tales, preserved by their dedicated hands, from which one could divine the wonders of heaven and the world, but Gereck didn't see that. He saw only the dark, the dust, the shelves and shelves of parchment that could only be useful in the vaguest of situations, and all the wasted time and space put into preserving such things.

Men fought and died for control of these kinds of libraries, but he couldn't see why. He hoped he would never be asked to defend a monastery. A dull way to lose your life, as far as he was concerned.

In spite of all that, he was here. He needed the library. He had to see those records; he had to know if they might tell him anything about Elaina.

He dismounted and tied Fendrel to the post outside, then walked inside the open doorway. It was barely warmer within than without, though at least they had it lit. A few torches and windows brought life to the place. He nodded at a pair of passing monks, who eyed his sword with trepidation, and said nothing.

He wasn't sure if it was out of habit, spite, or whether they had taken some vow of silence, but not a single man he saw stopped him or acknowledged him with words. Many simply stared. He thought of them as cows in a field, chewing their cud with little regard for the farmer.

The temptation seized him to jump out at a group of them and make a ruckus to see if they would fall over, but he restrained himself and continued to the back of the monastery. With any luck, the records he sought would be in the main recording room on this upper floor, and he wouldn't have to descend any further.

He walked up to the towering, black oak doors that led to the scriptorium, reached out and pulled them open, just wide enough to slip through.

Inside, monks bent over desks lit by a wide window that filled the far wall behind them. There must have been two dozen desks or more, from what Gereck could tell with a quick glance. The silence was stifling, with nothing to interrupt it but the stirring of parchment, scratching of quills, and the occasional shuffle of feet. A pair of those feet approached him now, almost imperceptibly.

Gereck turned around and came face to face with a set of wizened eyes. The man's stooped back made him much shorter than Gereck.

"What brings you here, sir knight?" The ancient, whispering voice cracked as if it hadn't been used this decade. Which, Gereck presumed, it might not have been.

"I'm here to see the records. I need..."

The monk raised his white eyebrows in alarm, and Gereck got the message. He lowered his voice to a whisper so quiet he almost couldn't hear himself. "I need to see a specific name."

The monk nodded. "What year?"

"I-I'm not certain," Gereck stuttered. He tried to remember what Elaina said about how long she had been in the tower, to give him a frame of reference. "From King Ambrosius's reign, I think. Towards the end of it?"

"Well then. Location? And the name," The monk shuffled away. He was remarkably quick; Gereck had to jog to keep up with him, and his own booted footsteps thundered in the silent room. Scribes looked up as they passed, some glowering, no doubt at the unseemly noise Gereck made.

"The first one would be Elaina of Astolat." He hoped that would be enough. He didn't have any other information.

"Astolat? Astolat..." the monk muttered, turning down a row of manuscripts. Some were in book form, others nothing more than folders or rolls of parchment.

He walked to the end of the row, Gereck following, and stopped to pull out two black leather volumes. The monk led Gereck to an empty desk, where he opened one of the volumes. A small plume of dust came from the book and made Gereck cough as he leaned in. Pages turned, and the monk's narrow finger trembled as it moved down the row of names recorded there.

Astolat, Bernard. Merchant of minor nobility, with a small holding. His wife had died young, and he had taken another, who also died. He had two sons by the first, both knights, Sir Torre and Sir Lavaine, and there were two daughters. Morgan and Elaina.

He took in the information like a starving man, knowing that this was all he was likely to ever see of Elaina's family. *Why hadn't she mentioned them sooner?* He wondered.

Because it didn't matter, did it, when she had been trapped in a tower for the length of their lives, never to see or to know what happened to them. So, this was his chance to find out, at least for some of them. Occupations, wives, children... They were all listed in the subsequent entries.

The monk gathered the volumes in his arms.

"Another name?" Gereck asked hurriedly. The monk gave him a look of impatience.

"Very well?"

"Asger? Same time frame."

The monk opened up the first volume again, only taking a moment to locate the entry. Gereck read the name, not sure what he was looking for. It was a minor noble family. A son and a daughter. A mother. A father. It was the son's name that caught his eye.

Mordred.

Hadn't Elaina mentioned Mordred? In fact, wasn't that the name of her supposed lover, the one who had abandoned her to her fate in the tower? Gereck paused, grateful for the silence around him, for it allowed him space in his mind to think. *How* could *Merlin have known about him?*

He looked at the entry again. No date of death. He cocked his head. He wasn't sure he had found anything of importance, but if this Mordred was still alive, perhaps that would mean something to Elaina. Hopefully, it wouldn't destroy her.

"Might I have some parchment? I'd like to copy this," he asked the monk, who lifted the top of a nearby desk.

He retrieved a small piece of blank parchment from the desk, and dipped a quill in ink, then left Gereck to his copying.

Gereck scribbled as quickly as he could, hoping what he could give Elaina would be taken as the gift he meant it to be. He recorded the two brothers' information, then paused. There was the sister's name, written boldly in black ink, but there was nothing beside it, except a birth date. No husband or children, and no death date.

He looked at the entry for Elaina, and noted that there was a date of death, the black numbers standing out morbidly on the page, for he knew she was not dead. Her family must have assumed. Then why wouldn't her sister's have been recorded?

Unless Elaina's sister *wasn't* dead after all.

CHAPTER TWENTY-TWO

"Why I am getting dressed if the king is requesting me at this hour? If he wants to have me he could at least have the decency to come to my bedchamber."

Guinevere muttered to herself as she allowed Alyce to pull the sleeves of a robe up over her arms, covering the thin nightgown that she wore beneath. She ignored the maid's wide-eyed stare and glowered at the cloak that was offered to her. "And why in the world do I need that?"

"H-He's r-r-requested you join him outside, Your Majesty," the younger woman stammered.

"Marks for creativity," Guinevere said, standing in front of the mirror and twisting her hair on top of her head while the cloak was clasped around her shoulders.

"Your Highness, would you like me to get some pins?"

"No," Guinevere let the hair cascade back around her shoulders. "No need for me to dress up. He gets me as I am or not at all."

Alyce nodded, clearly too appalled to say anything in response.

Guinevere knew she was being impetuous, but she was tired. It had been long day, a long four months without Arthur around and more responsibility than she knew what to do with, everyone looking to her to make decisions and run the castle. Never mind she had never done any of it before, and the politics made her head hurt and Merlin's magic made her mind drowsy and slow. And now Arthur was asking for her to come to him. There could only be one thing he wanted.

"Your Majesty? Shall I take you to him?"

"Tell me where I am to meet him. I don't need to be led like a child who has misbehaved."

"Yes, Your Majesty. He wishes for you to meet him at the stables."

"Very well. You are dismissed."

The maid curtseyed and fled the room. Guinevere made her way through the silent halls, wondering how near the dawn was. Not more than a few hours, surely. She yawned. Her footsteps echoed on the stone beneath them. She expected to feel excitement, or perhaps anxiousness, but she couldn't feel anything but tiredness at the moment.

When had she last taken a pill? She frowned, trying to remember, but her mind moved at a snail's pace, frustrating her. The cold air struck her face as she left the main keep and walked across the courtyard. It was snowing again, only lightly.

Arthur was standing in front of the stables. He held a lantern, so she could see his face. He was grinning. Her heart pounded in her chest. He was handsome. She had forgotten how handsome. Earlier, she had seen him in the courtyard as he returned, spattered with mud and blood and other filth she hadn't dared think about. It had been a good excuse to do no more than curtsey and smile. Now, in the soft, warm light of the lantern, stables in the background, it was much harder to remember her resolve to treat him indifferently.

"My Guinevere," he said, reaching his free arm out to her. She stopped just outside his reach, hands clasped around her arms, a barrier against the cold… and Arthur.

He closed the distance, sliding his arm around her waist and kissing her softly. His beard tickled, and his lips were warm. She relaxed, the barriers melting. Her body ached, and she suppressed a groan. It wouldn't be fair to give him false hope.

He pulled away and smiled again, and Guinevere stared back, conceding a small smile.

"I missed you," he said. "I hoped, while I was away, that…"

"Why did you bring me out here, anyway? It's freezing," Guinevere blurted. Arthur glanced around, almost as if he hadn't noticed. He must have, of course. Signs of spring had begun to show, but it was still quite cold at night.

He shook his head, turning back to her. "I have a gift for you."

"It couldn't have waited for dawn, at least?" A teasing tone crept into her voice. She couldn't help it. In her heart, she was glad he had come home; she had yearned for him. It was impossible to repel him now that he was here, standing so near, so real.

Arthur smiled and shook his head, then reached out a hand to her. "Come with me. It's warmer inside." His head gestured towards the open stable door. A warm glow was coming from within.

Guinevere eyed his hand.

Arthur sighed. "Guinevere, you know you can trust me."

She stopped suddenly, and Arthur tugged on her hand. “We could miss it if you insist on dallying.”

Guinevere followed Arthur inside the stables to a wide room filled with hay. Beyond it, other horses could be seen, some of them peering curiously over their stall doors at the two people who had walked in.

To Guinevere’s left, tucked into a corner, was a small arrangement of pillows and blankets. She raised her eyebrows at Arthur, who pretended to ignore her as he looked to the far end of the space. She followed his gaze to where a chestnut mare was standing, breathing heavily. Her sides were enlarged, swollen with pregnancy. Guinevere’s eyes widened and she looked at Arthur.

“She’s foaling, isn’t she?” Guinevere asked, her voice hardly above a whisper.

The mare snorted and shifted, kicking hay around the floor. Her knees shook and bent, then straightened again and the mare moved once more. She was close and would give birth soon, if there were no complications.

Guinevere’s throat constricted. Her head pulsed, on the verge of a headache. Perhaps she hadn’t taken her medicine as recently as she thought. She could feel a consciousness crowding into her mind, and the whispering started. It was quiet at first, easily mistaken for the wind in the trees outside or horses shuffling in their stalls. It only took a moment before it grew louder. She glanced at Arthur, wondering if he, by any chance, heard it too. No reaction.

She wasn’t prepared for Arthur’s touch on the small of her back, and she startled, barely stopping a shriek so it wouldn’t disturb the mare in her labor.

Arthur pulled her toward the corner with the pillows and helped her sit, then picked up a blanket and draped it over her shoulders. Guinevere managed to smile at him.

The mare suddenly lowered herself to the hay-strewn ground. She snorted again several times, and two dainty hooves appeared at the opening beneath her tail, surrounded by a glistening sack.

"Oh," Guinevere breathed.

Arthur sat next to her, close, but not too close. She let him, eyes only for the foaling mare. The mare was huffing and panting, letting out the occasional high-pitched whinny as her body worked to birth her baby. She laid her head on the ground, nickered, and gave another heaving push. More leg appeared. The opening swelled with the pressure of the horse pushing. Guinevere's breath caught in her throat. Arthur's arm was around her now. She hardly noticed as she watched the foal being born. The tiny nose became visible; in and out, in and out as the horse pushed and rested between contractions.

The mare's chestnut sides heaved, and in one final push, her baby slid into the hay, kicking its legs until the hooves broke through the sack over its mottled head. The baby had gorgeous coloring, white with large dark brown splotches covering most of its head and body.

Tears were in her eyes. She wiped them away. She felt normal for the first time since... Well, in a long time.

"Incredible, isn't it?" Arthur whispered.

Guinevere nodded, words caught in her throat. They watched the baby horse kick its way out of the sack, then scoot around, trying to get its legs beneath it.

"Let's give the mother some space to get to know her baby, shall we?" He stood and extended his hand toward Guinevere. She took it, allowing him to pull her up. They walked out in silence, the cold night air folding around them as they left the warm stable.

Arthur was holding her hand. Despite the cold air, Guinevere felt a warmth inside. They walked together, into the castle, up the winding stairs, down the dark and silent corridor. Dawn was still a ways off. They walked in silence, for which Guinevere was grateful. Her heart was pounding, her tongue thick in her mouth. She didn't want to speak and dispel the feeling that lingered after watching the beautiful mare give birth.

They came to a door, which was opened before them, and closed the moment they walked through. Arthur turned to face her, eyes peering into hers. She tilted her face upward, and their lips met.

She lost herself in the kiss, body moving forward instinctively, pressing against his. His hands gripped her shoulders, unclasping her cloak before pulling her into him. The cloak dropped to the floor. They came apart, panting, then came together again. Arthur's hands wandered further, up the length of her back and down again, lower each time. They rested at her waist, then rubbed up her side.

Guinevere's body reacted as if it was not hers to control. She leapt back from his touch, arms wrapping around her middle.

Arthur stopped. He looked at her. "Guinevere, I..."

"Arthur..." She looked into his eyes. There was hurt in them. She swallowed and looked away.

"Merlin was right," Arthur muttered.

"What?" Guinevere asked.

She discreetly put a hand to her head, as the pounding grew again. She had forgotten while Arthur was kissing her. She couldn't keep talking. She had to get to her rooms, to the medicine. The longer they spoke, the more danger Arthur was in.

"He said I shouldn't marry you, and he was right."

Guinevere stared at Arthur. "He said that?" she asked.

Arthur's face was taught with a hardness she had rarely seen. "Yes, he did. And I wish now I had listened."

Guinevere stared at him, mind void of any response. Arthur shifted his stance, fists clenching and unclenching.

"I could not anticipate what happened on our wedding night," he said, his voice strained.

"Arthur, I am sorry about that. I..."

He held up a hand, stopping her apology. "Let me speak."

\She swallowed. She had heard him use that tone with men who had disobeyed direct orders. It wasn't one she had ever thought would be directed at her.

"When I married you, I expected there to be difficulties. I knew about your fragile condition, I had heard the rumors and, for the most part, refused to acknowledge there was any substance to them. I spoke to Mary at length about you, about your character and your ways. She was confident that, with time, you would be well again. I wanted to believe her. I did." He paused.

The pain in Guinevere's head moved to the forefront, stabbing behind her eyes. She struggled to focus on Arthur's words. She had to remain aware. She couldn't lose consciousness now.

"And then, what happened on our wedding night, I just assumed you would overcome it, that your reaction was something normal, a simple fear that would disappear as you came to trust me more. Yet night after night, the same thing, until I left to deal with the Saxons. I told myself it would be all right, that when I came home you would be ready. Are you, Guinevere? Are you ready to be my queen, my wife?"

His eyes gazed so intensely into hers, and she cringed. Her mind reeled.

"Guinevere?" Arthur asked, turning towards her.

She couldn't hold his gaze any longer. She lowered her eyes to the floor. "No," she whispered. Tears pricked her eyes. Her throat had turned to stone and it was painful to swallow. She choked the words out. "No, I can't. Arthur, you know I can't!"

He hesitated for a long moment.

"Do you love another, then? Lancelot, perhaps? I know there was something between you, before. If you love him, speak now. I will not be made a fool."

"No!" Guinevere sobbed. His fingers dug into her arm. Her mind was in a vice, pulsing with pain. She couldn't breathe. "I love... you," she managed to gasp out. "Please, Arthur."

He released her, pushing her away from him. "If you loved me, you would not hesitate this way."

She reached out. "Arthur, please, listen to me. I want to be with you, I want to share your bed, I just..."

"You just can't, I know," he said bitterly. "I am tired of your excuses, Guinevere. You won't even try. How do you think I feel about that, being rejected by my own wife? You have been fortunate, you know. Other men wouldn't wait. Other men would demand their due as your husband and take it by force. It would be well within their right to do so."

"You can't mean that."

"I do. Camelot deserves an heir. If you can't give it to them..."

A rush of anger overtook Guinevere. "If that's all you want, go make a bastard with a whore off the street. She'll open her legs willingly enough when she sees your gold."

"You will not speak to me that way," Arthur said, voice low and dangerous as he stepped towards her.

"And I will not be treated this way, Arthur Pendragon!" she yelled. "You have no right..."

"I am your husband, I have every right!"

He grabbed her arm, pulling her to him. Guinevere struggled, hand beating on his chest, but he only pulled her tighter, bodyweight forcing her backward, towards the bed.

She almost gave in, and would have, if it hadn't been for Morgaine. In this moment, she surged forward, thrusting Guinevere aside in their shared mind.

"You're hurting me!" a voice screamed.

The words had erupted from Guinevere's mouth, but she hadn't spoken. It was Morgaine, seething with anger, livid and burning with fear.

Arthur froze.

Body shivering in nothing but a shift, every muscle tense, screaming at her to run, but Morgaine was in control now. She stared back at Arthur, a wild animal, trapped.

A long moment passed, eyes gazing, chests heaving, until, at last, Arthur released her and stepped backward.

Morgaine slipped back into the recesses of her mind, and Guinevere sobbed again, relief and horror and hurt balled up inside of her chest. She huddled in on herself, making her small, shaking so hard she had to sit down on the bed. Waves of sickness overtook her, and her body shuddered.

Sometime during the episode, Arthur left.

Guinevere curled up on the bed, her face in her pillow, crying until she ran out of tears to cry. She didn't want to stop, didn't want her thoughts to come back, forcing her to confront what had almost happened. Just as her body calmed and she could breathe again, she heard footsteps. She tightened herself up into a ball, head tucked under her arms.

The footsteps halted somewhere near the bed.

"Forgive me, Guinevere." Arthur's voice drifted, muffled, through her arms and the screen of her cascading hair.

No motion or sound escaped her. She was paralyzed.

The door closed behind him. It was ages before Guinevere could move again. When she did, her eyes burned from crying, her throat was raw. Muscles ached and complained as she moved. She picked her cloak up off the floor where she had left it before and held it neatly draped over her arms. She opened the doors.

Two knights stared ahead, stoic expressions on each bearded face. Guinevere lifted her chin and stepped out. From the corner of her eyes, she saw them watch her, though they made no other movement. She rounded the corner and let her breath out, then sucked it back in, focusing on her breath so the tears wouldn't start falling again.

The eyes of the knights followed her, burning into her. They knew. Or, at least, they thought they knew what had occurred between the king and his queen. They must have heard the screams, and now the rumors would flow. The queen would not bed the king. He had to force her. Tears pricked her eyes. None of them would know the truth, that Arthur hadn't used her.

The walk to her chambers stretched excessively long. She kept her head high as she passed into her rooms, doors held open by another set of knights. One of the men, Sir Tristan, smiled warmly at her as she entered. Once inside, she let them slowly trickle down her cheeks.

Mary's chair sat empty in the corner. The woman who had first been her nursemaid, after her mother died, then her governess, and finally her friend, had returned to Carmelhide. She was no longer needed, she claimed, now that Guinevere was married. She had stayed for only a week and then returned to help Guinevere's father run his household.

There was a hollow feeling in Guinevere's heart. She placed the cloak on her bed, then sat on it. She shivered, despite the fire crackling cheerily in the grate nearby. Her skin crawled. She wanted a bath, some tea, and bed. What she didn't want was to sit in silence, thinking about what had happened.

As if she had heard Guinevere's thoughts, Alyce opened the door a moment later. She appeared surprised to see Guinevere, but recovered well with a curtsey.

"How may I be of service, Your Majesty?"

"A warm bath, please," Guinevere said, weariness weighing down her words, "and tea."

While Alyce prepared her requests, Guinevere walked around the bed to the large, opaque blue jar that sat on the table. When she picked it up, a few small, lumpish balls rolled around the bottom. They were almost gone. She ought to tell Merlin. She tipped the bottle, and one of the brown herbal concoctions landed in her palm.

She set the jar down, bringing the pill to her mouth. Its bitter taste was familiar on her tongue, but somehow, today, it tasted of sadness. This is what her life had become. Pills, loneliness, responsibility, and survival. Where was the love? Where was the joy? How had she managed to ruin it all, when she was supposed to have it all?

"Your bath is ready, Your Majesty."

Guinevere pulled off the nightgown and shift and tossed them to the ground. "Have those burned, I don't want to see them again."

Alyce took them away without a word, then returned as Guinevere stepped into the tub. It was scalding, but when Alyce picked up a jug of cold water to adjust the temperature for her, Guinevere waved her away and asked to be left alone with the bristle brush and soap. Alyce obliged, obedient as ever, without inquiring further.

When she was gone, Guinevere soaped her entire body and scrubbed until the skin was raw and practically glowed red. The heat of the water burned everything away, every thought, every stress, everything that had happened since she had left home, and as she leaned her head back, her vision swam, and her mind spiraled deeper and deeper until she slept.

Her eyes blinked open. A shadow near the fire shimmered, and a figure slowly came into view. Guinevere shrieked and shrank down, causing water to splash over the sides.

Niviane stepped into the light, her bent back covered in a tattered grey robe. Her hair hung limply around her face.

"You!" Guinevere gasped.

Niviane hobbled towards the bed and Guinevere leaned away, catching a whiff of the woman's stench. Niviane grinned at her, patting her head with a knobbed hand.

"You have gotten yourself into quite the mess, my dear."

"Why are you here?" Guinevere hissed. She wished Alyce would return. Surely, she would walk through the door any moment.

"Get dressed. I have something to show you."

Guinevere climbed reluctantly from the tub and drew on her robe. She sat shivering at the edge of the bed across from where Niviane stood.

The old woman changed before Guinevere's eyes, her back straightening, the rough cloth of the dress morphing into beautiful green satin. Her grey hair extended into silvery blonde tresses that tumbled down her back. Guinevere gasped at the woman that stood before her.

"Nimue! You're...?"

"Not who you thought." The woman ran a tongue along her teeth and grinned. "I have been laying these plans for some time, *Morgan*. You will not get in my way."

"Don't call me that." Guinevere said. It was a childish response. Her face burned. How long had she been fooled by this woman's charade, even thinking of her as a friend?

Nimue... or was she truly Niviane... laughed, her green eyes sparkling. "But it is your name. And besides, it is high time you accept that *you* are not who you think either."

"Maybe I like being Guinevere." Guinevere replied. "My life is fine the way it is. Why do I have to know who I was, if such a thing is possible?"

The sorceress moved closer, placing a fingernail under Guinevere's chin and tilting it upward. "Because that past self made a bargain with me, and she could lose something very precious to her if you do not cooperate." Nimue turned away suddenly, walking towards the lit fireplace across the room. "It is in your best interest, trust me."

"How can I know you aren't plotting against Camelot, against me?"

Nimue laughed. "Against you? I have nothing to fear from you. And Camelot should not be your concern." She adjusted her gown, sitting in a large armchair beside the fire.

The glow made her eyes gleam, and Guinevere suddenly realized how dry her throat was. She reached for the wine that had been left for her on a nearby table, and before she knew it, the glass was empty. She frowned. Wine shouldn't be gulped. Neither should her hands be sweating, but her fingers were slippery on the glass. She set it down, afraid of dropping it on the hard stone floor.

She was too hot. The fire seemed to be reaching for her, baking her through the light robe. She glanced at Nimue. The sorceress lounged in the chair, not a drop of sweat evident on her face despite her proximity to the fire.

Guinevere's throat was constricting. She gasped for air. "Please," she choked out. "Why..."

The crushing pressure lifted off her and she lay on the bed, sheets twisted around her, gulping air into her lungs.

"To show you how easy it would be." Nimue stood, walking over to the window. "If you were my target, you would be dead now and I would have your place as Queen." She turned, gazing at Guinevere, who still knelt on the floor. "But petty crowns and titles do not interest me."

"Then what do you want?" Guinevere asked, her voice rasping. Her throat felt raw and sore, as if she had been screaming.

"Power."

Guinevere sat up. "You already have magic..."

"It's not enough. Another power exists in the land, greater than mine. I will have it." Niviane flexed her hand into a fist.

"What do you want from me? Arthur knows no magic. Surely he's not the one you are after."

"He is only the beginning. But in order for this to work, you need to remember, and I am certain there is only one way that can happen."

The woman walked toward Guinevere and leaned over her bed. Glittering green eyes met Guinevere's, and she could not look away from them. "You will go to the tower before the next rise of the full moon."

"I will go." Guinevere intoned. She blinked, and Nimue had straightened.

"Do not try to avoid it. The result will be excruciating for you."

Guinevere woke with a jerk, breathing hard. She sat up, her robe clinging to her skin, damp with sweat. Her chest heaved as she gulped air. How long had she been gone?

"Alyce?" she called out. "Alyce!" The maid bolted into the room, holding a basket of clothes for mending, face red. "What time is it, what day?"

Alyce gave her a strange look. "Your Majesty?"

"What day, Alyce?" Guinevere demanded. "Tell me!"

"The same day, Your Majesty. I drew a bath for you and left, as you asked. I was walking back just now to check in on you."

Guinevere closed her eyes and breathed in, then out, forcing her body to relax. "I must have dozed off. I am sorry to alarm you."

"Would you like help getting dressed, Your Majesty?"

"Yes, please."

Guinevere chose a flax-colored dress that draped elegantly over her figure. She felt at home in it today over the more brightly colored silk fabrics that glared at her from the wardrobe. Alyce brushed through her hair until it was smooth, then braided it with a silver ribbon.

"That will be all," Guinevere said when she had finished.

Alyce curtseyed. Guinevere had no doubt she would tell others about the queen's "episode" this morning. It was a wonder the girl hadn't had a nervous breakdown serving her.

Before Alyce left, however, a knock came at the door, and Alyce opened it to reveal a page. The boy bowed to Guinevere, then waited.

"You may speak," Guinevere said at last.

"His Majesty, King Arthur Pendragon, requests the audience of Queen Guinevere in the throne room."

Such a formal request. Did he intend to call her out in front of the entire court? A chill clutched her heart.

"Did he mention for what purpose he called for me?"

"No, Your Majesty. Only that he desired your presence."

"Very well." She stood, brushing her dress, then straightened. She eyed the bottle on her bedside table. Perhaps she ought to exercise caution and take one now. She looked to the page. He would see her take the pill and spread the rumors further of the queen's madness being treated by a strange medicine. She could ask him to leave, but that would only cause further speculation.

She straightened her dress again, then swept towards the door. She had taken one just before the bath. Surely it would be enough.

The page led her through the now-busy halls, maids and knights and servants of all varieties rushing back and forth to their various duties. They acknowledged her with nods, curtseys, or bows, followed by whispers the moment they had passed. What was it they said? Perhaps she ought to consider employing someone to tell her so she might try to quell the rumors.

Their journey through the corridors ended at the massive throne room doors. The page opened them and the announcement of her arrival rang through a silent hall.

"Ah, yes, Queen Guinevere," Arthur said. He didn't look up at first, and when he did, his eyes didn't settle on her. They looked past her, or at the parchment on the table beside him. Never once did they connect with hers, and she could not read the feeling in them, if there was any.

She swallowed hard, then curtseyed. "My king, what do you require of me?"

"There is a certain matter that concerns you," he said, still avoiding her stare. She waited. "It has become apparent that necessary measures must be taken to assure the safety and well-being of Camelot.

"I have appointed a counselor to you. She is your right-hand when you are well and able to attend to these matters, and will have authority to make decisions when you are not."

Guinevere's insides froze. "What are you saying?"

His brown eyes finally connected with hers. "You need help, Guinevere. As long as you are ill, someone needs to be handling your responsibilities, or there will be chaos. In this time of war, we need Camelot to be running as smoothly as possible, and that starts here in the castle."

"Whom have you chosen?"

He was watching her intently, no doubt for any sign of hurt. She steeled her expression. "Lady Nimue Cavender." Guinevere stared at him. Nimue, who was the sorceress Niviane. She had to speak, had to say something, but one look into Arthur's eyes told her that her words would not be heard, not today. She swallowed hard.

"She has heard my request for her assistance and offered to stay in Camelot to fill the position until such a time as you are well. I have seen you together, and it seemed you were friends. She has been appointed, but I would like your approval before it is made final."

"Do what you must," Guinevere said.

"This is for the best. I would see you better, Guinevere." She nodded, feeling frozen, unable to think. Like a mouse caught in the gaze of a hawk. "Is this agreeable to you?"

Guinevere gritted her teeth. "Yes, Your Majesty."

"Good. Then you are dismissed."

There was no warmth in his gaze, no familiarity in his manner towards her. He treated her as he would any subject, with an infuriating distant concern that refused to acknowledge what had transpired between them.

She curtseyed, then turned and walked from the room through the open doors. Her breathing came in ragged gasps, and her eyes burned with tears. Where had they come from? She tried to convince herself they came from anger, but the ache in her chest told her otherwise. She walked quickly to her room, shutting the heavy wooden door behind her and resting against it.

The tears flowed. The pain in her heart wasn't going away. Arthur's face came to her mind, the hurt and anger in it making regret swell inside of her. She had done that. He had reached out to her, and she had pushed him away, she had made him try to force from her what any wife, what any good wife, would give willingly.

"Your Majesty? I thought you may want tea." Alyce's voice came from the back of the room. Guinevere brushed at her tears.

"Yes, thank you, Alyce. You may leave. You are excused for the day."

"Are you certain, Your Majesty?"

"Yes, I am. Please go," Guinevere begged, gesturing towards the door and moving towards her bed. "I am just going to rest, I did not sleep well last night."

"Thank you, Your Majesty," Alyce said, curtseying before she left.

Guinevere picked at the tray of food on the table, nibbling at a few things. She wasn't particularly hungry. She left the food and picked up the cup of tea, only lukewarm now, and carried it to the window. She stared out over the land, past the houses in the city's lower levels, toward the farmland that was still brown, with only the faintest hint of green coming back to it.

Hopefully, war wouldn't destroy the delicate, growing plants.

Her eyes traveled toward the forest, about half a day's ride from Camelot. The trees were still bare and brown, their swollen buds having not yet released the green leaves of spring. . When had that happened? She had hardly been outside with the responsibilities of watching after the affairs of the castle while Arthur had been away. The sudden urge to get on her horse and ride among those trees consumed her.

No doubt there would be some responsibility for her here. She should do her best to perform it, try to change the peoples' opinion of her, if that was even possible… Her eyes were drawn northward, until they rested on the spire of a single tower. It stood on an isle in the midst of the wide river.

Her heart quickened when she saw the tower, and her eyes gazed at it hungrily, though she couldn't see much detail, except for a single circular window. In an instant, urgency gripped her heart like a vice. Guinevere gasped and fell backward. She stumbled as she tried to catch herself and her head fell back with a crack on the stone floor.

She awoke with a stiff neck and one desire consuming her mind: she must go to the tower. She stood and dressed, unaware of how much time had passed since her fall. It may have been hours, it may have been moments, but it didn't matter; all that mattered was that she go to the tower without delay.

Guinevere dressed herself and absentmindedly pulled a comb through her hair, not bothering to tie it up. She pulled on some tall boots, clasped a cloak around her neck, and left the room. No one approached her in the castle halls or the stables, excepting the young stable hand who brought her horse to her; a gentle gray mare.

"No, not that one," Guinevere said, stepping past the hand and going into the stables.

Most of the better horses belonged to knights, or the king. Guinevere moved toward the back, where she knew the king kept some of his stallions. His favorites. One of them had sired the colt she had seen born the night previous. She stopped in front of a stall containing a black stallion, a white star displayed on its forehead. He was lithe, and didn't seem too restless. The stable hand, who had followed her in to return the mare to her stall, glanced wide-eyed between Guinevere and the stallion.

"Are ye sure, Yer Majesty? That 'un is a might feistier than yer used to."

Guinevere opened the stall and stepped inside. She stroked the steed's nose and he snorted into her palm, then nudged her shoulder. "What is his name?"

"Ryker."

She looked into his eyes and could see fire, and a desire to run.

"Yes, I am sure. Saddle this one."

She fidgeted while she waited until the stallion was brought out. Her heart was pounding as if she had been running, and all of her muscles clenched, ready to bolt. That was why she needed speed. The stable hand came out with Ryker, then knelt at the horse's side, hands clasped to boost her. The horse was taller than her mare, that was certain. Guinevere sized him up, then took a few running steps and jumped. She gripped the horse's sides, slightly sideways, then used her arms to pull herself upright.

"Yah!" she yelled, squeezing the horse's sides with her legs.

Ryker bolted into action, and out of the corner of her eye, she saw the stable hand on his rump on the ground, staring after her, mouth agape. She let out a laugh, hair streaming behind her in the wind made as they galloped through the courtyard and through the first set of gates. She was forced to slow down in the lower town, due to the throngs of people going about their daily errands, but soon enough she was through the final gate and outside the city, urging the stallion faster and faster along the muddy road that led to the tower of Shalott.

There were few people on the road. A farmer and his wife, a small cart of belongings pulled behind them as they plodded toward Camelot, no doubt to trade or sell wares for things they needed to replace after the winter season. A single knight on horseback, perhaps out for a morning scout or just to ride. Guinevere didn't recognize who it was, and she didn't have the attention to return his bow with any sort of response. If she slowed, she might get stopped, and that wouldn't do.

She checked that her hood was still up and adjusted her grip on the reins as the stallion galloped toward the tower. It would be an hour yet before she saw it, and still more before she reached it. She leaned across the horse's back, urging him forward even faster.

At long last, the top of the tower became visible through the trees, and the rest of it came into view as Guinevere rounded the final bend. The tower was in the middle of the river, which ran high and fast with runoff from the hills. No doubt it was frigid as well. Guinevere slowed Ryker to a canter and let him take her past the tower so she could see around it.

It was surrounded on all sides with water, except at the side on the opposite bank, there was a small bridge of land that was covered, barely, by water, and it led up to the tower. She could see grass under the wavering surface. During the summer season, it was probably dry.

To get there, however, she had to backtrack half a league to the last bridge, and then wound through trees in the forest, trying to find the quickest way to the tower.

Why the rush? Morgan asked, her voice faint.

Guinevere hesitated. She had forgotten to take a pill before she left.

Guinevere?

Guinevere saw the river ahead, and through the trees, the base of the tower appeared, the path to it closer with every step. Her heart was pounding with anticipation, making her feel breathless.

Can you not feel how unnatural this is, your sudden urgency, the way your heart is beating from your chest? You can hardly breathe, and your hands are shaking. It's a wonder you are still atop this horse!

Guinevere frowned. Her breath was coming in quick gasps, like the air was too thin and she wasn't getting enough of it. She looked at her hands. They *were* trembling, but it was just adrenaline from the ride, she was certain.

"Niviane told me once that if I wanted answers, I needed to go to the tower. Well, I want answers."

It was only a half-lie. The urge to enter the tower, to climb the stairs, was so forceful she couldn't have denied it if she tried. "I am going," Guinevere said finally, nudging

Ryker's dark sides with her knees, urging him forward through the trees.

He stepped out from beneath their cover and stopped at the river's edge. Guinevere could see there was little room for him on the tower side bank, so she found a low-hanging branch and tossed the reins over it before sliding from the saddle. She hit the ground hard, jarring the bones in her legs. Ryker tugged at the reins and tossed his head, unsettled at being tethered.

Guinevere shushed him, patting his nose before turning to the tower. It stood tall and lichen-covered on the small isle in the water. A tall tree grew right beside it, reaching up toward the solitary circle-shaped window near the top. A chill passed over Guinevere at the sight of the window, and her heartbeat quickened painfully.

She gasped and put a hand to her chest, blinking back tears in her eyes. Something gripped her mind, vice-like, forcing her attention to the tower. She straightened and walked forward mechanically, her arms locked at her sides. Her shoes were soaked through as she splashed through the shallow water over the small bridge of land.

The cold water seeped into her stockings, chilling her feet, but Guinevere could spare no thought, no energy for them. She kept moving forward, aware only of the hand that seized her mind, directing her full attention to getting inside the tower. There didn't seem to be any doors, but there was a tall tree with low enough branches for climbing.

She gathered her skirts, looking for some way to tie them up. Fear gathered in her heart, and disrupted the total control of something, or someone, that held her mind. She blinked.

Why am I here?

Because Niviane wants us to be.

Her thoughts were jittered and confused. Was she Morgan or Guinevere? Had one of the other alters taken over?

The magic that had been laid on her regained control and forced her attention to be drawn elsewhere; a black, thorny bush on the far side of the tree. She edged her way around the tree, barely aware of the deeply pooled water just inches away. The plant was dense and the thorns sharp. Her hands received numerous cuts from the dagger-like barbs as she pulled the branches away from the tower wall.

Behind them, instead of stone, was a small, weathered wooden door. It had no handle. She dug her fingertips into the crack between the door and the wall, prying it open. Dirt cascaded into the entryway. It was dark inside, and she could see very little from outside, but she ducked inside, crouching in half to get through.

As her eyes adjusted, she found herself in a stairwell that wound both up and, surprisingly, down, perhaps to a cellar. She put her foot on the first stair and climbed. There was no railing to aid her, only stone steps and no sign of the top as the staircase continued upward.

Tiny, narrow windows, mere slits in the rock, allowed some light to filter through, and as Guinevere's vision gradually grew accustomed to the dim light, she noticed the walls were covered in large tapestries. Artfully woven and impossibly perfect, the colors vibrant as the day they were threaded, though they must have hung for decades.

They covered both sides of the wall. If she'd had a lantern, Guinevere would have stopped to look at the details. The glimpses she caught were exquisite; finer than anything she had seen before.

Even with a light, however, she couldn't have enjoyed them fully. The spell that gripped her had complete control, moving her legs forward, upward, climbing stair after stair until, at last, a wooden door came into view.

Her legs and lungs burned as she climbed the last steps. Her hand reached automatically for the doorknob. She could hardly breathe. She turned the handle, and the door creaked as it swung gently open.

CHAPTER TWENTY-THREE

All in the blue unclouded weather
Thick-jewell'd shone the saddle-leather,
The helmet and the helmet-feather
Burn'd like one burning flame together,
As he rode down to Camelot.
As often thro' the purple night,
Below the starry clusters bright,
Some bearded meteor, trailing light,
Moves over still Shalott.

Elaina looked up from her weaving. She expected Niviane, come with food and perhaps the last dress she had taken away for mending. Her eyes met identical pools of gray-blue, a set of eyes she hadn't seen in decades.

Her sister, Morgan.

She stood up from the bench and took a step towards her sister, arms reaching outward even as her heart wrenched painfully in her chest. The curse, reminding her that her life, and her body, were not her own to direct.

Her throat was suddenly seized with emotion, and she couldn't get any words out. Tears fell down her face.

Morgan's face was as young and beautiful as the last time they had seen each other, but her expression was hard to read; her eyes were wide, her mouth open in shock.

"I know you..." Morgan said, eyes narrowing as if she didn't quite understand what she was seeing. "How..."

"Oh, Morgan!" Elaina put her face in her hands, waves of relief and despair simultaneously crashing down on her. The pain in her heart vanished as the loom released her.

Then Morgan's hands touched her shoulders, hesitantly at first, before bringing her in for a full embrace. Decades of loneliness filled her heart with so much pain that Elaina couldn't breathe.

She opened her mouth to say something, anything, but before she could get a word out, her ears registered the sound of the latch being turned.

The door swung open. Morgan put an arm reflexively around Elaina.

It was Niviane.

The old woman smiled sweetly, serenely, looking at Morgan. "Hello, dear."

Morgan was staring at the old woman, eyes wide. "Niviane? No, you aren't... You didn't..."

"Of course I did. You asked me to."

"I never asked for *this*." Morgan cried, gesturing at the tower. "I asked you to keep her safe!"

Niviane's crooked back was no longer bent as she approached Morgan. "And is she not safe? Safe from your brothers? Safe from what any other man could ever do to her? Have I not kept my side of our bargain?"

"Yes, but..." Morgan looked at Elaina.

Elaina was frozen, her mind reeling. Morgan knew Niviane?

Niviane's ancient voice broke Elaina's concentration. "Let's make this fair, shall we? Give her something in exchange for her years of service at my loom. But where to begin? The beginning?"

"What? No!" Morgan cried. "Please, spare her."

Elaina stared at Morgan, uncomprehending. Spare her from what?

Niviane's hair had straightened and now shimmered down her back. Elaina blinked, trying to comprehend what was happening. The older woman raised a hand toward her, and intoned some words, keeping eye contact with Elaina. "*Is cuimhin liom é sin.*"

Elaina gasped with the strength of the vision that was forced upon her. She was standing in a room, swathed in the pitch dark of night. Moonlight from outside illuminated just enough to see the outline of a large four-poster bed with a canopy. The canopy was drawn back, revealing a sleeping form curled under the blankets. The door to the room opened, the latch clicking, then shut as the door closed behind a large, shadowed figure.

Elaina watched the figure approach the bed. The person seemed large and muscular from the outline, she assumed it was a man.

The man climbed into the bed and the little figure inside woke with a startled shriek, which was quickly muffled, though Elaina could still hear the young, feminine voice screaming through the hand that stifled her, and there was a significant amount of thrashing on the bed. The man cuffed the little girl on the side of her head, whispered something Elaina didn't catch, and left the bed. He re-buckled his pants as he walked towards the door.

Elaina's heart crawled into her throat, and her stomach churned. The sickness only grew as the vision continued, the door opening for a second time and another figure entered, this one also masculine, and repeated the earlier scene, only this time the little girl was struck several times, and there was a lot of furious whispering. The girl's sobs took a long time to quiet. Elaina's heart pounded as she waited for the door to open again. It did not, but the memory fast-forwarded, to another night.

The little girl in the bed had a larger form, and the covers draped over a curvy waistline, showing a young woman. The door opened and the young woman awoke rubbing her eyes sleepily and sitting up in bed. Elaina had to close her eyes this time, and her hands covered her ears. She couldn't stand to watch what was happening. Bile rose to her throat.

"Please stop," she whispered.

No one responded. She was trapped in the memory, and would see what Niviane wanted her to see.

A familiar sound came through her hands; a muffled knock at the door. Elaina removed her hands from her ears and opened her eyes. The figures on the bed paused. The man leapt off the bed, pulled up his breeches, leaving the young woman crying quietly on the bed. He went and opened the door, and a girl with pale hair was standing there, holding a small lantern. She peered around the edge of the doorway into the pitch-dark room.

Then the vision became a memory. A flashback from Elaina's own life. She was the little blonde-haired girl.

She was nine years old, creeping along the hallway outside her room in the dark. She was thirsty and needed a drink, and it was hot enough she had decided to leave her bed and get some herself. She passed her sister's room, and heard a sound. She stopped. Was Morgan awake too? Maybe she would like some water. Then they could chat and giggle until their nursemaid heard and made them go to sleep.

Elaina raised her hand to knock on the door, rocking on her feet in anticipation. She heard another sound, like a slap, and then a moan. Her hand froze and she lowered it, leaning in until her ear pressed on the door. Scuffling noises, some talking. Who was in there with her? Then the door opened and she stumbled back, coming face to face with her older brother Lavaine. He was tucking in his shirttails, and when he saw her his face seemed shocked at first, and then he grinned.

He tousled her hair. "What are you doing out of bed, imp?"

"I'm thirsty. Were you talking with Morgan?"

There was that uneasy look again. "Yeah, we were talking."

"Oh," she peered around him into the room. Was Morgan crying? "Is she thirsty too?"

"Let's ask." He leaned in through the doorframe. "Oy, Morgan, thirsty? El wants to get you some water."

"Just go away." Morgan's voice sounded weak, and sad. Lavaine shut her door before turning back. He shrugged his shoulders.

"Guess she doesn't want any, El." He turned and started down the hall towards his own room. Elaina watched him go, then glanced back at her sister's door.

"Why is she sad, Lavaine?"

"She got upset while we were talking. Nothing serious. Just another suitor refusal."

"Oh. Okay." Her brow creased in worry, but she didn't try to knock on Morgan's door again. She could hear sobbing from inside. Perhaps her sister would feel better in the morning.

Tears filled Elaina's eyes as she came back to the present, blurring Morgan's image.

"You never told me?" she whispered.

Morgan didn't respond. Her body tensed, and she wouldn't look at Elaina.

Elaina's heart reached out to her sister, aching to comfort the hurt that was there. She reached a hand out towards Morgan, trembling.

"No, it would not be better. Just stay where you are," Morgan hissed.

Elaina hesitated, retracting her arm slightly.

"You don't know what this is about. You will ruin everyth..." Morgan's voice suddenly choked and broke off, her eyes rolled in her head, then closed. Her body trembled, then shook.

"Morgan!" Elaina cried out, stepping forward.

"Do not touch her." Niviane said. "She will be fine in a moment."

Elaina clenched her fists, facing Niviane. "What have you done to her?"

"Nothing she didn't agree to. This was an unanticipated part of our bargain, a consequence of the enchantment on her damaged heart and mind. She will overcome it, or she will perish."

Elaina glanced back at Morgan, who still stood upright, her head lolling. Then, slowly, her head came up.

Her eyes were unfocused. She shook her head, stumbling to the side.

"What do you think of that?" she said out loud. Her voice was higher pitched and tinny sounding. Elaina looked around the room. Who was she talking to? She didn't seem focused on either Elaina or Niviane.

"I knew you wouldn't like it, that's the point, but you were hiding something from me, and I had to find out what."

Morgan paused. Her face became angry. "You wouldn't have! Time for me to find out for myself."

"Morgan?" Elaina said.

Her sister looked up, eyes wide, as if she was surprised to see her there.

"Who are you?" she asked.

Concerned, Elaina glanced at Niviane, who had a strange smile on her face. Which, now that she was looking at it, didn't seem so wizened anymore. Was she growing younger? Her hair was straight and silvery blonde, her skin smooth and unwrinkled. Her back was no longer crippled and bent.

Then Elaina recognized her. The beautiful woman she had seen in the mirror, on the day she was trapped by the enchantment. Elaina looked between Morgan and Niviane, and backed up until she bumped into the loom.

"What is going on here?" she said. "What happened to my sister?"

"She exchanged your freedom for her peace of mind, and her peace of mind to be part of my plans for Camelot," Niviane said, examining her hands. She glanced back at Elaina. "The spell was meant to revert her to infancy, causing her to live life again as her own self. There are minor memory lapses associated with the spell, but nothing to the extreme your sister has experienced. Her memory has split into several versions of herself because of the abuse she suffered at the hand of your brothers. Had I known the extent of the abuse, I may never have agreed to our bargain, but the oaths were made and now must be kept."

"What oaths?" Morgan, if it was still her, stepped toward Niviane, a strange expression on her face. "What am I bound to?"

"She doesn't know?" Elaina asked.

Niviane frowned. "She ought to. I hoped meeting you would trigger the rest of her memories. Perhaps it has, but they are being stifled." She gazed intently at Morgan.

"You are not Morgan," she said at last.

"No." Her chin was raised defiantly, a glimmer of Morgan's steely determination in her eyes, but the expression was still foreign.

"Then who are you?" Elaina blurted out.

"A body-thief," Morgan's familiar, husky voice spoke out of her own mouth. Her head was shaking angrily.

"It is my body, you are the intruder!" The high-pitched voice again. Elaina's head swam. The impostor in Morgan's body looked at her and smiled.

"I am Guinevere Pendragon, Queen of Camelot," she said. "Who are you?"

Elaina was frozen. No. She thought. *No. It can't be.*

Had Morgan married Arthur?

The woman... Morgan? Or was it Guinevere?... stared at her expectantly.

"I- I..." Elaina stammered. "I am Lady Elaina of Astolat."

Guinevere looked around the tower, glancing towards the window in the wall. "Ah! You must be the Lady of

Shalott. Of course you are. Why does Morgan care so much about you?"

"I am her sister. Well, half-sister." *And Arthur is my son.* She was paralyzed. "Where is Morgan? I need to ask... something."

Guinevere glared. "I am not about to give her control. I might not get it back." She paused, then looked at Niviane. "You trapped her in here? Why?"

"Her sister asked me to make her safe. She didn't want her brothers to do to Elaina what they had done to her. Since the magic was beyond her power, I agreed. She never asked what method I would use, and this one suited my purposes best, especially when I discovered Elaina was with child."

"What?" Morgan's true voice came through again. Her body shook for a brief moment, but clearly she was in control again. She stared at Elaina. "You were pregnant?"

Elaina closed her eyes and sighed. When she opened them again, she was met by Morgan, wearing a furious expression. Her shoulders were raised, arms tense by her sides, fists clenched.

"Yes. I didn't know for a while. Mordred and I had made love for the first time that morning. You sent me to pick flowers..."

"And you took him with you? Unchaperoned? He could have hurt you!" Morgan's voice became shrill.

"Why would he? He loved me!" Elaina shouted.

"Men cannot be trusted. He took advantage of you."

"Only because I let him. Besides, you trusted him well enough." Anger boiled out of Elaina, fierce and hot.

Morgan recoiled from her slightly, shock passing over her face. "What are you talking about?"

Elaina opened up her mouth to say she didn't know, to apologize, but another memory was thrust upon her and she couldn't speak.

She stumbled through the tall grass in the fire-lit night. Beltane was not a night to be out for the faint of heart. The drums echoed through the air, and circles of people danced wildly around fires lit in pockets throughout the fields, all throughout the land. Elaina avoided these fire circles and their whirling dancers. She was all too aware of the lust of Beltane, men and women falling where they stood in passionate embraces, ignoring marital status and age, caught up in the lust-spell of the festival of fertility. The wind carried the scent of passion as it blew past the celebrations, infecting everyone it passed.

It gave Elaina a headache. She reached behind her to grasp Mordred's hand. It wasn't there. She turned to look for him, but darkness met her gaze. In the near distance, by the lake, a fire circle. Heart gripped with terror, Elaina moved towards it. If he had been called by the music of Beltane, she might never retrieve him.

Her feet moved clumsily over the uneven ground. Her eyes kept searching, hoping to find Mordred before it was too late... and then she saw him.

The tall grass opened up into a small patch of cleared ground, just outside the fire circle. Two bodies intertwined.

Mordred's familiar dark head, his lithe body, moving in rhythm to the Beltane drums, arched over another, someone not her. Elaina's whole form choked at the sight. Her voice caught in her throat, unable to call out to him. He was lost to Beltane. She turned away, realizing what she was watching, but the face of the woman he made love to caught her eye and she stopped. She stared.

It was Morgan.

Her sister.

His heart belonged to her, but his body... now it belonged to Morgan.

Elaina gasped as she came out of the memory, tears brimming in her eyes, heart thudding painfully in her chest, the raw agony of the moment hitting her as fresh as the day she had witnessed the betrayal.

"You!" she yelled hoarsely at Morgan. Her sister took a step back away from her. Her eyes glazed over, and Elaina barely noticed the tremble as an alternate identity took over her sister's body. "How could you do this to me?" She was screaming now. "He loved me, he loved *me*. Were you so jealous you had to seek him out? Or were you so intent on my *safety* that you sought to destroy my happiness? He loved me!"

"Elaina, I didn't, I don't, please, it's not..." It was Guinevere's high-pitched, frightened voice that pulled Elaina from her rage. She stopped, and Guinevere was backed up against Elaina's bed, leaning away from Elaina's hands, which were inches away from her sister's pale throat.

Elaina took a deep, shuddering breath and leaned forward on the bed, looming over Guinevere. "Where is Morgan?" Her voice was hard and threatening, sounding strange to her own ears.

"I don't know. She went inside. I wasn't even trying to come out this time, I swear."

"But she is in there. She must hear me."

"I couldn't tell you. Only if she wants to, perhaps. I cannot hear her."

"Then you will tell her for me," Elaina said, eyes locked on Guinevere's. "For what she has done, I will never forgive her. And I never want to see her, you, again."

She stood, releasing Guinevere, who remained on the bed for a moment. Then, slowly, her entire body shaking, with fear, Elaina assumed, she got to her feet and walked to the door, passing Niviane, who watched her go without a word. She hesitated at the door, looking back toward Elaina.

"Are you going to release her, Niviane? There is no cause for her to be here any longer. Her... our brothers are long dead."

"It is not in my power to release her, just as it is not in my power to unite your mind. Rarely are these spells reversed with ease. She will remain here until such a time as she removes the curse or dies in the attempt."

Elaina looked away from Guinevere's pitying glance. Her heart felt empty and cold. The wall that held back her true emotion was about to collapse. She held onto it, desperately wanting to be alone before she broke down.

The door closed behind Guinevere. Niviane was still in the room.

Elaina had a question to ask. She swallowed her emotion and spoke without facing the sorceress. "Would you have done this if she had not asked you to protect me?"

"Yes," came the reply. "I recognized the seed growing within you. The Goddess gave me the signs and I found them all in you."

"Why do you need Arthur? Wouldn't the king's true son have done just as well?"

"The Goddess knew Uther's true son would die. Igraine could not produce a viable heir. She suffered numerous miscarriages, each malformed. Her body could not support life. I was gifted the ability to find the babe who would grow into a man who could be planted in the right place, bring Camelot to prosperity, and then the kingdom would be ready for harvest by a vessel of the Goddess."

A realization dawned on Elaina and she immediately whirled around to confront Niviane. "Then you mean to kill him?"

The words reverberated through the empty tower room. Niviane had gone.

CHAPTER TWENTY-FOUR

Gereck was woken in the morning by Sir Tristan, who, though he tried to appear solemn-faced as ceremony dictated, couldn't help offering a small, comforting smile to Gereck as he told him he would sit in vigil that night.

He was to be knighted, at last, and in the morning, he would leave to complete his quest with the Green Knight and likely never return.

It would be a day of feasting, first.

Gereck sat at the high table, surrounded by comrades in arms. They laughed and recounted tales of innumerable quests and glories of battle. There was no sadness this day, and little talk of the increasing Saxon efforts to enter Camelot, except for boasting of the success that King Arthur would surely have over them.

Mid-laugh after a fantastic joke by Sir Pellinor, Gereck looked to the king. His eyes were downcast, gazing into his cider. He swirled it in his hand, lost in thought.

"Oy, Arthur!" Sir Tristan called down the table. "Tell us about your hunt for the questing beast." The knight's cheeks were flushed and his eyes glittered merrily. Arthur smiled, sitting back in his chair.

"You lot have heard that story a hundred times. Sir Lancelot was there too, you might recall. Let him tell the tale!"

Sitting across from Gereck beside the queen, Sir Lancelot glanced up and half-smiled in acknowledgement, but immediately looked back at his cup without responding. He was as lost in thought as King Arthur had been only moments before.

The party did not wait for him. Arthur took up the tale, with great enthusiasm and large gestures. Gereck tried to ignore Lancelot, but his thoughts kept sending his eyes to watch the famous knight, who did little to join the celebrations. Other knights would try to bring him in the conversation, asking about one victory or another, but he deflected their attempts with half-smiles and apologies.

The knight had never liked Gereck, and had given no support in his journey to knighthood. No surprise, then, at his attitude, now that Gereck had achieved it. Gereck had always wondered what he had done to deserve the special disdain Lancelot spared for him, but he supposed he might always wonder. The knight wasn't likely to divulge anything to him, and time had run out for that sort of thing.

"Our newest knight has grown gloomy! Is there a curse on that end of the table?" someone called out; Gereck wasn't sure whom. He looked up and smiled.

"There's a curse on your tales, Sir Tristan. All those who hear them fall into a stupor." In the drunkenness of the hour, some food was thrown in the direction of the speaker. The king pounded the table for order, then stood up. The entire room quieted, and Gereck wondered at the power of one man to command such respect.

"The time for our feasting and merriment is drawing to a close. It is time to witness the knighting of Sir Gereck."

A cheer shook the hall. Gereck grinned, receiving numerous jarring claps on the back by his fellows at the table. With them, he made his way to the church. A squire met him in an anteroom, with a full set of armor to help him into. Gereck thanked him graciously, remembering humbly his own lengthy time as squire, and when his greaves at last were fastened, and a red cloak clasped in front, the squire bowed out.

Gereck took several deep breaths in the dimly lit room, then looked out into the hall of the church. Lords and ladies were taking their seats, the other knights in the foremost rows to witness his oath-taking.

At a sign from Bishop Ernald, Gereck stepped into the room. He walked to the front, where the king, bishop, and Sir Lancelot were standing. Gereck's heart was in his throat.

The bishop waxed on for the better part of the evening, the sun falling behind the horizon before he finished intoning the code of a knight. Gereck stifled a yawn and shook his head, trying to appear alert as King Arthur took the stand. He drew Excalibur, the sword ringing out loudly in the silent room. Its edge gleamed. Gereck stared at it, his body instantly trembling with excitement.

"It takes more than a great swordsman to make a knight of the Round Table. One must have the heart and courage of a warrior, the tenderness of a father, and the love of a husband for his country." The church was silent.

The king made eye contact with his knights, one at a time, until he reached Gereck. When he spoke again, his voice was quiet, but firm. "Any man can claim willingness to die for his country and his king in bloody and glorious battle," the king said, his gaze never wavering from Gereck's, "but it takes an extraordinary sort of man to live with honor, to bring peace without violence, and to love the people and his king as God loves us all."

Could he live up to that, truly? He had made so many mistakes, especially lately. Perhaps he wasn't worthy of knighthood after all.

"Before all of you and God as my witness, I dub thee, Sir Gereck Bauer of Camelot." Excalibur tapped each of Gereck's shoulders, once, twice, a third time. The king gestured to Lancelot, who handed him a metal token, engraved with a red dragon and a cross. The king's symbol, which all knights of the Round Table wore to remind them of their commitment to God and the king. He placed it over Gereck's head.

The silence in the room was thick. There was no roar of approval in the sacred hall of the church as Arthur extended his hand and Gereck took it, standing. His heart was full and his eyes were wet. He wiped the moisture away, looking into the king's steady gaze.

"Tonight you kneel in vigil," the king said for only Gereck to hear, clasping his shoulder. "You are aware of what this entails? That you must not speak, nor move, nor eat or sleep until morning breaks?"

Gereck nodded. He swallowed the knot in his throat. He didn't dare speak, lest he commit the sin of speaking before sunup.

King Arthur smiled. "Good. You begin now, friend. Luck to your journey tonight; I will come for you in the morning."

The church gradually emptied. Several more knights exchanged meaningful, supportive glances with Gereck, respecting that his vigil had begun. The bishop was the last to leave. He inclined his head toward Gereck, and in silence snuffed out all but one solitary candle near the front of the church where Gereck would kneel. He knelt in front of the raised dais, watching the candle's flame flickering in the darkness. It was a cool night, and he could feel the air reaching for him through his armor. Somewhere, a bell rang out the hour. Midnight.

His head kept nodding. He was supposed to be praying. He tried reciting the knight's code of chivalry in his head, but kept getting lost in thought halfway through and starting over.

The bell toned the first hour of morning, and the second. Soon after it had struck three times, Gereck's stiff body was complaining whole-heartedly. Determined to uphold the vigil, Gereck shook himself and carried on.

He heard voices.

At first he was confused, and thought perhaps his mind, aching for sleep, was creating hallucinations, but the voices grew louder as someone walked up to the church. They were not alone.

Gereck reached his hearing out to them. It was a man and a woman, from the sound of their voices. They must have stopped just outside the door. He could hear them, but not what they were saying.

He strained, listening, to catch anything. Most likely it was just two lovers, come to find a private place for meeting. He hoped they wouldn't try to disrupt his vigil.

Then he heard a name that sent his heart pounding.

"Lancelot, there is nothing you can do. She is lost."

The voice had raised slightly, perhaps in anger, and Gereck heard every word. A response followed, masculine, not as clear as the first.

Gereck turned his head. Whom was Lancelot speaking with, in secret, this time of night? The woman's voice was not young, so it couldn't be a lover; not that Lancelot had ever had one of those, and Gereck would be the one to know.

So who was it? It would break his vigil to try to hear more. He would forever be shamed if anyone discovered him. He would be cast from knighthood before he had ever begun, not to mention the eternal damning that was assumed if he broke ceremony. But what could Lancelot be meeting so secretively about at this hour?

Surely God was forgiving enough to allow this.

Gereck stood slowly, so as not to alert the outsiders to his presence. He walked down the aisle of the church, empty wooden benches gleaming in the moonlight on either side. The voices became clearer the closer he got.

He stopped just inside the door, listening as the female voice spoke again.

"Seeing her sister again did not have the effect I hoped for. She is hiding, now, and if my intuition is correct, her loyalty is divided. The influence on her mind is stronger than I originally thought, and I believe she grows sympathetic to King Arthur."

"She loves him?" Lancelot's voice was a growl.

"Be at peace, knight. I do not think it has grown so troublesome yet. She can still be redeemed, but we must act quickly and you must keep your head and keep to the plan. Can I trust you to do that?"

"I am willing to do what it takes, Niviane. Camelot will not see another season pass with Arthur on the throne. I swear it."

A chill washed over Gereck. Lancelot plotted against Camelot. *Lancelot*, of all men?

"How far are you willing to go, Sir Lancelot?"

"What are you asking?"

"There is a nobleman, Lord Melwas. He lives about three days' ride to the east. He has already agreed to support us with his men, and fortunate for us he also has a specific skill set. It could be arranged for him to kidnap the queen..."

"I will not endanger her."

"You said you would do anything."

"How could I have known you would ask this? Melwas has a reputation. This is not the first I've heard of him. If she goes in there, she might not come out whole."

"Do you believe she would let him try anything? She is not without power."

"But she is weak; she is not herself," Lancelot insisted.

Gereck's mind was reeling. Lancelot was plotting to betray Arthur, and possibly have the queen kidnapped. It was all the more confusing that Lancelot also acted concerned for the queen's welfare. Whoever this Melwas was, and whatever his reputation, Lancelot clearly didn't want the queen near him. Did he love her? Is that why he plotted against Arthur?

Gereck cleared the thoughts away, tuning back into the conversation.

"This isn't necessary. I can..."

"Defeat Arthur on skill alone? Against Excalibur? If you had not lost the shield..."

"It wasn't me! I told you, that beard-blasted squire fell into the river with it. I sent him to look for it time and time again, even went myself, but it is truly gone."

"Without the enchantment laid on that shield, you would die swiftly at the king's hand, leaving him very much alive and untouchable."

"There must be some other way. You could spell another shield, perhaps."

"Fool! We do not have time. That enchantment took years to build and bind in order to counteract the effects of his sword and scabbard."

Lancelot scoffed. "I do not see what is so special about them. A sword is only as good as the man."

"King Arthur is among the best in character and ability, no doubt you know that."

"I am better still. I beat him in all of our sparring and competitions."

"In sparring you are never gambling your life. Two men always hold back in the arena when they respect one another. You are no exception."

Lancelot protested, but the woman interrupted him.

"The sword alone is powerful enough; Excalibur has spells of victory in war placed upon its blade ages ago by Merlin. The scabbard was woven by others like myself, imbued with magic from Merlin when he first agreed to train me, centuries ago. As long as Arthur wears the scabbard, he neither ages as a mortal man nor bleeds as a mortal man. He can be killed, but not without receiving a great many wounds, or losing his head. Are you capable of performing such a task without dying first?"

Lancelot was silent. Outside, a bell tolled.

"As I thought. Then we shall clear the path for Melwas. The kidnapping ought to awaken Morgan and cause a more thorough integration. You will communicate with Melwas's men?"

"If I am caught, it will mean the end."

"Only your end. There are other pawns in play I can utilize, Mordred. Remember that. They are just as eager to gain the same power you seek."

Footsteps scuffled on the other side of the door. Lancelot greeted someone. The bishop. The bell had rung in dawn, and he hadn't heard. The bishop was no doubt returning to the church to prepare for the morning Mass. He sprang away from the door, forgetting his armor would clatter. It sounded loud in the death-quiet church. He ran from the door, praying no one heard, and breathlessly slid to his knees at the front of the room.

The bishop opened the door. Gereck bowed his head, as if in prayer, mostly to hide his flushed face. The sun was glowing brighter through the stain-glass windows. As ceremony dictated, the bishop left him in vigil. Until the king released him, he would not be spoken to, or violate any of the other requirements.

Shame crept into his heart. He had left the vigil. Surely God would forgive him, as he had heard something that King Arthur must be told; Sir Lancelot, his best and greatest knight, betraying the queen, the king, and Camelot as a whole.

Lost in thought, he didn't notice as the knights of the Round Table filed into the church. It wasn't until King Arthur had approached him and placed a hand on his shoulder that Gereck looked up into his liege's face. It was bright with a glad smile, blue eyes sparkling. He swallowed and stood.

Two young squires helped him remove his armor; he would not need it where he was going. With no squire to attend him on his quest to death, it would do nothing but hinder him. Left with only his chainmail, Gereck was approached by two knights on either side of the king, who bestowed Gereck with a shield, bearing the bright red dragon of Camelot, and a sword in its sheath. Gereck buckled the sword on and took his shield to hand.

Arthur clasped his shoulder. "You are ready, Sir Gereck?"

He didn't feel ready, but he nodded, then looked around the knights who circled him. Sir Lancelot stood among them, not looking at him, face placid, without any indicator of the conversation Gereck had just heard him having.

How could he accuse Lancelot when he stood there, calmly and blatantly unworried? It would be suicide. The other knights would defend him to the ends of the earth and think Gereck unworthy of his newly bestowed knighthood.

Numbly, Gereck allowed himself to be led from the church. Horses awaited the knights, held by numerous squires. One brought forward two steeds, and Gereck recognized Fendrel, saddled and bridled in the finest tack he had ever seen. Gifts for his knighthood. A smile came to his face as he greeted the horse, and as he swung astride, energy surged through him. Everything would turn out all right, he was certain of it.

So, he ignored the uneasy feeling rising in his chest, and spurred his horse forward, heading the party of knights at the side of King Arthur. A crowd was gathering in the city, watching as the newest member of the Round Table made his way through the lower levels of Camelot's great city. He waved and smiled at all of them, especially the young boys who crowded the horses, looking on in awe, pointing at various knights and speaking excitedly to each other.

He had been one of those boys, once.

They reached the lower gates, the final threshold Gereck would cross before his quest began. A squire ran up and placed saddlebags over Fendrel's rump; supplies for the journey. Gereck thanked him, then held his head up, awaiting the king's signal.

Arthur leaned over in his saddle, speaking into Gereck's ear over the cheering crowd. "Good luck. I would desire that we meet again, and that I have many knights serve me as loyally as you have throughout the years."

Gereck nodded. Arthur straightened and raised his arm into the air.

"I give you... Sir Gereck!"

The sound of the cheering crowd crashed around Gereck, and he had a moment where he could warn Arthur, plant the seed of Lancelot's betrayal if nothing else, but as Gereck opened his mouth and leaned toward Arthur, the king slapped Fendrel's rump, jolting the horse into a sudden gallop that almost threw Gereck to the ground. He righted himself and let Fendrel run, the noise of the crowd fading quickly behind him.

There was no turning back now. He would have to send a message to Sir Tristan from the first inn he encountered, and pray it found its way to Arthur. The king wasn't alone, after all. There were the other knights still loyal to their king, and Merlin would certainly be aware of such goings on.

Later that afternoon, the tower of Shalott loomed into view. Gereck stared at the rounded window, wondering what Elaina was doing, and if he should say farewell.

He slowed Fendrel by pulling on the reins, and directed the horse towards the bridge over the river he had to cross in order to get to the tower. His mind searched for what he would say.

He muttered out loud, staring at Fendrel's mane. "My deepest apologies, Elaina, but you ought to know the truth. I lied to you. I am married. And I am not actually a knight. Well, now I am, but I wasn't before, and I am riding off to my death anyway, so if you don't forgive me I will never know. Best of fortune to you, hope you enjoy weaving in your tower for eternity. Oh, and sorry I couldn't free you." His mocking tirade trailed off. He had failed. He closed his eyes, as if he could prevent the guilt and pain from rising inside of him.

She never has to know. He raised his head and gave the tower one last glance. *I am sorry, Elaina.*

He kept Fendrel facing northward on the road, steadily trotting past the tower. He was painfully aware of it in his peripheral sight. He kept his eyes forward and kept his mind blank as new parchment, unwilling to give himself any opportunity to change his mind. She would be better off not knowing, wondering what happened instead of being told the agonizing truth, that they could never be together.

He only made it a mile before he wheeled Fendrel around and, cursing himself and his own stupidity, went back toward the tower, crossed the river, tied up his horse, and climbed.

Elaina was sitting on her bed, knees to chest, dressed only in a shift. Gereck wasn't sure if he should look away or not, she seemed so distressed. He approached the bed.

Her eyes were red and puffy. She sniffed and wiped her face on her crossed arms. She didn't look at him. As usual.

"Elaina?" Gereck said softly.

"Where have you been?" she croaked, her normally smooth voice hoarse.

"I... well, busy," he said, somewhat truthfully. "We are in a state of war. The knights have many duties right now."

She straightened, unfolding her arms and legs, then appeared to realize how scantily she was dressed. She jumped up from the bed and ran behind her dressing screen.

"I am sorry I wasn't more properly attired. I- I haven't been well."

"Are you ill? I could petition a physician to come see you."

"No, no. I..." Her voice became muffled. "I have something to tell you."

She came out from behind the screen, attired at last in a wrinkled gown. Her hair was disheveled. Accompanying her swollen, red eyes, she wasn't the prettiest picture of a woman... but he shouldn't be so callous.

"I came to say something to you, too," he said, feeling impatient.

"Oh?" she asked, running her fingers through her hair. She braided it, plaiting the strands of hair over her shoulder. When she reached the end, she grabbed a faded pink ribbon from the top of the screen and tied it, then tossed the braid behind her. "You start, then."

She walked around the room, picking up articles of clothing, straightening the covers on her bed.

Despite his eagerness, Gereck suddenly felt guilty as he watched her. He had nothing good to say; he was only going to ruin her life, and he wanted to delay that as long as possible.

"No, you. Mine can wait."

She looked around the room. "I told you once I have a son, do you remember?"

"Yes," he said slowly.

"And you wanted to know if you could possibly be familiar with him?" She didn't wait for another response, rushing into the next part so her words stumbled over each other. "You do know him, I am certain of it."

"How can you be sure?"

"Because my son is King Arthur."

CHAPTER TWENTY-FIVE

With a steady stony glance—
Like some bold seer in a trance,
Beholding all his own mischance,
Mute, with a glassy countenance—
She look'd down to Camelot.
It was the closing of the day:
She loos'd the chain, and down she lay;
The broad stream bore her far away,
The Lady of Shalott.

Elaina's breath heaved in her chest and her heart pounded. Gereck had heard her, hadn't he?

He coughed. "Really?" He cleared his throat as if he had more to say, but then went silent.

"Yes. I know because... Well, I named my baby Arthur, and the woman who took him away told me she replaced Uther's real baby with mine, and there's something else you have to know."

Her words were tumbling over each other so fast she had to stop and breathe. He started to say something, but she started again, speaking over him. "And that is this: my sister, Morgan, is posing as Guinevere, queen of Camelot, and she's married to Arthur but really loves..."

Her voice choked on the word, but she swallowed and continued. “She made a deal with a sorceress, and she's planning to betray the king and... and...” She trailed off.

She hadn't figured that part out yet, exactly how Niviane planned to overthrow Camelot. She wished she could see his expression.

“Gereck?”

“I can tell you're upset about this, but there's nothing I can do, I'm sorry.”

“Sorry? You think I am mad!”

“That isn't what I said.”

“It was implied! If you believed me you wouldn't be brushing it off,” she said, crossing her arms over her chest. “My sister came here, to this tower, with Niviane. They told me she married the king in the guise of Guinevere, and that they plan to kill him. I know Camelot is in danger, and you don't believe me because to you I am some lonely, desperate woman locked in a tower, but I am so much more than that! I am Lady Elaina of Astolat, and though I am trapped here, I am not blind or deaf, or mad, as you might believe.”

Her face felt flushed. Her neck strained with effort to keep from looking at him.

“Did you even hear me? They plan to kill the king! As a knight, you should...”

“I am leaving!” Gereck blurted out. Elaina stared at him, her mouth open in mid-sentence.

“What?” Her mind emerged from its self-induced frenzy, trying to comprehend what he had said.

“I never told you. I defended the king in a challenge with a knight, almost a year ago. He made a bargain with me. I got the first swing, but if I didn't succeed in killing him, I would have to meet him exactly a year and a day later. He was a sorcerer in disguise, and some enchantment enabled him to place his severed head back on his shoulders. I'm honor-bound to uphold my word to him.

"What you speak of, a plot against Camelot, I believe I heard someone speaking of it last night. I'm not sure about the rest of it, the king being your son sounds so impossible, and yet, perhaps you are right about everything. But I cannot help; I'm leaving."

"So you would choose defending your own honor over the lives of hundreds of others? Camelot is going to fall, and the only one who can do anything about it is choosing to run away!"

"To my death, Elaina. This isn't a ride through the countryside for my pleasure," he said, his voice rising. "I have to leave today if I am going to make it in time. I gave my word."

"I think you're just afraid to fail, that no one will listen to you." Elaina said, surprised at the harshness of her voice. "One day wouldn't prevent you from keeping that word." She moved closer to him, eyes shut tight, grabbing his arm. "Please, Gereck. Return to Camelot. Tell Arthur, warn him. You will make up the time if you ride out quickly enough."

He shook her off. "No-one would believe us, Elaina. Those you accuse are in the highest positions next to the throne. I would be imprisoned for trying to bring these things to light. I am seen as but a squire, and you are a fae tale to most of them, a ghost in a tower." He took a deep, shuddering breath.

Elaina started. "But you are a knight. Sir Gereck. You told me, when we met..."

"You assumed that when we met, and I didn't deny it, as I should have. I was only a squire."

In the silence, she stared ahead at the wall, clenching her jaw, shoulders tense. What could she say? She hadn't found the words, yet, when Gereck started talking, his gentle voice resonating with sorrow.

"I was knighted this morning. This is my one chance to do something great, like the other knights of the Round Table."

"Since choosing to go to your death instead of warn the king so Camelot might be saved is so heroic," Elaina said, mocking.

"I'm just trying to keep my word. This decision isn't made lightly, Elaina. By meeting the Green Knight I..." He swallowed, then took a deep breath. His voice shook. "I will leave behind a wife and our two children."

She sat in stunned silence. What could she say? Her own affection for him seemed small and pathetic, now. A young girl's fancy.

"Don't go," she finally said. "Please, Gereck. This is your chance to prove your greatness, not some vague quest that will end in certain death. Save Camelot. Save the king."

"I can't."

"Then you are a coward, *sir* Gereck. Why I ever thought I could count on you is beyond me." *And to think that I loved you.* She wanted to speak the words, but her anger choked her, holding them in her throat.

He said nothing as his footsteps walked away. Her heart clenched, and the pain she had been suppressing released suddenly. She let out a small, gasping sob.

A breeze blew past her face, carrying a faint sense of warmth and flowers with it. Spring was here again.

CHAPTER TWENTY-SIX

Guinevere hid in her room for days, trembling like she was ill, mind flickering between Morgan and Guinevere, Guinevere and Morgan without settling.

She couldn't tell who was who or if she was herself at all. All of Morgan's feelings raged inside of her, and despite her best efforts, she could not sleep them away.

Most of all, Elaina's furious, hurt expression haunted Morgan.

She had never intended it to go so wrong. She had only wanted to keep her safe... Safe enough to exact revenge on their brothers, help Niviane, and then take her sister away, to a place where they could live away from the taint of the world.

Even now, thinking about that desire made her want to weep. She could see the small cottage Morgan had envisioned, hidden away in a mountain valley. They would have kept sheep, perhaps, and sold their wares in a nearby village to maintain a living, and she knew Elaina would have loved it.

But Niviane had made that impossible.

Elaina hated Morgan, thought her a horrible tyrant for taking Mordred from her. She didn't know that Morgan hadn't taken him. Morgan had been caught in the lust spell of Beltane the same as Mordred, and it was pure accident they had ever discovered their feelings for each other.

Of course, Elaina would never believe that.

"She would be right not to." Niviane's voice rang out in her room.

Guinevere jumped from her chair, her embroidery, long since abandoned, tumbled from her lap onto the floor.

"You can see my thoughts!"

"Only when you broadcast them in the full strength of your emotion, the way a child would," Niviane said disdainfully. She wore a red dress with silver ribbons and trimming, wearing the guise of the young and painfully beautiful Nimue.

"What do you mean, then, by what you said? Why would she be right?"

"Because Mordred never did love you. I enchanted him."

A pit formed in the bottom of Guinevere's stomach. Morgan raged inside of her. Would she be sick? She wasn't sure what made it worse; hearing the truth, or recognizing that Niviane, whom Morgan had trusted so well, had manipulated her so thoroughly.

"What other lives have you ruined to meet your own ends?"

"They are not my ends, but the Goddess's."

"Then she is evil."

Niviane turned and spoke a word, twisting her hands towards Guinevere. Her tongue stuck in her mouth and would not move.

"I will not hear wickedness spoken against our Goddess. She gave you what little power you have, and the wretched life you live. You will not speak of her with such depravity in my presence, understood?"

Guinevere nodded. Her tongue released, and she rolled it around in her mouth to be sure she was unharmed.

"What did you hope to accomplish, sending me to the tower?" Guinevere demanded.

"It was meant to integrate your splintered mind, which, unfortunately, has failed."

"Then why are you here?"

"To resolve the gaps in your memory, in the hope that you will remember all. It is your final chance for redemption." Niviane walked to a chair near the fire and sat down, gesturing across from her. Guinevere walked woodenly to the chair, not wishing to be near, but desiring less to draw the woman's ire again.

"Listen well, Morgan le Fay, and hear the truth," Niviane's voice intoned, a strange lilt affecting the quality of her voice. "You, and only you, may ask the questions, though be warned, your questions will determine your fate."

By enchantment, Guinevere felt herself thrust to the back of her own mind, and her awareness flooded with darkness even as Morgan's came into light.

Morgan flexed her fingers, used them to brush aside her hair, then hesitated a moment to be sure Niviane had finished speaking. Then, she asked her first question.

"Why did I marry Arthur? Was it Guinevere's desire alone, or was it part of our plan?" Guinevere asked.

"Marrying King Arthur was part of your destiny. I knew that when I sought for your oath to aid me," Niviane said.

"Why would that be important to you? What am I meant to do?"

"What destiny would have you do."

"But what is that? What would you have me do with the king?" Morgan asked.

Niviane gazed stonily at Morgan. "He must be killed."

Morgan's heart pounded. Her hands felt slick with sweat. She wiped them on the blue material of her gown. Then, something lit in the back of her mind, like a light in a dark room. A question.

"Who is Arthur?"

"The son of Elaina of Astolat and Sir Mordred Asger."

"But... how? How could that be? He is too young to be her son, and..."

"It was I who put Arthur on his throne. The goddess showed me what was to be, and I watched for someone to fit all of the signs. Your sister did, from the moment you told me of her. The timing was ideal. You cast the spell I gave you and I took care of Elaina, just as I promised I would. She birthed a boy, and I gave that boy to a miller to be raised.

"I simply waited a few short years until Igraine and Uther came together as King and Queen of Camelot, and when they did, I performed the same spell on Arthur as I did you, reverting him back to infancy. I became a midwife for the Queen. She was weak and sickly in pregnancy, and her labor was difficult. I was able to make the replacement easily enough. Uther never suspected the fair-haired boy was anything other than his own, and Igraine was blinded by her desperation for a living child to love and hold."

Morgan's heart beat in her chest, almost pounding. It was incredible to think she had ended up married to Elaina's own son. Technically, she was Elaina's step-sister, so there was no blood relation. And she loved Arthur no less knowing her sister had borne him.

Whatever she had agreed upon with Niviane still had to be done. Morgan continued. "Why did you not wait for a woman in Igraine's own time to bear a suitable child?"

Niviane's gaze narrowed. "Haven't you been listening? I saw no reason to wait, when I already had gathered all the resources to perform the change for you and Mordred."

"Then his past life... Won't it get in the way?"

"Ah, no. In fact, it will serve us all the greater. His past life as miller's son gives him no advantage as a military strategist; all of his strength as king comes from the knights that sit around his table, and we have already taken care of them."

"We have?" Morgan's mind moved sluggishly, and she fought to keep up with the conversation. Another light appeared, another piece that had been lost. "I don't recall agreeing to kill him. I thought... Well, I thought I was the key, that I would convince the king to change the laws through seductive persuasion and..."

Niviane's laughter broke the night hair, its high pitch causing bumps to erupt on Morgan's thin arms. "Seduction? You? You're too broken to even make love to him, much less seduce him. If I had known just how repressed your memories of abuse were, I never would have agreed to cast the spell.

"Memories as painful as yours grow stronger, compounded by the years of being hidden within, so when they resurface they leave you crippled forever. Admit it, you can't look at your new husband without trembling like a shrew before a cat. Your former self is gone, Morgan. Though I might have one last use for you."

Shame shuddered through Morgan. She had been used time and again by every person in her life, except Elaina. Elaina, who she'd saved from the world, but in doing so estranged the only person who truly cared.

Morgan's hands clenched into fists. "What makes you think I will let you do this?"

Niviane's green eyes glittered, her lips curling into a sneer. "I taught you everything you know, dear Morgan. You are not powerful enough to stop me yourself. There is only one man who is, and he has a weakness for young, enchanting maidens." Niviane stood and turned away, her silver dress shimmering in the moonlight.

"I'll tell Arthur!" Morgan called.

Niviane raised her hand in a dismissive gesture, and Morgan watched as she faded from sight.

Emotions roiled inside of Morgan. Her heart ached, for Elaina, yes, but also for Arthur.

Why should she care if Arthur was killed? If it accomplished the Goddess's will, she ought to be rejoicing in the prospect. Her training dictated that nothing mattered besides the will of the Goddess, and to be used in her plans was an honor given to only the faithful.

She readied herself for bed, not wanting Alyce's intrusion, and then she slipped between the covers, her body tossing and turning with her thoughts.

Hours later, she woke in the pitch darkness of her room. She sat up, looking around and wondering what had woken her. The half-formed moon let in very little light, but it was just enough to see that her bedroom door was ajar.

"Alyce?" she called.

No one answered. She glimpsed a shadow moving beyond her bed. She stiffened and her eyes searched for the form again.

It leapt out of the darkness at her, and an arm gripped her tightly. A hand holding a cloth muffled her screaming, and a cloyingly sweet scent filled her nostrils and muddled her senses until she lost awareness.

CHAPTER TWENTY-SEVEN

A cold, drenching rain had started hours ago, and it dripped down Gereck's neck through the seam on the hood. Night was falling with no inn in sight.

He cursed not having stopped at the last inn. He had watered his horse, paid for a meat pie, and, after much hesitation, asked for pen and parchment to write to Sir Tristan about Lancelot's betrayal.

Elaina's words weighed heavily on his heart as he wrote. He wished he had done more for her, but nothing would come by regret. So he had left the inn, hoping to arrive at the next before the rain came.

Now, with night falling dark and fast, and being soaked to the bone, Gereck scanned the horizon desperately for any sign of lodging. He would have even settled for a copse of trees if he had to, but he was fortunate to be able to see the road at all through the sheets of rain, and soon that visibility would be gone as well. Gereck urged Fendrel forward, careful not to go too fast along the muddy road.

An hour more passed and Gereck despaired. He shivered beneath his cloak now, numb to the icy water soaking through. If he spent much longer in these conditions, he wouldn't have to trouble the Green Knight with killing him.

But then, when Gereck didn't come as agreed, the knight would assume Gereck's dishonor, and return to Camelot and take the king's life in exchange. He couldn't let that happen. Camelot must keep her king, especially now.

A light flickered far in the distance, between the hills, flashing as Gereck passed. He reined Fendrel in and backed the horse up until he could see the light again. The winding road ahead of him would take ages to bring him to the source of that light.

Leaving the road would prove the shortest distance, but doing so would risk Fendrel's legs on the uneven, wet ground.

It was that, or risk catching sickness and death by extending his time in the frigid rain and hoping to come across another form of shelter. Another shiver shook Gereck. He grasped Fendrel's reins and urged the horse to step off the mud-ridden road. Gereck never took his eyes off of the light burning faintly ahead.

By the time he passed between the hills, a large estate spread before him. The rain fell so hard, he thought he might be imagining it. A single window burned with light, in an upper room of the castle. A shadowy figure crossed it and Gereck raised his arm to draw the figure's attention. The movement set him off-balance, and he toppled from Fendrel's back and landed face-down in the mud.

Aches and fatigue surged through his body in debilitating waves. His mind reeled in exhaustion-induced fantasy, the taste of gritty mud in his mouth becoming a warm and meaty stew to his mind.

Winna's face came into view. She knelt at his side, an endearing look of worry on her lovely face. Then the face became Elaina's, and she leaned in to kiss him, but a man's voice called out to her and she turned away, leaving his lips burning.

Gereck heard voices, and several figures with lanterns surrounded him, but he couldn't get to his sword pinned beneath him. Praying they were friends, rather than enemies, Gereck let them carry him away.

When Gereck awoke, his body felt tremendously stiff, and his mind remained fuzzy from sleep. The enormous pressure in his head told him he had caught a bad cold, but at least he had managed to find a warm place before he passed out; he was covered with a soft blanket near a happily crackling fireplace.

A quiet humming drew his attention across the room, where a woman with honey-colored hair busied herself, adjusting a tray filled with dishes with her back to him.

Gereck cleared his throat and she turned. Gereck gasped. Her face was an image of beauty incarnate; cheeks so perfect they must have been sculpted and painted by an angel. No, she *was* an angel. The woman's lips spread into a smile so lovely it almost broke Gereck's heart, and yet simultaneously healed all of its wounds and sorrows.

"How is our mighty knight of Camelot?" The woman's voice seemed to sing in his ears. Gereck returned her smile.

"Mighty grateful. Thank you for bringing me in. I would have been in a right mess if I hadn't found this place. And special thanks to you, Lady...?"

"Lady Albree." She curtseyed, then picked up the tray and brought it over and set it on a side table nearby.

She helped him sit up, propping and fluffing pillows behind him until he was comfortable. Gereck breathed in her scent as she leaned across him to straighten his covers. It was as familiar as his own name. Musty, like the earth, like hay and dirt and... He looked up into her face, but she did not meet his eyes, instead looking at the tray as she set it in his lap.

"Can you manage the spoon and cup on your own?" she asked in her lilting voice.

"Yes," he responded, head feeling clouded again.

What had he just been thinking? He wasn't sure. He picked up the spoon and dipped it in the richly colored broth before him. He sipped it, to show Lady Albree that he was speaking truthfully, and she smiled, straightened her bright blue skirts, and turned away.

"I am glad you are doing so well. I would normally spend more time making your acquaintance, gallant knight, but I'm afraid I must tend to the affairs of my house. My lord will be by to greet you no doubt, and hear the news of Camelot."

Gereck nodded. "I thank you for your kindness."

"You are very welcome," she hesitated before the door. "Might I have your name?"

"Sir Gereck Bauer."

Her smile widened, and she dipped into a curtsey. "Sir Gereck, my pleasure." Then she left, closing the door behind her.

Gereck finished the broth, drank the contents of both cups on his tray, one a delightful spiced cider, the other a bitter herbal concoction, and then he lay down and fell into a deep and healing sleep.

When he woke again, daylight still came through the window, but how much time had passed? A sudden panic took him, and he sat up with a start.

"What day is it? How many days until Beltane?" He stammered.

Lady Albree came to his side and gently pushed him back into the bed. "It is the morning now. Beltane is in five days, including today. My lord is about to leave to hunt game for our feast. He will be pleased you woke before he left. I will tell him you are awake."

Lady Albree rushed to the door of his room and spoke to a servant outside. Moments later, the door opened again.

Gereck wasn't sure what he expected of the lord of the house, but the man who walked in wasn't it. He was tall and well-built, toned and clearly strong. His salt and pepper hair and beard were kept short, in the Roman style. He strode through the room with confidence and stared at Gereck, his stern, bright blue eyes gleaming.

Gereck immediately liked him, before the man even opened his mouth to speak.

"I am Lord Aldus."

"Sir Gereck."

Lord Aldus nodded. "Found yourself in quite the predicament, young knight, didn't you?"

"Yes, I did."

"Why didn't you stop at the last inn? The storm came in around the time you would have reached it."

"I was staying there, and in truth I knew the rain was probably coming, but I am on a quest where timing is imperative," Gereck replied.

The man's eyebrows raised, and he crossed his arms. "Is that true? What is the nature of your quest? Or is it for no other man to know?"

"An Emerald Knight challenged my king to a head game last Beltane. I took the challenge in his place, and was given the first strike, on the condition that I would take the return blow in a year and a day. My sword struck true, but the knight must have been an enchanter, for he took up his own head again even as it fell to the floor. Now I travel to keep my bargain, but I seek a location none seem to have heard of, and have only four days left to complete my quest."

"You value your honor above your life?"

"Yes."

"Do you have a wife? Children?"

"Yes," Gereck said again, more slowly.

"And you value your honor above their lives and well-being? You provide for them, do you not?" Gereck caught a glance between Lord Aldus and Lady Albree.

"They left our home near Camelot some months ago, and currently rely on a relative for their caretaking. I am certain they will be well enough off." Gereck lowered his head, guilt and sorrow crashing over him in a wave.

"To be honest, I was never a good husband or father. I've been chasing the dream of knighthood for months now, and only recently achieved the title. I've neglected my family terribly, something I had hoped to rectify, though now I'm not certain I'll be able to, for I have not found a way to avoid death, as the Green Knight did."

"I am amazed at men like you, Sir Gereck."

Gereck looked up. "What do you mean?"

"I mean men who will give up everything to prove honor. Their lives, their livelihood, their families..."

It was clear the man was trying to goad Gereck, and the words hit too close to the place Elaina's earlier words had struck.

"It is true that there is a balance that must be found," Gereck said, "and I certainly cannot claim to have found it, but no man can judge another's journey through life. We all do the best we can, and hope it was worth it in the end."

Lord Aldus's blue eyes seemed to twinkle in the morning light, and for a moment, Gereck thought the man's aging face seemed very familiar, but the moment passed and the glimmer was gone, and Lord Aldus stood, straight-backed and straight-faced, eyeing Gereck for a long time.

"Then I will ask you, sir knight, as you face your final days: has your journey been worthwhile?"

Gereck had pondered this question all the days between Camelot and here. His life was about to end, far sooner than he expected, and not many men knew the day and method by which they would be killed. But he did. How had he spent the past year? Were his pursuits worthy? Could his time have been given to something better, higher, nobler? The answer he had found troubled him.

"Yes, and no," Gereck replied. "There is one thing I would change, and yet, by changing that one thing I would alter the course my life has taken. It would mean I never could have met some people, and that I would have known others better, but if I did change that one thing, it would bring me greater happiness than I know now. I am certain of that."

Gereck took a deep breath, surprised at the emotion welling up inside of him. "So if you measure the worth of a man by his happiness, I suppose I could have done better, but there's nothing to be done for that now, except carry onward and hope whomever I meet on the other side judges me less harshly than I would judge myself."

Lord Aldus nodded, then smiled. He gestured at the door of the room, and a servant pushed it open, balancing a tray with two large goblets. The lord of the house took one goblet, silver and ornate, and handed it to Gereck. It was warm and smelled of heavy spices and an alcohol Gereck didn't recognize.

"Then a toast, to our friend Sir Gereck, a worthy knight of Camelot." They both drank. Gereck coughed as the drink burned his throat, but the flavor was excellent. He took another drink. The man cleared his throat. Gereck lowered the goblet.

"The Emerald Chapel I believe you seek is not far from here, a mere half a day's ride. You are not fit to travel, and as you have several days remaining to keep your bargain with the emerald knight, I invite you to stay the remainder of these few days."

Gereck nodded. "I am very grateful to you. I accept."

The man's smile broadened. "Very well, then. How about a little... agreement to bring some entertainment as you recover?"

"What type of wager do you suggest?" Gereck asked.

"Innocent fun, I assure you. Each day I will be gone hunting with my men. I will bring back meat for the Beltane feasts. You will be served a prime cut of meat from the day's hunting each night, which will aid your body in healing and strengthen you for your quest, if you agree to give me anything you receive in the castle in my absence."

Gereck furrowed his brow, but nodded. "I am not certain I will be given anything, but you are welcome to it, in exchange for such a generous offering."

"A toast to seal our agreement!"

The two men toasted again, and the second time, the drink did not burn so much. Lord Aldus drained his cup, smacking his lips as he did, then returned the goblet to the servant's tray. Gereck drank more, then clasped the hand Lord Aldus offered.

"I'm off to my hunt, and if I'm not mistaken, Lady Albree has arranged for some entertainment for you while you recover, my good knight. I will see you at dinner this evening! And remember our bargain." The man winked, and Gereck could have sworn his face changed, again becoming more familiar, but he couldn't quite put his finger on where he might have seen it before.

So instead, he bid the man farewell and good fortune on his hunt, and put the issue of changing faces out of his mind, more than happy to turn his focus on the lovely Lady Albree.

"I do hope you like music," she said, clapping her hands. Three musicians entered and set up their instruments. A harp, a drum, and a flute.

"Where did you find musicians here, at the end of the world?" Gereck joked. He had personally only seen musicians at festivals in the crowded city of Camelot.

"Very few know of my deep love of music, and where I lived before music was considered a lavish thing, an excessive pleasure, but once I came here I was determined to have it. I found some talent among the servants, and together we've practiced until, from what I've been told, we're quite pleasing to hear. Would you mind?"

Gereck shook his head. "Not at all."

He settled back in the pillows and closed his eyes. It was a unique experience to be serenaded personally, like he was a lord or king, deserving of special attention. He was determined to enjoy it, and as the first notes were played, he let himself be drawn in.

The first song was purely instrumental, upbeat and cheerful, and Gereck felt his heart being lifted. Music was an incredible thing. Almost like magic, his muscles relaxed and the aching in his bones faded away.

Then Lady Albree sang. It was a song of the quiet love between an old man and his wife. The story was one Gereck had never heard. The man was watching his wife die, old age finally taking its advantage and sending her to her grave.

It seemed to be meant as a duet, one part the older man's, the other part the woman's, but Lady Albree sang both equally well, and Gereck found his heart filling with the sound and the story, and even wiped tears from his face now and again.

The story ended with the old man burying his wife and seeing their children gathered around, his hope for their future and the love he shared with his wife bringing a bright end to the song. Lady Albree's voice lifted above that of the instruments, clear and bright in the final notes, and shockingly familiar.

Gereck was thrown into a memory, one of the few times he had been given a week's leave to be with his family. He remembered Winna humming, sometimes singing, as she scrubbed the dishes, the floor, sometimes the children, or while she made supper, or while she mended the tunics he brought to her.

He had asked her if she sang like that all the time, and until this moment, he hadn't really thought about her reply.

She had said, "Only when I think of you."

It had been sentimental at the time, one of those things she said that made him smile, but now Gereck could see what her singing really was; a declaration of love to him, something that had carried Winna through the days he was gone.

Tears filled his eyes as he thought of her. Did she think of him now? Was there a tune on her lips, or in her heart? It had been months since he had seen her, and she had nothing but an empty guarantee that he would return to her. A guarantee that, indeed, meant nothing, since he had no way to survive the blow the Green Knight would serve in four days' time.

The music trailed to an end, another song finished that Gereck didn't recall hearing. Lady Albree knelt beside the bed and took his hand in hers.

"My dear knight, why are you crying?"

He looked at her and tried to smile. "Your song was beautiful. My wife... My wife would have loved it."

Her eyes looked into his, wide and innocent, brown as a doe's. "You must miss her."

Gereck took a deep breath. "Not as much, recently, as I should have." Bitterness leaked out in his voice. He never should have entertained pretend as he had with Elaina. He should have gotten someone else to help her, should have tried harder to keep their relationship more aloof. "My loneliness led me to find comfort in another woman's company. I never betrayed my marriage physically, but emotionally... any bishop could find me guilty of the worst of sins."

The woman stroked his hand. "You sound as if you wish you could change it."

"Yes, I would. I would that I had spent these months pining after my sweetheart, my Winna. Instead, I tried to recreate the love I had with her in the fantasy realms of my mind. I regret it immensely."

"I am sure your wife would understand."

"But I'll never get to explain it to her." A long silence filled the room. The musicians, Gereck noticed, had taken their instruments and left, leaving him alone with the lady of the house. "You know, when a knight of Camelot is slain, the king will send a party of his companions to the house of the knight's family. They will bear his body, if they have it, or simply his sword, shield, and other possessions. They extend their condolences to the family, and a feast is thrown at their home, all provisions gifted by the king.

"All of my possessions are with me, and I'm not certain what the Green Knight will have done with my body. Not to mention the kingdom being under constant threat by the Saxons. I wonder if the king will even send his knights on behalf of a man who was knighted for mere days. Will they even know where my family lives now, if she'll be told at all that I've completed my quest and died? And if they did manage to find her, and they did provide such a service, I wonder if Winna will shed any tears on my behalf? Part of me feels that she has already cried her tears, when I did not go with them those months ago. It's not really fair, then, for me to expect any more, but I wish I had something for her, to tell her I've gone. And that I loved her to the end, even though it must not have seemed like it."

Lady Albree straightened, a solemn look on her face. "This may seem morbid, but I could have your body fetched from the Emerald Chapel. You can tell this

Emerald Knight that you've made arrangements, and my lord's men will retrieve it, if he's willing. You can tell us where to find your wife, and Lord Aldus will be sure to lead the funeral procession to her new home, and gift her the feast she would have if King Arthur had made the arrangements."

Gereck stared at her, a knot tying itself in his throat. "You would do that? But I am a stranger."

Lady Albree smiled. "A stranger of the best kind; one who is honest, and noble, and good. I'll have my maid bring in some parchment and pen, you can write where your wife lives now, and what you wish her to know. I'll be sure it's delivered."

"Thank you," Gereck managed around the lump of emotion that had built up.

"You are welcome."

The lady stood and walked toward the door, but then paused and turned back. The look in her eyes was full of sadness, and Gereck also thought he saw longing, but before he could make anything of it, the lady rushed to his side, leaned down, and kissed him full on the lips.

Her lips were warm, and again the familiar, homey scent filled him. Before he could identify it, she separated and fled from the room, her shoes echoing down the corridor as she ran.

Lord Aldus returned home in the late afternoon. The castle was put into a frenzy to accommodate the men and the catch they had brought in. Footsteps rushed past his door for quite a time, until gradually the excitement died down and his part of the castle seemed almost deserted.

No one visited until the darkness had descended outside, and a servant came to light the lanterns in his room. He asked after Lady Albree, but was given a short reply about the preparations she was seeing to, and then the servant bowed out without so much as telling him when he could expect dinner.

And so, his body too spent with illness for him to get up and explore or be much help, Gereck slept. It was a fitful, strange sleep, spotted with dreams filled with people needing him, asking him to help them, but when he went to aid them he found his arms missing, or unable to lift his sword.

Then Elaina was there, begging him to believe her, to tell Arthur he was in danger, but Lancelot ran her through with a sword and her face became Winna's. Lancelot mocked Gereck for his tears, then the Green Knight was there, standing over Gereck with his gleaming emerald axe, and he brought it down…

"Sir knight? Sir?"

Gereck came flailing out of the covers, hand grasping for his sword, but it wasn't where he usually kept it at his bedside. He rubbed his eyes and looked around the room. For that matter, he had no idea where it was right now. Perhaps Lady Albree was having it sharpened? He focused his eyes back on the servant who had woken him. A plump-faced older woman wearing a very concerned look.

"Yes, then. What is it?" He sounded cross, he knew. He *felt* cross, as if he hadn't gotten enough sleep, but judging by the lanterns lit in his room, it was well past dark. He must have slept for hours.

"Supper has begun. The master and his lady are expecting you, but perhaps I should have it brought?"

"No, no, that's all right." Gereck cursed under his breath and threw off the bed covers. He was late to dinner. It wouldn't do to represent Camelot so poorly, especially with the hospitality he had been shown. "I'll just… I mean…" He was still in his underclothes. The heat rose to his face, and he pulled the blankets back over his bottom half. "I'm not certain I'm fit for company, at the moment. My clothes, if I had them, are travel-worn and nothing to impress."

"His lordship is not easily offended, sir knight. He would rather have your company than not, I assure you. Allow me to look around a bit, aye? I'm certain I can find something suitable." She eyed him up and down carefully, twice, then turned to leave. "I just filled your basin with warm, clean water. Have a wash up if you can manage it, and I'll be back in a moment."

Gereck waited until she had closed the door behind her, then stood, testing his legs' strength. They seemed to hold him well enough. He walked stiffly to the stoneware basin, leaning on the table it rested upon. He was weak, but recovering. The fever seemed to be gone, at least. He splashed his face, neck, and arms, noticing a slight scent to the water. Something spicy he couldn't identify. It made his skin tingle.

A knock at the door sent him hobbling back to the bed, where he grabbed the sheets before calling out for the maidservant to enter. It was a man this time.

"Miss Helda had me come to assist you. I have a chair waiting, as well." Gereck could see the edge of an odd-looking chair just beyond the doorway. It seemed to have wheels, like a wagon.

Ah, then he wouldn't have to walk. His relief was immediate, and he smiled. "Thank you, er…?" He trailed off, expecting the man's name.

"Geoffrey."

"Yes, thank you, Geoffrey." Gereck reached for the clothes, but the man suddenly turned to the side and laid the clothing out on the bed.

"If you do not mind, I would offer my services to you. I am Lord Aldus's personal serving man, and would be honored to dress you." Geoffrey bowed.

Gereck nodded, after a moment's consideration. "I am accustomed to dressing myself, but I won't begrudge your offer. My muscles ache something fierce."

Geoffrey got to work. There seemed to be too many articles of clothing for Gereck to possibly wear, but they somehow all found a place. Gereck was certain he never would have figured it out on his own. At the end of it, when Geoffrey led him to a tall looking glass at the other end of the room, Gereck certainly looked sharp. Like any nobleman, he imagined, and it felt rather nice not to wear armor for once.

Once Gereck was seated in the wheeled chair, Geoffrey took him to the dining hall, pushing him as if he weighed nothing at all. Gereck was impressed, and grateful he didn't have to walk to the other end of the castle.

The doors of the hall opened before him, and all of the guests at the table turned to look at the new arrival. Gereck's cheeks flushed as Geoffrey wheeled him in, taking him directly to a seat on the other side of Lord Aldus. He parked the chair in the empty space and bowed first to Gereck, then to Lord Aldus, who dismissed him with a friendly smile.

"Well, Sir Gereck. How have you found your accommodations?"

"More than adequate, Lord Aldus. And how was your hunt?" Gereck asked, as a plate was set before him. He reached for his fork, then hesitated, noticing the portion of meat on his plate appeared different than any other plate on the table. The liver of the animal sat alongside a beautifully prepared cut of meat.

Lord Aldus cleared his throat. “I have kept my end of our little bargain, Sir Gereck. Did you receive anything in my castle today to give in exchange?”

Gereck opened his mouth to say no, then stopped. He stared at Lord Aldus, then glanced at Lady Albree. His heart pounded, and he took a deep breath. His mouth felt dry. He licked his lips. “I received the greatest of hospitality, to be sure, but so far as something I could give you…” He stood from his chair, hoping his legs held him, leaned across the table and planted a kiss square on the man’s lips.

The table erupted in laughter. Lord Aldus sputtered and wiped his lips, then joined in, roaring and pounding the table. Gereck sat, face beet red.

Lord Aldus’ blue eyes twinkled. Again, there was a flash of familiarity in his gaze, but then it was gone. “Who gave you that?! No, don’t tell me. I’ll guess it. I’m certain it was one of my maids. I’ll have it by tomorrow night, I’m sure.” He seemed merry enough. Gereck wondered if he would be so merry if he ever did work out who had given it.

CHAPTER TWENTY-EIGHT

Gereck woke the second day and was immediately aware of Lady Albree sitting beside him, doing some mending. He had never seen a lady do mending. Embroidery, yes, but never mending. She noticed him awake and smiled, setting the cloth and needle aside.

"You are probably wondering why I am doing servants' work."

He nodded.

Lady Albree shrugged. "I enjoy it, actually. Even with all of my other responsibilities. I never did enjoy embroidery, not when I could be doing something helpful with my skills in thread and needle. So, I mend. It keeps me humble." She clasped her hands together. "So, sir knight, what will it be today?"

"Lady Albree, I must speak to you about..."

She held a finger up to her lips, eyes sparkling with mischief. "If it's about yesterday afternoon, no need to speak. And please know, I am faithful to my husband."

"But..."

"None of that, now. How about a game?" She stood and walked to a cabinet, pulling out a wooden box. The top was painted in two alternating colors of squares. She slid it open on the bedside table, and Gereck saw small round wooden disks. Checkers. He smiled. He had whittled a game similar to this for himself and Winna. They had played every time he went home during his years as a squire.

"I would enjoy playing you. I am sure you're a worthy opponent."

They talked as they played, Lady Albree asking him about his home life. He told her about Cai and Ada, about their farm and how Winna would rather live there than any palace. Lady Albree laughed at that, saying every woman dreams of finer things, but Gereck insisted.

He knew his wife. She preferred the animals and the simple life caring for them provided. Lady Albree was unconvinced, but said she admired working women. The way she said it made Gereck think she would have preferred to be among them, but she stopped short of admitting it and he decided not to assume anything.

"I myself appreciate a good horse. We have good stables here."

"Fendrel!" Gereck said suddenly. "My horse. How is he?"

"Is that his name? Better off than you. He is healthy and eating well. I think he is concerned about you."

"What makes you say that?"

"I have a sense for these things. Would you like to go see him?"

"Yes, but perhaps tomorrow? I am feeling tired now and would like to sleep."

Lady Albree packed away the game, leaving it on the table. "Good." She stood up. "One last thing before I go, sir knight."

Again, before Gereck could voice any protest, she leaned in and kissed him, her lips light and warm against his. She withdrew, then brought her lips down again. He pulled away immediately, and she managed to whisk herself across the room so quickly that she closed the door on his sputtered objections.

His dreams were mixed with images of the Green Knight and his gleaming axe, alongside Lady Albree's face. He wasn't sure which one he was afraid of the most. Why did the lady kiss him? Did she fancy herself in love with a knight? Was her marriage unhappily arranged? Or did her kisses have some other meaning, aside from strong affection?

Gereck's mind felt muddled and unhappy thinking about it. Awake and sitting up in bed, waiting for Geoffrey to come dress him for dinner, he had nothing more to do. He thought of Winna. Had he betrayed her?

Would she ever forgive him?

Would he even live to confess it to her?

He had been so determined, from the moment he went to say farewell to Elaina, that he would be faithful in his final days. Now it seemed this woman, Lady Albree, would make that impossible. He decided it would not happen again. If he had to refuse her company, he would. He would be faithful; Winna deserved that much from him.

Geoffrey finally arrived with an array of fine clothing similar to the night before. They were a handsome green color, like a forest of trees. Gereck admired himself in the mirror, glad he could stand on his own without trembling as a leaf. He insisted on walking, refusing the wheeled chair Geoffrey had brought again, and though he moved at a snail's pace, he was able to walk into the hall on his own two feet, just as the feast had begun.

He took his seat at Lord Aldus's side and, as before, a plate of steaming, juicy meat, of the finest cut, took up much of his plate. He looked at the man, who looked at him with expectant eyes gleaming. Gereck mustered his courage and, before sitting, gave the man exactly what he had received in the castle that day.

The table roared with laughter, Lord Aldus joining in with a hearty laugh. He clapped Gereck's shoulder as he sat down, and spent much of the meal making guesses as to who had kissed Gereck in the first place. Was it a different maid than the day before? Was she a ghost? Gereck shook his head at the ridiculousness of some of the speculations, carefully not making eye contact with Lady Albree across the table, whose expression was alight with amusement, making her even more beautiful than ever.

The talk turned to the hunt, to the fields and the hoped-for harvest. Gereck tuned them out, relishing the good food and trying to keep his thoughts from being too depressed. He was fortunate to be so well cared for in his final days.

Despite his best efforts, it was long after he remembered the fate that awaited him that he asked to be excused, retired to his room and undressed before climbing into bed. He pulled the covers over him, avoiding his own thoughts until he drifted off at last.

The sun shone brightly into the room when he woke the next morning; day three. The final day before he would journey to the Emerald Chapel and face the Green Knight for his return blow.

He tried not to think about it. A maid came to the room with a set of plain clothes, and said his presence was requested in the stables. When questioned, she wouldn't tell him who had sent for him, but he felt certain he knew.

He found Lady Albree waiting for him at the stable doors, dressed in a gown made for riding, but no less regal on her.

"I have been taking some of the less-ridden horses out for exercise all morning. I thought you might enjoy giving your Fendrel a ride, if you are up for it."

Gereck nodded. His thoughts, as much as he tried to ignore them, weighed heavily on his mind, but a ride would put them off. He insisted on saddling his own steed, then mounted and rode alongside Lady Albree in silence. She remained silent for much of the ride, perhaps sensing his mood, and then started to talk about this and that, nothing serious or requiring any response. Gereck was grateful.

They stopped briefly to picnic, meeting a small group of servants in a forest clearing. It was quiet and warm, and wonderful to be outside, to feel the sun. Gereck let it warm his face, and he listened to the birds. Everything seemed brighter, and perhaps it was due to his impending fate. Death, it seemed, put everything in a new perspective.

The sun reached high when they headed back toward the keep. Exhausted and yet somehow refreshed, Gereck thanked Lady Albree for the ride with genuine gratitude. She pulled her horse to a stop at the top of the last hill, wind blowing her honey-colored hair around her face.

"I have enjoyed our time together, Sir Gereck, I would have you stay longer if fate allowed."

"I cannot," Gereck said shortly, discomfort making his chest tight.

An indecipherable expression crossed her lovely face. She reached a hand out and rested it on his knee. "I wish you the best fortune, then, and hope death is swift and kind."

"I wish the same for you, milady, preceded by a long and happy life." He paused, then, "Do you think you will have children?"

She laughed, then. "But I already do! I suppose I never mentioned that, and they aren't here to meet you. They are away for the festival, visiting a cousin of mine and getting some schooling. I am sorry you couldn't see them."

"As am I."

He thought of Cai, the way he cried when Gereck had taken his leave, and Ada… she would never really know her father. The emotion welled up inside him, attempting to push its way out through his tears. He brushed them away quickly and tried to cover up his sniffling.

"It is all right to cry, sir knight."

"I would rather not, all the same. It will not change anything."

"It may make it easier," Lady Albree replied.

Gereck said nothing, but stared down the hill toward the stables.

"I have something for you," Lady Albree suddenly spoke.

"I do not think that is a good idea, milady," Gereck replied warily. Fendrel sidestepped beneath him, sensing his anxiety. If it came down to it, he would make the horse run to avoid betraying Winna and Lord Aldus again.

"It is not what you think." She rummaged in a saddlebag and drew forth a green sash. "It is simply this."

"A favor?" Gereck asked, taking it from her. "It seems too nice a thing for that."

Her brown eyes gazed at him, wide and gentle, like a doe's. "It is a magic girdle," she whispered. "Whoever wears it will be protected against any weapon."

Gereck gripped the silken material in his hands. "You would give me this?" His heart swelled with excitement. Perhaps he was not fated to die after all?

She nodded, almost shyly. "Yes. It is mine to give, and I want you to have it. The Green Knight used enchantment to survive your blow, now you have something to withstand his. My only request is this: receive his blow and leave this place. Do not look back, do not hesitate, but return to your wife and your children and live out your days with them."

"I will. I will bring them to Camelot with me, fulfill my duties as a knight and come home to them each day." Tears stung his eyes. "I can never repay you, milady, and I will never forget your kindness."

"If you do as I ask, you will repay me tenfold. I desire your happiness, Gereck."

"Surely there is some way I can show my gratitude?"

"One thing," she replied.

She nudged her horse closer to his, leaned over, tilted her head, and looked at him expectantly. Her proximity overwhelmed him. Perhaps it was the influence of Beltane, or that her visage was so like Winna's in that moment that it caused Gereck to let go of his inhibitions, close his eyes, and kiss her. Her scent carried past him on the wind: hay and musk, and he could imagine that he truly kissed Winna.

Lady Albree separated, but Gereck reached for her, pulling her as close to him as he could manage. He reached his mind out to Winna across the miles, putting his whole apology to her into the embrace he shared with Lady Albree, wishing he held his wife.

They stopped, breathless, and their foreheads touched. Lady Albree glanced upward, and her lips found Gereck's one final time, a sweet, short, gentle kiss. And then they parted, their horses both growing restless on the hilltop.

They made their way in silence, returning their steeds to the stables and going separate ways. Gereck remained outside for some time afterward, walking the grounds, taking everything in.

The blue sky. The gray clouds on the horizon. The trees, waving in the wind. The warm spring air.

He gave Fendrel a good brushing, made sure he was well fed, and made the decision to leave him in Lord Aldus's care. If the sash didn't work, for some reason, he would want Fendrel to be well taken care of. He sought out the stable master and informed him, also thanking him for his services.

Then he returned to the castle, procured his own clothing from a maidservant, and changed into it, glad at last to be wearing the familiar, humbly-spun cloth. He tied the sash beneath his clothes, out of sight, lest anyone question him about it.

The time for dinner arrived. Gereck refused Geoffrey's offer of finer clothing, thanking him for everything. The manservant bowed deeply and led him to the feasting hall. It was in full celebration, the feasting and merriment almost contagious. Gereck found himself smiling. He sat at his seat to the left of Lord Aldus, and looked at his plate. It contained nothing different than anyone else's. He looked at Lord Aldus, who shrugged.

"It was an unfortunate hunt today, I am afraid. We obtained nothing but this old fox skin." He picked it up from the floor to show Gereck. "It is yours, of course. In exchange for what you received today."

Gereck tried not to think about what he was doing as he planted three kisses straight on the lord's lips. The man sputtered, clearly beside himself.

"Is that all?" Lord Aldus said, laughing. "Who has been kissing you, my lad? There are no secrets in my hall." The entire table seemed to fall silent in anticipation.

Gereck glanced across the table at the Lady Albree, whose fork played with her food on her plate. She did not look up at him.

"It must have been a faerie, Sir Aldus, for I have never seen her like, and I am likely to never see her again."

Conversation resumed. His response was accepted, though Lord Aldus's eyes seemed tight around the edges.

He could hardly listen to the conversation around him. The sash burned at his waist, and several times, he almost took it off and admitted his withholding it, but the thought of living to see Winna again was too tempting.

He ate the food, which was certainly just as good as the previous nights, but it tasted wooden in his mouth, his guilt turning the flavor bitter. He finished his meal and immediately requested to retire from the revelry, to which Lord Aldus agreed, saying he needed the rest before his journey on the morrow.

Gereck fell into his bed fully clothed, grateful for the rural location of Lord Aldus's keep. He couldn't hear the drums of Beltane as loudly as they often sounded in Camelot. He sensed a faint pulse of them somewhere in the far distance, but it was only enough to make him aware of the energy of the night, and that was enough to keep him awake for a long time.

CHAPTER TWENTY-NINE

When Guinevere woke, something soft and heavy lay across her body. Her breath immediately seized in her body.

It was a blanket. A thick blanket made of patched fur. A fire was lit in the grate next to the bed. A table nearby held a metal pitcher and two cups. The room flickered in firelight, and she had to wait a moment for her eyes to adjust before she could see into the darker corners. They were empty, except for one. A chair, occupied by a man with fair hair and a twisted, smirking face. She gasped and pulled the covers up, only now noticing that she was naked, but clean.

"Look at her now, the regal Queen Guinevere," the man drawled. His speech was strange in her ears, not a dialect she had heard before. "So pious even her own husband hasn't touched her, and now..." He chuckled. "We shall see if he still wants her. He'll have to get in line, of course."

Guinevere let out a small, gasping sob, covering her mouth with her hand. The man's eyes glittered and he smiled.

"Turns out Camelot's lion-hearted king chose a church mouse for a wife. What would he say if he were here now? Not that he will come, no, I do not think he would want you, even if he weren't busy elsewhere. Better for him to give you up for dead and choose a worthy queen, one who can give a man what he needs."

It was strangely quiet in Guinevere's mind. The silence she had longed for over many months disturbed her now. She expected Morgan to voice her opinion any moment, to feel the familiar anger flare up, anger that was not her own but somehow lent her strength... Except, it wasn't there. Nothing was there. Morgaine's bitterness, little Morgause's fear, nothing. What had happened while she was inside? How much time had transpired? There was no one to tell her.

"Who are you?" Guinevere managed, her voice quivering. She straightened up, keeping the covers pulled up. "Why would you do this?"

"I am enemy to Arthur, the instigator of your capture and torture. What else to you need to know?"

Guinevere stared at his face. Where had she seen it before?

"The wedding," she said. "You were there, weren't you?" She racked her mind for the name. She remembered seeing him, standing in line, grinning at her lasciviously. It had made her skin crawl. And she remembered the look Arthur had given him, the white-knuckled grip on her arm as he accepted the man's congratulations.

"Lord Melwas!"

The man inclined his head at her. "Indeed."

"But then, why me?" Guinevere asked, trying desperately to discover memories of her capture. The last thing she recalled was her conversation with Nimue, who was also Niviane the sorceress, but nothing since. Had it been days or had it perhaps been months? Years?

"You aren't listening, Queen Guinevere." The man stood from his chair and Guinevere shrank back into her covers, but he only crossed the room and picked up a poker for the fire, adjusting the burning logs within, sending sparks flying into the air as they collapsed. He added another piece, then walked back to his chair.

"Are you? I thought it might be obvious, your capture. You are a desirable pawn. Especially for someone who wishes to distract a king and his knights. If he is foolish enough to come after you, he will waste time and resources that, at this point in the game, are vital. We shall see if he does. Until then, and forever if he does not, you are mine to play with. A pastime I shall enjoy, I assure you."

He grinned then, and his teeth gleamed in the firelight, even across the room. He came closer, unbuckling his pants languidly, eyes never leaving her. "Long have I admired your beauty, Lady Guinevere, and often dreamt of having you here at my pleasure, and now I do."

He crawled onto the bed, and Guinevere tried to back away, but her bare back met the cold stone wall beside the bed. Nowhere to run. Melwas paused in his advance. "I must be honest, though. For all the rumors of your spitfire nature, you have turned out to be meek as a church mouse. Disappointing as that may be, I may never have you at such an advantage again, and therefore I will take you as I find you."

Guinevere's mind froze with terror. Morgan surged forward, but Guinevere slammed her from taking control. She needed to keep her mind as her own. She needed to think of a way to escape.

She brought the fur blankets up to her chin like a shield, even as she realized that they would do nothing to stop the coming assault.

A week later, Guinevere had given up hope. She lay in bed most of the day, and gradually, visits from Melwas dropped off. She was no longer a novelty, and that fact relieved her, but she was still a prisoner, and Arthur had not come.

Neither, for that matter, had Lancelot, although she was certain he would make no extra effort on her part. She could hear Morgan's thoughts, feel her confusion and pain. Why did Lancelot not come? Had he ever loved her truly?

Her door opened. Guinevere didn't move, except to turn her head. Melwas. He didn't even speak to her, but removed his boots, his cloak, his shirt, clear in his intent.

Not again.

"Did you think I had forgotten you?" Melwas drawled. "I was out with my men. We're dealing with some skirmishes between Saxons and your king's men."

He stoked the fire, adding several logs. "Do not get any hopes in your pretty head, he's not coming this way. He is caught in a struggle to maintain the ground he has. No advances are being made in our direction. Your king is a wise man, not wasting any energy coming after you,"

Guinevere watched him reach for his buckle and felt her stomach heave. Her body was trembling, remembering the other times she had been used.

"How did...How did you...Why the Saxons?" she stammered.

Melwas frowned.

She continued breathlessly. "I mean, why combine forces with them? What does that give you?"

"A bigger piece of the kingdom when they take over, darling, and my lands will be untouched by war. Haven't you figured that out yet? And you'll be glad to know, Sir Lancelot has given me an even bigger part in it than that."

"Sir Lancelot?" Guinevere murmured, confused. "What does he…?"

Melwas laughed, his hands on his hips. "My, you are daft. A betrayal happening right under your nose. Lancelot is leading the knights to rebellion. They will join the Saxons, let them into the inner keep of Camelot, to slaughter your king. They would slaughter you too, if you were there, so you might be grateful I have you here, with me.

"In any case, your being here is actually premature. Lancelot might be peeved about that, but the plan took too long to execute. I thought I might… hurry it along." His eyes gazed at her hungrily, stripping her bare by looking.

Guinevere pulled her blankets more tightly around her and huddled against the wall behind the bed. She was so tired of being used.

"Please," she said, her voice cracking. "Please, just… leave me alone."

Melwas stepped towards her, ignoring her plea. His hands fumbled again with the belt holding his trousers up. They dropped to the floor.

Let me. A voice whispered in her mind, and in her shock, Guinevere let Morgan slip through and take control of their body.

Suddenly, she stood, blankets falling to the ground. "Do not touch me." Her voice held a cold and commanding tone. It sounded almost foreign to her ears.

At that thought, Guinevere felt the presence of two others step up beside her in her mind. Her mind's eye saw them, a young girl, no more than nine, and the second in her early marriageable years. The girl took hold of Guinevere's hand and smiled up at her on her right. On her left, the young woman gripped her other hand.

Standing before her, Melwas grinned. "I was afraid you'd had it all beaten out of you. A bit of fire always makes it more enjoyable." He grabbed her arms, forcing her towards the floor.

In that swift moment, she remembered. They all remembered. The abuse. The hiding. The fear. The anger. The hurt. It flooded through her with such force she gasped. It combined with the memories of what Melwas had done, and at last Guinevere understood.

She was brought back by a mouth crushing against hers. She struggled, then went limp, letting him fall on top of her. His filthy hands scrabbled against her. She had to do something.

Fire blossomed in her chest. Not the fire of passion that came when she was with Lancelot, or when she saw Arthur, but a different sort altogether... sorcery. Guinevere balked. *This* was inside of her? She fought it, tried to regain control. Morgan approached her. *I finally understand, Guinevere. We have power within us that can only be used if we work together. I promise, we will not be victims this time.*

Guinevere stopped. She felt no malice in Morgan's words.

Do what you must. And she gave control willingly over to Morgan for the first time since she had known of her existence.

We are one. Morgan said, and power surged through them.

They faced their attacker together, and in her mind, Guinevere saw their faces, each the same, and yet different, containing separate memories and experiences, and then the faces blurred until it was just her and Morgan, and she realized what she had to do. She let go, truly, at last, and forever. Because she, herself, was an alter too. She had started as Morgan, in another life. Morgan was who she was meant to be. She was whole.

"*Cnamh tallaght!*"

Melwas's eyes widened. Then he laughed. "What did you do? Curse me?"

"Something like that." Her right fist came up and caught the side of his face. He cursed and she rolled, pushing him off her. She jumped to her feet in an instant and ran for the door.

"Guards, to me!" Melwas yelled. He struggled to his feet and stumbled after her as she reached the doorway. Men poured into the room. She moved away, their weapons pointed at her. Melwas's horrible teeth grinned at her. "The man who immobilizes her gets his way with her first."

The men broke out in a frenzy. They shoved and pushed their way into the room, surrounding her. Spears, swords, and axes all pointed in her direction. The fire went out in her chest as terror surged inside her. Instead of fighting it as she might have before, she stalled and searched inside for her magic.

"Think about what you're doing, Melwas," she called out. "Without me, you lose your position in bargaining with King Arthur. How will you get what you want?"

"The plan wasn't to bargain but to lure him near enough to destroy him with my armies. I have word that he is already on his way. When he gets here..." Melwas grinned. "We will be waiting, and you will be dead."

There, a spark. She grasped her magic and held onto it. "I don't think so," she snarled, holding her hands up.

She couldn't spell them all at once, unused for so long, her powers weren't strong enough for that, but she would take down as many as she could.

Melwas shrieked; the spell she had laid took its effect. He fell to his knees, grasping at his chest, his arms, his legs. "What have you done to me?" he croaked. She grinned, but could not respond as the first man lunged for her, jabbing with his spear.

Shouting began outside the corridor, but she ignored it, and spoke two words and muttered a prayer to the Goddess. The man slumped to the floor, his neck broken. She felt the fire inside flicker. It had taken more power than she thought to kill that one. Her reserves were faltering, and the fight had barely begun. She took the legs out from under another man, the eyes from a third. Her fire was small, like a candle flame.

Men poured into the room, replacing each man that fell. Exhaustion crept in on her focus. The flame sputtered. A spear caught her side and she cried out, falling to her knees. A sweeping motion of her arm caused the man's intestines to burst; he died instantly. Another took his place, pressing towards her with lust in his eyes. Outside, the shouting grew louder. She looked up over the heads of stinking, filthy men and saw chaos in the corridor.

An axe handle struck her head, blinding her with pain. The men closed in around her. This was it. A dagger scraped across her ribs. A fist caught her jaw, blood filled her mouth, and then their hands were on her, fighting amongst themselves for possession of her. A body spread itself over her, claiming her.

"Would you make love to a corpse?" She spat blood in the man's face. Her body was on fire, but her own fire, the power of the Goddess, was gone from her. The man grinned toothlessly, his breath dank.

"You're not dead yet," he leered, and then the expression froze on his face.

He slumped and she pushed him off of her. The men who had gathered were now scattered, each fighting a silver-clad knight.

It was Arthur. The king. He had come for her. Guinevere's heart welled up inside of her, overwhelmed that she could feel everything as her own, without the confused muddle of other voices, contrary feelings. . She truly loved him, with a love that paled in comparison with the lust-love that she shared with Mordred. Tears sprang to her eyes with the goodness of the feeling, blurring her vision.

A body fell across her, one of Melwas's men. Guinevere struggled to get up, to push the corpse off, but her body was spent. Her soul reached toward Arthur, begging him to look at her.

He turned and saw her, his eyes growing wide at the blood on her naked form. He dispatched the man he had been fighting and shouted to the knights. Guinevere couldn't hear what he said. Her head swam. Someone grabbed her and she shouted, fighting the hands. He was so close, she was almost free, they would not have her...

"Queen Guinevere, it's me! Hold on!" He had a cloak that he wrapped her in before picking her up. Did she know that voice? Not Arthur, not Mordred; someone else.

"Sir Perceval?" she whispered, gazing into his face.

The face smiled. "Aye, that's me, Your Majesty."

"Oh," she sighed, then slumped against his chest as he carried her from the room. The knights followed him, cutting back Melwas's men as they retreated. They had what they had come for.

The torches on the walls swam before her. Pain numbed, her eyes darkening. "Arthur..." she muttered. She came in and out of the darkness, aware of horses, and riding, and agonizing pain.

When Guinevere woke again, she rode encircled in the arms of the king himself. She sat before him in the saddle, curled tightly against his chest. Her own chest was thickly bandaged, and ached abominably from the scrapes she had taken in the fight. She shut out every sound she could as they rode; the sound of other men talking, the birds chirping. She was shivering, trembling more from fear and aftershock than the cold.

Arthur did not speak, even after he had noticed she was awake. The thoughts that occupied her surprised her, that they were her own. Was Arthur angry with her? Did he blame her? Or was it simply the fact that she was spoiled now, spoiled before they had ever been intimate together, and other men had stolen the privilege and taken advantage where Arthur had waited and, for the most part, been kind... Did he regret the months of waiting?

Did he hate her?

She reached out in her mind, seeking Guinevere, to know if these feelings were actually from her, but her mind was like an empty field, nothing to hear but her own thoughts, and since the adrenaline of her magic seemed to have leached from her, those were scattered and filled with apprehension.

Gradually, she opened herself up to the conversations around her, and she learned they had three days of riding ahead of them. Surely Arthur would speak to her before then? She found herself hoping, desperate as a maiden waiting to hear from a recent suitor.

Her hope was well rewarded that night. The party stopped after dark and set up a small tent. No doubts about whom they intended it for. Guinevere retired within and found a dress laid out, plain-colored and woven of a heavy material. She pulled it on over her aching body and crawled into bed, not bothering to put out the small lantern lighting the tent's interior. . She pulled the covers around her body like a cocoon and her insides, raw and vulnerable, opened up to her tears and she cried. Her body trembled violently.

She exhausted her tears and slipped into sleep, but the nightmares that lurked behind her closed eyes came rushing into her mind with such force they thrusted her into wakefulness, and she vomited over the side of the makeshift bed. The sour bile burned her throat and mouth. She wished for water, but what would the men outside think of their queen if they saw her in such a state?

Pride kept her from calling out for help. After all, asking for help had gotten her into this mess, wasn't it? If she had never sought out Niviane's aid, for magic to have revenge on her brothers, if she had never sought Niviane's advice for keeping Elaina safe, she wouldn't be here, regretting every moment since.

She cried more, this time quietly, the tears trailing down her face. She avoided sleep, pinching herself to keep awake until the fire outside her tent burned low and she heard one of Arthur's men mention sleep, and they discussed the night watch while someone went to gather more firewood.

The expected shadow appeared at the tent's forefront, backlit by the low-burning fire as he opened the tent flap. Guinevere felt her body tense, and she shrank further into the covers when he walked in.

"I'm sorry," he said quietly, clasping his arms behind his back. She didn't respond, and he must have thought she was sleeping, for he turned as if to leave the tent.

"Arthur?" she said suddenly. He stopped and looked back at her. She swallowed, still tasting bile. "Me too."

He walked over and knelt by her bed. His face appeared dark and serious in the dim light. Her lantern flickered, almost out of oil. He found one of her hands and took it in both of his, and cupping it, brought it to his lips.

"It isn't your fault. None of it is."

His apology dissolved on her guilty heart. She shook her head, unable to speak. Arthur's hand rested on her face, and she looked at him. "It is never your fault when something like this happens."

To her horror, tears welled up in her eyes.

"How can you say that?" she whispered hoarsely. "How do you know?"

He took a deep breath. "Men like Melwas have one aim: domination. He took you from me the way a warlord might take land in a battle, to gain the higher ground and have control. He wanted to intimidate me into making a mistake."

Guinevere gasped and sat up. “He said you coming to fetch me would be a mistake. Arthur, he’s going to attack Camelot!”

“Of course he is. Or rather, the Saxons are, since they’re in league with one another. Did you think that I would leave the city undefended? Only a small number of knights came with me.”

A chill came over Guinevere, and she shivered. Arthur pushed her back into the bed and pulled the covers over her, mistaking her shiver for feeling physically cold. She opened her mouth to say something, to tell him it was Lancelot, to…

“Please rest, Guinevere. You have been through an ordeal, and I… I need you to be strong at my side.” He swallowed, glancing down. “I have not treated you as I should have all the time, but even just seeing you gives me certain strength. I wouldn’t have realized how much I need you if Melwas hadn’t… if you hadn’t been taken.” His blue eyes gazed into hers. Guinevere swallowed the words burning on the tip of her tongue.

She nodded and gave him a smile, though her throat had restricted until she could hardly breathe. The trust he showed her, and the pure love that shone unhindered through his eyes made her heart thud painfully with guilt. She would tell him when they arrived at Camelot.

Meanwhile, she could think of what to say, how to convince him that his most loyal knight and dearest friend had betrayed him, and how to explain how she knew it in the first place.

CHAPTER THIRTY

Gereck woke to the cock's crow. His light, restless sleep broke easily at the faint sound. He dressed, the green sash tied carefully about his waist. He fingered the fox fur he had draped over the back of a chair the night before; he had decided to leave it. He could not keep it in good conscience. With it, he left a note:

Lord Aldus,

One thing I was given while you were away, I could not part with. If we should chance to meet again, I will find a way to repay you for my lax honor.

-Sir Gereck of Camelot

Lady Albree and Lord Aldus awaited him, standing in the early morning chill outside the stables. It cut through his clothes, made stronger by a fierce wind that blew. Above the keep, dark clouds hovered, no doubt heavy with rain. Gereck hugged his cloak close, which kept the worst of the wind at bay. Chilly for the day after Beltane.

"Are you certain you'll not take your horse? We could have him fetched back for you." Lord Aldus said.

Gereck shook his head. “I will rather enjoy the walk, I think. No point in rushing things.”

Lord Aldus shook his head.

“We wish you a gentle journey and honorable passing.” His wife stepped forward, her brown eyes soft, her voice melodious as she spoke. She looked more like Winna this morning than ever, and Gereck’s eyes betrayed him into believing it *was* Winna. She came and kissed his cheek, and suddenly Gereck caught a vision of his wife dressed in worn, homespun clothing, tending a pot over a fire, two children playing at her skirts. He shook his head as she backed away, and tried to smile at them both.

“There are few people I would have rather spent my final days with. Your hospitality has been generous, and I wish you both all the happiness life can afford.” He bowed. They both inclined their heads in acknowledgement.

A maid came forward with a small satchel. “Food for the road, good sir.”

He took it, though his stomach churned at the thought. He wasn’t sure he would be eating this day. With a wave, he set his feet on the path and didn’t look back. He entered a tight copse of trees, and it became dark, the morning light blocked out by the trees’ foliage. He walked in silence, and the day wore on.

If Lord Aldus had told him correctly, it would take him most of the day to get to the Emerald Chapel. He whistled as he walked, he let his mind wander. To Winna. To the kids. To Elaina. To King Arthur. He wondered if he had been wrong, if he should have gone back to Camelot and told someone. Would they have listened? A knight, oaths of brotherhood and loyalty barely leaving his lips before the accusation that would destroy the Round

Table and all it stood for. It was difficult to imagine anything other than imprisonment, and pity or anger, would have been the reaction.

He had, at least, sent a note to Sir Tristan. When he received it, then he could choose to act or not as he saw fit. But if the green sash Lady Albree had given him did as she said and protected him from the blow of any weapon and Gereck lived, what then would he do?

The forest opened onto a moor, where the green grass peeked through a heavy fog. The rocky edge of a cliff appeared ahead. He watched his step on the grown-over path, fumbling over rocks, roots, and grass with barely a trail in sight. It was not an oft-trod path he took. The land remained still, as if every waking thing avoided this place, or slept. Perhaps it was under an enchantment, just as the man who dwelled there.

Moisture from the air beaded on Gereck's tunic, on the handle of his sword. When he touched it, for assurance, it felt ice-cold in his hand. He wasn't sure why he had brought it; he wouldn't need it here.

Ahead, the mist cleared. A building with a peaked roof came into view. It seemed abandoned. Moss and lichen discolored the stone walls, and vines wound across the windows and doors. It did, indeed, appear green. The Emerald Chapel. No light brightened the windows, no sound came from within. Had Gereck somehow miscalculated? Was the Green Knight inside, waiting, or had he come at all?

His hands felt numb with cold. He brought them to his face and, cupping them, warmed them with his breath. His breathing felt shallow, his chest tight with apprehension, with fear. Then he remembered the sash. His breathing eased. Perhaps he would not die today. He tore away the vines covering the wooden door, then put his hand on the knob and turned it, stepping carefully within the darkness of the Emerald Chapel.

Very little light filtered through from outside. He closed the door, letting his eyes adjust to the darkness. In the dimness, he could see a large, hulking form. The moment the door closed, the form moved and became a man, standing, his giant axe set before him on the ground, his meaty hands resting on the handle.

The Green Knight. Head still impossibly intact, billowing with the same dark, mossy hair. As Gereck's eyes adjusted, he could see more and more of his opponent, but the man's face remained obscured.

"Before you strike your blow, might I know your name?"

"I am the Green Knight." The deep, bellowing voice was like a low rumble of thunder. "I am known by other names, but this one serves my purpose."

Gereck didn't feel like protesting. It would not matter, soon, and if he lived... well, then he could ask more questions.

"Welcome to my abode. You have timed your travels well," the Green Knight said, hefting his axe in both hands. "Now, prepare to make good our bargain."

Gereck knelt to the floor, and the giant moved closer. Gereck bowed his head, and from the corner of his eye saw the knight raise his blade.

He flinched. The Green Knight saw and laughed, a deep belly laugh that boomed out into the tiny, enclosed space. "He flinches before he is struck," the knight mocked.

"When my head comes off, I cannot put it back," said Gereck, "but I gave my word, and I am here, aren't I? Go on, then. I will not flinch again."

The Green Knight brought his axe up again. Gereck felt a tingle on the back of his neck and shuddered.

"Strike and be done with it!"

The Green Knight lowered his weapon again. "Have patience, sir knight. Or are you so keen for death?"

Gereck shut his mouth. He leaned forward, exposing the back of his neck, and waited for steel. He did not flinch or cry out as the axe whistled through the air, its sharp edge coming down on his neck and splitting the skin.

His heart pounded. His breath came in quick gasps. Gereck reached up and felt his neck. His hand came away bloody. He sat back on his heels and looked up at the Green Knight to find Lord Aldus standing there in the knight's place.

"You are brave indeed, Sir Gereck Bauer. Three times I raised my axe, for the Lady Albree's three final kisses. She is not my wife, as you might have believed, but a woman who agreed, for my purposes, to determine whether you were a man of true honor. The cut on your neck is for the girdle you took but did not exchange, as was our bargain. For that, I let you feel how much sorer I might have struck."

Gereck stood and reached under his shirt, untying the girdle. He extended it to the nobleman. "I am sorry, Lord Aldus. My honor is tainted."

"Your honor is intact. Your debt with me is cleared. Keep the girdle, as a token. A reminder. It is truly as powerful as you were told, mortal weapons will not harm you. My axe is not of this world."

Gereck nodded and tied the girdle about his arm, momentarily lost in thought. "Forgive me, Lord Aldus, but I am having difficulty understanding one thing: what were you truly testing? Was it my honor you were after, or King Arthur's? After all, he was the one you challenged first."

"Indeed it was. My purposes are many; your understanding would not comprehend them all, but if you look more closely, perhaps we can discuss them further."

Gereck peered through the dimness at Lord Aldus's face. His blue eyes seemed to shimmer, and his form took on an otherworldly glow, then it faded. Again, the man had transformed. Again, it was one Gereck recognized.

"Merlin!"

The man smiled. "Not everyone would have recognized my true form through that enchantment. It is your pure heart, your honorable heart, which allowed you to do that."

"Then who was the lady?"

Merlin nodded towards the door. "She awaits you outside."

Gereck's heart swelled within him, and his throat thickened, making it hard to swallow. Merlin smiled, then his entire body faded into the darkness and he was gone. Gereck turned and thrust open the door, stumbling out into the damp, cool air. The mist swirled around him. A woman stood, the hood on her heavy cloak covering her face. Gereck ran to her and reached his hands up, pulling back the cloak to reveal Winna, smiling up at him.

His sweet Winna, here. His hand stroked her face, then he pulled her in tightly against him, feeling her warmth, her heart beating against his.

"I was certain I would never see you again," he said.

"So was I," she replied, holding him out at arms-length. "You have changed some."

"Facing death can do that."

She nodded.

"How did you come to be involved in this? Were you truly the Lady Albree? Why did you..." He trailed off, not certain what he was trying to say.

"Merlin came to my cousin's home soon after we arrived. He said my web was tangled with yours, that you have something great to accomplish, and that you need my support to do that."

Gereck thought of Sir Lancelot, his plot against Arthur. He thought of Elaina, and if her words were true, what that would mean for Camelot. He nodded.

"Yes, I do. Do you truly understand?"

Winna looked toward the ground and then nodded. She took a deep breath. "I do. The wizard and I had much time to talk. He taught me something of destiny, and the bigger part we all play. I'd never stopped to imagine myself as having any impact beyond my own family before now, and I'd never considered you might have some part to play in the great, wide workings of things. Merlin helped me understand that we all live in the same web of life, and that where one thread is tugged, the entire web vibrates... or something like that.

"I never before could accept the truth, but now I know I must," she continued. "I married one of the dreamers of this world, one of those so determined to succeed, every move he makes sends waves of movement up and down the threads of life, reaching back into the past and forever changing the future."

She looked up at him then, and the look in her green eyes pulled at Gereck's heart. "That's you, love. Not a king, not even a knight, not born into privilege or ease, and yet you dream and reach and thrive as no one else could, as no one else has. I can't believe I didn't see it before, and I'm sorry for my bitterness. I've been a poor companion for you."

Gereck reached out with his arms and pulled her in against his chest. To think he had almost given it all up. To think he had almost let selfish dissatisfaction keep him from the best person in his life.

"I haven't been my best, either. I could have been there for you, more often. I could have helped you more, visited more." Regret welled up inside of him. "I should have come with you."

"If you had, you wouldn't know half of what you know now."

What he knew now... Suddenly, an echo of voices came into his mind. The conversation between that woman, Niviane, and Lancelot. Urgency accompanied it. Camelot needed him. He looked at Winna.

Her eyes searched his, then her face relaxed. "You have to go again."

He nodded. "My work isn't done yet. I have information King Arthur needs. He may be betrayed, and it's my duty as a knight to be at his side, to tell him what I know. I must go."

"But you'll return?"

"That's entirely up to him," another voice interrupted. Gereck stepped in front of Winna, searching for the source of the voice.

Lancelot came into view from around a tree. "You're alive," he noted, sticking his drawn sword into the dirt in front of him. "How?"

Gereck shrugged. "The Green Knight let me go."

Lancelot raised his eyebrows. “Let you go? Just like that?”

“Gave me this first,” Gereck replied, indicating the blood on his neck where the knight had nicked him. “He said my honor made me worthy of life, or something like that.”

Lancelot eyed him. “You see, now this is why I followed you. To keep this from happening.”

“To keep what from happening?”

A cynical smile crept onto Lancelot’s face, and he took several steps toward Gereck. “To prevent ambitious squires from fabricating victorious quests to obtain knighthood.” He grabbed Gereck’s collar and jerked him around so his neck was in plain sight. Lancelot scoffed and shoved Gereck away, sending him stumbling to catch his footing. “You might have done that to yourself, for all I know.”

Gereck squinted at the sun, then spat on the ground. “Why would I do something that stupid?”

“Because you’ve wanted knighthood longer than anyone I’ve ever known or heard of, and when your little quest proved to lead to certain death, you couldn’t handle it, so you made up a pretty story about your ‘great honor’ to take back to the king. Well, I’ll tell you one thing, the king isn’t going to believe that for a moment, but if he does, I’ll be there to deny any of it ever happened.”

Winna made a sound of disbelief behind him. Gereck stared at the black-haired knight. “You aren’t serious.”

“As a priest.”

Gereck sputtered. “Lancelot, you know how much I want this. You can’t... how could you...”

Lancelot doubled over, laughing and pointing at Gereck. "You should see the look on your face!" He straightened, wiping his eyes, then slapped Gereck on the back. "Why would I do that? Truly. You've served me honorably, as my squire, for all these years. I would be honored to be seated beside you at the Round Table."

Gereck relaxed and grinned. "You really had me there, Lancelot."

"I'll give the king my highest recommendation of you, to be sure, but I need something in return, Sir Gereck."

The relieved smile slipped off Gereck's face. "What?" he asked, keeping his voice measured.

"Oh, it's nothing. Simple enough after what you just went through, I'm sure."

"What is it?"

Lancelot made a motion in the air with his hand, and from the brush and trees around him men appeared. Their clothes were dark and filthy, their hair ratted, faces unshaved. In their hands, bared weapons glinted in the sunlight. Gereck stepped back, raising his hands.

"Lancelot, who are these men?"

Lancelot looked at them, grinning. "These are my people. No cause to fear if you agree to help us."

"Help you what?" He drew his sword, slowly. His new sword. He hadn't used it against another man yet. He didn't want his first blow with it to be against a fellow knight.

"It is time the power shifted in Camelot," Lancelot said. "We are heading a rebellion against a weak and simple king, to change the face of Camelot."

Fury boiled up inside of Gereck. He had worked his whole life to serve King Arthur, and if Lancelot succeeded, he would never have the chance. He set his jaw and looked Lancelot in the eye.

"Who will rule? You?"

Lancelot laughed, as did the men around him. "We have a monarch chosen," he said. "No one would ever suspect them, and I'll not spoil the surprise by telling you now. Rest assured, they will give Camelot everything it needs to succeed."

Gereck's hands clenched into fists. His entire body shook. "I have looked up to you, Lancelot, all these years. I wanted what you had; friendship with the great man who is our king. How can you betray him? Did you never love him? Have you no honor?"

The smile disappeared from Lancelot's face, and he stepped toward Gereck. The men around him raised their weapons, readying themselves. "I have more honor than any man who sits at that 'table of equality'. Table of insecurity is more appropriate. The king has divided loyalties between the old religion and this new Christian movement. We are here to end that division and unify Camelot at last, under one banner, and return to the old ways."

"You will destroy us," Gereck said, raising his sword. "War divides. It cannot heal. King Arthur can still unite the people. And he will!"

"You always were an idealist," Lancelot said. "I assume your lack of protest means you won't join us?" The men advanced.

"Did you ever think my answer would be different?"

"No, but I owed you enough to try."

Lancelot pulled his own sword from its sheath and lunged forward. Gereck parried, barely keeping his feet as he stumbled back. His sword skill was no match for

Lancelot's; he could not win this fight. Unless... the sash was still tied to him. Lancelot's sword came down, and Gereck blocked it again. He could not be harmed. His sword skill might be lacking, but he had a chance if Lancelot could not mark him.

Gereck swung his sword toward Lancelot's shoulder, then felt someone shove him from behind. He fell forward, managing to right himself before he hit the ground. He turned right into an armored fist that knocked him backward. Two men leapt on him, forcing him to his knees.

Gereck struggled to fight them off, to reach his sword and defend himself, but the men held him tightly as Lancelot approached. The knight reached down and fumbled with something at Gereck's arm.

"What..." Gereck choked and couldn't finish speaking. Lancelot held up the green sash and tucked it into his belt.

"A little present someone promised to me. I'm just picking it up. Consider it payment for my shield." Lancelot stood and motioned to the men. "Take care of his woman first."

Winna stood to his left, eyes wide with terror as four men descended toward her. Their intent was clear. One grabbed her arms and threw her to the ground. She scrambled to her knees and tried to regain her feet, but one of the men flipped her over onto her back, then pinned her arms and straddled her. She thrashed about wildly, but the man cuffed her across the face. She lay stunned for a moment, and that's all it took. The three other men surrounded her, kicking her sides and jeering, urging the man on top of her to have his way so they could have theirs.

A red film colored Gereck's vision. His head swam with anger, his stomach felt tight and sick with it. No one would use his Winna in this way. Not if they wanted to live.

A harsh, inhuman sound escaped his lips, half-roar, half-battle cry, and with every ounce of strength he had, he brought his arms together in front of him, smashing together the two men who were holding him. His sword was within reach. He snatched it from the ground and before the men could draw their own weapons, each was wearing a vest of blood, courtesy of Gereck's sword.

There were at least a dozen left to advance on him. Lancelot was nowhere to be seen. Winna shrieked in the background, but for the press of men, Gereck could not see her. She was beyond him.

For the first time in his life, Gereck knew true anger. No coherent thought crossed his mind as he engaged each man in combat, there was only instinct, and the ever-burning presence of fury that kept him moving despite the strikes his own body was taking.

One of them men holding a wooden staff thrust it into Gereck's stomach, winding him through the chainmail, finally getting the pause they needed in his bloodbath. Six bodies lay around him, either dead or wounded beyond saving. Before he could draw breath, the men jumped on him, binding his wrists and feet, and then they set on him, beating and kicking anything they could reach.

The ropes on his hands and feet dug into his skin. Gereck threw his bound hands over his head and curled into as small a ball as he could manage, protecting what little he could.

A boot connected with his jaw and blood filled his mouth. Dark spots filled Gereck's vision. He did not ask them to stop. If he must, he would die defending Camelot. He would die trying to save Winna. But he needed to live. She needed him, and someone had to warn the king.

He couldn't move, couldn't defend himself. He wondered why no one finished him off; they all had weapons. Was it more sport to beat a man to death? There certainly wasn't more honor, not that these men cared much for that.

A boot landed on Gereck's head, pressing it into the hard-packed dirt. Dust settled around Gereck's face. It was in his eyes, in his mouth, and blood seemed to be everywhere. His blood. It filled his mouth with a metallic tang. The boot pushed harder until Gereck cried out, afraid his skull would be crushed. He struggled, but everything hurt, and he couldn't budge. Worst of all, he couldn't hear Winna any longer.

Lancelot's voice floated into his ear. "That was a taste of what you'll get if you return to Camelot."

Gereck spat blood from his mouth into the dirt and tried to lick his lips. "Why not kill me?" he croaked.

"I have more honor than that, Gereck, and I don't like to get my hands dirty."

"You have… no… honor," Gereck gasped. His ribs were on fire. It was likely several were broken. Lancelot straightened and aimed a final kick at Gereck's back. Gereck arched back in agony, then there was a distinct strike to his head and everything went dark.

When he came to, it was getting dark. Lancelot and his men were gone.

His mouth still tasted strongly of blood. He rolled to his side, letting out a yell as his body burned with pain. He panted, trying not to take deep breaths, as each time he did his ribs screamed in agony. He checked his teeth. Miraculously, none were broken. He reached his hands up, still bound, and felt his head. They came away wet with blood.

Where were the men? Why had they kept him alive? Perhaps they had assumed him dead, or as good as.

His next thought was of Winna. He glanced blearily around at the darkening landscape, eyes passing over brush and the bodies of the men he had killed until they found a more delicate form draped across the ground. He watched for a moment, but she did not stir.

"Winna." His voice was nothing but a hoarse croak.

His ribs were in agony. He pulled himself forward with his arms, which were still tied. Each movement forced him to stop and catch his breath and wait for the pain to subside. His breath became ragged. Tears of pain and frustration poured down his face. He tried calling to her twice more, but she did not hear him, or at least, she did not respond.

The half-moon hung higher in the sky when he finally reached Winna's form. He pressed himself against her, praying to feel warmth, breath, heartbeat. When his hand touched her shoulder to give her a gentle shake, he could tell her body had already stiffened.

Winna was dead.

Gereck barely had strength to mourn. His body seemed too stressed to even make tears anymore. He lay next to her, tearless sobs shaking him and sending racking waves of pain throughout. Somehow, he fell asleep like that.

The morning greeted him with birdsong, and a sunrise beautiful enough he felt like weeping. Seeing Winna in daylight was almost too much to bear. Unable to bring himself to look upon her face, the blood on her head and soaked through her dress on her side was enough for him to know that he didn't want to see. He touched her wheat-colored hair one last time, and caught her familiar scent of musk and fresh cut hay on the breeze.

Anger, fierce and burning, coursed through his body. His blood pumped through him, liquid fury. Lancelot would pay for this.

Gereck closed his eyes, braced himself, and rolled away from her, gritting his teeth against the pain. It took him half the morning to half-crawl, half-squirm to a sword belonging to one of the fallen men. He managed to hold it between his knees and saw at the ropes on his hands until they were freed. He untied his feet, then rested for a long time, staring out across the landscape. One eye had swollen shut and saw nothing but a strange blur. There was no one in sight, and nothing for miles.

He had to find help. He wouldn't make it back to Camelot in this condition, but he had no choice. No one would look for him; no one had expected him to live through this ordeal. No one else knew what he did, what Lancelot planned.

Gereck gathered his strength and slowly moved into a crouch, then pushed to stand, using the sword as a cane. He took a single step. Agony lanced up his legs and through his chest. He cried out and fell forward, hands not moving fast enough to catch him before his face struck the ground. He would not be able to walk.

He was tempted to give up. After all, no one expected him to do this, but no one else knew about the treachery within Camelot's walls, except...

Elaina. A memory swam into his mind through the haze of pain, his last encounter with Elaina in her tower. She had said something about the queen... What had she said? She thought the queen was her sister, and Arthur... Arthur was her son.

Gereck cursed. He felt like a child who was too distracted with play to see the snake laying in the grass, until the snake struck. How could he have missed it before? The name didn't match. Of course it didn't. He couldn't have anyone recognizing his surname, could he?

Lancelot Du Lac was Mordred Asger, Elaina's first sweetheart. The queen was her sister, and the king... Gereck's mind reeled at the possibility. How had it happened? King Arthur was her son, but not hers alone. The only man who could have impregnated her, at least according to Elaina, was Mordred.

Mordred, or Lancelot, had sired the greatest king to ever rule Camelot. Did he know? With his intent to overthrow the kingdom, Gereck assumed not. After all, he wouldn't have seen or spoken to Elaina since she became trapped in the tower.

Gereck didn't have the whole picture, but he had enough that he knew he would be responsible if the knowledge never reached Arthur. He deserved to know, for one, and he couldn't afford not to know, for another.

Another thought came then, making Gereck's heart ache with the reality of it. Winna was gone, and Cai and Ada would be alone, parentless, if he gave up now.

And Elaina. *She holds a promise from me too*, he remembered. There was too much left undone. He would see it through.

CHAPTER THIRTY-ONE

Guinevere longed to sleep. Her entire body ached with fatigue; to walk across her room took such great effort she had to rest for an hour afterward, but every time she closed her eyes, her mind filled with visions of Melwas and his men, reaching for her, touching her... She could almost feel their hands upon her, the weight of their bodies and how they used her, the pain...

And so, she did not sleep. Instead, she lit candles and worked on embroidery, the dim light doing nothing for the already poor skill she had, or snuck out to the stables to brush the horses and converse with the stable hands. Not that they said very much. They were terrified of their frail, mad queen who had strange fits and injuries.

She had caught, in passing, conversations by various servants about her insanity. Hushed debates on whether she practiced sorcery. Guinevere never would have believed that one herself, until she had used magic on Melwas and his men to escape.

The worst of the whispers followed her like tormented spirits, claiming that Arthur had left with his men to fight the Saxons at the border at the request of Merlin to escape the queen's wicked influence.

Arthur had gone, marching out with his men the day after she had been returned to the castle. He hadn't looked at her, hadn't spoken with her or spent a moment alone in her presence before kissing her cheek, mounting his horse, and leaving. He'd left his sick and injured wife at the mercy of a suspicious and aloof court.

Perhaps Arthur's consultant, Merlin, did think her mad, or a traitor to the kingdom, and had warned the king? Confronting the sorcerer himself would be the only way to find out for certain, but when she finally got up the courage to have him summoned to her chamber, the messenger returned with the news that Merlin, too, had gone, and no one knew where or how long he would be absent.

So the days passed, and Guinevere lost track of time. Her body, exhausted with her lack of sleep, collapsed throughout the day. She stopped eating, food having no appeal. The castle physician learned of her sleeplessness and prescribed a powerful herbal combination that forced her into hours of sleep at a time, to give her body the rest it needed, but each time she dutifully took her dose, Guinevere's mind became imprisoned in a torturous hell of nightmares, reliving her vivid memories of violent abuse, as well as those of her fractured childhood self.

They were her own memories, and no matter how much she screamed or fought to wake up, she couldn't escape the influence of the drugs. The physician ordered her to eat, but she vomited almost immediately upon finishing a meal.

On the outside, she appeared calm, though desperately weak, but on the inside, her mind raged with fear and pain. She took to staying in bed all day, reading or sewing, or listening to the gossip of her ladies in waiting, struggling to contain the madness that roared constantly through her thoughts.

Three weeks after her capture, just as rumors circulated about the king's return, Guinevere found relief. Her dreams changed.

Instead of torture and rape, she found herself walking up a flight of endless stairs, filled with anticipation and, oddly enough, peace. She would wake each morning filled with yearning, wanting nothing more than to find those stairs, to climb them, to know what she would find at the top. The dreams brought respite to her heart and mind, and some of her appetite and health returned, conversations included her, and people smiled when they saw her.

She was recovering.

After one night of endlessly climbing the same stairs in her dreams, she finally recognized them. They were the stairs in the tower of Shalott, where she had found Elaina. Did it mean that her sister would bring her peace?

The foreign guilt weighed in Guinevere's heart. This emotion belonged to Morgan, inherited by Guinevere in their recent integration. She could do nothing in her weakened state. Even if she could visit the tower, she could not break the spell on her sister.

Another week passed, and the rumors became knowledge. The king was, indeed, returning, victorious from a mighty battle he fought with the Saxons. One of many they would have to fight. He left half of his army on the border to keep the enemy at bay, but he was returning to Camelot. The kingdom rejoiced.

Guinevere looked forward to his return. She missed their conversations, missed his smile and laugh...and, now that Morgan and the others had integrated, where repulsion and disgust had once been Morgan's response whenever Guinevere thought of Arthur, now warmth blossomed inside of her. At first, the realization had unsettled Guinevere, but eventually, she became glad for it. Perhaps she could overcome the past and love Arthur completely. Now she could be the wife he needed her to be.

She went outside and stood for hours on the rampart, watching for signs of the king's return on the horizon. Each night, she fell into a peaceful sleep, no longer drugged, having eaten small meals that gradually returned the strength to her body.

The day finally came that King Arthur returned. His full, unruly beard told of the month he'd lived in the wilderness. He seemed gaunt, the skin tight around his eyes, but when he saw Guinevere standing in front of the castle, he seemed to relax and a smile showed through his beard.

He dismounted and Guinevere resisted the undignified urge to run, waiting until he had dismissed his men before she kissed his cheeks and embraced him.

"I've missed you," she said.

His blue eyes sparkled. "And I, you."

It seemed as if her fears were unfounded. He had come home, and there was no mention of her being a traitor, or of Merlin sending him away.

That night, the castle held a great feast. He grasped her hand throughout, and they talked for a long time in her room, about how she had been, and about what he had seen in his travels. Unpleasant things were ignored in favor of enjoying one another's presence more fully, and then he kissed her forehead and went to his room without ever once asking for anything more, and Guinevere's heart filled with warmth for him.

She noticed that Merlin had not returned with Arthur. Rumors in the court had it that Merlin and the Lady Nimue had ridden off together, possibly to perform some enchantment on the Saxon armies that would render them crippled or powerless against Arthur's forces. Guinevere felt relief at the absence of Niviane, but fear gripped her heart, wondering at the plans of the sorceress, and whether she intended harm against Merlin or the kingdom.

Guinevere managed to reassure herself; after all, if anyone could hold their own against the sorceress, surely it was Merlin.

She put the fears from her mind and continued as she had, healing and allowing her love for Arthur to grow in her heart, each day in his presence bringing her closer to him, as it should have been from the beginning.

CHAPTER THIRTY-TWO

Something snuffled Gereck's face, the smooth, wet *thing* pulling at his hair, bringing him round to wakefulness. Gereck sat up, his sputtering and coughing turning into yells of agony. Pain blinded him.

His arms gripped his sides and his breath hissed through his clenched teeth.

A horse stamped nearby, letting out a snort and a brief, friendly-sounding whinny. Gereck opened his eyes.

"Fendrel!" He whispered hoarsely, hardly believing his fortune. Tears pricked his eyes, and he took a moment to thank the providence that had brought the horse to him.

Then, gritting his teeth, Gereck grabbed two fistfuls of Fendrel's chestnut mane and heaved himself upright. He screamed aloud, startling birds from the trees. His ribs were on fire and his head swam. He panted and moaned, leaning all his weight against the horse's velvety side. His legs quivered, even with the horse's broad back for support. Only the strength of his arms kept him from collapsing back to the ground.

He wouldn't be able to mount in this condition. He stroked Fendrel's mane and rested his face on the soft, short hair, breathing in the honey scent of hay and horse. He tried not to think of Winna.

He took a deep breath. “Fendrel, let’s try something.” He reached agonizingly downward and tapped the back of the horse’s knee joint.

Fendrel stood still.

Gereck tried again, pushing where he held the horse’s mane, shifting his weight just enough that he almost toppled over. Letting out a pained yell, he righted himself and rested until the pain faded.

“Come on, Fendrel! I need you to kneel. I can’t get up on your back otherwise, and your finding me will have been for naught.”

The horse snorted, bringing his head around and nudging Gereck as if asking why he hadn’t explained that sooner, and then the animal lowered his front half toward the ground.

Gereck leaned over the horse’s bare back, took a deep breath, and swung his leg over. Pain arched through his legs and ribcage. He lay prostrate on Fendrel’s back for a long moment, just breathing, then patted the horse’s shoulder, causing him to rise to his feet. He clicked his tongue and Fendrel walked forward, on towards Camelot.

Gereck stayed conscious enough to stay on, but not much else. He was barely aware of how far they traveled or the direction they were going, but he kept murmuring “to Camelot” under his breath, hoping his horse would understand and return home.

He rode through the night and into dawn before Fendrel stopped at an inn. The innkeeper’s wife rushed out, clucking worriedly at Gereck’s injured state.

She called for help and two young men came out. They helped Gereck from Fendrel’s back and up to a room.

The innkeeper's wife, Cara, drew him a warm bath and had one of her sons wait on him, helping him get in and out, and then into bed. Cara came back in with a thick, heavy-smelling salve that she glopped all over his face and chest.

Despite the unpleasant smell, it immediately warmed Gereck's skin and soothed his aching muscles. He drank a bitter herbal tea in gulps, then relaxed into a deep and dreamless sleep.

There were a lot of questions when he woke. They had, of course, noticed the Pendragon symbol on the medallion King Arthur had given him, and they recognized it as a token of knighthood. As a knight, Gereck would be forgiven the costs of his care, since he was without his purse. The family wanted to be sure he hadn't taken it off a real knight's body.

Gereck answered all of their questions as thoroughly as he could. He knew if he mentioned Lancelot as his attacker they would immediately be suspicious, because everyone knew Lancelot's name; he was as widely known as the king himself.

So, Gereck told a simple story about scouting in a small party and being set upon by bandits.

They believed him. The woman, Cara, suggested he stay a week to be fully mended, but Gereck insisted on leaving after just two days. She seemed suspicious at his vehement insistence that he be off until he hinted that a lady waited for him.

His story had her chuckling and shaking her head as she left to gather some supplies.

He obtained a saddle and halter, promising to send payment and tell everyone of their generosity, and directed the two sons to tie him to Fendrel's back. He would be riding as hard and fast as his injuries would allow, and if he fainted, he didn't want to fall off.

They obliged, their mother *tsking* softly and smiling knowingly in the background.

The next seven days passed in a feverish, pained blur. Cara had given him some of the salve and herbs for a pain-numbing tea, both of which Gereck used as judiciously as he could. He ran out after four days.

The pain he was in without the tea sent him into bouts of unconsciousness as Fendrel pushed towards Camelot.

Fendrel seemed to sense Gereck's distressed state, and the horse kept trying to stop at inns and villages, almost insisting Gereck get help, but Gereck would not stop. He urged the horse onward, stopping when Fendrel needed rest and ignoring his own needs.

He reached the top of another hill, barely holding himself together. The land had started to look familiar; certainly he neared Camelot. His view from the top of the hill made him weep with relief.

The tower of Shalott rose through the early morning mist, and Camelot itself was faintly visible some distance beyond. One more day, if he rode well.

Gereck urged Fendrel forward, his aching body rocking with the steady rhythm of the horse's footsteps.

The king must be told of Lancelot's betrayal. Gereck could only hope he would get there fast enough.

CHAPTER THIRTY-THREE

She left the web, she left the loom;
She made three paces thro' the room,
She saw the water-lily bloom,
She saw the helmet and the plume,
She look'd down to Camelot.
Out flew the web and floated wide;
The mirror crack'd from side to side;
"The curse is come upon me," cried
The Lady of Shalott.

"It is a quaint tower. Why would you have us stop here, Lady Nimue, when it is only hours to Camelot?" The male voice carried up the stairwell to Elaina's ears. She sat up in bed, the clacking of the enchanted loom continuing without her. She yawned, wondering if she had imagined the voice, when another joined it, coming loud and clear through the door.

"It is late and I am weary; are not you as well? I thought it nice to rest, to eat, to sleep in a bed..." The female voice trailed off, perhaps suggestively.

People. Actual, live people, coming to her tower! Elaina leapt out of bed and made her way in the dark to her dressing screen. She grabbed the nearest dress, which hung over the top of the screen, and put it on. She didn't know how or why, or what might happen, but she wouldn't meet them in her undergarments.

She hastily put her feet inside, tangling one of them in the ribbons and toppling over onto her side. Her shoulder knocked the dressing screen to the ground and she thrashed about, trying to find which way was up.

"What was that?" the male voice asked. "I just heard a fearsome crash."

"I've heard tell that two lovers were once trapped here, the only shelter they could find in the face of a fierce blizzard unlike any seen before," the female voice said.

Elaina struggled to get herself upright with the fabric tangled about her in the pitch dark. As she righted herself, she listened to the conversation of the man and woman coming further up the stairs.

"Oh, do tell. These blasted stairs will get me yet, Nimue. Is it much farther? I mean, we could have been to Camelot by now. I am certain of it."

"Save your breath for climbing, old warlock. I won't be carrying you. Would you like to hear the story?"

"What story? Oh, that one. If you think you can tell it without losing wind yourself. Then no one would find our corpses on these stairs for a hundred years, and they will devise a myriad of tales to explain our bodies here, each one more romantic than the last."

"Well, you have all but guessed the end of my story. What is the point in telling?"

"Distracting me." The male voice huffed rather wheezily.

They were close.

"Well, the lovers died, frozen by the cold. They had no means for a fire, see, and when they were found, they were placed in a tomb within the tower, a magical tomb that preserved their bodies perfectly, the top made of clear glass so any who saw them might look upon the faces of the lovers and wonder at their story."

The clearer their voices became, the more familiar they seemed. Had Elaina heard them before?

"It isn't a very original tale, is it?" the male said, sounding more irritated and out of breath by the minute.

"It is romantic, at the least, and I like romantic," the female replied.

"What is romantic about freezing to death?"

What would they do when they found the door locked? Would they turn away? Her heart rate increased.

The handle turned with a loud click, to Elaina's great shock. Had it been open all this time? Could they somehow have a key?

Her eyes, adjusted as they were, could not see more than a vague outline of the two figures who came in. She hardly dared breathe.

"While we are here, we might as well pass a pleasurable night."

"Oh no, I know what you are thinking Merlin, and it will not happen tonight. Not here. I will not give in to that until I am back in a real bed."

Murmured protests followed, and judging by the woman's amused and muffled giggling, there was a lot of kissing going on.

Elaina wished she could shut her ears.

After a brief moment, one of the figures slumped to the ground with a thud, and a soft snoring filled the room.

"At last," the woman said, sounding repulsed. "That potion took far longer than it ought to have. Too long. I'm not sure I could have held him at bay that time. Elaina?"

Elaina started, hearing her name, and then, an instant before the lantern flickered to life, she recognized the voice.

Niviane wore her youthful guise and a dirty traveling dress. She tossed her hood back off her hair, which rippled with silver light down her back.

Elaina scrambled to her feet, discarding the dress that had tripped her. She didn't feel as confident facing the sorceress in her nightgown, but it would have to do.

"What do you want, Niviane?"

"I may be powerful, but physically I have little strength. Move him with me." She nodded towards the unconscious man. He had long white hair and a beard that fell over his sleeping face.

"Who is he?" Elaina asked.

"His name is of little importance. Come, take his arms."

"I am bound to the loom, not to you. I will not help you unless you tell me why he is here and what you intend."

Niviane laughed. "I could spell you and steal your mind, if you wish to insist on disobeying me. Either way I will have your aid."

"You will not," Elaina said, folding her arms against her chest, holding her chin high. "I do not answer to you, and I want no part in this."

Niviane chanted low, a guttural sounding tone that seemed to vibrate at the back of her throat, in a language that Elaina could not discern.

Her mind slipped away, as if she dreamed, but the dreams were dark and unclear, and Elaina did not remember them when she came back into awareness some time later, her arm muscles feeling strained.

Elaina stood bent over one side of a large wooden chest that she had never seen before. Intricate carvings adorned the surface. She straightened slowly, looking at Niviane, who stood across from her.

"You see? I said you would help," Niviane said.

"You enchanted me!" Elaina looked at the chest. "Is he... did we...?"

Niviane nodded. "The man is within. As for the enchantment, it was easily done, but not without price."

Elaina eyed her warily. "What does that mean?"

"It means I owe you a truth. Ask me any question and I must answer," the sorceress said in an almost bored tone.

Elaina considered the questions that flooded her mind. The obvious one blazed at the forefront of her thoughts.

"How can I break the curse holding me?" Elaina asked, squaring her shoulders.

Niviane laughed. "Isn't it obvious by now? You can't. No one ever has."

"That's not an answer. You didn't cast this spell without knowing how to break it."

"And if I did?" Niviane's eyes narrowed. "Not all magic can be undone."

Elaina's chest felt hollow. "Then...this is permanent? I'm here eternally?"

"The gift of an extended life with little strife, and no worldly care. Many would pay handsomely for the kind of security and comfort you enjoy here."

“Then they do not understand the cost!” Elaina cried, clenching her fists. “Why are you here? Why did you come with that man?”

Niviane walked toward the loom, her fingers trailing along its wooden frame. “I don’t owe you a second answer, but I will give it to you because it amuses me. I came to kill a powerful enemy that has been a thorn in my side for some time.”

“You have not killed me, Nimue. Or should I call you Niviane, now that you’ve revealed yourself?” The male voice, more familiar in close quarters, came from the wooden chest to Elaina’s right.

Elaina jumped at the sound. “What... how?”

Niviane examined her nails. “You are not dead, it is true, but you cannot be freed by anyone other than myself.”

Elaina averted her eyes, looking instead at the chest. She knew that voice, and the image of her intelligent bluebird friend came unbidden to her mind. It fit perfectly.

“Brennus?” she whispered.

“One of my many names. I am better known as Merlin,” the man in the chest replied.

Niviane wheeled around. “You know this man?”

“I think I do,” Elaina replied. “He came to me in the form of a bird, once. I might have been dreaming.”

“You were not. It was I.” The sorcerer replied from the chest.

“Then you knew this was my tower! How could you let Niviane trap you?” Elaina exclaimed.

“So I might aid you,” Merlin said calmly.

If Niviane felt any shock at the revelation, she did not show it. “A fruitless endeavor. She will never leave.”

“Why me?” Elaina asked, trying to block Niviane’s voice from her ears. It had to be possible. She had to keep believing that she would somehow, someday, be free, and if Merlin could tell her how...

“Because you understand.” It was Merlin. He sounded tired, like the chest was sapping his strength and energy to where he could hardly be heard. “You seek more than what is shown to you. You reach for what is beyond you. You dream with passion that can only be fulfilled by action, and you have the motivation to fulfill that action.”

Dreams? Passion? “What do I understand?” Elaina asked.

“It is an inner knowing, child. Look within yourself.”

Niviane cackled, walking behind Elaina, so close she could feel the heat from her body. “She is a simpleton, Merlin. Too naïve to ever understand that kind of power or how to use it.”

Merlin’s voice broke through the darkness of her thoughts. “Do not listen. Your strength of will and mind are far greater than you have ever imagined. Stop listening to the voices that demean and degrade you, Elaina. Find your strength. Trust your intuition.”

“Morgan,” she realized. “Morgan did this. She’s the reason I’m here.”

“Do you know why?” Merlin asked.

“Silence, you old fool! There is no cure for this curse.”

Elaina glanced at Niviane’s face only briefly, then turned to the enchanted chest as if she were speaking to a living person. “Because...she loves me. Or loved me. I’m not sure there’s much left of the sister I adored. Why would she imprison me to be with Mordred? I thought she hated men.”

“Magic can play with emotion,” Merlin said.

"Then... Mordred was enchanted? He never loved her?"

"Not beyond lust. Niviane made it easy for Morgan to receive the love she never had, love without pain, but in the end, it became as warped and twisted as her plans."

"The love she had never had from our brothers," Elaina realized, throat closing up with pain as she considered the abuse her sister had suffered.

"Niviane promised her the deepest desire of her heart in exchange for giving herself to dark magic that would train her to become what Niviane wanted her to be: a queen who would pave the way for the fall of Camelot."

"Which you did not halt, Merlin. It has begun in earnest. You will not triumph in the face of the Goddess, and I will live to see Camelot rise to true glory in her name." A sneer twisted the triumphant expression of the sorceress's fair face. She raised her hands, clasped them over her head, and spoke a word. A flash of bright, golden light filled the space, and then Niviane was gone, vanished through magic to some unknown place.

"What does she mean, Merlin?" Elaina asked.

"Camelot faces betrayal and war." Merlin sounded weary.

"What can I do?" Elaina cried.

The wizard did not answer.

Reeling and confused, Elaina turned about the room.

Her eyes landed on the loom. The shuttle moved back and forth, weaving as it always did even when Elaina did not sit at it. Orange thread passed through the shuttle, making a pattern of flames. Flames?

She looked more intently at the image in the thread to see what was burning. A human figure dressed in red stood, tied to a post in the midst of low flames in the courtyard of the keep of Camelot. A shadowy crowd looked on, including a man atop a horse.

"Morgan!" she gasped. "What is happening? Why is she burning?"

"The queen was found abed with the king's knight, Sir Lancelot."

She looked at the loom again as it wove Morgan's flowing black hair. All she had was herself, alone and knowing too much, with no one to tell, and no way to prevent any of it from unfolding.

"The loom weaves things that are happening now, in the present..." She trailed off, looking at the mirror. It showed the courtyard of Camelot without the flames and no Morgan tied to a post, no sign of the gathered crowd.

"How can this be?" She whispered.

"It appears the magic has shifted," Merlin said. "I spoke to the loom with my magic just before Niviane's potion took my consciousness. It was a small advantage I could give you, to see the future, rather than the present."

Elaina walked around the loom, staring at the foreshadowed scene. "But why does it matter? I can't do anything here, alone, still cursed. You heard Niviane. Even under the truth spell she couldn't tell me how to break it."

"Niviane cannot tell you what she does not know. Perhaps there is a way. Your heart has changed, has it not? You think of leaving."

"I have thought of leaving since the day I arrived!" Elaina cried.

"And yet now you are prepared to do it. You know the moment has arrived, where the benefits outweigh the risks. You are prepared to die for this, should that be your fate."

Elaina looked in the direction of the chest. She walked over and knelt beside it. She ran her fingers across the surface.

Despite Niviane's assurance that she could not open it, she tried the latch, which didn't budge.

She sat back on her heels. "What if I die before I do anything that I set out to do?"

"Then you die, and others take up the web of life. Elaina, your part in life can only be told by you. What you do matters an incredible amount, because no one else will ever do it for you, and yet, in the grand picture of the world, it would seem that it doesn't matter.

"Life's greatest lie is that what you do has no effect, when it does, immensely and grandly and without any doubt. What you choose to do today will change the face of Camelot. Not everyone has an opportunity to shake the foundation of a nation, but you, you who birthed the king who stands to defend Camelot this day, you do. The question is, what will you do with it?"

Elaina stood, crossing her arms. "Then you believe I should break the curse and tell Gereck...except he is dead... Arthur, then, or one of his knights. That my sister plots against Camelot? If she's burning at the stake, they must have already figured it out."

"What you have seen in the tapestry is the future; the future as you create it, Elaina."

"What evidence do I have?" Tears came to her eyes with the hopelessness of the situation. She realized Sir Gereck's stance now, why he had refused to return to Camelot.

"Why should I go at all? I could stay here, safe, curse unbroken..." She trailed off. Did dying frighten her so much that she would remain and weave for eternity?

"Elaina, what does your heart tell you?"

Her heart? Her heart was afraid.

Afraid to leave, afraid to die without ever seeing the sun again.

Afraid of meeting Arthur and all the pain that came with knowing she would never get to raise him as her own.

Afraid of Gereck and discovering why he had left her so suddenly, so wretchedly, to make these decisions on her own.

Afraid that he didn't love her, afraid to know why he had lied to her.

"How can I stop being afraid?" She asked.

It was as if she spoke to an empty room, and maybe she did.

The early morning sunlight filtered silently in, illuminating the loom and gleaming off the blank, clear surface of the mirror. Dust particles floated through the air, like bits of gold drifting about. A bird sang outside her window.

Elaina's throat constricted and she closed her eyes. It was true, what Merlin had said. She knew it was time; time to finally open her eyes and see.

Morgan had given everything for love. What would Elaina give?

She couldn't die not knowing for sure if Gereck, if her sister, if Mordred, had ever truly loved her.

She couldn't die without seeing Arthur, touching him, telling him who she was, even if he didn't believe her.

She held knowledge that could cause the fall of Camelot, or prevent it.

She could save the people she loved, and those who loved them, and so many others, but only if she loved them enough to break through the tower walls and risk death to find them.

Life blossomed inside her chest. Her lungs drew breath, and for the first time the air tasted sweet instead of stagnant. Strength coursed through her limbs.

Elaina turned slowly, deliberately, carefully, toward the window, eyes shut tight until the sunlight streamed red through her eyelids. Then they opened, blinded by the light.

For one, heart-wrenching moment she thought she had died after all, with just that one glance, but her eyes soon adjusted and the setting sun moved beyond the window. She stared at the bright spring green of new leaves on the trees outside. A patch of blue sky, bluer than anything she had seen in her life, peeked through the trees, and the gray river stretched beside the road, flowing toward Camelot.

Camelot. The castle and its winding city stood atop the hill in the distance. Elaina could make it before sundown if she left now.

Elaina moved one step closer to the door and a loud crack sounded. Glass flew through the air. She threw herself to the ground, covering her head.

The clacking of the loom fell still.

Elaina slowly lifted her head, glass falling from her hair onto the ground. The mirror had completely shattered.

She had broken the curse.

"Love is a powerful force. Far more powerful than any spell I know," Merlin spoke at last, his voice cracking with age and fatigue through the wood of the chest that trapped him.

Elaina stood, glass crackling beneath her bare feet. “Can I do anything for you?”

“Do not trouble yourself with my fate.” The sorcerer replied.

“Thank you, then, for all you’ve done for me. For giving me hope. And courage.”

“I merely reminded you they existed. You claimed them on your own.”

Elaina stepped over and around the gleaming shards as best she could, miraculously making it to the open door without cutting her feet.

She paused briefly in the threshold, hesitating, then squared her shoulders and put her foot on the floor on the other side of the door. Her other foot followed, and a smile spread across Elaina’s face.

She took another step.

Her heart wrenched in her chest. She rubbed the skin above her heart, frowning, then moved towards the stairs again. A stabbing pain took her breath away, then faded, just as quickly.

What was happening? Hadn’t she broken the curse? She looked at the long, winding stairs, then set her shoulders with determination and descended. She took some stairs two at a time as she went, each step sending shards of pain through her heart.

Elaina cried out, but kept running, determined to see the sun and feel its warmth on her face.

She reached the bottom of the stairs, panting and heaving, her heart pounding painfully in her chest, stomach roiling with nausea from the constant ache in her chest. She put her hand on the doorknob and threw open the door, bending down and stepping through.

Deep breath in, exhale. She'd made it out.

It seemed a quiet, normal morning after all the chaos that had happened. Birds chirped, the river rushed past, gurgling happily, water lapped the grassy bank a few paces from her feet.

Elaina wanted to collapse with relief, but the ache in her heart came back as soon as she moved forward.

It meant one of two things: either the effects of breaking the curse were taking time to settle, and Elaina would live, or she hadn't broken the curse at all, only violated the conditions of her staying alive.

She could be dead within moments, or hours, or perhaps days, she didn't know. She needed a quicker way to get to Camelot.

Elaina scanned the shore by the road, looking for travelers. There didn't seem to be any, but the tower blocked the portion of the road behind her. She looked along the bank near to the forest, where trees gaily waved their branches, almost welcoming her.

The green plants, the sun, it was such a relief to be among them again. Her throat felt thick. She breathed in, reveling in the smell of sunshine and grass.

Camelot wasn't getting any closer. Elaina edged along the bank and around to the side of the tower nearest the trees.

A bridge of land, covered with shallow, flowing water, connected her tower island to the shore. Some ways down the river, a small boat bobbed in the river, perhaps left by a fisherman gone to shore. Riding the river would be the quickest way to Camelot.

Elaina started towards the boat, trying to ignore the pain that pierced through her. She crossed the small land bridge and walked along the rocky bank, wincing as the sharp stones jabbed her bare feet. Mud squelched between her toes as she waded in, and the knee-high water grabbed at her dress, making it drag on her shoulders.

Ahead, a light gleamed, reflecting off of something metal nearby. Elaina blinked, getting her vision back, and looked for the source. It glistened in the mud between the thickly growing rushes, and she caught a hint of yellow.

Curiosity getting the better of her, Elaina waded towards it, lifting her skirts to make walking easier in the now thigh-high water. She grabbed the edge of the thick and metal. The smooth surface slipped from her fingers several times, until tugging and grunting, she dragged a heavy shield out of the water.

Through the grime, she could make out a faint image of a knight's coat of arms. She washed it in the river, wiping the thicker mud off with handfuls of grass until a yellow lion, rearing with its mouth open in mid-roar, stood against the shield's silver background.

Gereck's shield. He had been looking for it when he climbed her tower, she remembered, and seemed distraught that he hadn't found it.

If the Green Knight had been successful, then it wouldn't do Gereck any good now, but Elaina found herself unable to leave it on the muddy bank. Perhaps they could hang it up in the castle somewhere in Gereck's memory.

Elaina waded back to the boat and placed the shield inside, then held the far side with one hand, the near side with her other, and heaved herself over the edge. The boat rocked precariously, and she prepared to go over completely, but then it righted and she sat up, pulling her sodden skirts back over the side. They were drenched and heavy, but she didn't have any clothing to spare, so she settled back, hoping the sun would dry them in the hours she had before she reached Camelot.

She sweated as she worked to untie the heavy, thick rope from its mooring, struggling with the damp knot that had been tied for who knew how long. The boat rocked with her attempts, and her heart continued to throb with pain, as if something inside of her had shattered along with the mirror.

Her breathing felt constricted, but her head was surprisingly calm.

In spite of the fact that she could be dying, peace took up a place inside of her, along with a brightly burning determination to get to Camelot, tell someone what she knew, and see Morgan and Arthur again.

She finished untying the knot and shoved off from the shore, allowing the boat to get caught in the current.

Gazing at the trees and bushes on the embankment, Elaina drank in the sights she had longed to see for decades. A deer, grazing in the shadows of the forest near the bank, looked up as she passed. The peacefulness of the afternoon slowed the pounding of her heart, and gradually she relaxed. The agonizing pain dulled to a merely inconvenient ache, and she found herself enjoying the rocking of the boat on the water.

She looked back at the tower only once. The sun shone on its rocky walls, glistening off the leaves of ivy that trailed up toward the only window. She wondered what the loom would do now. Would it weave forever without anyone at the shuttle, as it so often had while Elaina had slept? Or would another maiden be led, unsuspecting, into its clutches, and would she, in turn, wait for someone to rescue her?

Not if Elaina had anything to say about it. As soon as she warned Arthur, granting she lived through that, she would return and seek Merlin's advice. Perhaps he had a spell that could destroy the loom and mirror.

Elaina sat back, adjusting her dress, splaying it out as widely as she could to dry, when a sharp pain sliced across her hand. She gasped as blood welled up, bright on her pale skin. It dripped down her hand.

She shook out her skirt, searching for the culprit, and a piece of glass tinkled as it hit the floor of the boat. Wrapping her bleeding hand in her dress, she picked up the shard of mirror and stared into it. A small portion of her own face gleamed up at her from the surface of the shard.

Taking a deep, shuddering breath, Elaina pulled back her arm to throw it in the river, to be rid of the cursed mirror forever, but stopped. She looked into the glass again. Perhaps some magic still remained. She thought of Arthur.

Men crowded around a table, the image so miniscule individual faces were nearly indiscernible. A figure at the head had to be Arthur, a crown gleaming on his head. His pale and golden hair was so unlike Mordred's curly black hair that they might not have been related, except Elaina knew the truth.

She resisted the urge to pull up Mordred's image, afraid of what she might find. Instead, she thought of Gereck.

The mirror blurred, then the image grew, focusing on a prostrate form laying on a muddy riverbank, legs halfway into the water. *Was he dead?* She couldn't see much more than the matted brown hair on his un-helmed head. She looked more closely, wondering where he was, when she realized that she recognized the riverbank, and the tower she saw behind it.

Her tower. He laid somewhere on the road to Camelot; the road the river rushed along, the same river she floated on now. The image in the mirror flickered out, turning the surface of the glass clear once more. Elaina set the piece on her lap, careful not to cut herself again.

She kept her eyes wide open, searching as the boat rounded each bend in the river. Time passed. She drew nearer to Camelot and despaired that she had missed him somehow, or that she'd misjudged the angle of the light and the tower and that he lay further south.

The river wound around another tight bend, and a rock jutted from the water, threatening to create a crater in the side of her boat. Elaina pushed off of it with all her might, the boat rocking as it rushed down a small rapid. When it bobbed back up onto a calmer length of the river, Elaina saw him.

Laying facedown, arms reaching upward as if he had been climbing up the bank. He wore no armor, and he had no supplies with him. Bruises blackened his face.

Elaina used the shield to scoop through the water, steering towards Gereck. The current seemed to help, and in moments Elaina could reach out and grab his foot. She pulled herself and the boat closer until it edged up onto the bank.

Climbing out, she knelt and put her damp hand in front of Gereck's mouth. He breathed out, and Elaina relaxed. She rubbed Gereck's shoulder.

"Gereck?" She swallowed. He looked so pale, and damp debris clung to his brow. He didn't respond to her call, and Elaina could not afford to wait for him to wake. She grabbed the man's legs and heaved.

It took her several awkward tries, and by the end her arms ached from the effort, but she finally succeeded in dragging him onto the boat.

His heated skin burned against her fingertips, and he moaned as she adjusted his legs and arms more comfortably. She arranged his feet over the shield so there would be room for them both. It was damp, and she had nothing available to give him a gentler place to lay his head than the lichened boat floor.

She pushed off from the shore, letting the boat be taken by the current. She sat at the back of the boat, trying not to kick him.

A cloud passed over the sun, blocking its light. The world seemed chilled with the sun covered, but it came back momentarily. Elaina gazed at Gereck's face, taking in his features for the first time.

He had thick brown hair, sort of mousy-colored. His strong, square jaw had several days' stubble covering it. She wondered what color his eyes were, and tried to imagine. Perhaps blue.

She would have liked to see him smile. Everyone looked better when they smiled. And when they weren't laying in the bottom of a boat looking like death, but that couldn't be helped.

Another cloud covered the sun, bringing on the chill again. Elaina shivered, feeling the dampness of her wet skirts.

What would Gereck say to her now, if he woke and found himself where he was?

Elaina looked up to find a clouded sky. The wind had picked up, blowing sideways across the river and whipping through the trees.

A drop of rain struck her hand, like ice on her skin. As she looked around, the world seemed more grim, and she was reminded of what she had set out to do; to warn Arthur, and Camelot, of the impending war and betrayal, to perhaps save her sister from a horrible death.

She clasped her arms around herself in a tight hug, wishing she had her shawl.

Looking at Gereck again, the words to a song Elaina used to sing came to her mind. She hummed the tune, then let her voice drift quietly over the damp, grey riverbank.

"*Sweet is true love though given in vain, in vain;*
Sweet is true love though given in vain, in vain.
And sweet is death who puts an end to pain:
I know not which is sweeter, no, not I."

Her voice carried out over the rushing water, clear and strong. It sounded so different than when she had sung inside her tower.

"*Love, art thou sweet? Then bitter death must be:*
Love, thou art bitter; sweet is death to me.
O Love, if death be sweeter, let me die."

Some found love sweeter, and some death. Elaina had experienced both. Now, however, she wasn't sure what she felt. She had loved Mordred, once. He betrayed her. Then she had loved Gereck, but he was not hers to claim.

Sudden fatigue and a rush of pain overwhelmed her, and with no other option, she lay beside the fevered man in the bottom of the boat, pressing right up against him on her side, one hand and her face on his chest.

As she listened to the constant thrum of Gereck's heart, the final verse of the song floated into her mind. She had only the strength to hum.

"*Sweet love, that seems not made to fade away,*
Sweet death, that seems to make us loveless clay,
I know not which is sweeter, no, not I.
I fain would follow love, if that could be;
I needs must follow death, who calls for me;
Call and I follow, I follow! Let me die."

The boat rocked gently as it bore them steadily toward Camelot.

CHAPTER THIRTY-FOUR

"Ah, yes. Sir Tristan." Arthur's face split into a smile. "The man who has risked a thousand deaths to bring us news of our enemy. Where do they gather?"

Guinevere tried to listen, she did, especially as Sir Tristan spoke of the number of the enemy. She would need the information if she had to take her husband's position, she knew, but she couldn't stop peeking sideways through her dark hair at Arthur.

He sat attentively in his chair at the table, and she saw he had shaved recently. Why hadn't she noticed sooner? His strong jaw stood out definitively on his handsome face. She wondered what it would feel like to stroke the smooth skin there, to press her face against his...

She shook her head, trying to refocus, but then she caught his eye and he smiled at her. She returned his smile and looked away before she could get lost in his deep blue eyes.

He looked back at the men in the room, absently stroking the thumb of his left hand with his right, nodding at what the knight said.

Her heart thudded from the effects of Arthur's smile. Her blood coursed through her body, warming her, creating a tingling sensation in her most sensitive areas.

The feeling confused her. She didn't remember feeling it before, except perhaps on their wedding night, and she had no name for it.

But Morgan did.

A memory came to her. Strange to think that they were her own.

The night Mordred had come to her, in the light of the fires of Beltane, and they had fallen down together, nothing between them, clothes in the grass on the bank of the river, trees and stars for shelter overhead.

Is that what this feeling is? Guinevere wondered, her face flushing. Guilt accompanied the warmth, but she pushed that away. She could forgive herself for her past actions. It was before Arthur, before she had known any of what she knew now.

She basked in the warm sensations that moved through her body, and without thinking, reached a hand under the table and rested on Arthur's thigh.

He tensed at first, not looking at her, but she kept her hand firmly there. She watched him from the corner of her eye, seeing him visibly relax. After a moment, he dropped one of his own hands and rested it on hers.

The meeting closed after Sir Tristan's report, and the room emptied, leaving the two alone. Now was her chance to tell Arthur about Lancelot. She couldn't have done it publicly.

Her heart beat fast. What to say? *Your most loyal knight has betrayed you? And I planned to do so with him, only I didn't know it; it was the madness within me.*

What might he do if he believed her?

She couldn't reveal how she knew about Lancelot without telling Arthur about her past self, Morgan, the deal she had made with Niviane, and her sister locked in the tower. In the best case, he wouldn't believe her.

He would be convinced she was lying, the fantastic nature of her story would be too much. Besides, since she had returned from Melwas' he seemed to have renewed his affections for her.

Guinevere would do anything to keep it that way, to feel loved, truly loved, by someone for the first time in her life. To tell him would be to sabotage that. How could he love her knowing that part of her had plotted to betray him.

All of the courage she'd built up scurried away, like a mouse to its hole.

She couldn't tell him. Not yet. Perhaps more evidence would support her claims soon, something undeniable, something that didn't put Arthur in suspicion of her as well as Lancelot.

So instead of speaking, Guinevere stood, feigning a yawn.

"Are you tired, my queen?" Arthur asked, placing his hand at the small of her back.

His touch there sent a surge of blood rushing through her body, and Guinevere lost her tongue.

She nodded, feeling shy, and glanced up at him through her lashes. "If my king allows it, I will retire early this evening."

"Of course," he replied, his tone disappointed. "I understand you must still be recovering. I will leave you to rest." He bent over her hand and kissed it, lingering.

"Would my king accompany me to my chambers?" she asked breathlessly. Her heart pounded, her blood rushing.

Arthur looked up at her, smiled, and then straightened. He offered her his arm.

"Anything for my queen." He escorted her from the room.

Guinevere vaguely noticed Lancelot's gaze following them, but she forgot it the instant the door closed behind them.

They walked in silence. Guinevere didn't want to risk losing the feeling between them with an awkward conversation.

They came to her door and Arthur opened it for her, standing on the threshold as she walked in.

"Shall I call your lady-in-waiting to attend to you?"

Her heart almost stopped in her chest when she turned back to look at him, seeing the longing in his eyes so apparent, he may as well have shouted it. She swallowed the lump in her throat, ignored the tightness in her chest, and turned her back to him, lifting her hair as she did.

"Would you do it tonight?"

She waited, hardly breathing, until she felt his hands on the ribbons at her back. Her muscles relaxed completely at his touch, the fumbling of his fingers as he unlaced her dress oddly comforting. He slipped the material off her shoulders, and his lips trailed against the base of her neck. He came around in front of her, taking her hands in his, eyes asking.

She answered by kissing him in a full, passionate embrace. Her body trembled, memories threatening to come crashing down, but Guinevere was not weak any longer. Part of her knew this needed to happen for the healing to be complete, so she gave herself completely to the feelings, ignoring any thoughts that leaked into her mind.

Each kiss drove them away, so she brought her lips against Arthur's again and again, pressing her body against his, relishing the feeling of his hands on her.

He picked her up, still kissing her, and laid her in the bed, then made a quick round to blow out all the lanterns.

The fire remained, burning low and hot, emitting a dim, reddish-orange glow in the otherwise dark room.

His dark silhouette undressed against the light of the fireplace, then he climbed into bed, pulling the covers over them both.

They lay side-by-side, only their arms touching. Guinevere rolled onto her side, and he looked at her. It seemed he wanted to be sure she was ready. Even with the obviousness of her advances he didn't presume anything, and she loved him more for it.

He whispered her name in the dark. She murmured back, and their lips and bodies met. His lips trailed across her skin, making it burn with pleasure.

Years afterward, she would remember his smell more vividly than anything else. Spicy and musky all at once, and the same tickle would come to her nose, almost making her sneeze, but not quite. Her heart would flutter whenever she thought of it, Guinevere's first time, her first true love.

After their passion quieted, satisfied, they lay together in the dark, holding one another. His chest moved against Guinevere's, his breath on her ear. She explored the new feeling within her. A tiny bud of true healing. A tinge of sadness filled her as they lay together, his body warm and still against hers. If only she had come to him sooner.

They had a lifetime ahead of them, a lifetime together, once the Saxons were defeated and Camelot knew peace again.

Morning dawned bright, the bed empty except for Guinevere. She was alone again, but her heart still sang with joy from the night before. She stretched in her bed, comfortably warm beneath the covers, and when she glanced toward the window, her eyes caught a glimpse of something she had never seen before.

On a table beside her bed sat an ornate engraved metal box. It stood on four delicate feet, a lock on its forefront.

Guinevere sat up. The top held a large, circular blue gem set into the metal, and words engraved around it.

She tilted her head to read the ornate script.

"*A love truer could not be found.*"

A key lay beside the box. Guinevere picked it up and turned it in the lock, then lifted the lid of the box. Inside, a beautiful necklace with three large clear stones set in gold rested on soft, dark velvet. Diamonds.

She touched them reverently, smiling to herself. He must have been saving it for their first time.

A wedding gift; a gift to represent their love. Now that it was finally sealed with the physical act, he had given it to her.

Guinevere dressed with Alyce's help, humming a tune so cheerful the maid managed a shaky smile.

A page came and delivered a request from the king for her to meet him in the throne room.

Guinevere received the request as Alyce finished doing her hair, then asked that Alyce get the box on her side table. The maid complied, bringing it and the key to Guinevere.

The maid's eyes widened as she picked up the necklace and clasped it. The metal felt cool at first, but quickly warmed against Guinevere's body. She touched the smooth surface of the gems, then stood and swept from the room, eager to see Arthur's face after the previous night.

She joined Arthur in arbitration, listening to the grievances of their people. Many were refugees, coming from farther reaches of the land, where the Saxons had already swept through and pillaged. They sought shelter and food, which King Arthur generously allotted them, though Camelot's own supplies almost weren't enough for the people who lived there.

However, he was a fair and wise king, and he required that the services and loyalties of the people be sworn to him, that they would respond if he called on them for anything he should need of them.

The people were grateful. They loved and respected him, and readily swore their fealty to him.

After several hours, Guinevere's back and head ached. She tried not to show it so she might stay at Arthur's side, but he noticed and he sent her to rest.

Guinevere smiled at Arthur; a true, sincere smile that she felt in her heart. She left the throne room, happy to leave the remaining arbitration duties to her husband.

He would probably be in council through much of the day. From what their council had decided the day before, he would be leaving within the next day or so to fight a crucial battle.

Camelot would be emptied of knights and soldiers alike. Arthur was confident they would win, and when they did, the Saxons would easily be pushed back to their own lands with little force required.

She neared her chambers, then had a thought light in her mind that made her smile. Why not surprise Arthur? She could go await him in his chambers, rather than her own.

She set down the hallway, a bounce in her step, until she got to Arthur's room. Guinevere opened the door and slipped inside, then unwound her hair from its tight coil on her head, lost in the warmth of remembering the night before.

An arm grabbed her around the waist, jerking her off her feet. She let out a shriek, then realized it was Lancelot.

"Let me go!" She struggled against his grip, but he held her tighter, silencing her objections with the press of his lips on her mouth.

She couldn't escape his grip without hurting herself, so she relaxed. He was like a wolf, ravenous for her body, hands plying all over her dress, searching for fastenings, fumbling over ribbons... She managed to get her hands on his chest and thrust him away, breathing fast and heavy. Her tongue tasted the metallic tang of blood. Had he bitten her? She touched her lip, fingers coming away with a tinge of red.

"What are you thinking?" She drew herself to her full height, fists clenched, trying to appear imposing.

Lancelot sauntered to the bed and sat down, drawing off his boots. He grinned at her, and revulsion coursed through her body. She said the first thing that came to her mind. "Arthur could come in here any moment."

Lancelot drew off his shirt, then languidly stretched himself out on the bed. "I happen to know Arthur is caught in arbitration with his loyal subjects, and soon will be in council with the knights, and as I was posted on rotation, I am fortunate enough to escape the chore of attending."

"But won't he expect you to be there, now that your post is up?" She felt dazed. This couldn't be happening. Everything had been going better than she thought possible, perfect, in fact, and now this.

Morgan had loved Lancelot, and he wanted her, but Morgan was gone, melded with Guinevere's own mind, unable to help Guinevere get out of the mess she had created. Her memories were one and the same, but her feelings were utterly changed.

Lancelot shook his head, that boorish smile still plastered on his face. "My shift will last until evening, and I got Sir Tristan to fill in for me." The grin widened, and he slid off the bed, coming towards her. "Seeing as we have hours until your husband makes his return, I expect you will be more than pleased to comply with what I have planned for you."

She didn't even try to resist as he pulled her near again. Fear clutched at her mind, betraying her desire to flee, to fight. She was fourteen-year-old Morgan again, her brothers telling her not to say a thing to their father.

"Will you not speak, my love?" He kissed her, rather softly, but she could feel the hunger in his grasping hands. His lips moved down her neck.

"I—I do not know what to say."

"Say you love me."

She could not.

"Say you want me."

His hands untied her corset, then moved to her shoulders and the dress fell free of her body, sliding to the floor. She knew she should do something, anything. Scream perhaps, but who would hear her? The guards were posted far enough from her room they would not make it in time to prevent anything.

The burly knight picked her up easily and carried her to the bed. Some part of her mind, the part that was not consumed with fear, observed that Lancelot's hands were under her slip, moving against her skin. Her mind raced while her body lay paralyzed. How could she escape?

She could magic him, like she had the men at Melwas's castle, but the words were lost in her mind, bogged down in the memories she had yet to sort through and learn as her own. She would get no aid from enchantments.

But she hadn't brought together all the broken parts of herself to become a victim again.

Lancelot pulled away from her and undid the fastening on his breeches. He had them half off when Guinevere's eyes landed on a sword that hung on a hook by the bed.

She twisted, grabbing the sword, and scrambled to stand on the bed above Lancelot. The blade was no Excalibur, but it would do.

She pointed it at Lancelot, who knelt, frozen and staring at her.

"Morgan..." He moved as if to come toward her.

"Don't," she said, shifting her grip on the sword. If it came down to it, she knew he would win this fight. The sword might as well be a fire poker, for what good it would do her, but it got the message to him, loud and clear.

"Morgan."

The sword felt heavy in her arms. Why had she never learned to use one properly?

"Morgan," he said again. There was an unspoken plea in his eyes. The wolf, the hunger, was gone. In its place she could almost see the man she had known before, as Morgan. The man she had fallen in love with almost from the moment he first called on her father, only to ask for Elaina's hand instead of hers.

Morgan had changed all of that. Her sister's lover became her own, bending over backwards to fulfill her will and bed her.

But bedding alone did not make two people love one another. Kindness, patience, respect; these Guinevere had found with Arthur, and now, she wanted nothing to do with Lancelot's paltry offering.

He was speaking. She forced herself to listen. "How could I have read you wrong? All these years I waited for you, since we first came together. You put me off time and again to protect your image of a virgin lady to marry the king, but now we are alone and free to do as we wish, Morgan. Arthur will never know."

She lowered the sword, shaking her head. "I have only ever wanted to live in a world where women could be *free*. Free from the unwanted advances of men, free from the lust of the likes of you." She spat. Something inside told her this was a mistake. Lancelot's face hardened.

He stared at her with eyes like fire. "You will give me what I have waited for."

He advanced on her, easily avoiding the blade as she swiped it at him, then tearing it from her hand with little effort. His hands pulled her roughly against him and his lips pressed onto hers.

She tried to pull away, but his fist tangled in her hair and yanked, painfully. His other arm caught her knees and pulled her off the floor, carrying her towards the bed.

She kicked and thrashed, but his muscled arms held her tight. He tossed her on the bed like a sack of flour, knocking the breath from her.

She rolled, but he caught her beneath the full weight of his body, stretching out on top of her.

"Please, stop!" she shrieked. "I don't want this."

"You do, I'll show you."

"Mordred, stop. It's not like it was. You have to stop." Her fists beat on his chest. Tears were pouring down her cheeks.

Understanding lit Mordred's eyes. "You love Arthur." His disbelieving laughter filled the room. "After all this time, after all the plans we set and your assurances that you could never possibly love another, you would throw it all away for this foolish king and his noble ideals? You have fallen farther than I thought."

She opened her mouth to reply when the chamber doors flew open and Arthur strode in. He stopped dead, taking in the sight of them. Lancelot half-stripped, Guinevere in nothing more than her shift.

"Arthur, I..." Guinevere said, just as Mordred leapt from the bed. He grabbed the sword from the floor, holding it out toward Arthur.

"Lancelot, what is the meaning of this?"

"Your precious queen has been playing the whore, Arthur. Open your eyes and see her for who she is. She would have your kingdom eating from the palm of her hand, and the men of the kingdom enslaved like beasts. I don't know what she's told you, but she isn't innocent as you might believe; a two-faced snake, no better than a street whore."

"You will not speak of my wife in this way, Lancelot Du Lac!" Arthur's voice roared through the chamber, and Guinevere noticed his hand on Excalibur's handle.

Mordred was breathing heavily, inching towards the door. He motioned towards Guinevere with the sword. "Ask her, if you must."

"Guinevere, is this true?"

"What? No!" she gasped. "Arthur, please, you must believe me. Lancelot attacked me, I..."

His eyes turned on Mordred. "My most faithful, trusted knight, worming his way into the bed of my wife. What could have possessed you to presume to usurp my rightful place?" Arthur seemed to grow a foot as he drew Excalibur and extended it toward Mordred.

"Prepare yourself, Arthur. You may have discovered us, but the plans we have set in motion will not be stopped. Camelot will fall before a fortnight, and you will fall with it." Mordred bolted past Arthur, still brandishing his naked sword. Arthur seemed stunned, and Guinevere wondered if he would pursue Lancelot, but he didn't move. She heard shouts in the corridor, then nothing. Why didn't Arthur do something?

"Is there any truth to his words?" He didn't look at her.

Guinevere's breath caught in her throat. It felt so swollen she couldn't get any words out. She shook her head. *What can I say*? If she denied it, denied all of it, she would be lying. But if she said anything, in the heat of the moment, Arthur wouldn't understand. He wouldn't be able to separate truth from lie. Tears came to her eyes. *I have to try*. She sat up in the bed, hands clasped in her lap. She looked down at them, unable to meet his eyes.

“Do you remember when I was having... episodes?”

Arthur hesitated. “The madness? Yes. Are you saying the madness did this to you?” Anger was plain in his voice.

“Yes... and no.” She took a deep, shuddering breath, gazing up at him, imploring with her eyes that he understand.

“Tell me what you mean,” he said slowly. There was a dangerous quietness to his voice now, a careful control of his temper. It wouldn’t last long.

She breathed in again. She had to say something now; there was no returning.

“I am not who you think I am. My name is not important, and neither is where I come from. What you must know is that the person I was... made an agreement with a sorceress. In return for the safety of someone I cared about, I would help her bring about the fall of Camelot,” she said, pushing herself off the bed. “It wasn’t me, Arthur. You must understand that. I was under an enchantment, I didn’t know... didn’t know who I was.

“My past self knew Lancelot. He knew the sorceress. He was to help with the plot against you. My past self... she...I, lost my memories and became who you know me as. I became Guinevere. I never wanted to hurt you, Arthur. You must believe me! When I met Lancelot, my memories started to return, and with it, the madness. And then the sorceress came to me, holding me to an oath I can’t remember making, an oath to destroy Camelot, and I couldn’t stop it. I couldn’t stop any of it.

"I've tried to be strong, but I've been so confused, so lost. Please," she stopped, choking on a sob. She put her hands to her mouth, trying futilely to prevent breaking down.

The sound of Arthur's breath filled the chamber. Guinevere's heart pounded in her chest and, without thinking, she moved forward, reaching out to touch him. The blow of his hand caught her across the face, throwing her to the floor. She touched her cheek, expecting blood. It came away clean.

"Do you truly expect me to believe you?" his breath heaved in his chest. "If what you say is true, then Lancelot was not wrong. You have plotted with him against Camelot, against me. And in your confusion, who's to say that you didn't share his bed? Who's to say you didn't seek Melwas, to trick me, to further your plans for the destruction of Camelot? If madness has been leading you, how can I possibly trust you?"

Guinevere couldn't stop her sobbing long enough to reply. The deepest regret she had ever known filled her inside. She didn't deserve him. It was her fault Lancelot had betrayed him. Her fault the kingdom was about to fall. She could not escape her past, and now the only person who had ever truly loved her was turned against her forever.

"I never... I never wanted to hurt you, Arthur," she gasped through a sob. "I couldn't... I didn't know how to tell you."

"You should have done so anyway!" Arthur roared, fists clenched at his side. Guinevere shrank away from him, trembling.

"I love you," she whispered. She had to say it, even if it changed nothing.

Arthur turned his head away from her. When he spoke again, there was a tremor in his voice.

“You give me no choice, Guinevere. I cannot trust you, and if I cannot trust you, then how am I to believe that you have changed? That you will not slip back into madness and stab me in our bed, while I sleep? Or plot further against Camelot, if I even succeed in saving the kingdom now? It has gone too far, and it’s too late.”

Arthur looked at her for a moment longer, the sadness and anger in his eyes breaking her heart, and then he walked slowly to the doors where several guards stood at attention, awaiting his command.

“Take her to a cell. I’ll see her in the throne room at high noon tomorrow. From this moment on, she is no longer your queen.” He spared her one last glance. “Put on a robe.”

Then he strode from the room without looking back. Guinevere didn’t move as the guards came to stand beside her. They pulled her to her feet. One handed her a robe, which she reluctantly drew on. Then she allowed them to take her away, half-dragging her down the hall. Void of feeling, Guinevere hardly registered when they passed by the throne room, still emptying from the council, and Galahad called after her.

“What are you doing with the queen? Hands off her, you…” He confronted one of the guards, who drew his sword and pointed it at Galahad’s throat.

“Orders of the king, Sir Galahad. You can ask him yourself.”

“Be sure I will, and if I find out otherwise…” He stepped aside, eyes confused as he watched Guinevere be taken away.

She closed them, unwilling to see who else was witnessing her humiliation.

They pushed her into a cell without a word, shutting the cell door with a final loud clang that reverberated through her soul.

Curled up on the floor with nothing more than a thin layer of hay between her and the hard stone, Guinevere shivered. She pulled her knees close and pulled the robe more tightly around her.

The robe was thin, made of rich silk that was a mockery to her in this dank place. It did nothing against the frigid cold of her cell. In one corner, there was a crumpled, coarse wool blanket, but she was loath to touch it. How many murderers, traitors, and thieves had left their blood, sweat, and filth on its surface?

But she had done that, and worse. She could not continue separating Morgan's crimes from her own. She *was* Morgan. Guinevere crawled over to it, shame filling her soul so completely that it overrode the instinct to run from this place, or fight. She deserved whatever Arthur gave her. She deserved his hatred.

CHAPTER THIRTY-FIVE

A longdrawn carol, mournful, holy,
She chanted loudly, chanted lowly,
Till her eyes were darken'd wholly,
And her smooth face sharpen'd slowly,
Turn'd to tower'd Camelot:
For ere she reach'd upon the tide
The first house by the water-side,
Singing in her song she died,
The Lady of Shalott.

Through a haze of pain, Elaina stirred into wakefulness. Something was tugging at her feet, moving them aside, making the boat rock violently. They weren't moving anymore. Had they gone to shore? Were they in Camelot?

"Stop… stop it," she managed, her tongue feeling thick in her mouth, her words slurring. "What're you… doing?" She sat halfway up, peeling her eyes open.

Her blurred vision made out the outline of a man, and he was at the end of the boat pulling something from under her and Gereck's feet. It gleamed in the daylight. A yellow lion on a field of silver.

The shield.

"Wait! That isn't... It isn't yours!" she said haltingly, fighting the pain and fatigue that weighed on her so she could sit up fully. The attempt was futile. She had not the strength to raise herself off her elbows. She leaned back on them, blinking furiously to get her vision to clear. The figure stared at her for a long moment, hesitating with the shield in hand.

"Elaina?" the voice asked.

"Mordred!" she exclaimed. The name practically pierced her heart as she said it, and she cried out in pain.

"Are you hurt? What is wrong?" He moved towards the head of the boat. "How have you come to be here?"

He didn't know. He didn't know Niviane had put her in the tower. He didn't know Morgan had seen her. She could almost forgive him for that. Tears filled her eyes. They seemed clearer once the tears started flowing. She blinked again, and was finally able to see Mordred's face. Such a serious expression. She wished he would smile, but she seriously doubted he would ever be smiling at her again.

"Why did you... not come for me?" she asked, though she knew the answer. Niviane's enchantment, sealed by the light of the Beltane fires.

He shook his head, seeming confused. "I have been..." He trailed off, glancing away from her. "I need to go. I am wanted here."

"What have you done?" Elaina whispered.

"How have you come here?" He asked, ignoring her question.

She took a deep, gasping breath, but drawing it in hurt almost more than it was worth. "Arthur... someone means to... kill him. I... warn him."

She had to lay her head back down. Her head felt fuzzy, but her vision stayed clear for now. She could still see him. Beside her, Gereck moved.

His expression darkened. "It's too late for that."

"What happened to you, Mordred?"

"Many things. Elaina, you must let me go. I do not know how you came to be here, but you must know I love you no longer. Farewell."

"I know about Morgan!" Elaina cried out. Her heart constricted in her chest and she coughed, hacking as it tore the breath from her. "It was ruined love, cursed love, not true... like ours." She didn't have much time.

Mordred shook his head. "You're wrong, Elaina," he said, eyes flaring. "You just don't want to believe I could love her more than you, after what we shared. But everything pales in comparison to what she and I..."

"Stop," Elaina gasped, the pain in her heart growing more intense by the moment. "I am dying, Mordred."

She gazed into his pale green eyes, eyes that once made her entire world light up, searching for any sign of remorse, but she found instead a cold, unpitying stare that could hardly belong to someone human, much less the man she had once loved. She gathered the last of her strength and lashed out with her words. "What was it like? Watching the woman you loved marry another?"

Mordred's face twisted into a grimace. "It's a tragedy that Morgan could not be saved from her madness. It has cost her greatly, a fact she will realize when she burns. She will regret how she has treated me then."

"Burn?" Elaina asked. Her heart pounded like a galloping horse on its last stretch, and she could hardly draw breath.

"Arthur caught us together. Even he won't ignore the law to save his own life. He must follow it. A queen caught in adultery burns for her sins."

"No," Elaina gasped, struggling to sit up. Pain lanced through her chest. She couldn't breathe, she couldn't move.

Mordred spat into the water. "She will be damned for sure, while I am made a saint when I rule the kingdom, Niviane at my side. It was supposed to be Morgan, but she has made too many mistakes, and I am finished with her."

He looked down, towering over Elaina, and her vision blurred so she could hardly see his face.

"I thank you for finding my shield." His voice took on a mocking tone. "I would have hardly had a chance defeating the king without it, and I don't know where you found that useless lump of a knight, but I hope he dies with you."

She reached a hand toward him, and a tear rolled down her cheeks. "Please..." Her voice was so soft and hoarse, she didn't know if he heard her. "Mordred, you... can still stop... this."

Gasping for air, Elaina watched Mordred walk away along the opposite riverbank. He didn't once turn back or reply, and her hand trembled in the air before falling limp to the bottom of the boat.

As her mind faded with the pain, she realized something she hadn't before. Mordred had been with the queen. Morgan. He must be known here, then, as the Sir Lancelot that Merlin had mentioned. The king's knight.

It made sense, now. He had gotten so close to the king that no one would suspect his hand in the betrayal until it was too late.

She heard voices and tried calling out, but they were just a murmur, too far to hear. Some of them shouted, and moments later her boat rocked as several men splashed in the river towards her.

"Where did he go?"

She muttered incoherently, but could not gather enough strength to motion after him. Beside her, the knight Gereck stirred.

"Gereck!" One of the men called out, making the boat sway and dip as they walked up to the side. "How did you come to be here? What of your quest? And this woman, who is she?"

He sat up beside her.

"I am certain he came this way, Sir Tristan. I bet my life on it," another man spoke.

"Send half the men up the river, half down. You there, find a physician for this woman and Sir Gereck."

Elaina shook her head, trying to voice her protests. Why was Gereck silent? He had to have heard the encounter between herself and Mordred.

"Quiet now, save your strength," Sir Tristan said to her.

Gereck murmured something she couldn't hear. Perhaps it was only her name.

But Elaina was dying, and more than anything else, there was one person she wanted to see before that happened. She managed a halting breath, drawing enough air in to breathe out his name. "Arthur," she said.

"Did she just ask for the king?" Sir Tristan asked.

"So I heard. Must be the death madness," another voice said.

They thought her mad. They wouldn't bring the kind, now. Not ever. Elaina slumped down in the boat, strength exhausted, pain spreading from her heart into her limbs and weighing them down. Her breath seemed to rattle in her throat.

Please. She thought, sending all of her prayers and intentions toward the heavens. *Please let me meet my son.*

CHAPTER THIRTY-SIX

Gereck moved beside Elaina, gesturing at a man in a brown vest and tattered pants. "You there, go get Arthur."

"Sir?"

"Just do it," Gereck said firmly.

"The king is in private conference," Sir Tristan's voice replied. "He does not have time for this dying woman, no matter how much he would pity her."

"He has time for this woman. I will get him myself." Gereck grasped Sir Tristan's arm and pulled himself over the side of the boat, ignoring the pain in his ribs and Sir Tristan's protests. He had become used to it, now, though it still hurt immensely.

He glanced at Elaina, laying in the boat, her eyes closed. How had she found him? The last thing he recalled was falling from Fendrel's back, having forgotten to get tied on at his last stop. Elaina's face was pale as the full moon, and her golden hair shone fair as ever.

She seemed to be sleeping, but as he stared, willing her chest to rise and fall, she remained still, as if made of stone.

"She stopped breathing," Gereck whispered. "Where is the king?"

Sir Tristan stammered something about the conference chamber, then gripped Gereck's shoulder tightly. Gereck brushed him off and staggered through the gathered crowd towards the castle.

He stopped in the doorframe of a servant's entrance. He didn't have the strength to go by himself. Days on a horse with minimal rest, food, or water had taken its toll.

He called out to a passing servant, who recognized Gereck and immediately came to his aid. Without asking any questions, the servant walked him through the castle and to the conference hall door, where two regular arms men stood sentry.

"The king will not be seeing common folk here. Go wait in the line if you want a conference with him." the soldier speaking jutted his thumb toward the throne room.

"No... you don't... understand," Gereck said, leaning on the servant to catch his breath. "I must see him. He'll want to, I'm one of his knights."

"Oh? Which one?" The smaller arms man challenged, his spear coming up toward Gereck's chin. "Ye don't look like a knight of the table."

Gereck pulled his medallion from his shirt. The red dragon and the cross gleamed on the painted wooden surface. "Sir Gereck Bauer."

"But you left on that fatal quest a whole moon ago!" The men gaped at him.

"I know. Clearly, I lived."

The two men exchanged looks, then looked back at Gereck. "The conference is for all Round Table knights not sent in pursuit of Sir Lancelot." they lowered their weapons and moved aside. Gereck nodded to his servant friend, who opened the doors for him, then closed them behind him.

Gereck immediately fell to the floor, catching himself on his knees.

"Sir Gereck!" King Arthur exclaimed. Several knights rushed to Gereck's side, helping him to his feet. "We expected we would never see you again. Has your quest failed?"

Gereck winced at the accusation. It hurt more than his ribs, which burned fiercely as he was led to a chair at the immense wooden table in the center of the room.

"No, Sire. I was fortunate enough to come across a generous and kind... lady. A lady who gifted me a sash which held powers to withstand the knight's blow."

It was easier than trying to explain the truth, of Merlin's presence, of his wife...

Gereck shook his head to clear it. A fatigued fog threatened to close in, his body requesting rest. He couldn't rest, not now.

"What of your condition, Sir Gereck? Who has so abused you?" another knight asked.

"I must tell you... Sir Lancelot..." Gereck stammered.

"Has betrayed the trust of Camelot, and her king," Arthur spoke, gazing off toward the door. His eyes seemed wet, and Gereck couldn't fully decide if he saw tears or not.

Arthur shook his own head, then bowed it. His hands brushed across the table, as if removing dirt or debris from the surface, only the table was clean. "It gets harder with each telling. I hope this is the last I have to speak of it."

Arthur gritted his teeth, as if in pain. "Sir Lancelot Du Lac was discovered in bed with the queen. He was unfaithful on more than one front, and it is due to his betrayal that we have a war on our hands. A war that could destroy Camelot."

"Yes, but..."

Sir Galahad interrupted him. "We are more than a match for Lancelot and a few renegade knights, Arthur. Surely you believe that much."

"They are not alone," Arthur replied grimly, "and he has the sword Clarent, stolen from my chambers."

Galahad shrugged. "But you have Excalibur. Clarent is a sword of peace, what could he do with that?"

"Clarent bestows peace in a way unique to a sword; by not fighting. However, it relies on righteous men to wield that power. If Lancelot has truly turned on Camelot, he will destroy all peace by using it in battle, for its very nature and power will be warped eternally the moment he spills another man's blood with it," Arthur explained.

"Then we must confront him without bringing him to use it," Sir Perceval said. Gereck shifted from one foot to another. He did not want to interrupt, but if he didn't, Elaina would die, having never met Arthur.

"We must prepare for the worst," the king said. "He will not back down."

"Arthur!" Gereck shouted. The hall fell as silent as a tomb. "There is a situation at the river. A woman is dying, and she has asked to see you."

The knights stared at him in disbelief.

"Is this what you risked fainting to tell me, Sir Gereck?" Arthur asked.

Gereck nodded, holding his head high. Let the others think what they would. They could all be dead tomorrow, and some things were more important than war councils.

"Camelot is going to war, Gereck. I am the leader of these men, and my people are depending on me. I do not have time to attend every one of my subjects, especially at a time like this. Find a physician, and if she lives, God granting we both live, I will see her at the end of this war."

"But, Arthur, Your Majesty, I..." Gereck started.

"Enough, Gereck," Sir Gawain said. "You heard the king. We must figure out how to deal with Lancelot and the Saxons. That is our priority now, not matters of personal preference."

Sir Gawain turned back to the king.

"Camelot is impenetrable, a fortress unlike any other. The hill surrounding protects our walls from being scaled, and the walls themselves are too thick to be broken through. Even the Saxons will not penetrate our defenses."

Arthur shook his head. "The knights of the Round Table were pledged upon Clarent's blade. If the sword is tainted with blood, all your oaths will be broken. The bond of fealty between us shattered. You will, without even realizing it, scatter yourselves to the four winds and leave Camelot to ruin."

Protests rang in the wide hall. Several of the knights stood, knocking their chairs backward.

Arthur smiled, but it was a sad reflection of his usual grin. "I know that, in your hearts, you will always be true, but you will not be able to prevent it. Notice, half our number are already missing, either deserted or joined with Lancelot." He held up a hand to the avalanche of objections. "I know what you would say, and it will change nothing. All we can do is pray this stops before Lancelot uses that sword."

"What would you have us do, Sire?" one of the knights, Gereck couldn't tell which, spoke out in the silence.

King Arthur stood, hand on the pommel of Excalibur. "We go out and find him. No one goes alone. No one is to draw their sword against him. I would rather you run from him than confront him while he wields that sword. Do you understand?" He gazed at each of them, almost individually.

When he got to Gereck, the knight's eyes felt locked in place by the king's ice blue stare. Gereck was suspended in that gaze, and then the king looked away and left his place at the Round Table, his footsteps echoing in the hall. He passed Gereck, clasping a hand on his shoulder, and Gereck could see in his eyes that he did not expect to win.

Arthur moved to leave and Gereck gripped his arm.

"Sire." He said it quietly enough only the king could hear. Arthur stopped and looked back at him. "That woman I mentioned; she is your mother."

Confusion passed over the king's eyes, but he made no comment. He simply walked away. When he reached the doors, he turned and looked back at the men in the room. Every eye was watching him, some glistening with unshed tears.

"Serving with you has been the highest honor of my life. I believe Camelot can rise against this evil, as we have against all others, but if this happens to be the final moment for our glory as the knights of the Round Table of Camelot, then there are no other men with whom I would rather end my days as king." Fist held over his heart, he bowed, and when he arose, the hall echoed with the resounding clash of each man's fist meeting his chest.

Then Arthur's piercing eyes found Gereck's again. "Take me to her."

Gereck had to be supported once more. He could hardly walk with the pain and weariness that overcame him. Arthur commanded two knights to hold Gereck on either side, helping him limp along.

The crowd had grown since Gereck left. One of the knights bellowed, "Make way for your king!" The people parted, letting Gereck and the King pass. The boat had been dragged ashore, and Elaina lay as Gereck had left her, damp and still. Her chest did not move, her eyes did not open.

Gereck watched Arthur's face carefully. When he saw Elaina's face for the first time, he visibly startled, stepping back, eyes widening.

"Arthur?" Gereck asked. "Are you all right?"

"I was not meant to be king," he murmured, gazing down at Elaina's face.

"What...?" Gereck started, cutting himself off as Arthur leaned over the boat's edge toward Elaina.

"It does not matter now," the king whispered. "What is done is done. I wish I had known you." He bent and kissed Elaina's forehead lightly.

For the first and last time, Gereck saw them together. Elaina's fair hair, the shape and color of her eyes, Mordred's structured face and broad shoulders. Arthur was Elaina's son.

He was also Mordred's, Lancelot's, and he didn't know it. Gereck wondered if he should say something, but decided against it as Arthur stood, sweeping his hair from his eyes with a toss of his head.

"Tell them to bury her on the chapel grounds." His eyes drifted over the crowd as it dispersed. Arthur fidgeted with one of his gloves, then looked at Gereck. "What was her name?"

"Elaina of Astolat," Gereck said.

"Was she your faerie lady, the one in the tower?"

"Yes."

Arthur placed a hand on Gereck's shoulder. "I am glad you found her and led me to her. You will have to tell me someday how you came to know of our connection."

Gereck returned the king's smile. "I will, Sire." Then his brow furrowed. "Then you believe she is who I have said?"

"When I saw her, I just..." Arthur shrugged. "I knew. She was familiar to me, I remembered her, but it was as from a past life, so distant, and yet, so clear I cannot deny it."

"What changed your mind about seeing her?"

"I know you wouldn't lie to me, and I also know that war spares few. I did not want to put this off for another day and risk... Well, it has come to naught anyway. Thank you for your efforts, Gereck."

The glove made it back on the king's hand, and Gereck handed him his helm, which he immediately placed on his head. Excalibur was drawn with a ringing sound. "To war, then."

"To war," Gereck replied.

The king made his way back up the bank toward the castle, then turned back toward Gereck. "Do not join us when we march to battle tomorrow, Sir Gereck. Only fight if it comes to you. When all is said and done, someone must stand and defend all we hold dear."

Gereck almost protested, then closed his mouth. His king had spoken. "Yes, Sire." Then, "Arthur, what of your wife?" *Elaina's sister.*

A dark shadow passed over his face. "She has chosen her lot. She will burn in the courtyard tomorrow. The church has spoken and the law has made its decision."

With a sinking feeling, Gereck watched his liege disappear into the castle. He glanced back toward Elaina, her face serene, her hands resting peacefully by her sides. He tried to cry, watching a few men bring her up onto the shore, but the tears had been wrung from him with exhaustion.

He clapped one of the men on his shoulder. "Put her in my room, for now. I will see to her arrangements."

Her filthy, wet dress trailed up the mud-ridden bank as they carried her toward the castle.

He had failed to keep Winna safe.

He had failed to warn Arthur in time.

And now, he had failed to free Elaina.

Heart heavy with regret, he followed the men up the embankment, the pain of each step a reminder of the people who had once depended on him, and now, had no need for him.

CHAPTER THIRTY-SEVEN

Guinevere was in too much shock to move her own legs when they finally came for her.

Sir Tristan and Sir Galahad half-carried, half-dragged her through the doors and into the throne room. They released her arms and she crumpled to her knees.

Arthur sat in his throne, straight-backed and solemn-faced as he gazed at her. He didn't speak for a long moment.

"Read the charges," he said at last, his voice heavy.

Guinevere pleaded silently with her gaze.

His expression did not waver.

The steward cleared his throat. "Her majesty, Queen Guinevere Pendragon, has been found guilty of adultery with the knight Lancelot Du Lac and is sentenced to death by burning according to law and by order of the church."

"No," Guinevere whispered. Her ears filled with the roar of whispers that broke out among the knights and nobles gathered in the hall. She scrambled to her feet. "No, please. Arthur, I never..."

Arthur stood abruptly, and the fierce look on his face cut off her choking plea. "You will address me as 'Your Majesty' or 'King;' informality is no longer your privilege."

Emotion gathered in Guinevere's throat. "But I love you," she choked out.

If he heard her, he did not move. He didn't even look at her.

The steward continued, but Guinevere didn't hear him until his last words, "The sentence will be carried out at dawn."

Two men took her arms and pulled her to her feet. In her last glimpse of Arthur, he rested his head on his hand and stared toward the high windows where strong rays of afternoon sunlight streamed in. The golden light caught on his hair, gleaming, and then the doors slammed shut.

Guinevere stared at the polished wood and cold stone and allowed herself to be led away.

Arthur was going to let her die. He had his reputation, and the law, to uphold. He had chosen Camelot over his wife, and she didn't blame him.

They put her in a different cell, one with a small window. Was it meant to be a blessing or a curse? To see the sun, but not stand in it. To smell summer on the breeze, knowing she would not be around to witness it.

No wonder Elaina had been so upset. She hadn't even the luxury of glancing out a window, and she saw only shadows in her mirror.

Guinevere thought about little or nothing as the afternoon wore on, though with each passing hour, thoughts of Arthur became harder to dispel. Her magic was weakened by her lack of motivation to escape.

Guinevere wrapped the blanket more tightly around herself. What awaited her out there? Mordred, furious and vengeful. Niviane, powerful and scorning. The Saxon armies, marching toward Camelot.

Burning would be a mercy in the face of it all.

CHAPTER THIRTY-EIGHT

They cross'd themselves, their stars they blest,
Knight, minstrel, abbot, squire, and guest.
There lay a parchment on her breast,
That puzzled more than all the rest,
The wellfed wits at Camelot.
'The web was woven curiously,
The charm is broken utterly,
Draw near and fear not,—this is I,
The Lady of Shalott.

Elaina had died.

She had never been more certain of something. But she had an impression of warmth, and soft, golden light, the feeling of being embraced by someone who cared for her dearly.

Then, with sudden harshness, she breathed again.

Everything hurt for an agonizing, blinding moment. She sat up, panting, her hands against her chest as if trying to hold her heart in until the feeling dissipated.

The small room held sparse furniture. There was nothing other than the bed she lay in, a small table, and a chair. The bed hardly fit in the room by itself, and there wasn't much space to walk around it. A sleeping form occupied the narrow space, curled in on itself.

"Gereck?" Elaina called softly. The figure stirred, then fell back into slumber. She tried again, louder this time. "Gereck?"

That got him. He woke with a start, rolling over and staring up at her with disbelieving eyes. "Elaina?" He rubbed his eyes. "Elaina, how…?"

He scrambled to his feet, wincing, and gazed at her, eyes traveling up and down her body, over her face, into her eyes. Then, suddenly, he let out a joyful whoop.

"You're here! You are really here! How did you escape? What broke the curse? I thought you were dead! You *were* dead."

"I was," she said quietly, hardly believing it herself. "I made a choice. I decided that I loved Arthur, Morgan, and you more than living in the safety of my tower. It was terrifying, but I looked out the window into the sun and the mirror shattered, and I was free. My heart kept hurting, and eventually, I think I really did die." She looked at him, wide-eyed, taking in all his features. He must have bathed and had his wounds tended, for his bruises seemed faded and he was wearing clean clothing. He looked much better than when she found him. "But then I was alive again, and it seemed like only a moment."

"Well, it was actually through the night. I don't know if Arthur's kiss had anything to do with your being alive now, but I am glad you are, either way."

"Arthur's kiss? Arthur… saw me?" She didn't remember seeing him. She looked up into Gereck's eyes. "Tell me."

"Well, our boat drifted ashore at the edge of the city, the two of us in it. Several knights found us, and you asked for Arthur as you passed out. I knew I had to try to convince him to come meet you, whatever it took, so I went to him and he agreed to come see you."

"Did you tell him who I was?"

"He knew the moment he saw you that you were his mother."

Elaina clasped her hands to her lips, unable to contain her smile. Joy, she felt joy. She couldn't remember the last time she had felt this way. She laughed, at the same time crying. Her son had seen her. He knew her. But she hadn't seen him.

"Where is he? Can I meet him?"

Gereck's face fell, and he ran a hand through his hair. "He is... readying to leave, as we speak. I do not know that I could convince him to come."

"I will go to him." She threw back the covers and got out of the bed.

Gereck cleared his throat and looked away.

Elaina glanced at the thin shift she wore. "Where are my clothes, then?"

"I wouldn't know. I wasn't certain whether you were truly dead; I didn't want to assume. I had a maid care for you. The dress was likely thrown out."

She climbed back in the bed and pulled the covers up. "You can look now."

They shared a smile, then a stiff silence filled the room.

"You never answered my question," she said at last. "What happened with him? With Sir Lancelot?"

"He was caught abed with the queen. He escaped with Clarent, the Sword of Peace, and there is a search being made for him, hopefully before he uses it. The queen is to burn at the stake. This morning, I believe." He looked at her matter-of-factly, then slowly his expression changed. “Oh, I didn’t mean… I mean, is she really your sister?”

Elaina climbed out of the bed again.

A very flustered Gereck turned his back to her.

“Where is this happening?” She looked around the room for any sign of a chest of drawers. “Do you have some clothes I might borrow?”

“The courtyard. Why would you want to know? You don’t want to watch, do you?”

“No, I want to rescue her.”

Gereck turned and stared straight at her, his expression utterly dumbfounded. “You… what?”

“Unless you want to help, I am going to run out there half-naked. Where do you keep your clothes?”

Gereck knelt and pulled several small boxes out from under his bed. From them, he took tunic and breeches. He handed them to Elaina.

“This is madness, Elaina. How do you expect to accomplish this? The king will be watching!”

Elaina took them and laid them out on the bed, then removed the shift and tugged on the clothes.

“I will have to be quick. Do you think I might get a horse?” she asked, voice muffled through the tunic as she pulled it over her head.

“I had a horse you might have borrowed. I suppose he may have made his way here after I fell from his back. That is, if he wasn’t stolen on the way. As that may be, I might be able to get you one.”

True to his honor and word as a knight, Gereck chastely kept his gaze fixed on the floor. “Why am I even talking with you about this? You can’t go, you are a woman. Do you even know how to use a sword?”

“I won’t need one. I’ll have you.”

“But I can hardly stay on a horse, much less swing a blade at anyone trying to stop us!”

Elaina pulled on the breeches and frowned. The shirt drowned her, as did the pants. She couldn’t keep them up without holding them.

“I need a belt. Or something.”

Gereck returned to one of the boxes and pulled out a strip of leather with a metal clasp on the end.

“Thank you,” Elaina said, taking it. She wrapped it around her waist and cinched it as tightly as possible. “I suppose not much can be done for shoes or armor.”

“Did you hear me? You are going to die if you go out there. And I cannot come with you.”

“I shall have to move very quickly then, shan’t I?” She looked at him, holding his gaze. She read the concern in his eyes, and her own heart thumped madly, but she would not back down.

Gereck approached her. “Your plan is to ride a horse into the center square, filled with people, avoiding the guards and any knights who might be there, including King Arthur himself, and cut a woman free from a wooden pole that may or may not be surrounded by a flaming mountain of wood?”

“Yes,” Elaina said. “I know it is foolish. I know you think me mad, but I can’t let her die, not like this.”

He stared at her.

“She is my sister, Gereck. Wouldn’t you do the same for your family? She loved me! That’s the reason I was in the tower, because she wanted to protect me. What kind of sister would I be if I stood by and watched her die?” Elaina’s chest heaved.

"I don't know if she loved the king or if she truly did betray him with Lancelot, but I spoke with him before I died and he didn't seem too happy with her, so perhaps it isn't what it seems."

"Wait, you spoke with him?" Gereck asked.

"He saw that I had found your... well, I suppose it was his, wasn't it? The shield?"

"He has the shield?" Gereck cursed. "Then he has the means to defeat Arthur!"

"But what of Excalibur?"

"The sword is powerful, but the sheath has the true power. The sheath gives the wielder untold strength and protection. While Arthur holds the sword, only one thing can kill him; a mortal blow to his heart, or complete beheading, but with the shield, Lancelot can defend himself against it. His swordsmanship is such that he might actually land the killing blow, and if he does it with the Sword of Peace he now holds, Camelot will be in ruins."

"Then we must prevent them from fighting. If I rescue Morgan, then follow Arthur and get close enough to tell him that Lancelot is Mordred..."

Gereck shook his head, "Holy Saints, Elaina. How could that stop them fighting?"

"Perhaps Mordred wouldn't kill his own son." This had gotten far beyond Elaina's scope of power. She had no fighting ability, no magic. How could she possibly expect to succeed?

Nevertheless, she had to try. No one else loved Morgan the way Elaina did. No one else would help her.

The way Gereck looked at her, she knew he realized what the odds of success were.

He sighed. “I can get you a horse, and I can get you armor. I can’t come with you, especially since there wouldn’t be room on the horse for three, and you’ll need a place for your sister. I can also get you herbs.”

“Herbs?” Elaina gave him a perplexed look. “Why would I want those?”

“The physician keeps them in his rooms. There are some that smoke so strongly they can obscure vision in a small room.”

“But this is a courtyard, outside, covering a large space.”

“They also,” Gereck continued, “cause the eyes to sting and burn, so that vision is impaired.”

“That would be wonderful!” Elaina exclaimed. “But how do I keep my vision from being harmed as well?”

“There is an antidote of sorts that can clear the herb from your system and clear your vision almost immediately. You’ll throw the herbs on the fire, if there’s one lit. If they haven’t lit it yet, you’ll need a torch.”

Elaina stood on her tiptoes and kissed him. His lips were surprisingly soft, yet firm, and though she had intended to give him a light kiss of gratitude, it went on much longer than she planned.

A knock at the door interrupted them, and they parted.

Gereck’s eyes tightened, his face far too grim for having just enjoyed a kiss.

But then, he was married, Elaina remembered. Shame filled her. She hadn’t meant to come between a man and his wife.

Gereck opened the door to reveal a maid, carrying a dress. “Thank you,” he said, taking the dress from her. She curtseyed and left immediately, glancing back into the room at Elaina, who knew her being dressed as a man must be a tad shocking.

Gereck laid the dress on the bed, fingering its soft material, then looking to Elaina, an expression on his face that she assumed meant he thought she ought to be wearing it instead of what she had on. To his credit, he said nothing.

"I need a hat," Elaina said suddenly. "I do not want to be stopped, and a woman dressed as a man is sure to draw attention. Do you have something for me? To cover my hair?"

Gereck nodded and took a floppy-brimmed cap of rough make and material from another box.

Elaina took it from him, holding it between her legs so she could braid her hair. She had no pins, but she tied it up as best she could, then pulled the cap over it.

"How does it look?" she asked.

Gereck reached up and helped her tuck a stray strand inside the cap.

She smiled at him.

"Explain something to me, if you can." He gazed at her with such intensity now that Elaina wanted to look away, but she couldn't. "How is it that a lady, such as yourself, comes to this? To saving my life, and rescuing another from death? I did not know you desired to be almost like a knight."

"I didn't know I had it in me either, but now that I live, I find that there are many things I never would have attempted before that I now hope to try," Elaina replied.

Gereck paused for a long time, then nodded, and without a word walked toward the door, opened it, and motioned for her to exit ahead of him. Elaina smiled. She may have been dressed like a man, but it still thrilled her that someone treated her like a lady.

CHAPTER THIRTY-NINE

Chains clinked, the thick iron bands heavy on Guinevere's wrists. She stumbled on the hem of her dress and fell to her knees.

Armored knights on either side caught her arms, pulling her to her feet. Mercifully, neither knight was someone she knew well. Their faces were impassive, unfeeling, except one of them, the younger, kept giving her wide-eyed glances, as if he couldn't believe her guilty of the crime charged to her.

The rough material of the borrowed dress itched on her skin. Guinevere longed to strip it off, to again be wearing her gowns made of velvet and silk, if only to be comfortable before she died.

Two maids had come at the first light of dawn and bathed her, brushed and braided her hair, dressed her, even. A final luxury.

Tears pricked her eyes again, and her throat felt thick with emotion. Why they bothered dressing her only to have her go to her death, Guinevere couldn't understand.

Propriety, it seemed, reigned supreme, even in the death of a traitor. And yet, the gratitude she felt for the simple act of... could it be considered kindness?... had made her want to embrace the women who waited on her. No doubt, they hadn't volunteered for the task.

Surely it was Arthur who had requested it be done. A sign that, no matter how much her betrayal angered him, he still loved her.

The corridor brightened as they rounded the corner, open arches brightening the white stone of the hall. The newly risen sun hadn't reached the top of Camelot's wall yet, so it was still chilly and shadowed.

The courtyard filled with people. The people who would watch her demise. A tall beam rose from a mound of carefully arranged wood and straw stood near the center.

Several of the king's men tucked bits of kindling and smearing pitch into the wood to help the fire catch.

Guinevere's bare feet padded on the cold pavement. Her heartbeat pounded loudly in her ears, and her breath quickened. She looked up at the pale blue sky, which grew brighter by the moment. Would the sun rise quickly enough for her to behold it in her last moments?

What will it be like to die?

She glanced at the wood mound. It rose as tall as a man, with enough wood to make a fire burn hotter and brighter than the ones she had seen at Beltane, and those could sometimes be seen for miles. She remembered the feeling of burning her fingers, once, on a hot pan back home. Her fingers had blistered, turning red-hot and agonizing when they were touched. Mary had nursed them, changing bandages and applying salve for weeks before they felt normal again.

Mary would not be here to nurse her back, this time, and Guinevere was immediately and immensely glad. She wished there was a way to be certain Mary never heard of her death.

Guilt flooded her heart, and tears came to her eyes. Mary would hear Guinevere's fate and no doubt mourn and wonder why, why had Guinevere betrayed the king? What cause had she found for infidelity?

Guinevere would never be able to speak the truth, to explain that she was innocent of the crimes charged against her. She hadn't betrayed the king; at least, not consciously.

She bit her lip against a sob and stumbled, but caught herself.

The knights halted their march, standing straight in the courtyard below a balcony.

Guinevere raised her tear-stained face, looking straight into the stony gaze of her king.

Arthur's eyes had dark circles beneath them.

Had he slept?

She supposed he hadn't. More evidence he cared. But not enough to save her.

He motioned to the knights and watched as they picked Guinevere up by her arms and carried her into the center of the courtyard. She held his gaze, hoping to see some softening of his face, but his expression remained hard and unaffected.

Her feet brushed something. Wood. The knights lifted her up to where another man stood on the mound. He pulled her up and forcibly held her arms to her sides as another man wrapped heavy rope around her, crisscrossing it over her chest.

Panic took Guinevere by force. Despite her determination to take death gracefully, knowing no escape would come, she thrashed about as the rope wound about her ankles, tying her to the hard wood beam at her back.

Struggle though she may, the knots held, and the ropes cut into the skin of her arms.

A knight took a torch from a nearby brazier. The orange flame leapt up, almost eagerly. It touched a patch of straw and it caught quickly, flames rising, licking toward her feet.

Guinevere pulled at her bonds, crying out from the pain of the ropes and the pain in her heart.

"Arthur!" she cried hoarsely. "Arthur, please!" Smoke rose around before her, and she could see through it that he turned his back on her and walked back into the castle, knights at his side.

How could anyone do this to one he claimed to love?

Guinevere let out a hoarse scream as the fire flickered against her feet. The heat grew unbearable, the smoke choking her and burning her eyes.

The terror of dying grew to be too much. She cried out and screamed over and over again until her throat burned and she coughed without ceasing.

Through her vision, blurred with smoke and tears, a helmed figure appeared, riding towards her through the haze.

Guinevere moaned hoarsely.

Her feet blistered, and flames licked hungrily at the fabric of her dress. Sparks flashed and wood popped. The smoke intensified, growing into an impenetrable screen, blocking out Arthur and the crowd that had gathered to watch their queen burn.

Her eyes stung viciously as the smoke reached them, and Guinevere cried out again, struggling against her bonds.

A loud *thwack!* bit the wood at her back, and then the ropes slackened.

Guinevere fell forward into the flames, shrieking, limbs flailing. She scrabbled around, trying to stand, to get out of the flames. Her hair scorched, the smell like manure. Her eyes still stung, barely able to see.

The helmed figure came around again and reached towards her.

"Take my hand!" they cried out.

Guinevere reached out her hand, missing the figure's grasp, then finally made contact.

The figure pulled Guinevere to her feet and Quinevere thrust herself away from the fiery pyre.

The armored chest cooled her burned face and arms as the horse leapt back and galloped across the cobblestone courtyard.

Soldiers and knights clamored after them, all on foot. The horse left them far behind. It ran through the lower sections of the city, barreling through groups of men attempting to close the three great gates marking sections of the city. They made it through each one, just in time.

The countryside blurred. Guinevere later recalled talking to the helmed figure, asking his identity, wanting to know his name. *Was it Lancelot? Or was it, perhaps, Arthur, disguised?* She had lost sight of Arthur at the end. She hoped it was him with every fiber of her being, but the figure did not reply to Guinevere's muttered inquiries, and eventually the agony of her burns sent her into a state of delirium.

She saw flocks of crows, flying overhead.

She saw Niviane, about to cast her enchantments.

She saw Mordred, lying with glassy eyes staring at the heavens, a bloody hole in through his armor.

Each vision felt more real than the last, as if her magic hyperreacted to the agony.

Guinevere cried out. Her rescuer put his arm around her, and the horse galloped on.

When the horse finally stopped and the figure dismounted, he carried Guinevere off the steed in his arms. They climbed in a dark place—a cave, or a castle, perhaps—for what seemed an eternity.

Guinevere could not figure out where they were or what they were climbing. Her mind still flashed with images from her multiple pasts.

Her father in Carmelide, her brothers, Elaina, Melwas, back to Elaina.

Her sister's face hovered anxiously over her, sweaty and flushed, mouthing something that Guinevere couldn't hear.

Guinevere tried to answer, but no sound came out. The image of her sister's face lit up with fire, burned and blackened at the edges until the flames consumed her, and Guinevere let out an endless scream filled with the pain of a thousand lifetimes.

CHAPTER FORTY

She will live. I will live. I will see her again. Elaina chanted in her mind as she rode away from the tower.

It had taken every ounce of courage she could muster to return to that place, one she had hoped to never see again, but she could think of no better place to hide the renegade queen. No one would search the tower, if Camelot could even spare the men in this time of war. And Merlin had promised to watch over Morgan, though there wasn't much he could do imprisoned in a chest.

The horse snorted beneath Elaina as he galloped back toward the great city. She hoped to get there before Arthur left with his remaining men to face the Saxon armies in battle. To warn him of Lancelot, of the sword Clarent and the shield that would make the knight nearly invincible.

She leaned across the horse's back and made him run until he wouldn't run anymore, and then she let him walk, so long as he didn't stop. Her back ached, and her rear end was sore, as were her thighs. She would barely be able to walk when she dismounted, she wagered.

Her breath sounded loud inside the metal helm her face. She threw it off, realizing she had to find a way to ditch the armor before word got out of the queen's rescue and someone recognized her as the rider who had accomplished it.

Elaina could hardly believe that she'd done it. She could still see the black smoke from the fire, curling into the air as a dark reminder of how close she had come to watching her sister burn. Smoke marks charred the armor as she shed it piece by piece, strewing it down the road for some fortunate peasant to find.

Morgan's screams had curdled Elaina's blood and set her own heart aflame, almost crippling her to the point of inaction, but she had acted, and she had succeeded. Now Morgan lay sleeping, though badly burned enough that she still risked death, but Elaina could not stay behind to treat her. Gereck was too injured to ride and tell Arthur the truth of Lancelot, so it fell to her. If she could stay on the horse. She simply had to pray that Morgan would pull through and live.

The sun edged further towards the horizon. Travel from the tower took roughly half a day. Riding fast, Elaina shaved off a few sun spans, but she could tell as soon as she arrived at the castle keep that she was too late.

Only the odd servant moved about in the silence. She asked the first one she saw, a young man whose eyes about made it out of his head at the sight of her clad in men's clothes, her blond hair probably in a great mess.

He stammered a reply, that the king had, indeed, gone out to meet the Saxons hours earlier, and then edged away from her and ran down the corridor before she could thank him.

Next she went to Gereck's room. It stood empty.

Feeling anxious and weary, Elaina lay across the bed, promising she wouldn't sleep, only rest a while.

The armor had rubbed her in certain places, making her especially sore. It didn't help that her muscles were screaming with each movement. All she had to do was stay on the horse long enough, riding hard enough, to catch Arthur before he confronted Lancelot as Mordred.

The thought made her want to close her eyes and go to sleep, but there was no arguing, not even with herself. No one else could go in her place.

The door swung open, and Gereck peered in. "Elaina?"

She sat up, muscles screaming in protest.

"Geez, you look like horse—" He stopped, clearing his throat. "Well, war isn't pretty, is it. You missed the king."

Elaina closed her eyes. "I know." She breathed in deeply.

"I've got provisions for you. I'll attend your sister as soon as I can gather some healing supplies. I don't know much, I'm afraid, but we can't trust anyone else with the knowledge of where she's hiding."

He paused, and when Elaina didn't comment, he pulled a bit of something from the bag he held and handed it to her. A lump of cheese. She nibbled it, feeling strength flow into her after a few bites.

Gereck continued. "The castle is buzzing about the daring rescue you made. Of course, everyone is speculating who the mysterious knight could be. The rumors talk of the queen having multiple affairs, but then, nothing can be done about that."

"Thank you, Gereck. I need another horse." She squared her shoulders and slid off the bed.

Gereck led her to the stables, talking on the way about the direction Arthur was most likely to ride, and she tried to commit it to memory. Her task seemed to grow more impossible with each passing moment, time narrowing like a tunnel before her, soon to close and prevent her from saving Camelot.

It felt like ages before Elaina sat astride a tall, dark horse named Ryker, ready to run. He shifted uneasily beneath her, and she patted his neck, wishing, not for the first time, that she had Morgan's affinity for horses. Elaina had tolerated them at best in the past, and now she was certain she had spent more time on the back of a horse in the past day than her whole life combined.

"May fortune ride with you," Gereck said, eyes scanning her face.

Fatigue gripped Elaina's mind and mouth. What could she say? She managed a small, grateful smile and nodded.

Gereck slapped Ryker's backside, sending the horse leaping forward.

Elaina shrieked and held on tight, listening to Gereck's laughter and cursing his name in her mind.

Crickets chirped as evening fell. How had the whole day passed so quickly?

After a short time, Elaina slowed Ryker to a fast walk. The growing dark made it too dark to gallop. Elaina's thoughts ran through all the ways she could try to convince Arthur to listen to her, a stranger claiming impossibly to be his mother, come to prevent him from being slain by his own father.

Dawn came, slowly at first, the light growing gradually until a dim gray color washed over the scenery. The sky lightened into a pale blue, and then the sun burst forth over the horizon.

Elaina's head drooped, and she kept catching herself a moment before falling asleep on the saddle. She couldn't stop. She recalled sitting at the loom, when, on occasion, the curse would force her to weave for days on end, through one night and into the next. It had happened more times than she could remember, and she had kept herself awake by singing.

It was, by Gereck's word, about a day before she would reach any land occupied by the enemy. So she let her voice ring out in the morning air, and she ate some bread and a soft, wrinkly apple, washed it down with a drink from her water skin, and felt much better.

For three days, she rode on, never once catching a glimpse of the army she chased. She saw plenty of signs of their passing, each village she passed sparser than the last. People had fled the war, afraid for the possibility of the king's army failing to hold back the Saxon hoards.

She stopped and slept in short bursts, managing to wake herself after a few hours and press on. Her meager supplies ran out on the third day.

On the fourth, faint sounds of battle rang out through the air.

Elaina spurred Ryker into a gallop once more, her heart pounding. Over the next hill, perhaps, or through the next copse of trees. Any moment she would come upon them. She took Ryker up another hill to get her bearings, and two towering cliffs rose ahead with a rocky valley between, and therein the armies fought.

There were few left on either side. Bodies strewed about the ground, some moving, others still and cold.

She could be there within an hour, but she had no skill in fighting. How could she get to the king?

Gereck had supplied her with a sword, which she had used to set Morgan free. Elaina had no delusions of using it in battle.

She made her way down the hill, dismounting and walking Ryker. She had hoped to catch them before the battle; none of her plans involved riding into the midst of one.

Her best bet would be to look as far from a warrior as possible, so no one would mistake her for an enemy soldier looking for a fight. She unwound her hair from their tight braids piled up on her scalp, shaking the crimped strands until they fell loosely around her face. A looking glass and a brush would have done her much good, not to mention a bath and a dress, but nothing could be done for that now.

No one could doubt Elaina was a woman. No one could mistake her for a man of either side interested in doing battle. She hoped they would not take her for a sorceress, there to work magic and destroy them all.

Ryker balked when she tugged on his reins and clicked him forward. He stamped his feet, refusing to enter the valley. No doubt the strong scent of blood put terror in him. Elaina patted his neck and murmured low. He would not budge, and his rolling, terrified eyes gave her the impression he would lash out at her or bolt.

She slapped the horse's rump as Gereck had done, and the horse reeled around, back toward Camelot. If she made it back to Camelot, she would do so on her own two feet. She couldn't expect the exhausted, skittish horse to wait in one place, even if no one made off with him while she was gone.

No one engaged her. Few spared her any glances, and she almost felt like a ghost, drifting through the battlefield and dodging dying men who moaned and prayed. Some reached out to her, calling her by the name of one martyred saint or another. Elaina's heart ached that she could do nothing to save them, only send her own prayers up that their passing be swift and painless.

Only a few straggling skirmishes were still being fought, the majority of which seemed to be knights of Camelot picking off Saxon warriors trying to flee. She relaxed. It seemed obvious they had won.

Then she saw Arthur.

Grime covered his face. Dirt and filth and so much drying blood, Elaina couldn't be sure whether it beloned to him or not. He swayed where he stood, leaning on the sword that still gleamed, despite the dark spatters across its metal surface. He hadn't seen her yet, but in a moment he would. She took every part of him in, the weary look on his face, the set of his shoulders, the several gashes in his thigh, arms, and side. None fatal, it would seem. At least he still stood.

But as she neared, before she could call out to him, he swayed to one side, then toppled to the ground, his head striking the hardened dirt, and the mortal wound poured out fresh blood from where it gaped in his chest.

Her shocked cry echoed against the cliffs that surrounded the valley.

She ran, stumbling over the uneven ground as she navigated around bodies and over broken weapons, past slain horses and pieces of scattered armor. She reached Arthur's side and knelt.

With some effort, she got him onto his back. The deep, oozing wound was too much for the enchanted sheath belted at his waist to heal. She had come too late. She had failed him.

Desperately, Elaina called out. "The king! I've found the king!"

The remaining soldiers glanced at her, but would not meet her gaze. They were exhausted by three days of hard battle, which they had won, but at a steep cost. Nothing would save Arthur now.

Elaina stared at the dead and dying men surrounding her, her eyes resting on one whose dark, curled hair gleamed in the misty morning light. Curls she had once run her fingers through, now matted with blood.

Mordred.

She could not mourn him now, not after what he had said and done to her and those she loved.

Elaina turned back to Arthur. His chest rose and fell with shallow, labored breathing, blood bubbling from the wound. She pulled his head into her lap and leaned down towards him, stroking his fair hair with one hand, the other bringing one of his hands onto his chest and holding it there.

"You do not know me," she whispered to Arthur, "but I have known you and loved you since you were born."

"My... mother." His eyes opened a crack.

Elaina's heart sang and broke all at the same time. "How do you know?"

"I saw you...at the river. I knew...A memory...from a past life. By all the saints, you could be no one else." His speech was halted and broken. Breath shuddered from his damaged lungs. He would not live, no matter how much Elaina wanted it.

She brought his hand to her face and smiled, tears filling her eyes and blurring her vision.

"I loved you. If I had not been cursed, I never would have let you go." Her throat closed up, choking on the flood of words she had planned to say.

Arthur nodded his head, ever so slightly. Then, the hand still holding his sword came up and moved toward her.

"Take...this." Arthur said, exerting all his effort, and dragging his sword across his chest. He extended the hilt toward Elaina. "My time... is done. Excalibur must be returned."

"Returned where?" Elaina asked, grasping the hilt and taking it from him. It appeared normal enough, the hilt bound in plain leather worn thin by Arthur's hands, but something in Arthur's voice and the gleam of the blade told her it was more than a simple sword.

"To... the lake." Arthur closed his eyes, and his breath stopped, then started again. Elaina's eyes did not leave his face. His lips moved.

Elaina leaned in to hear.

"Avalon," he whispered. "Throw it in. The lady... will take... it."

He reached for her hand, then, and Elaina put her fingers in his. At her touch, he sighed, and a small, relieved smile lit up his face.

"I wish I had known you, the boy you were, and the man you became," she said, voice quiet.

He did not respond. His eyes remained shut. The rise and fall of his chest could barely be seen, and then it stilled.

Never before had Elaina felt such simultaneous joy and utter sadness. Never before had her heart been so whole and yet broken. To live was to feel pain and love. To be blessed and tortured until the body gave out.

Tears made trails in the filth covering Arthur's armor.

Exhaustion settled into Elaina's bones, and she wanted to lie down next to her son and sleep, but the smell kept her from it. The smell and the blood soaking into the dirt and trampled grass.

The morning sun summoned a fog and cast it in gold, the ethereal mist hovering over the field of mangled corpses. Whether it was magic or nature's way of mourning, Elaina couldn't quite tell.

After a time, a small band of knights approached.

Elaina stood, naked sword in hand, and walked away without speaking. She didn't want to try to explain her identity or her intention. She thought they might protest that she carried Excalibur, but except for a single call after her, they did not pursue.

Another surprise came when she found Ryker grazing just on the other side of a hill near the cliff-lined valley.

She slid Excalibur into the scabbard on the saddle, replacing her borrowed blade with the one Arthur had charged her to return to Avalon, and then she mounted Ryker and urged him back along the road they had come.

She made few stops at the homes of villagers who had a morsel of bread to spare, so she didn't starve. She kept Excalibur hidden where possible, afraid someone might recognize the sword and wonder where she had gotten it.

Life seemed to be going on as usual for the people of Camelot. The land had not yet been touched by word of Arthur's death, and Elaina said nothing of it. She simply passed through, a woman dressed as a man with a horse and sword. She was fortunate no one challenged her, and she suspected some saint had blessed her with a sort of invisibility.

Three days later, the great city of Camelot came into view. A city full of people waiting to hear the fate of their kingdom.

Elaina longed to be there, to find Gereck and tell him what she had seen, and then rest.

But her quest remained unfinished.

For the third time, she went to the tower and climbed the winding stairs to the non-descript wooden door. It stood ajar, creaking slightly as a breeze nudged it.

Elaina pushed it open, afraid of what she would find.

The bed in the corner had been neatly made up, as if no one had ever slept in it. The loom stood still and empty, no colored thread moving with the shuttle, and the tapestry Elaina had seen the future in was gone.

Shards of glass still littered the floor, crunching beneath Elaina's feet as she walked through the room. Her dressing screen remained as well, her few remaining dresses hung over the top. The little table. The large wooden chest.

"Merlin?" Elaina called out.

No response.

Her heart chilled. She ran to the chest and knocked on the lid, then tried the latch. Nothing. Her heart pounded.

"Merlin?" She said again, louder.

Had he escaped? Or died? Or had Niviane returned and done away with him? Had Niviane taken Morgan? Or had Gereck succeeded in finding a place for Morgan to rest and heal?

"Ah, Elaina," a wheezy, whispering voice sighed through the lid of the chest. "You have returned."

"As I said I would," Elaina said, heart pounding with adrenaline and relief as she gazed at the intricately carved chest lid.

Swirls of wood made the image of two trees, bowed towards each other, circled by a ring of birds in flight.

"Merlin, what happened with Morgan? She isn't..." Elaina swallowed, "She isn't dead, is she?"

"Avalon came for her."

"Then she is dead?"

"No. Or perhaps yes. Either way, Avalon wasn't finished with her."

"What do you mean?"

"She trained as a priestess there, did you know? She will have been taken, healed, and perhaps brought before the goddess for judgment. You might find her there."

"At Avalon?" Elaina asked, hesitating. "Is it even a real place? I thought it was a faerie story."

"Much that is told in stories is often found to be true. Why else do we tell stories, except to hide truth where the worthy and wise will find it?" Merlin said faintly.

Elaina had to press her ear against the chest to make out the whisper of his ancient voice.

"Merlin, are you dying?" she asked, her own voice nearly at a whisper.

"Ah, yes, I am. It seems time has caught up to me. I return to nature, as all do."

Tears pricked at her eyes. She hadn't known Merlin as more than a simple blue jay, but in her last years in the tower he had brought her hope, and enough truth to save her from her own fate. She wished she could do the same.

"Is there nothing I can do?" she asked.

Silence met her. Dust motes floated through the sunlight that streamed through the window. Light glittered across the floor.

Elaina breathed in this last sight of the tower, the room that had held her for decades of time.

"Merlin?" she said aloud. She could feel it now. The tower had become a tomb.

She wiped her eyes and stood, boots crunching across the glass. She walked through the door without turning back. Nothing remained for her there.

She reached Camelot before dark and returned Ryker to the stables. No one knew the fair-haired maiden, her name, or where she had come from. They questioned her. Not about the king or the battle that had been fought or even where she'd come from, but about the horse and how she'd gotten him. Her soft-spoken voice and polite demeanor turned away their suspicion. And then, when no one was looking, she slipped away.

Elaina knocked on Gerekc's door, and he opened it, more haggard than he had looked six days past. He glanced over her form, perhaps examining her for injuries. Then, with some hesitation, he came forward and embraced her.

Elaina swallowed the hard lump that rose in her throat.

Gereck stood back, holding her at arms-length and looking her over again. "You are unhurt?"

"I am."

"Did you reach the king?"

Elaina heard the unasked part of the question. *Did you reach the king in time?*

She looked around, hesitating to share in a place where she could be overheard.

Gereck gestured inside the room.

Elaina followed him in, closing the door behind her.

"Arthur?" Gereck asked again, sitting on the bed.

Elaina took a seat in a chair in the corner. She shook her head, biting her lip. "The king died in my arms on the battlefield. Mordred was already dead. I do not know the details of how the battle went, only the final result."

"Has Arthur named anyone as regent in his stead?"

"He had no heirs. Typically, the queen would reign on his behalf." A shadow passed over Gereck's face. "I went to the tower. Your sister was not there. Someone took her. I- I'm sorry."

"I already know. Merlin says she was a priestess in Avalon, and that they took her to be judged for her crimes."

Gereck furrowed his brow. "Merlin? What does he have to do with this?"

"The sorceress, Niviane, seduced him somehow, perhaps under another guise here in Camelot. She brought him to my tower and trapped him in an enchanted chest, and I believe... I believe he might be dead, now."

Understanding lit Gereck's eyes. "No wonder Arthur wasn't warned of Lancelot's betrayal. I knew Merlin had to be aware, but I believed he was too powerful to be fooled. And yet, he was as mortal and faulty as any of us."

Elaina stared blankly at the wall. "He didn't even try, in the end. He knew Niviane would trap him. I still don't understand that part."

"Merlin once said life was a web, or something, and that every movement we make sends vibrations across thousands of strands at once, that we can't avoid the influence we have, and some of us have a bigger influence than others. Perhaps Merlin's time to influence others had ended. I think you are one of those people, too. Everyone here is indebted to you. You birthed a king."

Elaina shook her head. “I am no more than anyone else.”

“I think everyone is more than they think they are. That one motion on your part has impacted thousands of lives, Elaina.”

“I suppose you are right.” She smiled, then sobered. “What news of your wife?”

“Lancelot, Mordred, rather, killed her.” His lips pressed together, and he looked down at the floor.

“No! What of your children?”

Gereck turned, looking over the far side of the bed, and Elaina stood to see two little figures sleeping on straw mats on the floor.

“Oh,” Elaina breathed. Her heart ached for them, ached like the day she had lost Arthur, for the first time, and the last.

It took a moment for Gereck to respond. “They were staying with a cousin of Winna’s. She brought them to me here in Camelot at my request.” He wouldn’t look at Elaina, keeping his eyes glued to his hands. “I betrayed Winna. Betrayed her love, and the promise I made when I married her...If I only had been satisfied with them instead of pursuing this foolish dream of knighthood!”

He shook his head. “And it all came to naught anyway. The knights of the Round Table are gone, divided forever, and Camelot will come to ruin.”

“Maybe not,” Elaina said softly. She came to him, sitting beside him on the hard mattress and resting one of her hands on his. “Perhaps there is hope yet for Camelot.”

Gereck stared at her. “And what of us, then?”

“Us?” Elaina blinked, taken back. Her heart swelled, each beat taking up more space in her chest.

He reached for her hand. “Elaina, I know that I have no right to ask this of you, and that you won’t prefer it after spending so long in that tower, but...”

“You want me to stay,” she finished for him.

“Would you?” he asked hoarsely. He cleared his throat. “I mean, you don’t have to, and we don’t have to marry, there’s no expectation, no assumption...”

Elaina wanted to say yes, but the word stuck in her throat. She couldn’t agree, not without knowing her sister’s fate. “I can’t stay, not yet.”

Gereck swallowed hard, then nodded. “Of course, I understand.”

Elaina’s heart lurched in her chest. “I will return, Gereck,”

“I know,” he said, voice breaking with emotion. “I know you will try.”

Try. The word stung, but not in the way Elaina expected. *Try*. She might not succeed. She might never see Gereck again. She might die.

The thought didn’t sting as much as it had before. Death no longer frightened her into paralysis. Never again would she keep herself locked in a tower, too afraid to leave.

That night, she and Gereck talked long into the night, wrapped in a cocoon of darkness and silence, the only souls in Camelot who knew the fate of the king.

The next day, Elaina rode out on a new quest to take the sword Excalibur to the Lake of Avalon. To find her sister, Morgan, should she still live, and to seek the aid of the priestesses of Avalon.

Perhaps in doing so, she might save Camelot.

Morgan's story continues in The Queen's Quiet End

The Lady of Shalott

Part I

On either side the river lie
Long fields of barley and of rye,
That clothe the wold and meet the sky;
And thro' the field the road runs by
To many-tower'd Camelot;
The yellow-leaved waterlily
The green-sheathed daffodilly
Tremble in the water chilly
Round about Shalott.
Willows whiten, aspens shiver.
The sunbeam showers break and quiver
In the stream that runneth ever
By the island in the river
Flowing down to Camelot.
Four gray walls, and four gray towers
Overlook a space of flowers,
And the silent isle imbowers
The Lady of Shalott.
Underneath the bearded barley,
The reaper, reaping late and early,
Hears her ever chanting cheerly,
Like an angel, singing clearly,
O'er the stream of Camelot.
Piling the sheaves in furrows airy,
Beneath the moon, the reaper weary
Listening whispers, ' 'Tis the fairy,
Lady of Shalott.'
The little isle is all inrail'd

With a rose-fence, and overtrail'd
With roses: by the marge unhail'd
The shallop flitteth silken sail'd,
Skimming down to Camelot.
A pearl garland winds her head:
She leaneth on a velvet bed,
Full royally apparelled,
The Lady of Shalott.

Part II

No time hath she to sport and play:
A charmed web she weaves alway.
A curse is on her, if she stay
Her weaving, either night or day,
To look down to Camelot.
She knows not what the curse may be;
Therefore she weaveth steadily,
Therefore no other care hath she,
The Lady of Shalott.
She lives with little joy or fear.
Over the water, running near,
The sheepbell tinkles in her ear.
Before her hangs a mirror clear,
Reflecting tower'd Camelot.
And as the mazy web she whirls,
She sees the surly village churls,
And the red cloaks of market girls
Pass onward from Shalott.
Sometimes a troop of damsels glad,
An abbot on an ambling pad,
Sometimes a curly shepherd lad,
Or long-hair'd page in crimson clad,
Goes by to tower'd Camelot:
And sometimes thro' the mirror blue

The knights come riding two and two:
She hath no loyal knight and true,
The Lady of Shalott.
But in her web she still delights
To weave the mirror's magic sights,
For often thro' the silent nights
A funeral, with plumes and lights
And music, came from Camelot:
Or when the moon was overhead
Came two young lovers lately wed;
'I am half sick of shadows,' said
The Lady of Shalott.

Part III

A bow-shot from her bower-eaves,
He rode between the barley-sheaves,
The sun came dazzling thro' the leaves,
And flam'd upon the brazen greaves
Of bold Sir Lancelot.
A red-cross knight for ever kneel'd
To a lady in his shield,
That sparkled on the yellow field,
Beside remote Shalott.
The gemmy bridle glitter'd free,
Like to some branch of stars we see
Hung in the golden Galaxy.
The bridle bells rang merrily
As he rode down from Camelot:
And from his blazon'd baldric slung
A mighty silver bugle hung,
And as he rode his armour rung,
Beside remote Shalott.
All in the blue unclouded weather
Thick-jewell'd shone the saddle-leather,

The helmet and the helmet-feather
Burn'd like one burning flame together,
As he rode down from Camelot.
As often thro' the purple night,
Below the starry clusters bright,
Some bearded meteor, trailing light,
Moves over green Shalott.
His broad clear brow in sunlight glow'd;
On burnish'd hooves his war-horse trode;
From underneath his helmet flow'd
His coal-black curls as on he rode,
As he rode down from Camelot.
From the bank and from the river
He flash'd into the crystal mirror,
'Tirra lirra, tirra lirra:'
Sang Sir Lancelot.
She left the web, she left the loom
She made three paces thro' the room
She saw the water-flower bloom,
She saw the helmet and the plume,
She look'd down to Camelot.
Out flew the web and floated wide;
The mirror crack'd from side to side;
'The curse is come upon me,' cried
The Lady of Shalott.

Part IV

In the stormy east-wind straining,
The pale yellow woods were waning,
The broad stream in his banks complaining,
Heavily the low sky raining
Over tower'd Camelot;
Outside the isle a shallow boat
Beneath a willow lay afloat,

Below the carven stern she wrote,
The Lady of Shalott.
A cloudwhite crown of pearl she dight,
All raimented in snowy white
That loosely flew (her zone in sight
Clasp'd with one blinding diamond bright)
Her wide eyes fix'd on Camelot,
Though the squally east-wind keenly
Blew, with folded arms serenely
By the water stood the queenly
Lady of Shalott.
With a steady stony glance—
Like some bold seer in a trance,
Beholding all his own mischance,
Mute, with a glassy countenance—
She look'd down to Camelot.
It was the closing of the day:
She loos'd the chain, and down she lay;
The broad stream bore her far away,
The Lady of Shalott.
As when to sailors while they roam,
By creeks and outfalls far from home,
Rising and dropping with the foam,
From dying swans wild warblings come,
Blown shoreward; so to Camelot
Still as the boathead wound along
The willowy hills and fields among,
They heard her chanting her deathsong,
The Lady of Shalott.
A longdrawn carol, mournful, holy,
She chanted loudly, chanted lowly,
Till her eyes were darken'd wholly,
And her smooth face sharpen'd slowly,

Turn'd to tower'd Camelot:
For ere she reach'd upon the tide
The first house by the water-side,
Singing in her song she died,
The Lady of Shalott.
Under tower and balcony,
By garden wall and gallery,
A pale, pale corpse she floated by,
Deadcold, between the houses high,
Dead into tower'd Camelot.
Knight and burgher, lord and dame,
To the planked wharfage came:
Below the stern they read her name,
The Lady of Shalott.
They cross'd themselves, their stars they blest,
Knight, minstrel, abbot, squire, and guest.
There lay a parchment on her breast,
That puzzled more than all the rest,
The wellfed wits at Camelot.
'The web was woven curiously,
The charm is broken utterly,
Draw near and fear not,—this is I,
The Lady of Shalott.

Lord Alfred Tennyson
1832

THANKS

This one is for my mom. Thank you for encouraging me to do what I love, and for giving me the writing prompt that became this book.

Also, thanks to my writing group and my husband for dealing with writer's block breakdowns, plot changes, and expressions of inadequacy, all of which have been met with the most incredible support anyone could ask for.

Thank you to Phase Publishing for believing in me and giving this book its first life.

Special thanks to all of the authors of all the books I've ever read: your stories inspired me to become a writer, and continue to make me a better one.

Bree Moore lives in Utah with her amazing husband, six children, and two cats. When she's not busy homeschooling or folding laundry, she sneaks off to write more urban fantasy.

Bree has a passion for pregnancy and childbirth, which influences her female-led stories. She loves shopping for groceries like other women like shopping for shoes (no, seriously), movies that make her cry, and Celtic music. She likes both her chocolate and her novels dark.

Subscribe to her newsletter for a FREE Fantasy story!

Also by Bree Moore

Shadowed Minds Series

Thief of Magic

The Lost Souls Series

Raven Born

Serpent Cursed

Coven Bound

Serpent Turned

Rebel Sworn

Short Stories and Anthologies

Second Star

Beyond Instinct

www.ingramcontent.com/pod-product-compliance
Lightning Source LLC
Chambersburg PA
CBHW020601310726
48979CB00008B/1304/J